CORREUS

A brave soldier whose fierce loyalty to the Empire blinds him to treachery close to home.

YGERNA

Correus's exquisite wife, desperately in love with him, unsure that his son will ever accept her.

FLAVIUS

Correus's half brother, the Emperor's principal staff aide and confidant, a man more sure of his courage than of his heart.

DOMITIAN

The Emperor's weak-willed younger brother, eager heir to a mighty empire that could come to ruin under his clumsy rule.

VETTIUS

The shifty man whose so-called friends could be the unluckiest men in Rome.

FIORGYN

The lovely, fair-haired German woman whose forbidden love for a Roman soldier threatens the safety of her own people.

THE CENTURIONS SERIES
VOLUME III

THE EMPEROR'S GAMES

Damion Hunter

 Created by the producers of
The Worldshakers, Wagons West, Covered Wagons and
The Kent Family Chronicles.

Chairman of the Board: Lyle Kenyon Engel

BALLANTINE BOOKS ● NEW YORK

Library of Congress Catalog Card Number: 83-91128

ISBN 0-345-29827-6

Produced by Book Creations, Inc.
Chairman of the Board: Lyle Kenyon Engel

Manufactured in the United States of America

First Edition: February 1984

For Jeff and Felix

Contents

Cast of Characters

THE HOUSE OF APPIUS

Appius	Flavius Appius Julianus the Elder
Correus	Correus Appius Julianus, adopted slave-born son of Appius
Ygerna	Flavia Agricolina, British wife of Correus
Felix	Frontinus Appius Julianus, Correus's son by Freita, a German freedwoman; formally adopted by Correus
Eilenn	Correus and Ygerna's daughter
Eumenes	slave belonging to Correus
Flavius	Flavius Appius Julianus the Younger, half brother to Correus, legitimate son of Appius
Aemelia	wife of Flavius
Aemelius	father of Aemelia
Valeria Lucilla	mother of Aemelia
Julia	Appia Julia, sister of Flavius, half sister of Correus
Lucius Paulinus	husband of Julia
Tullius	free servant of Paulinus

Antonia	wife of Appius, mother of Flavius and Julia
Helva	slave mistress of Appius, mother of Correus
Forst	German freedman, Appius's horsemaster
Emer	freedwoman, Forst's wife
Julius	slave of Correus
Diulius	horsemaster of the chariot ponies

ROME

*Titus	emperor of Rome
*Domitian	brother of Titus
Marius Vettius	senator, a crony of Domitian
Gentilius Paulinus	uncle of Lucius Paulinus
Faustus Sulla	a *triumvir capitalis*
Roscius Celsus	a wealthy merchant
Nyall Sigmundson	former chieftain of the Semnones

GERMANY

Theophanes	a pirate leader
Cerdic Ennius Wulf Commius	men of Aristides's band
*Velius Rufus	the emperor's general in Germany
*Julius Frontinus	the chief engineer of the Roman Army in Germany

Sulpicius Clarus	governor of Lower Germany
Quintus	a centurion of the Eighth Legion Augusta
Labienus	chief field surgeon
Rhodope	a madam
Marbod	chieftain of the Chatti
Morgian	mother of Nyall Sigmundson
Fiorgyn	wife of Nyall Sigmundson
Signy	wife of Ranvig
Barden	priest of the Semnones
Arni	a lord of the Semnones
Steinvar	a lord of the Semnones, husband of Morgian

I

The Emperor's Games

"Request permission to transfer." Correus slammed the wax tablet containing his request down on the desk. The wax cracked off at the corner, and he glared at it, thumbs hooked in his belt.

The optio in the headquarters at Misenum Naval Base scooped the tablet into one hand. "I'll see that it goes through," he said, blank-faced. Centurion Correus Julianus put in for a transfer once a week, regular as sunrise. Another tablet in the stack wasn't going to make any difference, but the optio wouldn't have dreamed of saying so. Centurion Julianus was a senior officer and a man plainly on the thin edge of his temper. "A bad week, sir?" he inquired carefully.

"Oh, no," Correus said sarcastically. His aquiline face was tight-stretched, and a few locks of brown hair stuck out untidily from beneath his helmet rim. He looked as if he had jammed it on his head in a hurry. "I'm a professional soldier. I put in nine years in the field so I can come here to ship fourteen lions and a hippopotamus up the Tiber! Along with a herd of goats to *feed* the lions. Have you ever slept on a ship where they've been slaughtering goats? Have you ever *smelled* a lion? Mithras

1

god, I can still smell their stench on *me*, and I soaked in the bath with half a bottle of my wife's scent!"

"Well, I expect the next run won't be so bad, sir," the optio said soothingly. The duties of a peacetime navy got on most men's nerves, but Centurion Julianus looked ready to go around the bend.

"No, this time we'll get to ship a hold full of sand. *Sand*, mind you—we'll need half the whole damned fleet because Italian sand isn't *pretty* enough! And now the emperor wants a water fight, bless him, to cap off the big day for his games. On the old Augustan lake by the Tiber. It hasn't been filled in thirty years, and we'll probably drown half the audience. If I'd wanted to be a damned actor, I'd have put on a gold wig and a dress and gone into the theater!"

The optio nodded sympathetically. A water spectacle meant two navies of condemned men in fake uniforms, fighting each other for the promise of life if they came in on the winning side. That was all right for the civilians and the mob, of course, but not really an amusement for the professional man. And Centurion Julianus didn't much like arena games, anyway. "I'll put your request through, sir," he said, "with the rest of 'em. But I wouldn't be holding my breath." The centurion had nearly a year yet to run to the end of a standard tour, and the Misenum commander didn't like training new officers when he could help it.

Correus nodded, growled, and turned on his heel. The optio watched him go. Centurion Julianus was really going to be unhappy when he got the specific orders for the water fight. The optio had heard about the emperor's water spectacle already—very little information missed a headquarters optio— and word was that it was to be a carefully choreographed rendition of the Battle of Actium, not the usual free-for-all. It would take a lot of training to get the condemned men to put their backs into learning military formation on the slim hope of coming out alive. And Centurion Correus Julianus was going to get to train them.

This posting was a favor to him, and Correus knew it—a chance to get fleet experience and mark himself as a well-rounded military man destined for great things. His brother,

Flavius, who was on the emperor Titus's staff, had no doubt had a hand in the appointment. But Correus had had a year of it by now, growing daily more rebellious, and had put in for transfer to an active command more times than he could count. Still, here he sat, shipping lions and condemned men up the coast to Rome or, sillier yet, a cargo of nothing but African sand to keep the arena floor clean. The men condemned to fight in the arena crept into Correus's dreams at night, shackled together and bleeding, lost eyes fixed on his own.

After he and Caritius, captain of the flagship of the Misenum Fleet, had begun to work out the details of the emperor's naval spectacle, Correus awoke at night, sweating, to discover that he had kicked off the covers trying to rid his own leg of an imaginary shackle, and to find his wife, Ygerna, also coverless, huddled into a chilly ball beside him with her hands over her face as if somehow his dreams had crept into her own. One night he had actually sat up screaming, convinced that he was drowning, chained by the leg to a sinking ship.

Ygerna sat up too, her thin face scared in the moonlight. She had seen him afraid only once before, and then it had been of her. He had let loose his grief for his son's dead mother, enough to fall in love again. This was different, a cold fear from inside the mind, like a dark snake that slithered out with the sunset. She put her arms around him as far as she could reach, and after a minute he stopped shaking.

"Mithras god." Correus flopped back down on the pillows. He put a hand to his face. The skin felt clammy.

"The same dream?"

"With a few refinements." He shivered. "I'm sorry, dear. This is the third night running I've waked you."

"I don't mind. I just don't understand. You've seen worse things. Why does the arena do this to you?"

That was true enough. He hadn't been a professional soldier for nine years without stacking up a few horrors to remember. But they didn't come crawling into his dreams at night. "This one's a birthright," he said sourly.

"That is a lot of years down the road," Ygerna said. "And you had more pampering than most free children."

"I know." Correus made a face. He always felt foolish when the subject of his slave birth cropped up. In truth he had led a charmed childhood, running tame on his father's estate, being freed and formally adopted at eighteen, and helped to a military career that would take him as far as he had the ability to go. His mother, Helva, still lived on the estate in the privileged position of the master's longtime mistress and mother of his second son. There had never been any prospect of the gladiators' school or a slave galley for Correus. But somehow the arena and the slave market always gave him the same feeling: There but for the grace of the gods and Appius Julianus went Correus. As a result he "collected strays"—his old commander's phrase—a parade of the lost and hopeless who had crossed his path and found Correus unable to let them go by to their fate. Julius, his body servant and stable boy, was one. His son Felix's mother had begun as another—bought by Correus to spare her from a worse master.

"It isn't fear for yourself, you know," Ygerna said quietly. "It's—you are mad because you can't change things . . . can't save them all." She switched from Latin into the soft dialect of the Silure hills, her homeland in West Britain, as she still did when she wanted to explain something carefully, not in a language that she still found stiff. "You want to be the god who is lowered on a wire at the theater, in a mask, with gold spikes on his head, and makes everything work out properly."

Correus started to laugh, softly, and pulled her down on the bed beside him so that he could rest his head on her breast. "You *are* a witch." His hand traced the delicate five-petaled flower that was pricked into the skin between her breasts with blue dye: the mark of the Goddess, the Dark Mother.

"I am not needing the Sight to tell you that much," Ygerna said. "You know it yourself, but it gives you bad dreams, anyway. I thought once that the dreams might be because of me—that the Mother might be angry, for stealing her priestess—"

"No, love. I've had them before." His voice was tired.

"I know. And the Goddess doesn't come to me anymore, so I doubt she cares what I do. I have grown too Roman for her, I think. And your dreams are out of your *own* mind. You'll have them until *you* get rid of them."

"How?"

"I don't know. They aren't my dreams. Learn to think like your brother, maybe."

Ygerna had always been able to figure him out, and, somewhat to his surprise, he had found that she could generally tell what his half brother, Flavius, was thinking, too. "You might as well tell me to think like a maenad or a Nubian from Africa," he said about that. "I can't even *understand* his thinking half the time." It was only in the last few years that he and Flavius had learned to put childhood rivalry far enough behind them to be friends. But each still found the other a puzzle, an oddity only partly comprehended.

"You and Flavius are like that god with the two faces—" Ygerna said.

"Janus," Correus said.

"Janus. The back and front of the same thing. You are more alike than you think. You just can't look at each other straight on and see it."

"Maybe." He was beginning to be sleepy. The nightmare drifted away with the sound of her voice. Sweet reason in a white night shift, with her long hair braided into two thick plaits and the front curls incongruously tied up in a wild array of rags. He kissed one breast sleepily, and she ran a light hand across his forehead.

"Go to sleep. You don't dream when I hold you."

No, nothing ever touched him in Ygerna's arms. But he couldn't spend his life huddling in his wife's embrace to close the demons out.

In the morning Correus found a family row brewing up over breakfast, to take his mind off his dreams. He eyed the storm signals warily.

"Felix may *not* go to a barbaric water battle. He'll stay at home in Misenum with me." Ygerna gave Correus a horrified look that made it quite plain that she found her countrymen revolting in this guise. When a Roman spoke of barbarians, he meant a people like the Britons, the half-tamed folk who were Ygerna's kin. Ygerna's expression said clearly whom *she* meant.

Since Felix, who was five, rarely saw eye to eye with his stepmother—or anyone else in charge, for that matter—the conversation quickly degenerated into an exchange of "I won'ts" and "You wills," until Correus sent him off wriggling like a squid under his nurse's arm.

Ygerna slumped down at the stone table in the secluded, shaded courtyard that was the center of their house at Misenum Naval Base and put her head in her hands. "Correus, it's no use. I'll never be able to manage him." She sounded nearly ready to cry, but she gave a rueful chuckle. "And in another few years he'll be bigger than I am, and *then* what am I going to do?"

"I don't know," Correus said. "Carry a club, maybe." He put his hands on the nape of her neck, where a few fine black curls were coming loose from the intricate knot on her head. He would rather discuss Felix than the emperor's water fight, he thought. "Dear heart, he'll come round. He is already. He's a willful little demon, but he does like you. And me, I hope. It's not so easy, being suddenly handed over to a father you don't even remember. It's my fault for leaving him with Julia for so long."

"You didn't have anything else to do with him," Ygerna said practically. When Felix's mother had been killed, Correus had been a cohort commander in the wilds of West Britain, and the rest of his household had consisted of a fifteen-year-old slave and a cat. Correus's half sister, Julia, had been sent straight from the gods when she offered to take the baby. It was giving him back again that had proved to be the problem.

Felix, or Frontinus Appius Julianus, to give him his full name—he had been named for Julius Frontinus, then the governor of Britain—had lived the first four years of his life with Julia and her husband, Correus's old companion Lucius Paulinus. Julia thought of Felix as her firstborn; not even two babies of her own had changed that. When Correus had come home at last, with a seventeen-year-old wife and a determination to meld his oddly assorted household into a family, Julia had gritted her teeth and given him back his son, but she hadn't liked it, and neither had Felix.

It didn't help, Correus thought, that Felix was so plainly not Ygerna's child. Ygerna was white-skinned and dark-haired, with black eyes and dark, winging brows in a sharp-pointed face. She hardly came up to Correus's collarbone. That was the sidhe blood in her, her grandmother's folk, the little Dark

People, the Old Ones of Britain who had ruled before the golden Celts had come. She had been a royal woman and a priestess of her tribe, the Goddess-on-Earth through whom Earth Mother made her presence felt, before she had been a hostage to the Roman governor and then, in the end, a Roman citizen—Flavia Agricolina on the official papers, in honor of the governor who had requested the citizenship and the Flavian emperor who had granted it.

Felix's mother, Freita, had been a German woman, tall enough to look Correus in the eye, and if there was something of his father in the shape and features of his face, Felix's coloring was all his mother's. His thick hair was the sleek gold color of ripe barley, and his eyes were as green as sea grass. He was strong and big boned, like the half-German colts his grandfather raised for cavalry remounts, and as much in need of discipline. By the time he was eleven, he would be taller than his stepmother. Correus wouldn't be surprised if Felix outweighed her two years before that.

"He'll come round," Correus said again. He didn't think that sounded like much help, but no other thoughts occurred to him. "You were doing fine last night."

"I was teaching him to play Wisdom," Ygerna said. "I learned it when I was his age. As long as I act like a sister, we do well enough. It's when I try to be a mother and say no that we get into trouble."

"I don't doubt it," Correus said. "It's not Felix's best word. But you're right about the emperor's games. I'm not taking a five-year-old to watch men kill each other. There will be races at the Circus Maximus next week, and he can go to those."

Ygerna snorted. "I suppose men don't kill each other in your chariot races."

"Not intentionally," Correus said. "At least I don't think so. They're certainly no worse than some British races I've seen. And there'll be trained elephants and whatnot. Felix'll love it. You tell him he can go to that and see if it takes the sting out of the other. You ought to see the circus yourself, before you get too fat to be comfortable sitting so long."

He put a hand on her belly, and she glared at him. "I am not fat," she said with dignity, "and I don't even show yet." Ygerna was more than five months along with her own child.

Most days she was pleased with that, but there were times when she would have liked to let Correus try being pregnant and see how much *he* cared for the experience.

"Yes, Princess." He bowed gravely to her, and she grinned at him. For some reason, Ygerna never looked like a Roman when she showed any emotion. There was something about joy or anger or just plain disgust that would bring out the sidhe blood in her and give her face an odd, exotic cast. Correus's own mother always explained to people that her daughter-in-law used to be a witch, and Correus had long ago given up trying to point out to Helva the difference between a priestess and a witch. Helva knew it well enough, anyway. And, looking at Ygerna, Correus sometimes thought that there *wasn't* all that much difference.

Julius put his head through the doors that opened from the atrium to announce that Captain Caritius was hot to cast off and about to split his gut for fear of missing the tide; the centurion had better hop to it.

"The centurion will be with the captain directly," Ygerna said repressively. She was trying to train Julius into a proper majordomo, but so far no one felt that she had had much success. She stood up and kissed her husband. "Go and attend to your sailors. We'll meet you in Rome at your father's house."

The one bright spot of the emperor's latest assignment, Correus thought as he walked up the boarding plank of the Misenum Fleet's flagship with Caritius, was that Ygerna had agreed to brave the rigors of a full-fledged family gathering, and spend the time that he was posted to Rome at his father's house outside the City. At least he would have her warm company at night instead of a century of sailors and the dubious comforts of the Praetorian Guards barracks. And maybe that would keep the dreams at bay.

The whole world came to the emperor's games that year—a hundred days of spectacles, horse races, and trained elephants, wild beasts, gladiators, and, always, blood—an endless celebration of anything that anyone could think of to celebrate, from the emperor Titus's accession to the purple to the completion of the newest wonder in that city of wonders, the Flavian Amphitheater: four tiers of smooth travertine stone from the quarries of Albulae, brought to Rome on a road especially built to carry it, soaring skyward above Doric, Ionic, and Corinthian columns, above gilded statues in their niches, to the great, multicolored canvas awnings that shaded the inner bowl and the arena floor below. The light flowed brightly red, blue, and yellow, like paint poured through the awnings, giving a circus gaudiness to the gilded statues and the spectators in their seats. From the marble boxes of the privileged on the first level, up through the public tiers to the galleries on the top, the seats were filled with pages, attendants, message carriers, and laughing, pushing holiday-makers, trailing cushions and hampers of food.

Titus, dedicating the amphitheater constructed by his father, the Deified Vespasian, on land once occupied by Nero's private palace, had decreed that it belonged to the people of Rome, and all, down to the humblest, were to have their place in it. There was even a terrace above the third public tier to give standing room to the few slaves and foreigners too lowly to receive one of the 45,000 entrance tokens distributed each day.

Crowded into the doorways that led to the third tier of the public seating, a half century of seamen in the naval green tunics of the Misenum Fleet jostled each other for a view of the arena floor, while Correus Julianus, resplendent in the golden oak leaves of a *corona civica* and the gilded parade uniform of a senior centurion, his vine staff tucked under his arm, leaned in an arch beside a statue of Athena Nike and watched them. The man who didn't behave himself would rue the day, his expression said plainly.

To the bored peacetime sailors of the Misenum Fleet, a week's duty in the emperor's grand new amphitheater was a high treat, theirs merely for the price of running the awnings out on their rigging when the sun became too bright for comfort—an easy enough task for a man used to doing the same thing on a pitching ship in a thunderstorm. They shoved at each other for places in the doorways or scrambled up the stairs to the upper terrace to push the lowly out of theirs.

"Centurion Julianus, sir!" A short, sandy-haired seaman with a scar on his nose bobbed up in front of him and saluted, and Correus glared at him. "There's a bit of a fight up top, sir—Lucan and that silly Greek and somebody's slave!"

Correus hefted his vine staff and made an exasperated noise in the back of his throat. He headed for the stairs.

By the time he had sorted things out, to the accompaniment of cheers and whistles from the rest of the gallery, Seamen Lucan and Demetrios found themselves deprived of the rest of their tour of arena duty, and the slave, loudly protesting that he belonged to Marius Vettius and the centurion had better watch out, had been told to sit down and pipe down.

"And if there's another squawk from up here, whether it's my men or not, I'll have the whole gallery cleared," Correus snapped.

Across the arena, on the top tier, he could see more flashes of naval green, the other half century under the watchful eye of Caritius. The captain of the Misenum flagship was having a fine time, Correus thought. When the emperor had personally requested their expert advice and assistance in planning the naval spectacle and mock battle that was to be the highlight of the day's events, Captain Caritius had set himself to the project with the enthusiasm of an impresario. Correus had gone kicking and dragging his feet until his brother, Flavius, who was staff aide to the emperor, told him to keep his opinions to himself if he didn't want a hitherto shining career nipped in the bud.

"How'd you like to grow a long gray beard at Misenum?" was the way Flavius had put it.

Correus gave a final baleful stare of admonition to the top gallery and returned moodily to his post in the shadow of Athena Nike's gilded wings.

Most of the house of Appius Julianus were at the games today. The master himself had remained at home, claiming bad health (Appius Julianus was never fool enough to insult an emperor), but Julia and Lucius Paulinus were below in the senators' boxes, and Flavius and his wife were in the emperor's own box. And in the public tiers the free staff of the house of Appius had found seating.

Emer, dressed in her best, her red hair shining, was squeezed in between her husband and old Diulius. Diulius had driven in the Circus Maximus itself in his young days and could never resist a spectacle. The heady excitement of the crowd and the danger were in his blood. Emer's husband, Forst, merely liked to watch men fight, with the scientific appreciation of a man who had done much of it. He was a German from beyond the Rhenus, tall and blond and big boned, with the fairness of the North. He wore the plain tunic and sandals of a Roman freedman, but his face sported a drooping mustache, and his pale hair was long, pinned in an odd, exotic knot at the side of his head. He had been a weapons master to the sons of Appius before he had been freed. Now he was a head horseman, settled, married, and master of the stock that the estate bred for sale to the army. He lounged in his seat and wrapped a long arm around Emer as a roar went up from the crowd.

The gladiators swaggered up from the chambers under the floor, marching smartly to the harsh music of drum and trumpet. They made a circuit of the arena, while a little rain of flowers and coins showered down on them from patrician admirers in the marble boxes of the first tier. They smiled their thanks with a raffish gaiety that made the crowd roar out its approval. The spectators had no love for a man whose face showed his fear, and later their approval would matter greatly. The music reached its height and stopped, and there was a sudden hush like an indrawn breath as the gladiators formed up in ranks before the emperor's marble throne to give the old salute:

Ave, Caesar. Morituri te salutamus.

We who are about to die . . . There was an extra spice to that greeting today, in the knowledge that for this spectacle alone, a hundred death fights had been purchased. These were not the hopeless and condemned, doomed to be slaughtered wholesale, but the highly trained warriors of the gladiators' schools, expensive pieces of property. It was a mark of the emperor's free spending that of the two hundred smiling swordsmen who stood with arms raised before him, half would never leave the white sands of the arena with the breath still in them . . . unless the crowd should choose to spare them. The spectators shivered, eyes bright, and waited.

In his garlanded box, the emperor Titus Caesar Vespasianus Augustus—a stocky, bull-necked figure with a gilded laurel wreath set somewhat incongruously on his carefully curled hair—sat to receive the gladiators' salute. Titus's head, like that of his father, Vespasian, always looked as if it belonged under a helmet. Beside him, amid the flutter of gold and purple ribbons and the sweet scent of rose-and-lily garlands, was the emperor's brother, Domitian, his own dark curls adorned with flowers and his face bored and slightly surly. He shifted his feet restlessly under his consul's robes, and his fingers tapped the marble arm of his chair in a maddening rhythm, until in irritation the emperor slapped his own hand down on his chair.

Domitian shrugged and began to toss dice with the cronies who attended him. A young blond boy with the face of a marble Apollo stood behind his chair, draped over Domitian's shoulders like a cloak. Titus winced. He had put his own vices behind him when he took the purple, and he found it irritating that his brother could not manage to do likewise. Although, Titus thought grimly, he preferred the blond boy to the dubious company of Marius Vettius and his ilk.

Vettius, cheerfully swilling the emperor's best wine and throwing dice with Domitian while the gladiators' parade went by, was an influence that Domitian could have done without. In the manner of sandal lickers throughout the ages, Vettius's stocks-in-trade were the lavish compliment and the outstretched hand. He sang Domitian's praises to his face, encouraged him to drink too much and spend too freely, and feathered his own nest with the posts that such tactics gained him. His latest plum was a prefecture in the City Shipping Offices.

Titus swung his head around and glared at him and noted with satisfaction that Vettius lowered his voice and dropped down a little in his seat. It would have given Titus great pleasure to drop Vettius off the Capitoline, but enough blood had flowed during the civil wars before Vespasian took the purple to give Titus nightmares even now. He had marked his own accession with a public vow to Jupiter Capitolinus that if there were no concrete proof, there would be no executions. He had since wondered occasionally if that had been wise, but one didn't go back on a vow, not of that sort, without looking over his shoulder ever after.

Titus shrugged and turned his attention back to the arena, gravely raising his hand in answering salute to the gladiators' ranks. If he were lucky, someone else might see fit to get rid of Vettius for him. The emperor wouldn't overly object to Vettius's blood on someone else's hands. Young Flavius Julianus, maybe, he thought with a half smile, catching sight of his aide's aquiline face and crisp dark curls under the golden glint of a *corona aurea*. "For bravery above that normally expected of a Roman soldier..." Flavius had paid for that *corona aurea*: The long, slim hands resting on the marble railing of the emperor's box had only four fingers each. The other two had stayed behind him in West Britain, hacked off with a dagger by a British chieftain who wanted to know a military secret. Flavius's brother—up there with his seamen and glowering at the spectacle, no doubt, Titus thought with a quick grin—had got a *corona civica* for pulling Flavius out of that, and they were both currently in very good odor with the army command—which meant Titus. Titus glanced again at Flavius. He was facing the arena, but his eyes were slued sideways so that Vettius was in his line of vision. He had the expression of someone keeping an eye on a snake.

The dark-haired girl beside Flavius put a hand on his arm, and Flavius turned his eyes away from Vettius.

"Dear, you've got your eyes all turned around like an owl's. What are you looking at?"

"Owls turn their heads, sweet, not their eyes," Flavius said absently, but he gave his wife his attention.

"Well, whatever, it makes you look very odd from this side." Aemelia slipped an arm through his. "And you'll miss the show. What fun to sit in the emperor's box!" She giggled. "Half my friends are giving me dirty looks, and just look at the expression on Papa's face!"

Flavius turned his head toward the senators' boxes on their right, where the plump face and round blue eyes of his father-in-law, Aemelius, radiated satisfaction as he admired his daughter's dark beauty in the emperor's own box. Beside the senator, his wife, Valeria Lucilla, was enjoying herself hugely, being condescending to an old acquaintance whose daughter, a tall, sallow girl two paces behind her, showed no signs of catching any husband, much less a staff aide to the emperor.

"Your vanity is showing," Flavius said, teasing. Aemelia laughed and nodded, but it *was* fun, and the emperor leaned forward and patted her hand.

"You must come to the games with us more often, my dear," Titus said, in an avuncular tone carefully older than his years in case anyone should get the wrong ideas about his fondness for his aide's young wife. Titus had never cared for schoolgirls, and it would be a shame to start a scandal. Aemelia was much too unknowing to deal with it. "You make the scenery much prettier." He waved a slave over to refill her wine cup and push a standing tray of sweets and iced fruit a little closer to her reach.

Aemelia gave him a smile and a sigh of content. "Are they going to start soon?"

"Very shortly," Titus said. "Flavius, you may cease watching my brother and his unfortunate friends. No one is going to attempt my assassination at a public spectacle. I am not Gaius Caligula. Watch the games instead—unless you share your brother's views on the arena?" he added with a raised eyebrow. A man's opinions were his own, but the crowd wouldn't care for it if they thought the emperor and his staff found the public's amusements beneath them. And a City mob got out of hand all too easily.

"Not at all, sir," Flavius smiled. "I'm quite enjoying myself." He turned to the arena again, arms crossed on the railing. Unlike his half brother, Correus, who always got sick to his stomach, or their father, Appius, who merely disapproved, Flavius liked the harsh combat of the arena, the blood, and the strident music. He had long since ceased to wonder if that said something unpleasant about himself. Although Seneca had claimed that the games rotted the soul, Titus's court had no choice but to attend, so it was just as well to like them.

Aemelia also turned her face, a dark rose among the rose-and-lily garlands, to the arena floor. She hadn't been allowed to attend the games until she was married, and they never seemed quite real to her. In truth she hadn't the imagination to see the cold-eyed warriors below her as real men or the doomed and condemned as a higher order than that of the beasts roaring in their cages beneath the floor, so she enjoyed herself with the happy pleasure of a theatergoer. And afterward there would be the dinner party, which six senators and their wives, a poet and a philosopher and the emperor himself had promised to attend. Aemelia gave another little sigh of pleasure. Life had become very exciting since Titus had risen to the purple.

Athena Nike's face was splashed with red from the red canvas of the awning. *One more month*, Correus thought. *I can take one more month of this*. He made himself look down at the arena as the gladiators lifted their swords and the crowd noise swelled around him, a hungry sound, half-animal. Maybe Ygerna was right, and he was closer kin in the soul to Flavius than he had thought. Maybe it would be too easy to be lost in the blood and the harsh cry of the trumpets. Maybe that was what he was afraid of.

II

Charon

THE CROWD HAD STIFFENED TO ATTENTION, LIPS PARTED, EYES eager now for the first fight. A sword-and-shield man circled warily about his opponent—a brawny man, half-naked, armed with Neptune's fishing net and a long-handled trident that ended in three gleaming tines. That rapt attention would only last a few fights, the swordsman knew. He was lucky to be the first, while the crowd was still fresh and appreciative, eager to spare the warrior who acquitted himself well. Later, after five or six more fights, the other combatants would fight ten and twelve at a time, and the crowd would be eating sweets and gossiping, bored again, interested only in the blood and not the skill. The man who went down then would stay down.

"The man with the sword," Emer said. "He's limping, I think."

Forst narrowed his eyes. "He has a bad ankle," he said, watching the swordsman. "Just enough to slow him. He is going to lose. He's playing to the crowd, I think."

"Aye." Diulius, the wiry old man on Emer's other side, gave her a gap-toothed grin. "He's givin' 'em a good show

and prayin' for a thumbs-up when the net man gets him." He
settled in to watch.

Emer wished she hadn't mentioned it. It was one thing to
watch the pageantry of the games for the excitement of it. It
was another to be suddenly put inside a gladiator's skin. She
put her hand on her husband's arm, not wanting to watch now
when that snaking net reached out for the limping man's feet.
"I think everyone within fifty miles of Rome is here." She
waved a hand at the jammed tiers rising above the arena floor,
from the marble boxes of the nobility to the standing space in
the top galleries.

"That should please the emperor," Forst said, watching the
swordsman.

A bowlegged man balancing a tray of iced fruit came down
the sloping corridor and through the crowd, shouting his wares
in competition with the constantly roving vendors of sweets,
cold drinks, seat cushions, and other comforts. Forst waved a
long arm at him, and the man pushed his way through the seats
to them. Forst bought two pears and handed Emer one, cold
and dripping with melted ice. She bit into it hungrily while
Forst complained to the bowlegged man about the price. That
was understood, part of the ritual. The fruit seller departed,
stuffing Forst's coin into a grimy pouch.

Forst was as Roman now as a man like him was going to
get, Emer thought, watching her husband. Only his long, knotted hair marked him for an oddity, and Emer suspected that
he clung stubbornly to it because of that. Forst was not a man
who liked to blend into the scenery. What had he been like,
she wondered, before the war in Germany, before the slave
collar, before Rome? Before her?

On the sand, the swordsman had gone down. The trident
fighter's net was tangled over the swordsman's head and arms,
and one leg was bent awkwardly under him. He lay twisting
frantically in a pool of blue light, under the multicolored awning, until the trident man laid the bright sharp tines against his
throat. The swordsman froze. The trident man turned toward
the emperor's box and bowed. He raised a hand, looking at
the crowd, asking for life. Were the victor and victim friends?
Emer wondered. A man couldn't live and eat and fight with

another in the gladiators' school and not form some kinship. She turned her eyes away, back to the crowd.

The emperor was debating, making much show of consulting the white-robed Vestals in their box, but it was the faces in the tiers that his eyes were assessing.

Emer found that she didn't want to watch that, either, and moved her gaze along to the foreign dignitaries in their special box. They were sitting near the front of the long axis of the oval arena, where Emer could look down and almost face on to them. They were an exotic company, brightly clothed, with odd, barbaric jewelry and their own contingent of guards. Enormous black men in feather-crowned helmets glared impassively out over the heads of the foreign princes from the four corners of the box. They would be there as much to keep the foreign royalty in as to keep unauthorized troublemakers out, Emer suspected. The box's occupants were client kings and chieftains of conquered lands, politely invited to spend some time in Rome. It was unlikely that any of them would go home again. They could make too much trouble at home. And it pleased Rome's citizens to see evidence of success in her foreign wars.

Each had his own entourage about him, slaves and a woman or two, and small boys with fans. There was a table overloaded with food. *They are pets*, Emer thought, and then put a hand to her mouth. There was a red-haired man in a dark green shirt and trousers embroidered all over with gold thread. He sat near the center of the box. His mouth was half-hidden under a drooping mustache, and his hair was long and pinned into a knot at the side of his head.

"Forst."

Forst raised his eyebrows at her inquiringly, his mouth full of pear.

"Forst, there is a man in the foreigners' box. At the center—"

Forst looked. Emer saw his eyes cast about until he found him, and then his skin, tanned to a light gold under the Italian sun, went pale. Pale and cold...clammy. There was a thin film of sweat on his forehead.

"Forst? Who is it?"

Forst shook his head. He stood up, leaving the gnawed pear on the seat. "Stay here."

"Forst—"

He didn't speak to her again, but just pushed his way out into the wide, sloping corridor that led down to the first tiers and the walkways that circled each level.

"What's taken him?" Diulius asked. "Coming on sick?"

"No. No, I don't think so."

"Well, he looked gut-sick to me."

He had looked sick to Emer, too, and it had been the man in the box who had caused it. Only the tribes of the Suevi, the loose confederacy of which Forst's people, the Semnones, were a part, wore their hair in that fashion. Emer knew that much, but so little else of what Forst had been before he came to her that she had never considered whether or not she should point out the red-haired man to Forst before she had impulsively done so.

She had lost Forst in the crowd now. Nervously she watched the little group that milled about the foreign princes. Beyond them, the emperor beamed mercifully and turned a stocky hand palm up. The swordsman rolled free of the net and stood, with all his weight on his good leg.

Forst came out of the outer corridor onto the sloping ramp that ran down through the boxes of the elite, and a large black hand pushed politely on his chest as he stopped at the entrance to the box where the foreign princes sat.

"Not here, sir," the guard said politely. Firmly. His voice echoed the pressure of his hand.

"I—I have—" Forst swallowed. He'd never get in if he acted like a raving lunatic. "I have business with the German lord. With—with Nyall Sigmundson."

A name out of the past, the dead time, out of the years he had so carefully erased in Rome. A name out of memory, which carried other memories in the sound, like laughter . . . boys' laughter. Three boys, ten years old and restless with the energy of youth and summer, wrestling in the cold shallows of a stream, rolling over and over in the water's edge. . . . And later, years later, the same three, himself and Nyall and Kari Half-Blood, standing in a ring of torches while the priests chanted and made magics and stared solemnly at the night sky. . . . The three of them, moving over the new snow past those torches to the bright heat of the Council Fire, Forst and Kari on either side, while the priests and the council made Nyall Sigmundson chieftain of the Semnones in his father's place. . . .

"I don't know. . . ." The Nubian's voice was dubious, and Forst frantically jerked himself out of memory, trying to think of something, anything—

"The chieftain has asked me to find him a suitable mount," he said, forcing indifference into his voice. "I am horsemaster for the stables of Julianus. If you don't let me in, old Julianus will probably be unhappy about it. I expect you've heard of him. His son is the emperor's aide." He gazed loftily at the Nubian while the man paused to consider.

"I'll ask," the guard said after a moment. He made his way majestically back into the box and bent to speak to the red-haired man.

A small boy with a palm fan stared curiously at Forst, and a girl in a peach-colored gown that went just beyond the edge of decency lifted her head from a jumble of cushions and gave him an interested eye. The swarthy man beside her, in a costume that looked vaguely Eastern to Forst, leaned down and said something, and she turned her head away petulantly. There were a great many cushions and boxes of sweets and half-drunk wine cups strewn about the box. Rome had a large contingent of foreign residents. It would be easy enough for a client prince to resign himself to captivity, surrounded by fellow countrymen and the pleasures that Rome could offer a man with time on his hands.

In the midst of this picnic atmosphere, Nyall sat like a wood carving. There was a slave at his elbow to keep his wine cup filled, but the slave could have been put to better use. The wine was untouched. When the Nubian bent down, Nyall's eyes were straight ahead on the arena, but Forst didn't think he was seeing it. When the Nubian spoke, Nyall just shook his head, then slowly, as if curiosity had dawned, he turned slightly until he could see Forst standing beside the entrance while someone in the box behind them shouted furiously at Forst to sit down. His eyes were cold, Forst thought, gray, dead, as if everything in them had gone out. But after a moment Nyall nodded to the Nubian. He stood and took a step toward Forst.

There was something wrong with his leg. With a cold contraction somewhere inside him, Forst thought of the gladiator lying under the net in the garish circus light. It was more than a limp. The leg was twisted outward so that Nyall walked with a dipping, hobbling gait. The lines of old pain spread like a web across his face. He said something to the Nubian, and when the man looked dubious again, snapped in Latin that still had the old, familiar accent of the North, "Do you think I am going to run, maybe, back to Germany?" He put a hand on the twisted thigh and grimaced. "I want to sit in the corridor with this man and talk about a horse."

The Nubian thought it over and nodded. It was no business of his if the German chief wanted to get cheated personally over a horse instead of sending his slave to do it, like a gentleman.

Forst stiffened as Nyall limped carefully through the debris in the box. What should he say? What should he say to a man who had been the chieftain, now that the gods had reached down and taken that from him? Worse than the shame of a pleasant prison in Rome, worse than defeat, worse than anything, was that twisted, dragging leg that had taken Nyall Sigmundson's chieftainship away. Nyall halted beside him. "I thought you had died," Forst said, choking.

"Close." Nyall put a hand on Forst's arm, carefully, as if he thought the other man might be an elf-gift that would vanish with the touching. "You . . . we keened you, the Companions and I, after the raid on the Forts-by-the-River, when we lost you."

"The Romans found me," Forst said. "I wasn't . . . quite dead yet."

"And now?"

"I wore a slave collar for a while, but I am free now. I . . . never went back. When I could have gone . . . the sons of the man who freed me—they are army men—they told me what had happened in the Black Forest lands. And that you had died."

"I expect they thought I had, then."

"I gave a bull to Wuotan Father for you." It was the last prayer Forst had made to the gods of his home.

Nyall smiled crookedly, the lines in his face twisting sharply with the turn of his mouth. "Maybe he will be remembering it, when the time comes."

"Typhon take it, *get down!*" someone behind them shouted. The other foreigners in the marble box were beginning to stare at them. Nyall came through the gate of the box, and they worked their way past the other boxes onto the sloping ramp that led upward to the first corridor. Behind them the gladiators had begun again, and a trio of musicians played a spritely melody in counterpoint to the fight. The sound of a water organ came faintly over the crowd's noise as they stepped into the shadows of the corridor. In the arched windows, more statues stood, heroes on this level, Ulysses and Hercules and Hector of Troy. There were stone benches between the windows, and they sat on one, where the statue of Ulysses blocked the sun from the open arch. A trio of girls in bright dresses hurried by, giggling and sharing a sack of candied plums among them. Forst and Nyall sat in silence, the music battering at their ears. Of all the things to be said, there was none that didn't seem a mockery.

"Who is chieftain now?" Forst said finally. Surely there would be something left to be chieftain over.

"I don't know." With his face in shadow, Nyall sounded more like the man Forst remembered—remembered and had mourned. In the light outside the box, Forst had thought that man might still be dead. There had been something flat in Nyall's eyes, like a corpse unnaturally wakened. "I made the council promise they wouldn't choose until I had gone," Nyall went on. "I would only have wanted to meddle."

"*Why* did you go?" Forst's voice was anguished. Once he had been closer than most brothers to the twisted man beside him, he and the rest of the Companions. Only Kari had been closer.

"It was . . . time," Nyall said. "There was little enough else left I could do, and a new chieftain had to be chosen." Some Roman's sword stroke had brought that choice on the tribe. A maimed man could not be chieftain. The chieftain was the land, in the tribe's eyes, and a maimed chieftain would bring a maimed land. "I told you, I would only have wanted to meddle, and I am still strong enough to make trouble."

With Nyall like a ghost at his shoulder, a new chieftain would never have been able to rule. "But to give yourself to the Romans—" Forst knew now that Kari was dead. Kari would never have let him do this.

"It was to buy time. To mend. We made enough widows in that war. With me here, the Romans would have little cause to go *there*, into the Free Lands, and maybe finish the job. Now they will have peace, the ones who are left."

"How many . . . left?" Forst wanted to weep. Worse than all the deaths was what had happened to the man beside him.

"Of the men, few enough. A fourth of our fighting men, *maybe*, counting the Black Forest men who came to us when the Romans took their lands. But there would be children to grow up if the Romans didn't come, so I came here, to them, instead."

"The children—yours?" Nyall had been single in the old days.

"I don't think so. I had a wife, but . . . no, I don't think so." There was a sharp flare of pain in Nyall's voice, and then it too went cold, dead as the eyes that had looked at Forst out of the box. "I found I was little enough use to her, either. And she was a chieftain's daughter and kin to the Black Forest lords. Better that she stayed."

Would *she* have thought so? Forst wondered. Emer would never have let him go alone. But Emer was a freedwoman, British by blood, but third-generation slave stock by birth. She would have no loyalty to the land, only to him. Nyall's woman though—what was she doing now, neither wife nor widow? He looked at Nyall and didn't ask.

"What can I do?" he asked, tormented, trying to reach out to a ghost. It was almost more than he could bear to remember Nyall as he had been, and to see him now, a broken thing, a pet in Titus's zoo. And Forst had thought he was growing very Roman.

"Nay, I am well enough treated," Nyall said with a smile that was like a death's-head twin to his old one. "As you can see." He waved a hand at the inner bowl of the arena, and the box full of slaves and wine cups and sticky, half-eaten sweets. "They have even given me new clothes."

His shirt and breeches were cut in the German style, but the workmanship had a foreign look to it—made in Rome, Forst thought, by someone not a German.

"Luxury, in fact—an allowance from the state—enough to buy your horse." Nyall's voice was suddenly alive again, bitter as acid. "And nothing to do for it but dance for my supper, like any tame bear." With that, he rose and limped away, back down the sloping corridor, while Forst sat clenching and un-clenching his hands behind him. After a while a small boy in a slave's tunic trotted by.

"Here, you—" Forst reached out a hand.

The boy halted and eyed him suspiciously.

"Where are you going?"

"My mistress wants her shawl." The boy began to edge past him.

"Do you want to earn a bit of silver?"

The child edged back again, plainly weighing the lure of the silver against the thumping he would get if he were late with the shawl.

"This is my seat." Forst handed him a bronze token with his seat section and number on one side and a likeness of the emperor on the other. "It will only take you a minute. There is a lady with red hair in the next seat. Tell her that Forst said that he will be late, and she is not to wait for him. Also that he said to give you a silver bit for the message."

"Forst." The child considered. "Is that you, lord?"

"Yes."

"And she will give me a whole silver bit?"

"Yes."

"Why do you wear your hair like that?"

"I'm a German," Forst said in exasperation. "Among my people, it means I have killed a man."

"Who did you kill?" The child appeared willing to keep his mistress waiting indefinitely as the stranger grew more inter-esting.

Forst half rose. "Do you want a spanking or a piece of silver?"

"The silver, lord."

The boy trotted off, and Forst leaned back against the wall with his feet on the bench. Emer would ask questions, too, but there was a question Forst wanted to ask first, of Correus and Flavius, who had known and fought Nyall in the Rhenus days and who would surely have seen him here in Rome. And who had told Forst that Nyall was dead.

The air was wet and full of old fish, overlaid with the scent of rotting cabbages and other, more mysterious garbage that Rome threw daily into the Tiber. Augustus's artificial lake along its banks was nearly filled now—they had filled it a week ago, and it had leaked. The pipes from the Alsietina Aqueduct were running full spate, and the brightly painted warships bobbed higher on the water. The shields slung along their sides and the oars, now held aboard ship, had a fresh coat of paint, and the sails of "Augustus's" galleys were newly dyed scarlet. Across the lake, "Antony's" galleys bore the horned headdress of his lover, Cleopatra. It was all show. The galleys marked for the naval spectacle were ready to be scrapped, leaking steadily from all seams, their inner fittings rusted into uselessness.

"I hope the old bitch makes it across the lake." Caritius cast a professional eye on the "Roman" flagship. "She probably *saw* Actium."

"I expect she'll make it," Correus said. "If there's any water in the lake, of course. Your damned galleys aren't the only things leaking. I've had 'em leave the water channels open full. I wish I knew where it was going."

"Into some senator's cellar, probably," Caritius said. "You'll get the bill tomorrow."

Correus growled. The aggravations of the day had been numerous. But the leaks in the galleys and the lake did serve to distract him from the men marked out to fight on them. The emperor had promised freedom to any man on the winning side still alive at the end of the fight. But Augustus's victory at Actium was too dear to the Roman imperial heart. A victory by Cleopatra and Antony's ships wouldn't be overly well received, so the fight was carefully weighted to the Roman side, and Antony's troops were in no good frame of mind.

Correus had as good as lived with them for the better part

of two weeks, teaching them to fight like marines, while Caritius showed them how to handle the ships. They were soldiers, some of them, Roman and foreign, fallen foul of their commanders and sentenced to the arena for their crimes. These were the ones who bothered Correus the most, more than the civilian lot of thieves and cutthroats. Admittedly, most of the civilians deserved any fate that Rome chose to hand out—but this was no way for a professional soldier to die.

He groaned and gave a last look at the murky waters of the lake. They'd had it dredged before they filled it, but nameless things still floated to the top and washed ashore on the islands in the center. He looked at the sun. It was time. The last spectacle in the new amphitheater would be winding up, the last criminal killed, the last lion hunted down. The tamer entertainments, the tumblers and mimes, would be rolling up their gear. When the emperor gave the signal, 45,000 spectators would come pouring out of the arena, blocking traffic all the way across the river, to see the capstone of the days' amusements. And if they weren't ready, there would be 45,000 *angry* spectators seated around a leaking lake. The new arena could be flooded, and Correus fervently wished the emperor had done so, but the old lake was bigger and easier for launching their fleet.

"I'll go and get them set," he said to Caritius. "Stand by in case there's trouble." If someone wanted to make trouble, the possibilities were infinite. The sailors from the arena were stationed at the lake now, with three more centuries of their fellows and a cohort of the Praetorian Guards from the City.

There were 1,250 men to a side, enough for five ships each. The Augustan ships were manned already, prodded along by the Praetorian Guards, and Correus stood by while the Egyptian crews, hair dyed black and skin stained brown, filed on board. (That most of Antony's crew had been Romans fighting Romans was tactfully forgotten.) Correus would have liked not to watch, but the Guards' troops were there, so he stood at attention, while across the lake, the first of the imperial party arrived and settled in to the special enclosure reserved for them. He hoped he didn't look as sick as he felt.

"No stomach for it, eh, friend?" The voice was biting, but somehow amused.

"Get back in line, and mind your tongue." There was the smack of a vine staff on flesh, and Correus picked out the owner of the voice, a thin, fair-haired Macedonian whom he remembered seeing before, his pale eyes startling now behind the red-brown dye and the blacking in his hair. For good measure, the junior officer gave him another smack with the staff.

"All right, you lot, get on board." As they came to the foot of the jetty, another officer held out his staff as the Macedonian marched past. "The rest of you wait here for the next ship. Behave yourselves, and you might come out of this. Give me any trouble, and you won't live long enough to fight for it. Clear?"

Beyond him, the Macedonian turned around. He seemed about to retort and then shrugged. With death snapping at his heels for certain this time, there didn't seem to be much point in it.

AVE CAESAR!

The sound came from 2,500 throats together, over the slimy green waters of the lake to the emperor in his imperial box by the shore.

"May you go down to Avernus behind me," Eumenes the Macedonian muttered from his post at the middle oar bank in the trireme's hold. It was too much like the rowing benches of the slavers in that hold, even if he wasn't chained to the deck. He'd tried to think that this was a quicker way than the slavers, and maybe better—they ground a man to death on the slave ships, with weariness and diseases and bad food. But he'd never been able to resign himself to death, not even now. The mallet strokes began to beat out their rhythm and pick up speed. He gripped his oar and gritted his teeth.

It was a windless day. The only ripples on the lake came from the open water channels and the trireme's oars as they rose and fell. She shot out ahead of her fellows to meet the Roman fleet. Behind her, two other galleys had tangled oars, snapping them off as they tried to extricate themselves.

The untrained rowers of the opposing fleet were not doing much better, but the lake was small enough for them to close quickly, and the crowd didn't want skill, it wanted carnage.

A fire arrow shot a sun-colored bolt across the sky and lodged in the trireme's furled sail. Tongues of flame ran down the rigging. Eumenes looked up through the open top of the rowing deck. *Fire! On this piece of kindling!* He dropped his oar with the rest of the rowers, victory forgotten. They herded frantically onto the upper deck as the oars snapped off in the oarlocks behind them and the trireme caromed sideways off a ship of the Augustan fleet.

The Augustan ship's oars sheared off on that side, and the trireme's crew managed to swing the *corvus*, the spike-tipped boarding ramp, around to catch her. The iron crow's beak punched through the deck of the larger quinquireme, holding her fast to the burning trireme. The quinquireme's crew, their own oar decks abandoned, hacked at the boarding ramp and the men who were pushing their way across it.

The rest of the ships were little better off. Two more were on fire, the flames glowing brightly in the dimming light of early evening, reflecting off the dark waters. Most had lost at least half of their oars and drifted awkwardly on the lake current caused by the open water channels. One galley had let her sail down, or it had come down, and one of the light stone-throwers that each ship carried sent a shot through the sail that took the mast with it, crashing down across the deck and crushing the curving prow into splinters.

Other shots whistled overhead as each ship tried to sink its opponents' galleys—and as often as not landed its shot on an allied deck or wide in the water. The stone-throwers made more show than damage—they had been carefully calibrated to have a range far short of the spectators on the shore—and the crews soon abandoned them for fire arrows or direct boarding. Each ship was also equipped with an underwater ram on her prow, but it took more training than these makeshift crews had had to time a ramming run properly.

Eumenes pushed his way across the ramp, his sword out and a shield in his hand, snatched up from the row along the ship's rail. An Augustan in a Roman naval tunic lunged at him awkwardly with a short sword, and Eumenes parried easily. He brought his own sword in under the other's wavering guard and pushed him backward, his blade in the other's chest. The man fell sideways off the plank. In another step Eumenes was on the quinquireme, clear of the burning trireme.

"Come on, damn you! Push 'em off!" he shouted at the crew of the trireme, while both ships bumped and fumbled together. Across the lake, beyond the larger of the two artificial islands, he could see another ship burning and a third going down prow first, accidental victim of a direct hit with a ram. "*Fight*, you bastards!" He was screaming above the sounds of battle until his throat was hoarse, but these poor fools in fake Egyptian armor had never been soldiers. They stood, almost paralyzed with fear, and hacked at each other clumsily, half the time forgetting which side they were on, while the Augustans did likewise, and slowly the fire on board edged closer to the quinquireme.

"Sons of whores!" With a parting scream of fury, Eumenes gave up and began chopping desperately at the boarding plank with the edge of his sword. An Augustan beside him recognized him for the enemy and abandoned his own efforts to free the boarding ramp to dive at Eumenes, sword out.

"You're on fire, you fool!" Eumenes shouted. "Get the plank free first!"

But the Augustan could think only of the last desperate hope: freedom—*life*—for the winning side if they killed all of the others. Eumenes was from the others, a life that stood between the Augustan and his own. Another of the quinquireme's crew, desperation outweighing sense, joined in the hunt, and Eumenes abandoned the plank and ran.

There were Roman tunics before him and behind him, too many to fight off even if they didn't know the hilt from the blade of a sword. He jumped between them onto the rail and dived.

The slimy green waters were as cold as the streams that fed the aqueducts. He caught a choking mouthful as the abandoned oars of the quinquireme swung over him. Something cracked against Eumenes's skull with a bright, sharp pain.

The sun had long since sunk down beyond Ostia Harbor in the west, but there was a full moon riding in the tree branches of the island, giving the lowering waters the unhealthy phosphorescent shine of decaying weeds.

"Almost low level, sir." The soldier from the Corps of Engineers nodded at the lake. "We'll have it clear in an hour or so." The lake had to be drained immediately and the dead pulled out of it. A handful of the Augustan crews had gone free at the battle's end, to the cheers of the crowd, but most were here under the dark waters. "You can go on home, if you like, sir," the engineer said, "and leave us to finish."

Correus thought wistfully of a hot bath and his brother's dinner party, which would be getting to the lobsters and asparagus now. "No, I'll stay. How many have you got out?" One unnoticed corpse in the mud of the lake bottom and a winter of heavy rains could contaminate the whole Alsietina Aqueduct, and he didn't want to be the man responsible when the water supply commissioner had to go and clean it out.

The engineer looked at his tally sheet. "One thousand seven hundred and forty-two. And twenty-three freed. The rest'll be on the bottom, most like, or caught in the galleys. We've one ship left to pull out."

"Well, have at it." On the shore Correus could see the broken hulls and charred remnants of the nine salvaged galleys, silhouetted in the moonlight. "Have you checked the islands?"

"Not yet, sir," the engineer said. "I can pull some men off the dredging to do it. We're a mite shorthanded."

"Never mind," Correus said. "If you've got a boat and two men, I'll do it. Let's get this finished. The sooner away from here, the sooner I can go get drunk."

"I'm with you there, sir," the engineer said, looking out across the water with its debris of dead things. "It's an unhealthy job. I'd as soon go wash my hands as quick as I can."

The oars on the little boat that the maintenance crews used dipped in and out of the water with a soft plopping sound. The only other noise was the grunting of the men hauling the last of the ship's carcasses onto the shore and the oars of the boats that were dredging the bottom waters with a net. They beached their boat on the sloping edge of the artificial island well below the high-water mark, and Correus unshipped three lanterns while the two rowers dragged the boat up on the mud. The lake was as low as the drain channels could get it now, and they could have walked across, Correus thought—if anyone had wanted to walk through the last two feet of water and what was probably still in it.

They found three bodies straightaway, caught in the brush on the low slope of the island when the receding waters had flowed away. "I'll take the north end to the second stand of trees," Correus said tiredly. "You two take the middle and the south point." He trudged away, the lantern swinging from one hand. *Diogenes in search of his virtuous man*, he thought. *The dead are always virtuous*. The emperor had sent a congratulatory message as the trumpets had sounded a triumphal tune and the last of the galleys with the insignia of the woman that most Romans still thought of as "that Egyptian witch" had slipped in flames beneath the water. There had been one Augustan ship afloat and twenty-three Augustan crewmen freed with a fanfare: a propitious omen and one that was likely to make the emperor grateful. *I'd be grateful if his damned lake sank into the Tiber*, Correus thought sourly. His lantern caught a pale gleam—a hand, white as a fish, wrapped around the trunk of a sapling where the first stand of trees grew down to the waterline.

The man lay face down in the damp earth, the blacking nearly washed from his fair hair by the lake water. His other hand was outflung as if it, too, had scrabbled for some purchase, some hiding place from death. Correus bent and turned him over gently. The body gave a shuddering cough, and a little water ran from the corners of his mouth.

"Oh, Mithras." Correus pulled the soaked Egyptian trappings from him and turned him over again, squeezing more water out. "What do I do with you now?" he murmured.

The body gave another racking cough and turned himself over this time. "Put a knife through me, I should think," he wheezed. "It would make it simpler."

Correus helped him to sit up, then sat back on his heels watching while the man retched and brought up more water. With the brown stain washed from his face, he looked as pale as the corpse he had almost been. He sat hunched over until the spasms passed. "Who the hell are you?" he said finally.

"Charon, maybe," Correus said shortly.

"Come to row me to Hades yonder?" the man asked. "I've been expecting you," he added politely.

Correus couldn't tell if he was mocking him or was still half-drowned and dreaming. Or maybe he was serious. "Who are *you*?" It seemed important somehow, in this mad, moonlit scene, to be introduced.

"Eumenes," the man said.

"How did you end up like this?"

"Still alive, you mean? Or on your fucking galley in the first place?" The man's tone was pleasant, at odds with his words, polite conversation in a madhouse.

"On the galley in the first place," Correus said.

"Off a slaver," Eumenes said. "Not so much difference there, really."

"What did you do?" A man, even a slave, had to be condemned into the arena. Plainly he had done something.

"Killed a man. Or I thought I had. I heard later he lived, after all." Eumenes sounded regretful.

"An overseer?"

"Yes."

"Understandable but foolish." Correus gave him a thoughtful look. He remembered him now. There had been something about the way he walked—like a man with a parade ground in his past. Most men never lost that once it had been drilled into them. "How did you get on a slaver?"

"Tried to kill my decurion," Eumenes said shortly.

"Do you make a habit of that?" Correus inquired.

"No."

"Twice in one career seems excessive. Auxiliaries?" Correus asked.

"Yeah."

"Be a little more informative if you want to save your ass!" Correus snapped.

Eumenes blinked, and his eyes opened wide. "Sorry, friend. I didn't know that was on the list of possibilities."

Correus sighed. "I'd sooner put a knife in a man than send him to the arena again. Since I haven't yet, I suppose I'm not going to."

Correus put out a hand and pulled Eumenes to his feet.

III

The House on the Aventine

DAYLIGHT. CORREUS GROANED AND STUCK HIS HEAD DEEPER into the pillow. Something warm snuggled up next to him, and he wrapped an arm around her. Ygerna. He was sleepily glad that he had made the ride to his father's house last night, wet and unpleasant as his mood had been. He didn't think he could have stood waking up in the Praetorian Guards barracks this morning.

There was a clatter outside the door and Julius edged his way around it, precariously balancing a silver tray. "Everyone has eaten," he said reproachfully. "I brought you this." He set the tray on the marble-topped dressing table, pushing Ygerna's flasks of scent to one side. He removed the napkin to reveal fruit, olives, bread and a honey pot, matching jugs of wine and water, and a pair of silver cups.

Ygerna sat up suddenly as the scent bottles rattled. "Julius! Be careful!"

"There is a man in the slave quarters who says he belongs to you," Julius informed Correus. He gave Ygerna a sideways glance and carefully poked the fragile flasks back from the edge of the table. "And Forst is here. He wants to see you."

"I don't doubt it." Correus groaned. He had Typhon's own headache. He pushed Ygerna's cat off the bed and sat up. Forst had been trying to see him since last night, and Correus had been dodging. "Tell him I'll come find him at the stables."

He knew what Forst wanted—Correus had also seen the foreign princes in their fancy box—and he simply hadn't wanted to deal with Forst's indignation and the emperor's water fight at the same time. So he had dodged. And now it was going to be worse than ever. He shuddered, remembering the night before. . . .

Correus and Eumenes had come upon the screaming girl quite by accident as they squelched their way over the old Pons

32

Sublicius across the Tiber, damp and smelling of rotting weeds.
The girl stood outside a house on the lower slopes of the
Aventine, just by the bridge. She had on a night shift, and
there were curling rags in her hair. She stood on the top step
of the house, shrieking hysterically into the darkness.

Without much thinking about it, they went up the steps,
shook her, and said, "Stop that! What's the matter?" In the
madhouse atmosphere of that night it seemed quite ordinary to
find in their path a screaming woman in her nightdress.

She pointed a shaking finger back toward the dimly lit atrium
beyond the open doorway, and Correus saw that there was
something dark and liquid on her hands.

He and Eumenes looked at her and then at each other before
sprinting into the atrium. There was another dim glow from a
guttering lamp set in a wall bracket in the passageway beyond,
and farther still an open doorway with a bright pool of light
spilling out. The girl came behind them, moaning. Correus
turned to her.

"In there?"

She nodded dumbly, putting her hands to her face, then
jerking them away as she realized the dark stain had smeared
on her cheeks. Inside the brightly lit room, the stain became
red—red as the pool that had soaked into the white bedclothes.
Nyall Sigmundson lay on top of his unwrinkled blankets, one
arm folded across his chest, the other trailing over the side of
the carved wooden bed frame. The knife lay beside the bed on
the floor. His throat had been cut from ear to ear.

"Oh, no . . ." Correus whispered, looking down.

The girl, a slave of the house by the look of her, continued
to gibber in the doorway.

"Stop it, woman, for the gods' sake!" Eumenes snapped.
"He's past hurting anyone, the poor bastard."

"The murderer—he could be hiding," she wailed. "Waiting—"

"There isn't one," Correus said. "You fool—he did this to
himself."

"Himself?" She hiccuped and looked curiously at the centurion. She took a step into the room. "Why ever would he do
that?"

Correus just stood looking down at the chalk-pale body on

the bed. The flaming hair had come partly unpinned, and there was blood in it. "I expect he had his reasons," Correus said. "The knife's there by his hand. Didn't you notice?"

"No. I just saw the blood—I leaned over and put my hand in it!" She began wailing again. "And the guards are all asleep—I think they've been drugged—and I couldn't wake them, and I didn't know what to *do*!"

"Well, standing outside screaming doesn't seem to have been very useful," Eumenes said acidly. "Run along and get the City guards, for the gods' sake, like an intelligent girl."

"Y-yes, sir." She hurried out, apparently finding no reason in their mud-stained garments to question the voice of authority.

"Thank you," Correus said. "I should have sent her for the guards right off."

"You looked like you had other things on your mind," Eumenes said. "You knew him, didn't you?"

Correus looked down at the copper-colored hair, the green shirt and breeches, and the right leg that was twisted outward.

"Yes, in a way. I knew him."

Correus put his hands to his temples. And now there was that to tell Forst as well. And Eumenes had to be explained to the courts, which had condemned him into the arena. Correus had taken the Macedonian with him the previous night on the strength of his dubious authority as overseer of the water battle, but there were complications and legalities involved in buying a condemned slave. He would have to bribe someone, he expected.

Julius returned to say that Forst had gone back to the stables, but if the centurion didn't go down there soon, he'd be back on the doorstep, most like. And would my lady like him to send her maid to her? And this had come for the centurion. He held out to Correus a wax tablet sealed in purple.

Ygerna, who had been about to get up and dress without her maid, dived back under the covers and said tartly that what she would like was for Julius to quit popping in and out, so that she could dress.

Julius turned beet red, looked wildly at the floor and walls, and fled. Ygerna collapsed on the bed, giggling.

"You shouldn't tease him," Correus said reprovingly, but

she just grinned at him. Correus sighed. Ygerna was even
younger than Julius, and occasionally she could be a bit stupid
about things. He thumbed open the wax tablet, and his eyebrows shot up in surprise.

"What is it?" Ygerna watched him as he got out of bed and
went to hold the wax under the light from the window. She
still liked just to look at him. She had been in love with Correus
since she was thirteen, but she still hadn't got tired of looking
at him.

"It's my transfer! Back to the Rhenus, to—*damn* it, to the
fleet again! But out of Misenum, at any rate." His eyebrows
went still higher. "I'm to have an audience with the emperor
on the subject. Do I detect Flavius's hand in this again?"

"You shouldn't be so suspicious. He means well."

"I know he does, bless him. And if he's got me out of
Misenum, I'll kiss him."

He found a clean loincloth in the clothes chest, knotted it
around his hips, and shrugged on an old tunic that Ygerna
thought must be a relic of his boyhood. The hem appeared to
have been let down twice, and the sleeves rode high on the
muscles of his upper arms. He ran a comb through his hair,
peering into her dressing-table mirror. The cowlick over his
brow lay flat for a moment and then sprang into its usual untidy
wave. "You'd think all these years of putting a helmet on my
hair would at least make it lie down," he said. "I'm going to
have a ride, if possible, after I talk to Forst." He picked up an
apple from the tray and bit into it. "Don't forget to eat something."

She grinned. "Don't worry." Ygerna had always had a light
appetite, but with her pregnancy she seemed to have developed
a state of perpetual starvation. Correus wasn't sure where she
was putting it, but she was going through more food than he
could eat.

"Do you want me to explain Eumenes to your father?" she
asked. "Someone had better."

"Yes, *please*." Ygerna was on polite if wary terms with
Lady Antonia, Julia's and Flavius's mother, and did her best
to ignore Correus's mother, Helva, but for some reason the
most formidable member of the family, his father, Appius,
held no terror for her. He took another apple and headed for

the stable and Forst. Whatever he encountered with the Rhenus Fleet wasn't going to be worse than this.

Two colts, a black and a gray, improbable stilt-legged creatures racing the morning breeze, careened wildly past the lower pasture fence. Correus and Forst leaned with crossed arms on the fence rail, not watching them. Forst was watching nothing, some invisible point midway over the horizon. Correus was watching Forst.

"So he is dead," Forst said finally. "Truly dead this time."

"Should I have told you?" Correus sounded half-helpless, half-angry. He would have liked to throw something. "I thought you would only grieve."

"Yes."

Wrong to have robbed him of that, maybe, Correus thought. And then, *He will grieve now.* There was no proper "should" or "shouldn't," no easy way to tell Forst that Nyall—his friend and chieftain—was alive, or that he was now dead. There was no easy way out from under the burden of his own knowledge. Finally he had blurted it out and watched Forst wince and crumble a little and then turn around and look at the line of fir trees that lined the road in the distance and masked the horizon. Now Correus wanted only to be gone, back into Rome to talk to the emperor and then onto a horse and north across the Alps, where there were simpler things to cope with than Forst's grief.

"I would like to know where he is to be buried," Forst said.

"I will find out."

Forst nodded and slipped through the fence rails into the pasture. "Tell your father that the red mare foaled last night. It's a colt, if he would like to see it."

It was a dismissal, and Correus took it gratefully. "Yes, I expect he would." He picked up the bridle he had hung on the fence post and very nearly ran back up the hill to the upper barn.

The emperor Titus Caesar Vespasianus Augustus settled himself on a couch and tugged the purple and gold folds of his toga into place. "Distressing how quickly muscle turns to fat," he said ruefully. "I should go back in the field. Twenty miles a day is the best way I know to keep a flat belly."

"That and the army's cooking, sir," Flavius said with a smile.

"Fortunately I command enough privilege to save me from that," the emperor said. He motioned at two other couches, luxuriously upholstered in silk. "Make yourselves comfortable, gentlemen."

Correus stretched himself out on one, wondering what horrible things his parade armor was doing to the silk. He had dressed in full kit for his audience with the emperor, the gold scale polished and shining over a full-dress harness tunic of white leather and gold fringe, with every decoration he owned strung across his chest. He felt vaguely like a racehorse. At least the gilded oak leaves of his *corona civica* made his hair lie flat. Flavius, equally resplendent in the light silvered cuirass and purple tunic of an imperial staff aide, took the third couch, crossing his long legs at the ankles and leaning on one elbow.

There was an ebony table edged in brass in the center, laden with a green glass bowl of figs, two-handled silver drinking cups with gilded edges, and the usual pitchers of wine and water. A pair of slaves hovered beside it, and one of them passed Correus a cup. The wine was a deep, rich ruby, out of the emperor's private stock.

Occupying a fourth couch, pulled slightly away from the perimeter of the conversation, the emperor's brother, Domitian, reclined, and looked bored and sulky. Flavius and Correus nodded to him respectfully, but the co-consul merely eyed them over his wine cup and continued drinking.

Titus looked at the Julianus brothers' attentive faces turned toward him, then glanced at his own brother. *He hasn't enough to do*, Titus thought. And not much that the emperor could *trust* him to do if it came to that. Titus had no sons, and Domitian was heir presumptive to the purple—but Titus was thirty-eight and healthy, and it looked like a long wait. The effect on Domitian was unpleasant. Titus had made his brother co-consul with him last year in the hope of soothing his restlessness, but under the empire, there was no real power attached to the title, although it was a great honor. The emperor was generally a consul, and the second consul, if he had any sense, agreed with the emperor. Domitian knew just what his consulship was worth. It was like being given *one* bite of someone else's cake, Titus thought, looking at his brother's heavy face, a younger, cleaner-lined version of his own. It only set Domitian to thinking how to get the rest of it.

If his brother had shown more sense when their father took the purple, the emperor thought, suddenly irritated, he wouldn't have a problem now. Instead, when the grim days of civil war had ended with the acclamation of Vespasian as emperor, Domitian had reacted to the heady power of being the only member of the new emperor's family as yet in Rome with all the restraint of a street urchin let loose in a bake shop. Domitian had handed out appointments and commissions with a fine free hand while his father and brother were still on the march from the East. Finally Vespasian had remarked wryly that he was lucky that Domitian hadn't thought to appoint a new emperor while he was at it. There had been a slight unpleasantness when Vespasian arrived in Rome, and although he had let most of the appointments stand, that episode had set the mark for the amount of power he was willing to allow his younger son. Domitian was appointed *Princeps Juventutis* and allowed to adopt the name of Caesar, and they both looked very nice on paper and meant next to nothing. The army command for which Domitian had hoped had never been forthcoming, and so far Titus had not seen fit to change his mind on that subject, either.

"So, Centurion Julianus." The emperor ignored his brother and set his cup on the table. He nodded at Correus to distinguish between the brothers—Flavius also held senior centurion's rank. "I understand you want to get back to the field yourself."

"Yes, sir," Correus said fervently, and hastily qualified it. "I'd be more use to the army there, sir. I don't feel I'm earning my keep at Misenum."

"You mean you're bored." Titus smiled.

Correus gave up. "To be truthful, sir, yes." He glared at Flavius.

"Your brother didn't tell me that," Titus assured him. "When an officer puts in thirty-seven requests for transfer in the course of a year, I can draw my own conclusions."

Correus looked embarrassed.

"Well, I think we can oblige you," Titus said briskly. He waved a hand, and one of the slaves trotted over with a map. He spread it for the emperor on the brass-bound table. "Here."

The emperor's thick finger jabbed at the map. Correus recognized the river delta that spread away under the emperor's hand—the mouth of the Rhenus where that great river widened out to sink into the cold waters of the German Ocean. "We've always had a certain amount of trouble with river pirates around Rhenus mouth," the emperor said, "but the Lower Rhenus Fleet has kept them in hand. Lately, though, the pirates have been multiplying like flies in the summer, and they've been raiding farther down the coast with every foray. The fleet can't find them, but they seem to have no trouble finding the fleet. The few identifiable goods from their hauls have been turning up in the damnedest places or never surfacing at all. If—" Titus broke off and glanced at the slaves, standing straight-backed against a wall, with the expressionless stares of well-trained servants. "Leave us," he said brusquely. When they had gone, he gave Correus a long, troubled look. "If the pirates aren't controlled, they could put a halt to the entire German Ocean trade." He ran his hand swiftly down the coastline as if in erasure. "And somebody who knows too much about our shipping is courting a treason trial."

Correus turned on the couch and sat up to get a better look at the map. "Someone's feeding them information?" That sort of arrangement with a pirate fleet was about as safe as going into partnership with a family of crocodiles—unless a man was operating from a very secure position indeed.

"Someone's holding their hands like a nanny," Titus said. "Or bribing them to keep us busy. Or both. You're going to find out, Centurion. And you're going to find out where their home harbor is. Then you're going to take the Lower Rhenus Fleet and knock them into kindling." The emperor bent his head over the map again, motioning Flavius into the conference, too.

Behind them, Domitian cast a disgusted glance at the three men and the map, and rose, lifting his bulk from the couch with unexpected grace. He was heavyset like his brother, a stocky, businesslike figure, but with a touch of the courtier in his walk. He ambled down the palace hallways at random, partly bored with this matter of pirates that seemed to occupy his brother's mind so thoroughly just now, and partly angry that Titus hadn't seen fit to ask his advice. He wasn't overly surprised when, a few minutes later, Marius Vettius appeared at his elbow. Vettius generally knew where Domitian was. Vettius made it his business to know anything that might be useful.

"A fine day, Consul," Vettius said genially. "Too fine to spend on affairs of state."

"I haven't been requested to!" Domitian snapped. Vettius put on a bland, soothing expression. The shipping prefect was tall, with a smooth, pale cap of prematurely graying hair and a toga that fell in perfect, graceful folds. His tunic displayed the broad purple stripe of a senator. Domitian knew that Vettius was not above provoking trouble between him and his brother the emperor, but today he felt like having someone treat him with the respect that Titus so pointedly denied him. "My brother is exercising his brain over a bunch of raggedy German river pirates," Domitian said. "He does not feel the need of my assistance in the matter."

"Oh?" Vettius's pale eyes looked interested, but he only said, "How tiresome for you. But hardly a matter of great importance. I am sure the consul has more pressing matters before him."

"Certainly," Domitian said. "I can go and inspect the Praetorian Guard again—it keeps them on their toes. Or I could bring a few decrees before the Senate for the fun of watching my brother withdraw them. Or I could go and inspect a whorehouse—they might actually pay some attention to me there. There's supposed to be a new one, with a *most* interesting stable, just below the new amphitheater."

"Hardly in the province of a consul," Vettius said.

Domitian cocked an eye at him. "Too proud for a whorehouse, Vettius?" He shrugged. "Then don't come." The shipping prefect came from a family that was nearly as old as the City of Rome itself, and had what Domitian regarded as a fastidious streak. Domitian had a taste for whorehouses and the wineshops that were little more than holes in the wall along the Tiber docks, and it amused him to drag Vettius there.

Vettius gave him a genial smile that masked a fleeting look of distaste. "Certainly I will come with you, if that's what you're in the mood for." Domitian's appetites were repellent but useful. He wasted his lust on fleeting pleasures; thus he was easily controlled. Marius Vettius had only one lust, of the abiding sort, and that was for power. "I only thought it a pity," he said carefully, "that the emperor doesn't see fit to give his heir more responsibility during the, uh, emperor's lifetime."

"That will come," Domitian said sourly. "So my brother says. There is, unfortunately, plenty of time."

"I cannot help feeling that that is shortsighted," Vettius said seriously. "I should not wish to criticize the emperor, but— one never knows what the Fates have in store, does one?"

Domitian gave Vettius a sharp look. "Don't pussyfoot with me, Vettius. Are you suggesting I have my brother killed?"

"Certainly not!" Vettius made a shocked face, but he kept his words plain and unable to be misconstrued. This was dangerous ground. "That would be treason. I do not suggest treason. Ever." *And you will come to it yourself in a year or two*, he thought, watching Domitian's surly, discontented face. "Only that it is well to be prepared."

Domitian scowled, but the seed was in his mind now. Eventually it would flower. "Who are these pirates your brother is so exercised with?" Vettius changed the subject.

Domitian shrugged. "No one so important. A nuisance merely." Titus had forbidden him to discuss the matter with anyone, he remembered now. He wasn't ready to risk his brother's wrath just yet by disobeying. The word "treason" hung in the air. The matter of the pirates was nearly as dangerous as murder.

While Domitian found his amusement with Marius Vettius in the whorehouse by the amphitheater, Correus and his brother trotted down the Via Salaria out of Rome.

"Merciful Athena! Oh, my departed ancestors!" Flavius leaned over the saddle horns and hooted weakly. "Well, you wanted a field command! Pirates and treason! You can't say he didn't oblige you!" Flavius's mount, a big gray, sensed his master relax and took advantage of the moment to swing his head around, teeth bared, at Correus's kneecap.

Correus punched him hard in the nose, and the gray jerked his head back with a snort. "Your concern for my skin is touching."

Flavius grabbed the reins and dug hard into his horse with his heel. "Mannerless bastard!"

Correus chuckled. "That's one of Aeshma's colts, isn't it? They all bite."

"They make good troop horses, though," Flavius said, "once you knock it out of them. The third-generation lot seems to be a touch tamer."

"I miss that demon," Correus said wistfully, thinking of the big gray stallion he had brought back from Germany at the end of his first posting there. "You and Freita and Julius and I were the only ones he *didn't* bite. It will be odd, going back there now."

Flavius watched him sympathetically. Correus had ceased to grieve for his first wife after he had found Ygerna, but he wasn't going to forget her, ever. "I expect you'll have enough to keep busy." His voice was serious now. "Don't be too big a hero. I don't doubt you can take on a fleet of pirates, but if they've got a connection in Rome, *that* part could get dangerous."

"Don't I know it. Palace intrigue scares me a hell of a lot more than pirates and Germans put together."

"What are you planning?" Flavius asked him. "Getting yourself held for ransom?"

Correus grinned at him. "How well you know me. I don't really see any other way, do you? I can hardly go and say I've heard they have a profitable venture and I'd like to sign on. Even if I could find them. Successful pirates are not generally stupid by nature. If we want them to bite, we're going to have to let them take a ship with me on it. Then you and Father can argue with them about the ransom while I nose around their camp. We'll have to work out some sort of code."

"That's dangerous," Flavius said.

"So's war."

Correus noticed that his brother looked more interested than disapproving. He wondered if Flavius was getting bored with his palace post.

"You've done this before," Flavius said thoughtfully, remembering that Correus's commanders had found that his ear for foreign tongues and his ability to slip on another man's skin made him an admirable spy.

"A time or two."

"Well, see that what you're up to doesn't get around in

Rome," Flavius said. "If there *is* a connection here and he gets wind of it, the pirates will drop you off the deck in midocean and never mind the ransom."

Correus put his heel to his horse's flank. "Kick that menace of yours up a bit. Julia and Lucius are coming to dinner. It occurs to me that this is right up Lucius's alley." Their brother-in-law was an unofficial adviser to the emperor and knew most things that went on in Rome.

"Anything Lucius can tell us," Flavius said, "he'll have told Titus already. And if Titus didn't want to tell us, you can bet that Lucius won't."

"Dear gods," Correus said disgustedly. "Spies and secret messages! A nice war will be a pleasure."

Their sister Julia's husband, Lucius Paulinus, proved annoyingly evasive when Correus and Flavius cornered him by the fish pool in the garden before dinner.

When they had recounted their interview with the emperor, he merely said, "Oh, dear," in a mild voice and contemplated the fish. Flavius ground his teeth, but Correus thought that he could probably winnow what he wanted out of Lucius later, unless Lucius had orders from the emperor to keep it confidential. Lucius Paulinus was a slim, sandy-haired man with a plain, pleasant face and ears that stuck out too much. He looked younger and more innocent than his twenty-eight years. Correus and Flavius had first encountered Lucius in the Rhenus country when the brothers had been very junior centurions on their first tour. Ostensibly Lucius was a historian, occupying himself as did most gentlemen of letters, with publishing his most recent work, a *History of Modern Rome*, and with extensive revisions of the work that would one day make him famous. What Lucius really did, Correus and Flavius had since discovered, was serve as the emperor's eyes and ears. In those days it had been the emperor Vespasian; now it was his son Titus.

"Pleasant evening," Lucius said. "Did I tell you I saw old Porcus in the Forum? He's trying to find a husband for that youngest daughter of his again. The last prospect bolted for Greece!" He launched into a lengthy, gossipy description of poor Porcus's tribulations in attempting to buy respectability for his errant offspring. Lucius's homely, freckled countenance presented an animated imitation of Porcus's doleful one. "And the mystery is how she manages to *be* so depraved, because she's got a face like the back end of a carriage horse and a figure to match!"

Flavius chuckled and drifted off. Correus looked at Lucius consideringly. When he set himself so determinedly to be amusing, it was generally because there was something else that he didn't wish to discuss. Correus looked around the garden. It was crowded with slaves and children. The ladies of the family made bright spots of color against the espaliered fruit trees and rose-colored brick walls. Lady Antonia began a move toward the dining room, trailing the thin wrap that was as much warmth as fashion allowed.

Correus eyed his brother-in-law, amused. "You slither like a sacred snake. Let's go dine." He would catch up to Lucius Paulinus later. Lucius needn't think he wouldn't.

Dinner was a crowded, noisy family gathering. The children threw food at each other at one table, and the adults commented proudly on their respective offsprings' accomplishments at the other. Correus's mother, Helva, did not dine with the family, but undoubtedly she would contrive to present herself later. Correus had been to see her already, and Ygerna, gritting her teeth, had made a dutiful visit. Helva had told her she looked thin and that she certainly hoped Ygerna would be able to carry the child a full term.

The dining room was a pleasant area, open at one end to the evening breeze and looking out into a vista of trellised vines and a fountain where three marble dolphins danced on their tails. The mosaic floor suggested an appetizing meal of fruits and lobsters, and the walls were fashionably painted with legendary scenes and vistas supposedly conducive to good digestion. Correus was pleased to note a new one on the far wall: An unappetizing banquet table laden with dead game had been replaced by Europa and Zeus, in the form of a bull. The bull was white and muscular, with a little wreath of roses between his horns. Europa seemed to be enjoying herself. He thought that might have been his father Appius's idea; it didn't look like Lady Antonia's sort of wall.

Appius Julianus shared a couch with Lucius. To one side of them, Correus and Flavius were sprawled on their own couch, and on the other side, Appius's wife, Antonia, and daughter, Julia, reclined, happily catching up on a week's household news. On the fourth side of the table, conversation had ground to a halt, and Appius could see his daughters-in-law wildly trying to think of something to say to each other. It was a lost cause, Appius thought, mildly amused. Ygerna thought Aemelia was a featherhead but was willing to be polite, while Aemelia in turn couldn't help thinking of Ygerna as something foreign and mysterious and therefore not quite *safe*. It was a Briton, after all, who had cut off Flavius's fingers. It made conversation difficult.

Appius felt a little sorry for Correus's wife. He knew his son well enough to know that there would be little on Correus's mind just now but the new campaign. The army had been Correus's life before either Freita or Ygerna had entered it, just as it had been Appius's. Although Correus was capable of giving his wife equal attention (something Appius had never been), she occasionally had to remind him to do so. Right now he had undoubtedly forgotten that Ygerna, nearly six months with child, was going to have to stay here while he was chasing pirates. That was going to be awkward.

There was a shriek of fury from the children's table, and a sharp admonition from one of the much-tried nurses in attendance. Very awkward, Appius thought, watching Julia out of the corner of his eye. The shriek undoubtedly came from Julia's daughter, Paulilla, who was three, and the perpetrator, equally undoubtedly, was Felix. The other two babies at the table were too young to be the culprits.

Julia half rose from her couch. "Felix! Now whatever did you do that for?" Paulilla's tunic was liberally splattered with stewed pears, evidently a direct hit.

Felix looked thoughtful, green eyes considering. "To see if I could," he said finally. "It was a catapult." He held up his knife and pulled the blade back with his finger. Paulilla continued to shriek.

"Pauli, that will do. Felix, dear, that's very smart of you, but you mustn't make catapults at the table."

"I really think we should let his nurse deal with him for now," Ygerna said with considerably more calm than she felt. She had no intention of entering into a dinner-table competition with Julia for the privilege of disciplining Felix, but she was also of the opinion that Felix had a bit more coming to him for plastering his cousin with stewed pears than a compliment on his creativity.

"An excellent suggestion," Appius said. "That is the function of nurses. I am prepared to admire my grandchildren at dinner, but not to enforce their table manners."

"You have to understand Felix," Julia said. There was a sharp note in her voice, and her eyes were unhappy. Felix looked at her curiously.

"I'm trying to," Ygerna replied pleasantly. Her Latin had the soft, clear accent of the educated classes and no discernible foreign traces, but Appius had the feeling that under it there lurked a stream of exotic British bad language. Correus, he noticed, looked aggravated but was eyeing Ygerna and Julia with the air of a man reluctant to step between two bowmen.

Lucius Paulinus rose to the occasion. He caught his wife's attention, and she bit her lip. "That is not your affair, Ju," he said quietly.

Julia looked ready to burst into tears, but she managed to control it. Lucius gave her a look that wasn't without sympathy. *A forceful young man, Paulinus*, Appius thought, not for the first time.

Ygerna appeared to be counting to ten.

Felix looked from one woman to the other, dubious now, catching their tension.

"Perhaps Felix would get Paulilla one of his tunics to wear," Lucius Paulinus suggested gently. "Nurse, you might go with him, please."

Felix, aware now that he had stirred up more with his catapult than he had bargained for, put his napkin down and scurried out of the room. Paulilla stuck a finger in the pears on her tunic and licked it. Dinner proceeded.

"Now see here, Felix." Correus swung the boy up into the chariot beside him and put the ponies into a gentle trot around the training track. "I thought this would be a good place to talk," he said. "Just us."

"Can I drive?"

"If you listen while I talk, yes. If you interrupt me to ask about ponies or catapults or why fish have scales, then no."

Felix thought it over. "How long do I have to listen?"

"Until I say you can stop," Correus said. "This is important. Don't think I didn't notice what was going on last night, because I did. You are not to shoot your cousin with a catapult anymore, but that's not what I want to talk about. I hope you're old enough to understand this, Felix. There's going to be a war between your mother and Aunt Julia if we're not careful."

"She's not my mother," Felix said firmly.

"No, she's not," Correus agreed. "But neither is your aunt Julia. I'm your father, and Ygerna is my wife, and that makes her your mother in everything but blood. Your real mother died when you were born."

"On account of me?" Felix looked worried now, and Correus took the ponies' reins in one hand and put an arm around his son. Death in childbirth was a fact of life, but there was no reason that Felix should think it was his fault when it hadn't been.

"No. You had nothing to do with it." Felix seemed satisfied with that, to Correus's relief. *She was dying anyway, and they took you from her dead body.* That was nothing to tell a child. "Now, see here. I'm going to have to go away for a while— to the Rhenus country, where your mother's people come from— and you and Ygerna are going to have to stay here until her baby is born and is old enough to travel." *And don't you fight me about it, because I went through it last night with Ygerna and one of you is all I can stand.*

"She can stay," Felix said helpfully. "I'll go with you."

"You can't," Correus said.

"Why not?"

"Because there won't be a house for you to live in, not till spring."

"I could sleep in your tent," Felix suggested.

"It's not allowed." Correus was beginning to feel a little harassed. "Now that's not what I wanted to talk to you about. While you're here, I want you to be very careful how you behave around Ygerna and Aunt Julia. They both love you, you see, and they're both afraid that you like the other one better. So you must be very careful not to take advantage of that and try to make them spoil you."

"Why not?" It seemed like a useful opportunity.

"Because it will make them both unhappy if they fight. And because I will smack you when you get to Germany if that's what you've been doing."

"All right. Can I drive now?"

"Have you been listening? Carefully?"

"Yes."

He didn't look like it, but Correus gave up. "Come on, then. Hold the reins . . . like so. Good. Now put your feet like this. . . ." He moved Felix's legs apart until they were braced at the correct angle to take the swaying of the chariot. "Can you hold them?"

Felix nodded.

"All right. Let's go." They made a sedate circle of the track, with Felix holding tightly to the reins, his green eyes dancing.

A second chariot and a team of black ponies swept by them, drew rein, and waited until the red roans that Felix was driving caught up. Flavius lounged over the side of his chariot. "Race?"

"Can I stay?" Felix bounced excitedly and tugged at Correus's tunic.

"All right, but put your helmet on or Diulius will never let us hear the end of it." Diulius, the ex-Circus driver who had charge of the racing stable, had laid down the law about helmets in Correus's and Flavius's youth, and it had stuck. Correus adjusted his own, and Felix picked up a smaller version, made by the estate blacksmith, that lay on the floor of the chariot. He knotted the strap under his chin.

The red ponies, smelling a race, began to dance sideways across the track. Correus pulled them in and lined them up with Flavius's blacks by the starting pole. "Give us a signal!" he shouted to Diulius, who was tightening a harness strap on a third team outside the track.

Diulius pulled a grimy scarf from around his neck, waved it once, and let it fall. The ponies shot forward. Diulius watched them with satisfaction. They rode and drove like centaurs, both of Appius's sons. If they hadn't, Diulius would never have let them put a finger on his precious stock, even if they'd been the *emperor's* sons.

The blacks shot out ahead, well locked into the inside position, and Flavius gave Correus a grin over his shoulder, then settled down to keep them there.

Correus gave the red ponies their heads and inched up until he hung on Flavius's chariot wheel. He'd driven those blacks; a team on their wheel made them nervous. They swept around the second turn into the long, straight side of the track. The blacks were almost but not quite in stride with each other. Flavius could feel it and was trying to distract their attention from the red team. Correus let his team drift just a hair closer. They careened into the third turn. Felix held onto the chariot rim with both hands, his eyes bright.

Flavius shot Correus a quick look. He shook out the blacks' reins, and they lengthened their stride with one last rush. Flavius pulled their heads around so that they shot across the front of the red ponies' noses. Correus drew rein. Flavius had slowed him, but he had also given up the inside slot. Rounding the last turn, that would make a difference. Correus slipped the red ponies to the right and leaned forward. They thundered onto Flavius's heels, then to wheel level, on the opposite side now, before he could move back to the fence. They rounded the last turn and came into the straight, nearly neck and neck. And there they hung as the starting pole flashed past.

They drew rein and trotted the ponies around another half turn before they slowed to a walk. They pulled their helmets off and shook their hair out, waiting to catch their breath.

"I don't know why I bother to race you," Flavius said, mock-serious. "No challenge to it."

"I had extra weight in the chariot," Correus said indignantly, "or I'd have taken you."

Flavius grinned. "Hah! I'll swap you teams, put my wife in the chariot, and still walk all over you."

"Hah yourself. Diulius!" Correus shouted as the old trainer strolled over. "Who's the better driver?"

"Neither one of you's fit to drive a goat cart," Diulius said. "My old granny can outdrive you both."

They laughed, and Diulius grinned at them. "You could have gone into the Circus Maximus, either of you, and had all the old ladies tossin' flowers. Master Correus, I want to borrow that slave of yours for a day or so. Three of the stable lads are down sick, and that Julius can handle about any team in the place. There's a sale coming up, and half the ponies are going stale for lack of training."

"You're welcome to him," Correus said. He looked thoughtful. "He takes to the chariots, does he? How good could he get?"

Diulius thought. "Good as you. Better, if he wanted to work at it."

"I told you, sir, I'd as soon let it go by." Julius looked up from a polishing rag and a rusty pile of Correus's field armor.

"Well, you don't have a choice," Correus said. He felt like a mother robin throwing her chick out of the nest. "And nobody said anything about the auxiliaries." He'd said plenty about the auxiliaries before, but the suggestion had met with no enthusiasm from its intended beneficiary. Since Correus had first bought Julius, he had intended to free the boy when he came of age and help him to some career. Julius had been of age for two years now, but the career had failed to materialize. Julius had seen as much as he wanted to of the army in Correus's service. The idea of joining up personally to get a spear stuck in him held no charm.

"Diulius tells me you're a passable hand with a chariot team."

"Fair enough." Julius looked suspicious.

"Good. You're his for the next year."

"Why?"

"You don't want to be a slave all your life, do you?"

"I dunno. Maybe."

"Horseshit. Go with Diulius. If you don't like it after a year, we'll think of something else."

"Who'll you take to the Rhenus with you?"

"Eumenes. I've got to do something with him. And if it comes to that, I'm not so delicate that I can't polish my own armor. Just think about it for a year." Julius was City-bred. The Circus would catch him if he gave it half a chance. Correus grinned. "Think about all the beautiful girls throwing money when you drive by. Think about what a top driver makes in a year." *It'll keep you from thinking about my wife.* He didn't say that. Julius couldn't help it, and it was making him miserable: another good reason to shove him out of the nest. "Think about a big house in Rome. Think about not having to spend the winter on the Rhenus this year."

Julius laughed. "Colder than a river sprite's kiss. All right, I'm thinking, I'm thinking. Old Diulius thinks I could make the Circus, does he?"

"He does. So you'll try it?"

"Do I have a choice?"

"Not for a year." It wouldn't take more than that, Correus thought, looking at Julius's thoughtful expression. He could see the Circus at the back of Julius's mind now, growing solid...enticing. Rome was where Julius had been born. He was part of it. It would hold no horrors for him.

Having dealt with Felix and Julius, Correus went to hunt up his brother-in-law, Lucius Paulinus. Correus found him finally, after a tour of house, gardens, and bath, sitting under a hayrick, watching four field slaves scythe grain. Lucius had a sheet of papyrus propped on a board in his lap, and he was drawing on it with a piece of charcoal. Correus peered over his shoulder.

"I wish I could do that."

"You could, I expect," Lucius said, "if you'd sit still long enough."

Correus sat down beside him in the shadow of the rick. "I'm not a gentleman of leisure, such as yourself."

Lucius Paulinus chuckled. He and Correus Julianus went back a long way. Each affected a profound horror at the other's mode of life, and each had an affection for the other that went far deeper than the mere kinship formed when Lucius had married Correus's half sister, Julia. "So now you're chasing pirates," Lucius said thoughtfully. He sketched a broad sweep of grain behind the M-shape of two slaves bent to their scythes. "It may be that all the pirates aren't in the Rhenus mouth."

"So the emperor implied."

"Oh, did he?" Lucius sounded noncommittal. He *never* admitted out loud, even to Correus, who knew it perfectly well, that he was invaluable to Titus.

"A clam has more conversation," Correus said.

Lucius put the charcoal and papyrus down and weighted it with a rock. He clasped his hands behind his head and leaned back in the hayrick. "I'm not being obscure on purpose," he said seriously. "Last night at dinner—well, my wife and yours know enough to keep their tongues behind their teeth, and certainly so does Lady Antonia. But Aemelia has dandelions where most of us keep a brain. She's the most indiscreet woman I ever met, and she's too much about court these days."

"You're being a bit hard on her, don't you think? There's nothing malicious about Aemelia."

"No indeed. She's a sweet little thing. But she does get things tangled. I make it a practice not to discuss anything but fluff in front of her."

Correus chuckled. Maybe Lucius was right. The emperor certainly wouldn't like it if Aemelia brightly asked him one day who it was that Lucius was spying on this week. "Now that we have adjourned to your private office"—Correus indicated the hayrick grandly—"maybe you will tell me what your long ears have picked up about these pirates."

Lucius looked worried. "There's the trouble. Nothing. Or at any rate nothing more than moon dust. I'm almost certain that someone in the City is feeding them information, which is bad enough, but frankly that's only one man's treason, and one man can be eliminated. What worries me is that he seems to be so hard to nose out. If he has *very* high protection, it could be embarrassing."

"Do you mean Domitian?" Correus asked bluntly.

Lucius winced. "That's treason, too. Domitian is the heir. For the gods' sakes, shut up. But yes, since you ask, I do smell a connection. Maybe not a direct one. I haven't got any evidence, mind you, just a feeling."

It wasn't much to go on, but Correus was inclined to give Lucius's "feelings" a good deal of credibility. "What's your feeling about trouble brewing in Germany? On top of the City connection?"

Lucius sighed. "Titus will have told you everything I know. That's the army's province. But frankly, yes, if you've been wondering where these pirates' loot has been disappearing to, so have I. And the thought 'into a German war chest' does come to mind. You've been wanting to get back to active duty, friend. I think you've got it."

* * *

We are always saying good-bye to someone, Lady Antonia thought. In the early years it had been her husband, Appius, midway through a career that had taken him from birth in a respectable but obscure equestrian family with a tradition of legionary service to a post as legate of a legion of his own and finally to a military governorship. Now that he had retired, the children seemed always to be scattered to the four winds— even her daughter, Julia, whose husband, Lucius Paulinus, was writing a modern history of Rome's provincial wars and believed in looking at them firsthand—or so he said. Privately, Lady Antonia suspected that most of what Paulinus saw went into a report to the emperor and not into his *History*. They probably would be off again soon. And Flavius, her son, the child of her heart. The emperor was a soldier, too. There would be a campaign somewhere, and Flavius would go with him.

Today it was Correus. He was leading the big gold gelding his father had given him the day he went into the Centuriate, with the new slave behind him on a spotted horse from the cavalry stock. As always, the whole house had turned out to bid him farewell, not just out of respect to the master but for love of Correus.

Forst and Emer—she had been a kitchen maid before Forst had requested her freedom when his own had been granted— were there; Forst still had black circles under his eyes, but he was there nonetheless. Old Thais, who had been nurse to both boys; Sabinus and Alan, who was almost as old now as Thais, and Diulius—men who had taught the brothers to fight and ride and drive a chariot; Philippos, the steward of the house; and Helva, of course, hanging onto Correus's arm, and, at forty-three, still looking beautiful enough to stop traffic, in a sky-blue silk gown that was highly unsuitable for a morning at home. She gave Correus a proud maternal smile. Helva had never been much use as a mother (it was Antonia or Thais who had bandaged skinned knees and banished nightmares), but she did have her priorities firmly in mind—the more successful Correus's career, the more comfortably Helva would live when Appius died and freed her. Helva occupied a privileged position in a wealthy household. She didn't *want* to be freed at the cost of that.

Antonia sighed. The older she got, the less she wished that

it wouldn't be such a scandal if she had Helva beaten within an inch of her life. But there were still times. . . . Antonia's marriage to Appius had been an arranged one, as alliances among the privileged generally were. She didn't begrudge Helva the nights that Appius had spent in her bed. But Helva could be such a *nuisance*. . . .

Julia and Lucius were there to say good-bye, and Flavius and Aemelia, and of course Correus's British wife on his other side, her thin arm through his, her dark eyes upturned to him. She still didn't look much more than fourteen, but Antonia suspected that Ygerna had been a forceful personality from birth. She had Felix by one hand, scrubbed, his thick, corn-colored hair brushed down flat, and wearing a tunic as yet unstained.

Correus gave Helva a hug, and bent and kissed Ygerna, his eyes smiling into hers. Then he swung up onto the gold geld-ing's back.

Ygerna, glowering, watched him go, leaving her abandoned among his family.

Flavius and Aemelia waved good-bye, and Aemelia leaned her head against Flavius's shoulder for a moment. She had tried living on the frontier, and it had not been within her strength, although she had once sworn it was. But that had been when she wanted to marry Correus. Looking back on it, she had lately begun to think that it was as well that she hadn't been allowed to. Correus had become a stranger in the last years. And he would have wanted her on the frontier with him. Flavius understood her. Flavius was . . . safe. And he loved her. Al-though this last week, she had begun to wonder if his brother's wandering feet hadn't been rubbing off on Flavius: There was a thoughtful, gone-away-over-the-hill look in his eye, and more often than not she would talk to him for a while and then realize that he hadn't been listening at all. Was he wishing for a chance to chase pirates, too? Aemelia looked at her husband's hands and gave a delicate shudder. Let Correus have the pirates.

"What will he do when he gets there?" she asked. "To the Rhenus, I mean?"

Flavius gave her a startled look, as if the answer was ob-vious, or as if her words had pulled him back out of some daydream. "Walk into their den, of course," he said, watching his brother's back disappear down the tree-lined road that ran from his father's lands to Rome. "And hope he looks innocent."

Marius Vettius flicked his fingers through the shipping schedules laid out before him on his desk, sliding them back and forth across the smooth black marble top, making patterns with them. The information in them was too valuable not to sell to the pirates, even with the emperor poking his stubborn nose into the matter. Vettius weighed the emperor's interference against the profit when the Rhenus pirates paid him his percentage. Finally he stacked the wax tablets into a neat pile, corners aligned, pulled another tablet out of his desk, and began to write. When he had finished, he sent for Fulminatus, who was a junior clerk in the City Shipping Offices and not overly burdened with honesty.

Fulminatus held out his hand for the tablet and gave the prefect a cocky smile. "Same place, Chief?"

Vettius ignored him and left Fulminatus standing there until he got the idea. The clerk's smile faded, and he stood up straight. "To be delivered as usual, sir?" he asked crisply, but his eyes shot Vettius a look of dislike. Fulminatus considered the prefect too fine in his ways for a man who was up to something shady. Still, Vettius paid well for service, and Fulminatus, like a great many other people in Rome, was too afraid of Vettius to push him very far.

"Yes, to the usual place," Vettius said. "Just give it to the man who tells you his name is 'Mercury,' with no chat, please."

Fulminatus nodded. He looked curiously at the sealed tablet. He'd unsealed one, very carefully, once, but he hadn't been able to decipher what was written on it. Fulminatus thought Vettius had found out; he had been set on by robbers in an alley afterward. They hadn't taken anything, but they beat him black and blue. Since then Fulminatus had kept his curiosity to himself.

When the clerk had gone, Vettius tapped his long fingers together idly, waiting for the incense that burned in a silver pot on the desk to clear the air of the dank river smell that had come in through the open door with Fulminatus. All the shipping offices occupied a row along the Tiber docks, and most had subsidiary offices at Ostia Harbor, twenty miles downriver.

All smelled vilely of rotting garbage—the City merchants burned more incense in their offices than they sold at a profit. Vettius poked with one finger at the silver burner so that a half-burned piece crumbled on the grate in a cloud of scent. Titus would probably send a fleet after the pirates, Vettius thought. Equally probably the fleet couldn't catch them; they were hidden too well in the labyrinth of the Rhenus delta. But it would tie up the Rhenus Fleet for a while. If there were any anti-Roman elements at work in the Rhenus delta, as Vettius was beginning to suspect, that might be all to the good. A war gave an ambitious man a wider scope. A war had put Titus's father, Vespasian, on the throne. The next war could put another man there. Vettius watched the red heart of the incense reflected in the silver burner, and smiled.

IV

Julius Caesar

THE MARINES ON THE GALLEY'S UPPER DECK WERE NO MORE than scarlet splashes in the fog. It was a gray, clammy mist, blanketing everything and muffling sound. The dip and splash of the oars seemed to come from above as well as below and to the sides of the galley, and the cry of the sailor taking soundings in the bow had a thin sound behind the mist.

The marine commander looked dubiously into the whiteness.

"We'll find 'em; don't worry." The captain's voice beside him made him jump. The captain was a disembodied head above a gray wool cloak. He had taken off his helmet, and his hair hung dankly like seaweed in his eyes.

"The timing is extremely important," the marine commander said. "There won't be a second try at this."

"We'll find 'em," the captain said again. "Or rather they'll find us, which I thought was the idea."

The marine commander compressed his lips into a tight line. The galley's captain knew perfectly well how tricky it was going to be. He *said* he knew every inch of this coast with his eyes closed, and the marine commander hoped he did. He peered into the fog. "Can't you signal her?" Somewhere out there was the second ship, a small, fat merchantman with the insignia of the Veii Exporters' Guild, and beyond that somewhere, presumably, the pirates, their quarry.

The captain ignored him.

"Thirteen feet, sir, in the channel," the seaman in the bow called out. "Twelve and a half."

"She'll run aground," the marine commander said. "She draws more water than we do."

"Aye, well, I expect her captain will be keeping that in mind," the galley's captain said.

The marine commander looked gloomily at the fog. The prefect of the entire Lower Rhenus Fleet was on that merchantman. If they lost him, they might as well jump overboard and save a naval court its trouble.

A liburnian loomed out of the thinning fog—long, low in the water, dangerous as a crocodile. There was another behind her, nearly invisible, painted the same seawater blue. Pirate craft.

"Ships to port, sir," the captain of the merchantman said. There was a curious note of satisfaction in his voice.

"Right on time." Correus, the merchantman's passenger, pulled the folds of his toga around him. It was damp almost clear through. "This isn't a mist; it's a rain that doesn't fall down. Have we picked up our escort again?"

The captain shook his head. "They should be behind us. Beyond that last headland, I'm hoping."

Correus looked over his shoulder. The bank of dunes along the coast was only an amorphous splotch, a darker shade of gray. "Can they see us? I won't risk the crew. We'll run for it if we have to."

"I'm afraid we're committed now, sir," the captain said. "Even with Poseidon pushing her, this wallowing sow couldn't outdistance those liburnians. And if the mist burns off a little more, we're going to glow like a campfire when the sun hits." The merchantman was brightly painted red and yellow, with a gilded bird's head on the stern and a bright stripe of purple along the oarlocks. "We'll hug the coast. If we've missed them, they can pick us up from shore. These waters are cold enough to freeze you fast, even in midsummer. You'd better put on your show before they take it into their heads to heave you overboard."

Something whistled over their heads, and the merchantman burst into life. Crewmen in civilian tunics scurried into the rigging as the captain shouted to put on more sail. Belowdecks, the purple-painted oars were run out, and the hortator's hammer set a double-time stroke. Merchantmen relied mainly on sail to move their heavy ships, but they carried a slave crew of rowers, and in pirate-infested waters the oars could make the difference. This merchantman moved with more agility than most. Her hold held not a half-starved crew of slaves, chained to their benches, but seamen of the Rhenus Fleet, trained to the exhausting maneuvers that moved a war galley. Still, the merchantman's weight and fat-bodied build made her an easy target, and she had no intention of fighting back.

An iron pike from a bolt-thrower crashed into the deck, and the captain yelled at Correus, "Get in your quarters!"

Correus took a look at the liburnian closing on them and ran. Most merchantmen were equipped to carry a passenger or two in better style than the common traveler would find in the hold. The cabin was built on the main deck, with the captain's quarters on one side and the passenger's to the other. Eumenes looked up as Correus dived through the door.

"I take it we've picked up some company." He was thoughtfully polishing a dagger.

"We have." Correus did a last check of the cabin and himself for any noncivilian gear. "And you're not to use that knife, you fool."

Eumenes put the dagger in his boot.

"They'll search you," Correus said.

"And be surprised if they don't find a knife," Eumenes said. "A fellow who doesn't carry a dagger is going to keep a slave that does."

"You take to this game in a hurry," Correus said.

"I place a fair value on my hide, especially these days." Eumenes looked a little embarrassed. "It occurs to me that I haven't thanked you yet, not properly."

"If we bring this off, you'll have paid your selling price and more," Correus said. He glanced at the open trunk with the good woolen togas and tunics folded inside, the tray of cheese and expensive wine, the carrying case full of scent and hand cream, and tongs and brushes for curling his hair. "I don't like the arena," he added. He gave the curling tongs a disgusted look. "People who use these go to it."

Eumenes chuckled. "I didn't think this was much in your line. Ever slipped this skin on before?"

"Once or twice," Correus said. "And a few other skins as well. My brother-in-law taught me some of the trick of it. He says it's a matter of who you *think* you are."

The merchantman ran with oar and sail along the coast, with the liburnians like hunting wolves on her flanks. Behind them, veiled in the mist, the watchdog galley coursed along the dunes.

The liburnians closed in, and another bolt sang overhead into the sail, tattering the lower edge. Half the rigging came away with it, and the sailors scrambled to take in the sail before the ship heeled over.

The merchantman's oars gave a last stroke and stopped, and the ship stood still in the water. In the lead liburnian, a black-haired man with a badger's streak of gray in his beard gave a quick grin and waved a second man over.

"They take a warning, it seems. Board her, but keep your eyes open."

"I doubt we'll hit an ambush," the second man said. "Look."

Three figures climbed the merchantman's starboard rail and dived. More came running behind them, up from the rowing decks, and then they were pouring over the rail into the sea, the ship abandoned behind them. On deck a lone figure in a toga stood screaming curses at them.

The black-haired man started to laugh. "Stranded, by all the gods! They've even unchained the rowing crew. Either this one can't swim or he won't. We'll see what we've got, and then we'll pick up the crew. They'll be glad enough to see us by then if they haven't drowned."

The other, a red-haired man with a drooping mustache and a dirty tunic embellished with gold thread under the grime, gave an order, and the liburnians came up on either side of the merchantman, shipping the inside oars as they sidled close. Boarding planks were run out and secured, and the black-haired man strode across with his crew behind him. The captain of the second liburnian came aboard, also. The passenger in the toga had disappeared from the deck.

"Cerdic, go find our straggler," the black-haired man said. "Ennius, check the hold." The second captain nodded and started down the ladder to the rowing decks and the hold below. Cerdic was breaking down the door of the passenger's cabin.

The mist had begun to burn off, and the black-haired man looked about him with satisfaction.

"Full of wine and cloth in the bolt," Ennius said, appearing topside again. "Looks like silk. And three crates of gold pots and two of ingots." His crew came up the ladder behind him, carrying tall clay amphorae and the brushwood in which they had been cushioned.

"Get it on board. Them too," the pirate captain added as Cerdic returned, dragging a blond slave by the scruff of his neck. Two men came behind him with the man in the toga. His arms were pinned behind his back; his expression was furious.

"You'll pay for this, you fools!" he sputtered. "There will be an investigation—"

"Pipe down or I'll have you gagged," the black-haired man said. He strode back across the boarding plank to his own ship and sat in a chair on the deck, to watch the cargo being transferred.

They cleared the hold and stripped the merchantman of every fixture of value with a locustlike efficiency. Correus protested as his trunk and dressing case were carried past. Cerdic gave him a threatening look and raised a hand, so Correus subsided, pulling the folds of his toga around him angrily. It was greatly disheveled, and he had the beginnings of a black eye. Eumenes sat down on the deck beside him and glowered at his captors.

The liburnians backed carefully away from the merchantman and unshipped the rest of their oars. "Ram her," the pirate captain said.

The liburnian made one precise, expert pass, and her ram punched through the merchantman's hull. The liburnian carried only a slave crew at the oars, but they were well trained and afraid. The penalty for disobedience came too high. They watched as she listed, settled in the water, and sank. For just a moment, the gold bird on the stern caught the first shaft of sunlight as it broke through the fog.

"Turn about and pick up the crew."

"Better not," Cerdic said softly. "Here's company."

Behind him the lean shape of a Roman patrol galley had appeared, and the swimmers in the water were making for it.

"Out oars! Double-time!"

The drumbeat began in the hold, and the blue oars rose from the water, dipped, and pulled. The liburnian leaped away into the thinning fog.

"You'll regret this!" Correus's voice was high-pitched with hysteria. The black-haired captain swung around slowly to look at him.

"I am Theophanes," he said distinctly, "and this is my ship. Now you are mine, too." He had a fillet of gold in his black hair, and a tunic and leggings of fine, bright blue wool. There was a gold collar around his neck, and at his belt a sword with a finely worked hilt inlaid with gold. He had a broad, heavy-boned face with a sickle-shaped scar on the cheek, relic of an old knife fight. His eyes were blue and unexpectedly amused.

"I am a Roman citizen!" Correus said. He was wet and practically quivering with fury. "My father has a great deal of power! I demand that you put me ashore *immediately*!"

Eumenes opened his mouth as if to say something, then shrugged and closed it again. The pirate captain looked at Correus thoughtfully.

"Cerdic, go and get this gentleman a clean toga. One of his own, mind, and keep your hands off the rest." Cerdic glared at him and disappeared into the liburnian's small hold. There was a hoot of laughter from the steersman in the stern, and Theophanes shot him a look that shut him up fast. "I must apologize for my crew," he said with a half bow, but there was a small smile on his lips. "I make it a point to stay on good terms with Rome."

Cerdic returned with the toga, and Correus unwound himself from the wet one and huffily adjusted the clean folds. "If you want to *stay* in Rome's favor, you'll take me ashore immediately. To the nearest port," he added, noticing the appalling bleakness of the coastline—sand dunes and salty grass and a few stunted trees above the waterline. Theophanes looked like the sort of man who might take that request literally.

"Your father's a rich man, eh?" Theophanes tried to put a little worry in his voice, but it wasn't entirely successful.

"He is." Correus appeared to be angry enough to remain oblivious to the pirate's expression. Theophanes stood stroking his beard, his hand over his mouth. "And he'll spend every penny it takes to wipe you off the face of the earth, when he hears of this!"

"Well, now," Theophanes said, considering, "he'll be sending a mite to me first, I expect—for our trouble, you know—if he wants you back again with both your ears. And seeing he has so much, I think we'll up the price a little."

Eumenes had been sitting stoically beside his master with the look of a man to whom one slave market is much like another, but a look of amusement passed over his face at that.

"Now see here—!"

Theophanes poked Correus in the chest with one finger. "If I were you, I'd behave. You don't look like you'd fetch much in the slave market as it is, and I wouldn't want to damage you by mistake."

There was another hoot of laughter from the men lounging on the liburnian's deck, and this time Theophanes made no objection. "I'm afraid my crew are somewhat lacking in manners," he said gently. "I should avoid antagonizing them." His expression was pleasant, but his eyes were veiled, opaque, Correus thought, like dark stone.

"When that patrol galley catches up, they'll crucify you from the closest tree."

"I wouldn't put your faith there," Theophanes said. "Look."

Correus turned to the stern where the liburnian's wake rippled away in a torrent behind the steering oars. The Roman galley was losing distance fast. As he watched, the oars slowed from their frantic stroke to the measured movement of a ship in no hurry. Slowly the galley began to turn.

The camp lay among the sand spits and islands that made up the spreading delta of the Rhenus. The coast was always shifting here, the sand dunes changing shape with each new season, and the mist hung low over the sodden fenland almost unceasingly. It was a fine hiding place, Correus thought, for a few ships and a crew that wanted to go unnoticed. There were more galleys beached above the waterline and covered in brushwood. As long as they weren't followed back by boats from the shipping lanes and the Roman canal that linked the north channel of the Rhenus with the coast, there was little chance that they would be found. The man who discovered them by chance would go missing in the fenlands somewhere, Correus suspected.

The defenses were the fenlands themselves and Theophanes's three concentric rings of pickets. Within, the permanent camp had become a village, self-contained. The longhouses had cattle pens at one end and sleeping cubicles for the ships' crews at the other. Three women sat mending a net on the threshold of the largest house, and another was nursing a blond baby with a coral bead around its neck. There were a surprising number of women about.

Dogs and chickens ran barking and squawking among the outbuildings, and there were slaves, apparently permanent residents, who moved freely about the camp. A locked slave house held the rowing crews and the prisoners not worth ransoming, who awaited transport to the inland slave markets. The transport, both for slaves and loot, must come from outside the camp, Correus decided. The pirates didn't keep enough pack animals to manage it on their own. He filed that observation away thoughtfully.

Theophanes and the young liburnian captain, Ennius, came for them the next morning, having left Correus and Eumenes to spend the night with their hands tied behind their backs and then to each other's wrists, in a bare, wood-floored cubicle that made their muscles ache like fire after a few hours. Ennius (Roman, Correus thought, by birth, at any rate) untied their hands and shoved a grimy scrap of parchment into Correus's.

"Now," Theophanes said, "you will write. You will explain your situation to your father, and then I will read it."

"Yes." Correus reached a hand around and rubbed the small of his back. "Uh, look here——" His toga was filthy now, and his hair was sweat-dampened and hanging in his eyes. He had the look of a man who has been thinking things over, overnight.

"I don't want you to think . . . uh, that is, if I was rude yesterday . . . well, what I want to say is, I'll cooperate."

"Good. I am glad that we see eye to eye on that," Theophanes said. "Now write." .

"Yes, of course." Correus began to inscribe his message on the parchment.

Theophanes whistled. "Both of you? Your father must be richer than you said."

"No, no," Correus said hastily. Theophanes might decide to up his price again, and while the money that the emperor was willing to spend was substantial, it did have its limits. "But I couldn't leave Eumenes. Father wouldn't hear of it. Eumenes's father served my father for years. He'll pay for us both, I assure you."

Theophanes looked at Eumenes and set the sum at twice his slave-market value. The old fool probably would pay, he decided. If he didn't, well, there were always the slave markets. He took the parchment from Correus and inspected it, his expression daring Correus to make remarks. Correus wisely kept his mouth shut and wondered where on earth Theophanes had learned to read.

When Theophanes had satisfied himself that the message was suitably conveyed, he stuck it in his tunic, and Correus let out his breath.

"I take it you were a touch uncomfortable last night?" Theophanes's amused look was back.

"I'd rather sleep on a pile of rocks with a Fury for company," Correus said frankly. "My father will pay better if I'm not returned to him bent double like a hairpin."

"I'm glad to see you so sensible," Theophanes said. "It's amazing what a little discomfort and thought will do. Now that the preliminary unpleasantnesses are finished, Ennius will take you to your quarters."

They followed Ennius out across the sandy open space between the houses. A stocky, brown-haired woman with large, practical-looking hands was washing out clothes in a rain barrel.

"Do you have wives here, or are they all slaves?" Correus asked curiously. Somehow the brown-haired woman looked like a wife.

"Some one, some the other," Ennius said. "Sometimes it

changes. If a man takes a fancy to a woman in a market lot, he can always meet Theophanes's price for her. It can be risky, though," he added with a grin. "Old Commius took a liking to a woman off a merchant ship and spent half of his last share to buy her. Now he leads a hell of a life, poor old soul. She was a lady's maid and very high in her ways. She stuck a knife in his foot the first night when the dinner didn't suit her. And now he doesn't get in her bed unless he's bathed."

He led them to one of the larger longhouses and held back the hide flap over the door. "You'll be comfortable enough in here. But don't get any notions. Those fen bogs are tricky. The last man who ran got stuck in one, and we couldn't get him out. He screamed for about an hour before he went under."

Eumenes shuddered. Ennius pointed at a cubicle with straw and hides on the floor and prodded the other occupant with his toe. The sleeper opened his eyes, and then widened them at Correus, taking in his toga, somewhat the worse for wear, but draped over a tunic with the thin purple border that denoted an equestrian house. The fine, soft wool and the heavy gold ring on his left hand meant money.

"Come in," he murmured. "We are all fish in the same net."

"Don't pay attention to Ranvig," Ennius said, shooting him an odd glance. "He draws his philosophy out of a beer horn every night."

Ranvig sat up and brushed the straw off himself. "There is very little else to do," he said with dignity, "but sit in a swamp and count how many days it will take your thieves to get to my family and back again with your blood money."

Ennius looked as if he were about to retort but thought better of it and left with a parting admonition to Correus and Eumenes to remember the fens and the pickets and stay put. Correus wondered how often Ranvig baited Ennius. They seemed to have settled into a grudging acquaintance. He studied Ranvig curiously. The man looked to be close to thirty and was a German by his dress and speech. Theophanes had spoken a rough dog Latin, which most of his crew seemed to understand; but Ennius's Latin had the sound of a native tongue, and Ranvig had followed it well enough to answer in the same language, although with a strong German accent. Ranvig had had some education, then.

He was blond, as most of the Germans were, with long, pale braids that hung over his shoulders, and he was clean shaven, with an odd, crooked face. His blue eyes were set slightly askew, and his front teeth were crooked also, and vaguely wolflike. When he smiled, his mouth slanted upward farther on one side than the other. His hands were long fingered, and the fingers were very nearly all the same length; Correus remembered a German telling him once that that was supposed to be a sign of the elves' blood. The whole effect was surprisingly pleasing, as if one oddity somehow balanced another.

"I can't say I'm sorry to see you," Ranvig said. "The company here hasn't been overly pleasant."

"We ain't found it much to our taste, either," Eumenes remarked. There were straw and hides to sleep on now, an improvement over last night, and a woman had brought them soup and barley bread to eat as soon as Correus had written his letter. But the cubicle had little else to recommend it. "I could go plain crazy in here in a hurry," Eumenes said.

"As long as you aren't thinking of running for it, they won't take much notice of you," Ranvig said. "Go where you want to. Just don't try to cross the fence." The village was bordered by a low wooden palisade, intended more as a protection for the stock that roamed the compound than as a defensive barrier.

"I'll remember that." Eumenes hitched up his soiled cloak and repinned it. "It might be I can talk the trunks out of them. We'll have lice if we live in these for long."

Correus shuddered expressively. "Do try." He sat and leaned back against the upright that supported the wickerwork partition between their cubicle and the next. "I'm too tired to move."

Correus's accent had undergone a subtle change, Eumenes noticed. It was still the educated Latin of the upper classes, but it had acquired a stilted tone and a mild drawl. It was fashionable in Rome these days to sound slightly bored. The drawl had come on when Theophanes's crew had first boarded the merchantman. Eumenes suspected it would disappear again when they left the village. If they ever did.

Eumenes went outside and stood for a moment under the overhang of the eaves. There was a fine drizzling rain coming down. A chicken darted up to him, clucking furiously, and settled herself in a flurry of feathers in the shelter of the eaves.

She bobbed up and down, and after a moment an egg rolled away into a mud puddle.

"You aren't much of a mother," Eumenes said. He picked up the egg and stuck it in his cloak. Eumenes wasn't sure how much Theophanes was planning to feed them, and he had been hungry before.

Theophanes had every reason to feed the hostages who were to be ransomed. If Eumenes had thought with his brain instead of his belly, he would have known that; in the end, somewhat self-consciously, he gave the egg to a man from the rowing decks. Eumenes had earned his own respect for food on an oar bench. Bad diet brought disease, and a sick man didn't pull his weight, although generally he was left on the bench until he died. To a man on an oar bench, one egg could make the difference for a while between living and dying.

The prisoners to be ransomed ate freely of whatever the pirates ate, which was better fare than in most of the German coastal villages: wine and grain and strange delicacies from the captured ships; fruit and vegetables bought in some careful, roundabout fashion from the town markets of the German coast; fish from the rivers; and pig and deer meat from an occasional day's hunting when no ship was expected in their waters. And they always knew the night before when a ship was expected, Correus discovered.

He could measure their knowledge in their drinking, although he was careful not to notice. Twice in his first two weeks in the camp, the pirates launched their ships and came back on the last tide with amphorae of wine or olive oil, raw wool in bales, or the Eastern spices that were almost worth more than gold. Usually there would be a frightened handful of men and women tied to each other in a line like pack ponies. There was always a market for slaves, both in the Roman zone and the barbarian country.

On the night before these expeditions the crews stayed scrupulously sober, with Theophanes's wrath to face if they didn't. Otherwise there was wine and beer in plenty, enough to drown in, Eumenes said, and any other distractions a man could find to take his mind off the bleak fenland and the constant cold and drizzle.

Except for the fact that Correus, Eumenes, and Ranvig stayed carefully within the limits of permitted territory, the pirates treated these three much as they might one of their own. Eumenes taught old Commius to play a game with colored pebbles and spent much of his time thereafter cheating him at it. Correus was regarded with a sort of tolerant amusement when he threatened them all with immediate extinction as soon as his father should discover that they held his only son hostage. Only the young captain Ennius kept his distance from the Roman, and Correus wondered what it was that Ennius might have run from in Rome.

Theophanes seemed to find them all of little interest until he discovered that Correus could speak Greek, which proved to be the pirate captain's native tongue. Correus was startled to find that Theophanes spoke it cleanly, with none of the cant that characterized Eumenes's speech. How a man born to a good family, or at least a good education, had come to this ill-fated profession was something Theophanes was plainly disinclined to explain. But they slipped into a peculiar truce marked more by the factor of birth and class, by their difference from the others, than from likeness to each other. Correus found Ranvig pleasant, occasionally humorous, company, but Theophanes remained an enigma, a brigand who could quote Homer.

For further entertainment, there was a battered harp, taken from some long-ago captive, which was passed from hand to hand in the central hall of the largest longhouse. Each man knew a story or song of some sort, and each was loudly and drunkenly applauded whether his language was intelligible to his listeners or no. Theophanes's first mate, Cerdic, had a woman—a dark-haired creature, reputed to have the evil eye and possessing also a heart-stopping beauty—who sang like a bird and was much in demand. Cerdic didn't care who looked at her, but Correus noticed that no man got close enough to touch her, even by accident. Whether that was the evil eye or Cerdic's temper, he wasn't sure.

Ranvig, when the harp came around to him, played inexpertly on it and sang a song that made Correus's ears prick up. Ranvig's singing wasn't appreciably better than his playing, but Correus had heard the words before—Forst had a habit of singing the same song to calm a restive horse. Ranvig took long drinks from his beer horn between verses, but seemed to grow no drunker. He forgot the last verse, but they cheered him, anyway.

When Ranvig had finished, the harp came around to Correus, and they looked at him expectantly, their faces curious. The Roman might be too proud to play, their expressions said. Correus thought, fingering the harp. The songs the legions marched to were out if he was to maintain his disguise, and he didn't know much else. He had thought of Homer, parts of which he knew by heart, or Vergil. Suddenly he grinned. Theophanes might as well have a history lesson.

"Don't sing very well," he said. He flicked a finger across the harp strings. "I can whistle," he added, "but that's not much of an entertainment. So you'll have to settle for a story." An evil grin crossed his face. "Little something to give you nice dreams. This is about Julius Caesar—I expect you've heard of him?—and the pirates of Cilicia."

They looked up expectantly, and Correus smiled again, not particularly sweetly. "These pirates, you see, had begun to overreach themselves. Interfering with shipping, making themselves a menace, abducting respectable ladies. They even got up the nerve to come into Ostia Harbor and wreck a consul's fleet. It's always a bad idea to annoy a consul, but this one must not have been very tough because he let it go by, and so the pirates decided that they must be invincible. That's when they took a ship and abducted a young passenger on his way to Rhodes to study law."

"Gonna take 'em to court, was he?" someone shouted. "And have the magistrate give 'em a nice fine?"

"Not exactly." Ennius, who must have heard the story, glared at him, but Correus went on cheerfully, in the voice of a man telling a nursery tale. They settled in to listen, suspicious but interested. "Well, these pirates hadn't much imagination—they thought they'd ask twenty talents for him. Figured someone would want him back that bad. Caesar thought that was insulting. Early on he had a pretty good idea of his own worth. Thought it was embarrassing to have his price set at twenty and told them he was worth fifty, at the minimum. They laughed a lot, but they asked fifty. They figured he ought to know, and if he wanted to make them a present of thirty talents, they weren't going to argue with him. The only trouble was, a man worth fifty talents was a little frightening. When he wanted to sleep they kept quiet, and when he wanted an audience to practice his speech-making on (speech-making is very important to lawyers) they all came round and listened. But pirates not being very bright"—Cerdic bristled, but Correus went on as if unaware of having insulted them—"they *didn't* listen when he told them he'd see them again. See them crucified was what he said, actually."

"Anyone ever pay the ransom?" old Commius yelled. "*I* wouldn't 'ave wanted him back!"

"There were a few who thought later it would have been as well if they'd left him," Correus said. "But *someone* paid the ransom, and as soon as they turned him loose, he got to Miletus, which wasn't too far away, and raised a fleet and sailed right back to make good on his promise." Theophanes looked as if he were laughing, and Ranvig had a thoughtful expression on his face.

"What happened?" a tall, balding man called out. A good story was almost better than a song. A man could save it and retell it next winter, even if he couldn't carry a tune.

"Oh, he caught most of them," Correus said, as if that should be self-evident. "But they'd treated him pretty well, so he wasn't ungrateful."

"He let 'em go?" Commius asked.

"No. But he cut their throats before he crucified them."

There was a short silence while Correus wondered if he hadn't rather overdone it, and then they burst into laughter. "It's a good thing you ain't a Caesar!" Commius shouted.

They were still laughing when the picket came in, dripping wet as usual—it rained almost continually now that autumn had begun. He leaned down and said something quietly to Theophanes. Theophanes looked at Correus and Eumenes.

"Go back and sleep." Theophanes stood up, and the rest followed, pushing purposefully out through the door. Cerdic stayed behind and motioned to Correus and Eumenes to follow him.

Ranvig raised his eyebrows. "I also, I suppose?"

Cerdic swung around. "Yes."

They followed him out into the rain and the gray half-light

of a full moon. The gates stood open, and Correus could see the shaggy shapes of ponies in the misty light. Already the men were loading bales onto their backs. *Transport*, Correus thought.

"Move it!" Cerdic said.

They stepped up their pace, Eumenes craning his neck curiously back to watch the ponies. Ranvig paced along beside them with apparent unconcern, his head turned away from the ponies and their drivers. Correus remained thoughtful. There was no particular reason why he and Eumenes should be hustled off so quickly. It was as if Theophanes was afraid that they might know the men who came so quietly in the night to take away the booty stored in the outer sheds. But they didn't, and there was no reason to think they might. And if they didn't, who did? Ranvig?

V

Veii Market

EMER PUSHED THE BARN DOOR OPEN AND HELD UP HER LAMP to peer inside. Forst was there. He had come here again to sit in the dark and brood over Nyall Sigmundson, she thought, exasperated. "Forst. If you don't come to bed, you will catch cold out here. You are not a horse." She pleaded with him from the doorway, shivering in her night shift, her red hair hanging in braids over the cloak that she had put on wrong side out. She was barefoot and shifted from foot to foot, wiggling her toes on the cold stone.

Forst looked up. "You will get a worse one. Where are your shoes?"

"I couldn't find them," she said impatiently. "I woke up, and you were gone again. This is the third night in a row."

"I know. I'm sorry." He was sitting on an upturned feed bucket. He had a twist of straw in his hand and was tying knots in it. The horses in the loose boxes on either side watched him, puzzled.

"What do you *do* out here?" Emer's face was bewildered, and Forst shrugged his shoulders. "You will make yourself sick if you do this any longer."

He pitched the knotted straw into the dung channel that ran past the stalls and looked around on the stone floor for another.

"Forst!"

"I sit here and wonder what would have happened if I had stayed away from Nyall," Forst said tiredly. "If I had been Nyall, I would not have wanted to see anyone from the old days, either. I am a fool."

"You talk like one," Emer said tartly. "If I understand you— and I am not sure that anyone could just now—you think that it is your fault that Nyall Sigmundson has cut his throat. You are very conceited."

Forst found another straw and began to knot it. It snapped, and he flicked it into the dung channel with the other.

"You have told me about Nyall before," Emer said. "How could a man like that live the way he was living?"

"Or with what he had become," Forst said bitterly. "But I—I showed him what that was, I think. I held a mirror under his nose, and I shamed him."

"You provoked what would have happened anyway," Emer said flatly. "A man like Nyall Sigmundson does not 'adapt' to being maimed. Not when it loses him the chieftainship after he has already lost a war and the man who was closest to him— and his wife, too, because I think I know how he reacted to *her* when it happened."

"Nyall wasn't like that."

"Men are fools," Emer snapped, "and your Nyall was a fool, too! Men like that cannot adjust when they lose something, and so they die of it! How much longer do you really think it would have been before he slit his throat without your help?"

"Go to bed!"

"The more fool *I* for showing him to you," Emer said. "And what do you think you can do to atone for it all? Sit on a feed bucket all night?" She turned on her heel and stamped out, letting the double doors swing shut and slam behind her.

Forst sat looking into the dirty water in the dung channel. Emer wasn't going to understand, not ever. It wasn't because she was a woman, for all her furious remarks about men. It was because she had not been born free. Or maybe simply that she had not been born German. The Free Lands were as alien to Emer as were the slopes of Olympus. There was no way to explain to Emer what the Free Lands had been, what Nyall had been before Rome, because for Emer there had never been a before.

And what did it matter whether or not Emer understood? What was he going to do that would require that she understand? After all his thinking, Forst still didn't know. Nervously he got up and took his lantern from its hook on the wall. Forst couldn't shake the feeling that he owed Nyall a debt—and that somehow he was going to have to pay it.

Ygerna looked over the rooftop balcony into the sunlit garden. Felix had disappeared. One minute ago he had been patiently doing his lesson with Nurse in the next room—or, rather, Nurse had been doing the lesson and Felix had been looking at the green-and-gold lotus flowers painted on the walls and wanting to know why there were no frogs on them, and if there were frogs, what would they eat. The next minute he had simply been gone; "slipped through my fingers," Nurse said.

Helva was in the garden, sitting under the trellis, her beautiful white face further shaded from the sun by a parasol. She was dressed in trailing layers of butter-yellow silk, her gold hair pulled into a knot of ringlets on her head with a big amber pin. She was wearing an amber necklace and four bracelets, and there were amber drops in her ears. She was not, so far as Ygerna could tell, doing anything, although a spindle trailed from one hand for effect. Lady Antonia, who was herself busy from morning to sunset, overseeing the multitude of slaves belonging to the estate, had never yet succeeded in getting any work out of Helva and had long ago given up trying. Ygerna never ceased to wonder that anyone as restful as Helva should have produced a child with the nervous energy that Correus possessed. Correus was almost entirely his father's son. Except for a slight advantage in height and his hair, which was brown and waving rather than dark and curling, it was hard to tell him from Flavius. The long aquiline face, the strong bones, the sharp-angled brows, all belonged to Appius. There must be something of Helva in him somewhere, Ygerna thought, but she hadn't been able to find it, except perhaps for his almost intuitive understanding of what made a Celtic mind tick. Helva was a Gaul, born of one of the hundreds of tribes that had spread over Europe and Britain before the Romans came and who had all been kin to each other once. Helva had no such intuition for her own people or any other, although she had learned over the years, for self-preservation, to handle Appius as well as anyone did. This trick did not extend to Appius's offspring, Ygerna had discovered. Correus listened to his mother patiently or irritably, according to his mood, and then went and did what he wanted to. Julia loathed Helva, and Flavius was alternately bored and amused, although Ygerna suspected that Flavius was not immune to Helva's overpowering physical appeal; no man could have been. It just would never have occurred to him to have a try at his father's mistress.

Ygerna leaned farther over the balcony. She was willing to bet that Felix was in the garden somewhere, probably trying to get to the gate into the kitchen gardens and go unnoticed down to the hay fields. Felix had most of his grandfather's slaves firmly under his small thumb. He could generally find someone willing to abet him in his flight from Nurse and lessons.

The doors from the atrium onto the colonnade opened, and Ygerna craned her neck to see. Julia and her mother strolled out into the rose garden, with baskets and clippers in hand to prune the late roses, and Ygerna swore as she saw Felix dart out after them. Now she was going to have to cross Julia's path. It was really too much to ask Nurse to beard that lion in her den.

"I'll get him, Nurse. He's gone into the garden." Ygerna walked carefully down the stairs to the colonnade that ran outside the ground floor, bordering the garden. It was beginning to get chilly, and a flurry of leaves from the fruit trees trained against the rose brick wall blew around her ankles. Felix was sitting with his feet among the water lilies in the fish pond.

"Felix, that will ruin your sandals. And Nurse wasn't through with you, you know."

Felix looked up from the pond. "There's a new fish," he

said. "Lots of new fish." Little specks of gold skittered about among the larger ones.

"There will still be new fish after your lesson," Ygerna said firmly. She pulled him to his feet.

"Oh, Felix, you haven't run away from Nurse *again*?" Julia put her basket down and came over to kneel beside him.

"I was through," he assured her.

"*You* may have been through," Ygerna chuckled. "Nurse assures me she was not." She occasionally thought Felix must be some goblin's changeling, but she couldn't help liking him. No one could.

"You never did this before," Julia said. She put her hands on either side of his head, which was the only way to get Felix's undivided attention. "Look at me, Felix. What is the matter?"

Felix shuffled his feet uncomfortably, scuffing his sandals on the edge of the pool. He ran away from Nurse *all* the time, but it didn't seem like a good idea to say so.

"Julia," Antonia said. She handed her daughter her basket. "I think that Ygerna can deal with Felix."

Julia sighed. "I suppose I shouldn't visit when he's having his lesson," she said sadly. "Then he won't be tempted to run away to me."

Ygerna gritted her teeth. "I don't think you should worry about that. I imagine Felix was on his way to some other hideout when he met you."

Felix looked from one to the other. This was what his father had meant, maybe. Whatever he said, it was going to make someone upset. "I think I'll go back to Nurse now," he said unhappily.

Watching his small form trudge away through the roses, most of which were taller than he was, was more than Julia could bear. "He's afraid of you!" she said tearfully.

"I am not a beast with three heads!" Ygerna snapped. She could feel her emotions about to boil over. "He likes me well enough until you start prodding him! Now he's crying because he loves you, and his father has told him not to be rude to me." She felt like crying herself.

"Of course he loves me!" Julia said. Her jaw was set, and there were tense lines around her mouth. "I'm the only mother he's ever had! How can you yank him away from that to live with a—a *stranger*!"

"How can you try to make him think I *am* one? He's Correus's child! He belongs with us!"

"I don't notice Correus here to raise him!" Julia said.

"Julia." Antonia's voice had a touch of iron in it. "You are being unreasonable. And unpardonably rude."

"I don't *care*!" Julia said. "He's *my* baby, Mother. You know he is!"

"I'm sure the poor little thing thinks he is. It's all been very hard on him." Helva fluttered over to put her oar in, her lovely face smiling sweetly.

Suddenly the garden was full of screaming women. Appius laid his quill down on the desk in his private office and looked out. Julia was weeping, and Ygerna practically spat flames. Appius had not been in Pompeii when Vesuvius exploded, but his sons had. He thought he was getting a better idea of the force of the volcano from his daughter-in-law than from all of Correus's and Flavius's descriptions. Beside her, Appius was startled to see his normally calm and intelligent daughter crying furiously like a child who knows she is being bad but can't seem to stop. Every so often she would stop crying to snarl at Ygerna or her mother.

Antonia, whom very few things unnerved, had simply waded into the fray and told Julia to behave herself. But then Helva drifted over to participate and something in Antonia seemed to snap. When Appius looked out, Antonia, her handsome patrician face set in an expression that would have done a Fury proud, was screaming at Helva all the things she had wanted to say for the last twenty-seven years. Helva stood there with her blue eyes wide open and her commentary on matters silenced for once, but Appius thought she looked just a trifle amused.

As he watched, the doors from the atrium in the central core of the house swung open again, and Flavius and Aemelia appeared on the threshold. Flavius took one look at the scene in the garden and dived back into the house, but Aemelia scurried solicitously over to Julia.

Appius's normal reaction when his wife and his mistress butted heads was to duck, but this was getting out of hand.

"Juno help me." He went out into the garden. As he approached, they all stopped screaming and looked at him. There was something to being the head of the household, he thought. Julia was hiccuping uncontrollably, and her father glared at her mottled face.

"This is disgraceful."

"I know." Julia hiccuped again.

"Stop that."

"I c-can't!"

"No, I suppose you can't," Appius admitted. "You ought to be glad Lucius isn't here. He'd ask for a divorce on the spot—I never heard such a racket. I thought it was a cat fight."

"It was," Antonia said with a touch of humor. She seemed to have got a grip on things again and was her usual unruffled self except for the bright spots of color on her cheeks and the dangerous look in her eye.

"Talking of that," Helva said brightly, "did you hear that Pausanias has made his son divorce that unsuitable girl he married? So sensible, I think."

"*Helva!*"

Helva smiled at him.

"Be quiet. And go somewhere else. This doesn't concern you."

"Felix is my grandson," Helva pointed out.

"Then confine your remarks to Felix."

Helva looked as if she might be about to draw a connection between Felix, Correus, Ygerna, and the benefits of divorce, when Ygerna said through gritted teeth, "That is *enough!*" Her hands were clenched into fists at her side, and Appius wondered if she wanted to punch Julia or Helva or possibly Aemelia, who was fluttering about Julia, trying to pat her on the shoulder and keep up a running twitter of dismay.

"Felix is *my* problem, not anyone else's, not even his grandmother's." Ygerna shot Helva a look that made even Helva twitch. "If Correus wishes to divorce me, I am sure that he will mention it to me."

"My dear, there is no question of—" Antonia began.

"I can put up with Correus's mother," Ygerna said. "I have put up with worse."

Helva opened her mouth and closed it again, and Appius almost laughed. Very few people had ever silenced Helva.

"What I will not put up with," Ygerna said, "is meddling between me and Felix. He will *never* adjust if we quarrel over him, and it will frighten him besides." This time she looked at Julia. "If you can't leave it alone, I will take Felix and go someplace else. Is that clear?"

"My dear, you mustn't do that." Antonia put an arm around Ygerna's shoulders. "That wouldn't be safe at all. And you mustn't listen to Julia, who is behaving very badly."

"I don't *want* to listen to Julia," Ygerna said frankly. "But she makes me too mad. I do not have a very good temper," she added, and this time Appius did laugh. Ygerna smiled back at him. "That is an understatement, I expect. I am going to go now and try to explain to Felix why everyone has been fighting."

Appius watched her walk away, with a thoughtful expression. She wasn't much bigger than Felix, but Appius thought that he would back Ygerna against most people any day. She would certainly make good on any threat she chose to make. If they didn't wish to find themselves explaining to Correus how it was that they had chanced to lose his son, his wife, and his unborn child, Julia was going to have to mend her ways.

"She'll leave," he said to Julia, "if you prod her into it. And if you do, so help me Isis, I'll put you over my knee. It was a mistake to let you have that child in the first place, and I should have known it."

"You didn't have anything to do with it," Julia said. "It was Correus. And what else was Correus going to do, leave the poor thing with that filthy wet nurse in that filthy fort while he went off with the army?"

"Better if he had, maybe," Appius said. "Babies have been surviving a little dirt for years. But Felix isn't going to survive you quarreling with his mother."

"She's not—"

"She *is*. So get it into your head. She's right about Felix, and you know it. You are not stupid, Julia."

There was very little answer to be made to that. With a frosty glance Julia swept past her father and into the house. Aemelia fluttered behind her, pausing to extricate her trailing mantle from a rosebush. Appius found himself alone with Helva and Antonia.

Antonia gave him a look of distant dignity. "I have things to attend to. Thank you for speaking to Julia. I've been trying to make her see sense for weeks. It isn't as if she didn't have babies of her own." She picked up both baskets and the clippers and swept away. Helva might have been another rosebush in her path.

Appius gave Helva an exasperated look. "You've been making trouble again. Can't you behave for more than three hours at a stretch?"

"I have every right to be concerned about our son," Helva said sweetly.

"Correus is doing very well unassisted," Appius said. "Don't meddle. And don't bring up divorce again or I'll beat you."

Helva giggled. "You wouldn't. You only tried that once, remember?"

Appius laughed. He couldn't help it. It had been in his young days when he had first been fool enough to buy Helva in a slave market in Gallia Belgica. She had done some forbidden thing, and when he had decided that she was getting totally out of hand and had tried to give her a thrashing for it, she had feigned the sounds of a woman in the throes of such passion that in ten seconds there was a crowd of cheering, hooting legionnaires outside his tent, and Appius had given up. Then she had refused to sleep with him until he apologized and bought her a new pair of eardrops. Helva's body and the flower-garden beauty of her face had induced him to buy her in the first place, and she had quickly learned to use them to her advantage. Sometimes she still could. She was his one extravagance, his one silliness, the one thing he owned for its bright, impractical beauty alone.

"I should sell you," he said sourly. "You're a distraction." He had said it before, but it wasn't a possibility. He had adopted his son by her, given him his name. If he turned her out now, the scandal didn't bear thinking about. And he wasn't sure he wanted not to have Helva to look at anyway, not after all these years.

She linked her arm through his.

"When did you get all that amber? You have too much jewelry."

"I bought it myself," she said reproachfully. He made her a generous allowance. "I have so few pleasures, Appius. Don't begrudge me this one."

"I'm going bankrupt buying my wife jewelry," he said. "Trying to keep her ahead of you."

"What difficulties you have," Helva said sympathetically. She patted his hand. "I'm sorry I'm such a trouble."

A piercing shriek erupted from the bath.

"Master *Felix*!"

Nurse's voice. Felix must be having his bath. Ygerna poked her head in and followed the sounds and the trail of dropped clothing to the warm room. No one had ever been able to convince Felix to take a cold bath by any method short of brute force. Since the cold bath was not to clean so much as to promote health, it had finally been decided by all concerned that Felix was healthy enough.

Felix erupted from the depths of the pool like a porpoise, naked except for the gold bead around his neck, the lucky amulet that all Roman boys wore until they came of age. He hurled himself at the bank of the pool in a shower of water.

"I'm a fish!" he announced proudly.

"Well, Nurse is not," Ygerna said. Nurse was wringing the water from the ends of her apron. "I am going to go into Veii, to the market there. If you will stop being a fish and let Nurse dry you, you may come with me."

Felix was one of those children to whom a trip to anywhere was worth the going. He would cheerfully accompany anyone who would take him, to the fish market, the law courts, to the barn to dose a sick horse, to the fuller's shed with the dirty laundry, to the smith to mend a pot. He got around a good deal that way, attached to one or another member of the household. Maybe if she took him to the market at Veii, it would distract him from wondering why everybody in the family started screaming as soon as his name was mentioned.

Veii was an old Etruscan town to the north of Rome, the third point of a triangle between Appius's lands, Veii, and the city of Rome itself. Ygerna sent her maid to the stables to ask for a carriage and a slave to drive it, since Julius had been given over to Diulius's tutelage now. Ygerna was mildly surprised to find Julius driving the carriage anyway, but Felix greeted him delightedly and demanded to sit beside him.

"Diulius has gone to show a team to some old general who wants to make the green team famous this year," Julius said. There were four factions in the circus races: blue, green, red, and white. "And there wasn't anybody else handy." He checked the traces and readjusted a strap.

"What you mean is, you ducked off since he wasn't there to watch you," Ygerna said. "Well, I won't tell on you." She settled herself on the cushions of the carriage, with her maid Cottia beside her. "But you can have Felix." The sun was out, and the weather, with the capriciousness of fall, had turned warm again. Felix was a much more restful companion when he traveled outside.

"Right. Come and sit up here, and if you behave, you can drive some. If you don't, I'll smack you."

Felix seemed to find this arrangement reasonable and settled in beside Julius. They set off down the long drive that joined the big house to the main road beyond, Ygerna fidgeting among the cushions in the carriage. If one wanted to get somewhere, it seemed simpler to drive a chariot or just saddle a horse and ride, but Correus assured her that ladies did neither of those things in Rome, and Ygerna got no pleasure out of being considered an oddity. She was too pregnant to ride or drive now anyway, and the carriage, tedious as it was, was a retreat, a respite from treading on eggs in her father-in-law's house. She didn't know what she was going to buy in Veii, besides peace and quiet.

Peace and quiet proved to be relative. It was market day in Veii, and before they reached the city gates the road was jammed with traffic. There were private carriages and litters, litters-for-hire, horses, donkeys, and two-wheeled carts pushed by the countryfolk and loaded down with turnips and live chickens. A flock of sheep went *baa*'ing across the road and snarled the traffic hopelessly, while a white-haired gentleman leaned out of his litter and swore at them. A duck, escaped from somewhere, ran past in the other direction, quacking, a piece of string still tied to one foot.

"We'll never get through this," Julius said. He maneuvered the carriage up to the city gates and stopped, looking disgusted.

"We'll walk," Ygerna decided. "Leave the carriage here and go and buy a drink. *One*," she added. "Then come and stay with it until we get back."

Julius didn't protest. There was a wine stall he knew of just inside the gates, which were always open during daylight. Its small outdoor terrace commanded a view both of the gates and of the street that led to the Veii market. It looked like a good place to settle in.

Ygerna took Felix by the hand, and they strolled off toward the market, with Cottia in attendance. The day was warm, and Ygerna slipped her cloak off and gave it Cottia to carry. She always seemed to feel hot now. Felix tugged her into a quicker pace toward a stall filled with jointed wooden toys, brightly painted with black and red patterns. The shopkeeper, a round man in a red apron, held up a dog with a movable tail and a collar of red stars.

Felix put his hands on the counter top, which was nose-high, and peered up over it.

"Are you sure this is what you want? I will only buy you one thing."

Felix nodded. If he saw something else, the chances were good that he could make a great enough nuisance of himself to acquire that, too.

Ygerna paid the toymaker and laughed. Every time they shopped, Felix wanted the first thing he saw and she asked him if he were sure and they ended by buying something else as well on the way home. Felix laughed, too, and she winked at him. It wasn't that Felix didn't listen to her because he didn't like her, she thought. Felix didn't listen to anybody. There was a certain amount of comfort in that.

They prowled on among the stalls, inspecting oil of jasmine and attar of roses in small stoppered bottles; jewelry made by the Veii Metalworkers' Guild, glowing against a backdrop of black silk and little piles of uncut gems; baskets of red and brown straw; iron pots and fire dogs; pots of eye ointment and bottled remedies advertised to cure lung disease, bad humors of the blood, and all female ailments. In the butcher's shop, a goose hung upside down, awaiting its fate, while beside it hung a dressed lamb. The lamb was black with flies, and Ygerna choked and looked away. Her stomach gave a little protesting heave as they stepped out into the center of the street. It was crowded with market goers and shopkeepers off to buy their noon meal in one of the chowder stalls or bakeries that clustered together at one end of the market. The butcher brushed by them in a bloody apron, and Ygerna thought the smell would choke her.

"Are you all right? My lady?" Cottia looked at her anxiously.

"I . . . I think so. It's just hot. And that meat smelled so bad." Her face was chalky, and her insides felt empty. "I think maybe I had better sit down, though."

"Oh, Isis!" Cottia wailed, looking around them at the crowd jamming the market square. "Where?" It was impossible even to stand still here for very long. And what was she going to do if her mistress fainted?

"Here, I think," Ygerna said suddenly, and sat. Odd lights were beginning to dance across her field of vision.

"Ygerna?" Felix tugged at her mantle. "Mama?" He was beginning to be frightened.

"Here, move back from her. It's only the heat and the crowd, I expect," a low, rich voice said, and Ygerna looked up to see a dark woman in a deep red gown bending over her. Her skin was gold, and her hair and eyes were black. There were small gold drops in her ears and a delicate gold necklace around her throat. Her gown was plainly made, with no embellishments except a band of embroidery at the hem, but it was of silk. She was probably fifty if one looked closely at the fine web of lines around her eyes and throat, and she was the most beautiful woman Ygerna had ever seen.

"I saw you wobbling on your feet a minute ago," she said gently. "I was afraid you were going to be sick—I always was with my babies. Go and get her some water," she said to Cottia over her shoulder.

"It was the smell," Ygerna said faintly. "And I was so hot." She sounded indignant. Nothing ever made her sick.

Cottia brought the water, and Ygerna drank it thirstily while Felix stared silently at the lady. He'd never seen anyone so pretty, not even Aunt Aemelia. She looked like the statue of Aphrodite in the Temple of Venus and Roma, except that Aphrodite was a blond and this lady had a pile of thick black hair like jet, pinned up with gold pins with little knobs on the ends.

"Are you queen of something?" he asked. The queens in his nursery stories were always more beautiful than anyone else, unless they were evil ones, and then, of course, they were ugly.

The lady opened her eyes wide and looked at him with an odd little laugh. "Not these days," she said. "Now hold onto my skirt so you don't get lost. We're going to go and sit in that litter over there—do you see the one with the blue curtains?"

"I'm all right now," Ygerna said. She felt dreadful and conspicuous sitting on the ground in the middle of market day.

"You'll be better if you lie down for a while," the woman said. "Please come. I'm not in any hurry, and I remember how awful I used to feel when I was pregnant."

Ygerna stood up and balanced herself carefully. "Thank you, then." The woman gave her an arm, and Ygerna leaned on it as they crossed the square, with Felix trotting on one side and Cottia behind them, carrying Ygerna's cloak and Felix's wooden dog.

The litter must have been the woman's own. It was far better appointed than the litters for public hire, and the slaves standing beside it gave her a respectful bow as they approached. Inside was a sea of gold and deep red cushions; a light inner curtain of pale silk gauze let the occupants see out without passersby seeing in when the blue outer curtains were opened.

"Is there someone to whom I can send a message for you?" the woman asked.

"No, there's only my driver. It was so crowded we left the carriage at the gates."

"You're not from Veii?"

"No. My husband's in the army. I'm living with his family. His father is Appius Julianus."

"Ah, I have heard of him. I met him once, when I was younger."

"My name is Ygerna." Some introduction seemed to be called for, although the woman had volunteered none. "It is Flavia Agricolina on my citizenship papers," she added with a face of distaste.

"You are foreign?"

"British," Ygerna said. "My uncle was a king of the Silures."

"And you left that to marry a Roman soldier?" The woman's face had a peculiar expression, as if she were looking back into some time that was gone now. "My name is Berenice," she said.

Ygerna nodded. She had the feeling that the woman expected her to know the name, and was braced for her reaction. "I left all that because the Roman governor wanted to make me queen of the Silures," Ygerna said, "and my uncle Bendigeid wanted to kill me to stop him. He was a terrifying man, my uncle. The god was very strong in him. It was like looking at a fire that has jumped the hearth."

"The god?"

"The Sun Lord, the Shining One. Lugh Long-Spear."

"I see. I knew a man like that once. He heard God speak to him. Or maybe he only thought he did."

"What happened to him?"

"He started a war with Rome, and he died."

Ygerna looked at Berenice curiously, wanting to ask more and not sure that it would be polite or that the woman would tell her if she did.

"It was in Judaea," Berenice said after a moment. "He took the Holy Temple with him, and most of his people. A whole country gone because one man started a war."

Judaea—the name turned over in Ygerna's mind, and something Correus had told her about the emperor Titus came back to her. . . . Titus, who had triumphed with his father, Vespasian, after that war. Titus, the conqueror of Judaea. Titus, who had brought back a Jewish mistress and made a scandal . . .

Berenice watched the recognition in the other woman's eyes. "You'll do yourself no good by being seen with me," she said. She sounded as if she had said it to other people before and they had agreed and left. Titus had sent her away twice when public opinion against her ran too high. The last time he had made it plain that those who wished to remain in his favor should stay away from her also.

"My husband always said the Senate should have minded its own business," Ygerna said.

"He was wrong," Berenice said. "They were too afraid of me."

She had been "that foreign woman," and the Romans still remembered Cleopatra. Berenice was immoral. She had had three husbands and had left one of them to live with her brother, and rumor said it was incest. She had been a queen, first of Colchis and then of Cilicia. She had been queen in everything but name when the Romans gave her brother Ituraea to rule. She was the daughter of Herod Agrippa, the last king of the Jews. She had done her best to stop the massacre that the Roman procurator Gessius Florus had let loose on Jerusalem and nearly been killed in the trying. Later she had tried to stop the revolt that followed it. There had been no stopping either. It was all too late, and she had watched the city fall down around her. She was over forty when Titus fell in love with her and took her to Rome.

"They are still afraid," she said. "A leper wouldn't make them more nervous. You had better go, child. Your father-in-law won't like this at all."

Ygerna wriggled up in the cushions until she could sit up straight. "No one ever won a war with Rome. Or with my father-in-law, either, I expect. But I don't tell him things I think he wouldn't like."

Berenice laughed. "I forget. You aren't a Roman, either."

"It can be very lonely here," Ygerna said, "not being a Roman. Things . . . go away from you. The Goddess, the Great Mother . . . I used to be her priestess. I was Goddess-on-Earth, and when she spoke, she spoke through me. She left me when I left Britain. My husband says the Jews only have one god and won't worship the others." That seemed odd to her. *I am very insular*, she thought. *I don't know anything*. "Does he go away from you, too, if you leave his place?"

"Our God never goes away," Berenice said. "But it grows harder sometimes to find him, especially if you doubt how well you've served him. Our priests would tell you that I've served him ill indeed, but I don't know. . . . I tried. . . . There was no winning that war for my people. Titus knew it. We tried so hard to make them see, my brother and I. But they didn't understand. They thought that God would strike the Romans down with a blast of fire and an angel with a sword, and save the city. My people have never understood the Romans. And no matter how much I explained them to Titus, he couldn't understand the Jews. So much tragedy from that."

And now she lives here by herself and can't go home again because the priests don't like her, Ygerna thought. *I have been lucky.* Helva didn't like her, but Helva wasn't the Senate. Correus could marry whom he wanted. Felix was fidgeting with the tassels on the cushions, and Ygerna poked her head through the curtains to Cottia, standing outside. "Go and get us something to eat, and take Felix with you and feed him. I am *always* hungry," she explained to Berenice as she handed Felix down from the litter, "and I thought it would be as well if Cottia went away for a minute. Are you being polite?" she asked seriously. "Will it make trouble for *you* if I stay?"

Berenice smiled. "My dear child, no. I could have very little more trouble than I have already. But I didn't want you to stick your head in something you didn't understand."

Ygerna nodded. "I only thought that maybe you were lonely, too."

Berenice smiled. "Less lonely now than I was. I have lived with men too much, I think. A woman needs another woman for a friend."

Ygerna smiled back. "There are too many women in my father-in-law's house, but no friends."

"Will they let you come to see me?" Berenice said. "If you don't tell them you're coming?" That didn't make much sense, and she giggled. It was a low, amused noise, and it sounded like she hadn't done it in a long time.

So sad to be trapped here, after the man she had come to Rome for had left her, Ygerna thought. "Do you live in Veii?"

"No, I have a house in the country where I won't be . . . such an embarrassment," Berenice said. "Send your maid to let me know when you're coming. It will be nice to have company again." She put a hand on Ygerna's and smiled.

Her age showed in her hands, Ygerna thought, but when she smiled, her face was still beautiful enough to take your breath away. How could a man give up beauty like that? And then the thought came to her, very quietly: *He couldn't.* And that was too dangerous a notion even to think about, so she put it quickly into the back of her mind.

Cottia came back with a straw plate of figs and olives, and they ate them, and then Ygerna collected Felix from behind the litter, where he was putting olive pits in the gilded fretwork that decorated the frame. They had better find Julius, she thought, before he settled in at a wineshop . . . if he hadn't already. Julius was drinking too much lately, sitting in the stables with Forst and a wine jug, Cottia said. Although maybe that was mostly Forst. Correus had told her about the German chieftain and Forst, and Ygerna thought it was little wonder Forst was drinking. So many people who couldn't go home again, she thought, all caught in Rome now, trying to grow into Romans and not mind.

Julius saw them coming and was waiting at the carriage. Ygerna settled Felix inside with her—it was beginning to grow cool—and he snuggled into the cushions beside her, with his head on her knee.

"That was a very beautiful lady," he said thoughtfully.

"Yes, she was."

"Did she make you feel better?"

"Yes," Ygerna said, "a lot better."

"That's good." Felix wriggled deeper into the cushions, his eyes half closed. "I'm glad you aren't sick, Mama," he said sleepily.

VI

The Man in the Office

WHEN WINTER CAME TO THE RHENUS DELTA, IT CAME WITH A hand as cold as Hel's. They were only on the edge of it, but already the sour, salty grass was frost-tinged, and in Theophanes's camp, they had to knock the ice off the water barrels with a knife hilt in the morning. They began to keep most of the food taken in their raiding, building up a store against the bad weather when the autumn storms would finally grow too strong and the shipping would cease altogether until spring.

This must be the worse time of the year, Correus thought,

when there was no raiding to be done, and bad weather would block the roads inland, even if a man was willing to show his face in the towns. There was always the chance of meeting a man whose ship had been raided, who would scream for the soldiers if he saw a face he remembered. Theophanes's crew would spend the winter in camp and grow bored and quarrelsome with it, like any winter-bound village. He hoped they grew bored enough to talk.

Ranvig, at any rate, was willing to talk. He rarely stopped, chatting cheerfully about hunting and women and his father's vineyards near Augusta Treverorum.

"We had a good year this season—dry summer, you know—good for the wine. So I suppose he'll be willing to pay Theophanes to get me back."

There was something slightly forced about Ranvig's inconsequential chatter. It occurred to Correus that it reminded him of his own.

"How did you happen to land in Theophanes's net?"

"I was supposed to be hiring on with a winegrower in Gaul. For the experience, you know. Parents always think you'll learn more if you make a long, uncomfortable journey and live in a hut for a year. He'll have hired someone else by now, I expect," he added philosophically.

"Bit old, aren't you, for taking up an apprenticeship?" Correus said.

"That was my thought," Ranvig said. "But my father built his vineyards up from not much. He hadn't enough to worry about until now." He looked at Correus and said frankly, "*You* don't look like the type to choose the provinces for a pleasure trip."

"I'm not," Correus said gloomily. "I have an old aunt who inherited property out here, and the family decided that I was the one to come and deal with it for her. They seemed to feel I had time on my hands."

Ranvig's crooked face looked amused as he passed Correus the wine jug. He had been lying down, and there was straw in his hair. They were drinking out of the jug. "It'll be a long winter with nothing to do but drink and prowl around after the slave women," Ranvig said. "I'm afraid Gaul will look good by spring."

"Will it take your father that long to pay?" Augusta Treverorum was in Upper Germany, a fair-sized city on the Mosella River. Theophanes's ultimatum should have been there and back by now.

"Oh, I expect so," Ranvig said. "He'll have to sell up a few things, you see, and that's not so easy in winter." He didn't sound worried, though. He took the wine jug back and raised his arm to take a swallow. There were old scars on it, just visible where his tunic sleeve fell back.

Correus thoughtfully pulled his own sleeves down. He had packed his togas back in the trunk once he had made a sufficient nuisance of himself over them, and had asked Theophanes for the shirt and breeches and fur leggings that the pirates wore. It was cold.

Ranvig handed back the wine jug and crossed his arms behind his head, lying back in the straw. However much Ranvig drank, Correus thought, he never seemed drunk.

The door latch at the far end of the longhouse rattled, and four or five of Theophanes's crew stamped in, shaking away the mist and drizzle like wet dogs. One of them kicked at the fire to stir it up. Another rummaged in the sleeping cubicles at the far end and came up finally with a length of rope.

"Hah! I knew I had it. Come on, I want to get that last lot tied on and gone before Theophanes starts yelling. Ranvig, is that beer?"

Ranvig shook his head. "Wine. Out of deference to the gentleman here." He nodded his head at Correus. "But it'll warm you just the same."

"I want beer," the man said. "Wine is for Romans and women. No offense meant," he added with a grin at Correus.

What he meant was that wine gave him a hangover. They thought it unmanly to water it the way the Romans did, and consequently it made them very drunk indeed.

"Where in Hel's name are the thralls? *BEER!*" he shouted at the top of his voice. After a minute a sleepy slave came from a cubicle and trudged out through the door. She came back with a pitcher, and the man picked it up and drank from it.

"We'll be back. Bring some more. And get this fire going."

He kicked it, and a shower of sparks spat at him. The thrall girl gave him a sour look and went to get more wood.

"You stay here," the man said to Ranvig and Correus, and they all went out again, taking the rope with them.

"There must be a packtrain tonight," Correus said when the men had left. "Where do they come from, do you know? They just pop up out of the fog, as far as I can tell. Sometimes the only way I know they're here is one of Theophanes's men comes along and shoves me in the first handy room and says to stay put."

"I expect maybe some of the pony drivers are a bit more respectable by day than by night," Ranvig said. "They wouldn't want you to put the finger on them in the market square one day."

"Do they think I'm a damned owl?" Correus said grumpily. "I wouldn't know my own mother in the dark in this fog. And I don't care who distributes their damned loot for them. What *I* want is to go home and have a hot bath, preferably some time in the next six months." He leaned back in the straw and frowned at the opposite wall.

The thrall girl, prodded along by the returning pirates, came back with more wood.

"Cheer up, friend," one of them said. "There's a ship on its way with a nice lot of slaves on board, and we're gonna make a bid on 'em, like!" The others laughed, and Correus thought they were all a little drunk. "Ought to be some women among 'em—we'll lend you one! A gentleman needs something better than this!" He smacked the thrall girl on the bottom. "Where's that beer, girl?"

They sat down around the fire and poured their beer horns full from the pitcher. Someone brought out the harp. Ranvig inspected the wine jug and eloquently held it upside down, and one of them passed him a beer horn. The beer horn was a point of pride. A man had to finish it or sit holding it—it couldn't be set down. Ranvig, who didn't seem to be feeling any ill effects from switching drinks, drained his. His long-fingered hands reminded Correus of Flavius's. Flavius would have his letter now, the fact that Correus needed more time carefully encoded into his plea for ransom. Flavius would tell their father to promise to pay it, and stall. Then they would wait for Correus's next letter, and Correus could hope Theophanes didn't get impatient in the meantime.

Correus was almost sure now that someone was feeding Theophanes shipping schedules—they seemed to know not only when a ship was due, but what she carried. But no amount of careful questioning or outright eavesdropping had given Correus a clue as to who was at the other end of those messages or even how they were sent. And there was the matter of the pony drivers no one would let him see. There had to be a reason for that. Otherwise, Theophanes let him run free in the camp. Correus looked at Ranvig thoughtfully. Was it Ranvig who was less respectable by night? Smuggling was always a problem— very few traders saw any reason to give Caesar his due unless forced to. If Ranvig had been smuggling, it would be easy enough for him to have fallen afoul of Theophanes's raiding parties—the pirates were no great respecters of other outlaws' liberty. And if Theophanes was also using a smugglers' band to transport loot, he would be careful to keep Ranvig out of their sight, and anyone from mentioning his presence, until his ransom had been paid to some unidentifiable third party. Theophanes was perfectly capable of dealing with the smugglers with one hand and kidnaping their associates with the other. And it would explain why Ranvig was lying to him—he wouldn't admit his smuggling to a Roman. Correus was almost sure Ranvig was lying. He wondered if Ranvig knew *he* was lying. And if so, would Ranvig feel inclined to point that fact out to Theophanes? Correus ran a hand through his hair, which was beginning to get too long. Ranvig gave him a headache.

The door opened again, and Eumenes came through it on the toe of Cerdic's boot.

"Stay where you're told next time!"

"It was colder than a witch's backside in there!" Eumenes sat down by the fire, looking aggrieved. Cerdic stood over him with his hands on his hips. "Why are you so touchy?" Eumenes growled.

"You know the rules," Cerdic said. "One more time, and I'll have you tied up."

Eumenes got up and gave him a black look. He went and sat by Correus. Ranvig appeared to have gone to sleep.

"What did you do?"

"Got too close to their precious ponies," Eumenes said in a low voice. "They hauled me into the first place handy when the pony drivers showed. It was a storeroom and the roof leaked, and after I'd sat in there for a while I thought it was as good a reason as any to go someplace else. They were loading the ponies in front of that house by the fence, and I went in the back door and through to the front and stood close enough to hear things. That was when Cerdic came through. I thought he was going to kill me." Eumenes looked a little unsettled.

"Next time do what you're told," Correus said in a loud, disgusted voice. "If Father pays your ransom and you aren't available because you've made that hothead Cerdic mad, I doubt Theophanes will send your price back again."

"Huh." Eumenes shot Cerdic a black look. "Ever hear of a tribe called the Chatti?" he asked under his breath.

Correus looked at Ranvig and lowered his own voice to a whisper. "They're the pony drivers?"

Eumenes nodded.

"Go get me some beer." Correus leaned back against a post. Around the fire, the group had grown to a dozen and started to sing. Theophanes slept in the largest longhouse, where most of these men belonged. If they wanted to drink the night before a raid, they knew better than to do it in his presence. Eumenes handed Correus a horn with the strong, heavy beer brewed in the village, and he sat drinking it and considering.

The Chatti held land across the Rhenus in Barbarian Germany, in the Taunus Forest district, and of late the frontier scouts maintained that the Chatti were getting entirely too powerful. Correus put a lot of faith in the frontier scouts. They looked like brigands, lived off the land, and found out things that the army needed to know. Occasionally they got caught, and then the army either never heard from them again or they found them in pieces in a tree. When the frontier scouts handed in a warning, a commander with brains paid attention. If the Chatti were acting as middlemen, it explained why a lot of the loot was disappearing out of the Roman zone into the wilds. It also meant that the Chatti were taking a cut, and it might mean that the cut was going into a war chest. When a tribe like the Chatti grew rich, the Rhenus commanders started posting extra pickets. And with the pirates keeping the Rhenus

Fleet occupied . . . Correus thought he had part of his answer for the emperor. But it wasn't the Chatti who were sending Theophanes Roman shipping schedules.

The singing waked Ranvig, and he sat up and pulled the straw out of his hair. He seemed disinclined to join in, and Correus, eyeing him in the firelight, thought suddenly that Ranvig might be older than he looked. There was something in his face that Correus, try as he would, couldn't equate with a man who had spent his life growing vines in Augusta Treverorum. Tonight, Correus thought, he looked a little lonely.

Ranvig caught him staring, and gave him his odd, crooked smile. He didn't seem offended. "If you are bored now, it will get worse over the winter."

"I don't doubt it," Correus said gloomily. "I had some books in my trunk, but I've read them all four times."

"What do you do in Rome, for amusement?"

"Read, hunt, drive—my father raises chariot ponies." He felt inclined to be truthful, insofar as he could. It was simpler. Or maybe it was just that he liked Ranvig and was tired of telling lies. "Go to the theater." He cast about him for some other harmless amusement. "Here, I will teach you a game. It's called Wisdom. I learned it from a slave of my father's, a Briton." Admitting to a British wife didn't accord with his carefully built character. He rummaged around in the straw for pebbles and bits of mud, and laid out a board with straws to mark the squares. Ranvig leaned over and looked interested.

He proved to be a quick pupil. They played several games, and Ranvig won the last one. He picked up the stones and laid them out again while Correus watched him, out of the corner of his eye now, still trying in some fashion to take his measure. Chatti boys wore an iron collar, like a torque, until they had killed their man in battle. Some continued to wear it afterward, a sort of reverse badge of their ferocity, to show that there were more enemies left to kill. Generally it left a gall mark. Correus looked at Ranvig's throat, where it was bare above his tunic neck, but he couldn't see any marks. Maybe it had faded since boyhood. Or maybe he wasn't Chatti. But more and more Correus was sure that Ranvig wasn't a winegrower's son from Augusta Treverorum, either.

Ranvig made a move on the Wisdom board and sat back. "I will play you again. I am beginning to like this."

Correus thought that that wasn't all they were playing. He moved a piece carefully, suddenly aware that Ranvig had been watching *him*.

"An odd way to make a friendship," Ranvig said.

Curiously, Correus thought that Ranvig meant that honestly. For an instant Correus's face twisted into the old bitterness that comes to any spy over the number of lies that shape the paths open to him. Then he said lightly, "We have much in common." He nodded at their captors, drinking beer by the fire. He hoped violently that he and Ranvig were not so much alike as he was beginning to think.

Nothing else surfaced until the night Theophanes killed one of his own men. Correus had spent most of his time playing Wisdom with Ranvig, or staring at the ground and trying to figure out where in Hel's domain he was. (Odd how quickly he'd picked up the old Rhenus slang again. All the soldiers stationed on the Rhenus began to invoke the German gods once they'd been there a month or so. They seemed to belong to the dark, tree-shrouded mountains and the mist-wrapped lowlands more than the bright rulers of Olympus did.)

Every time Correus got the chance, he would scratch in the dirt the pattern of the channels and islands and the gray coastline that he remembered from the voyage to Theophanes's hold, afraid to make a permanent record lest it be found, afraid not to lest he forget. A fleet could hunt Theophanes's pirates for a long time in these inlets and never get a smell of them without a guide.

When the pack ponies and their drivers had been and gone, there was a sharing out of the payment the next morning, and any particular booty or slaves, women mostly, that one of the men had an eye to were kept back from the shipment and could be bought with their share. These were quarrelsome sessions, and Theophanes kept order like a man with a pack of ill-tempered dogs.

The morning after the pony train left, the expected ship was due. And so there was a raid, and the sharing out didn't come until evening, when the long crocodile shapes of the liburnians had been beached again and the cargo unloaded. As predicted, it was mostly slaves taken by the ship's captain in raids of his own along the north coast beyond the Roman zone. The slaver captain was drowned with his ship, a death for which Correus found it hard to grieve, and the slaves were no worse off than they had been.

But there was trouble among them, in the form of a blond woman with the face of a virgin goddess and the body of a wanton. Wide blue eyes gazed out on the men above full breasts and the wide curve of her hips, all too visible through a wet, torn gown. Theophanes should have known better than to let the men bid on her at all.

The slaves were huddled in a ring of torchlight while Theophanes and Cerdic sorted them out, and Ennius stood looking at the blond woman with a hunger in his eyes that made Correus nervous just to see it.

"I'll give half of my share for that 'un." A tall graying man called Wulf put out an arm and pointed at the blond woman. Correus turned to see that Wulf's eyes had the same hungry look.

The woman stood motionless. Maybe she didn't understand the dog Latin they spoke in the camp. Or maybe she didn't care anymore which man she went to.

"No." Ennius started out of his trance. "No, Theophanes, I want her."

"I spoke first!" Wulf growled. He looked like a wolf, gray and scarred, in rough gray tunic and breeches. There was a dagger with an amethyst in its silver hilt stuck through his belt, an incongruous touch of riches against his worn clothing. He laid his hand on it and looked at Ennius.

"No!" Ennius said again, louder. The woman turned her blue eyes toward him, and Ennius said, still watching her, "I don't ask for favors often. I want her."

There was a sharp indrawn breath next to Correus, and he turned to see Cerdic's dark woman standing beside him. "She is trouble, that one," Cerdic's woman said. "Better Theophanes sell her fast, away from here. Or slit her throat."

"I spoke first!" Wulf said again. He sailed on Theophanes's ship, not Ennius's. Two of Ennius's crewmen edged toward him watchfully.

Theophanes looked from one man to the other, and then at the woman.

"Theophanes——" Ennius said. His voice was almost pleading. The woman moved a little so that her pale hair rippled around her shoulders. It glowed like ripe corn in the torchlight.

"You are both fools," Theophanes said. "But Ennius has the rank. Take her," he said to Ennius. "But look you that you don't take to spending all your time in her bed. Grow soft, Ennius, and I'll find another captain."

"No," Ennius said. "I will remember." He was still looking at the blond woman. He took her by the arm and led her away out of the torchlight. She went quietly, her walk docile, her beautiful face unprotesting. She made Correus nervous. Beside him, Cerdic's woman made the Sign of Horns as they passed.

Wulf stood staring after them, his eyes still hungry, and angry now. Then he turned away and stalked into the shadows.

No one saw gray Wulf for the next two days while Ennius took the blond woman into his bed. Presumably Wulf was lying low and sulking, and presumably Theophanes knew where he was and would knock some sense into him when he thought he needed it, if Wulf didn't drink away his bad temper in a day or two.

Theophanes left it one day too long.

The mist came down with the sunset as usual, and Correus was prowling among the buildings of the compound less because he thought he might learn something than to walk away his own restlessness. Ygerna's pregnancy would come to term with the onset of winter, and it was maddening to be unable to get word. Meanwhile he could imagine the baby coming too early, or too late, or Ygerna dying, or . . . The possibilities were endless. Worse, the only person he could talk out his fears to was Eumenes, who slapped him on the back and said jovially that women came through these things all right; his mother had had five.

He browsed moodily through the camp and almost fell over Wulf propped against the wall of the armory with a beer horn in his hand. He was drinking wine from it, unwatered, and there was a half-full wineskin on the ground beside him.

"What are *you* doing, Roman?" Wulf said sourly.

"You will be sick if you drink all that," Correus said.

"Not as sick as some," Wulf said.

"Why didn't Theophanes let you have that woman?" Correus asked. He sat down beside Wulf. The man looked as if he might talk, if suitably prodded.

Wulf growled and didn't say anything further. He took another drink and sat staring at the wineskin. Finally he said, "Ennius can pay more. He's a captain. He *gets* more to start when we split the take."

"That doesn't seem fair," Correus mused. "You all risk your necks, same as the captains."

Wulf snorted. "Tell that one to a sailor on a horse. Four shares for Theophanes, three for Ennius and the other captains, two each for Cerdic and the mates, and one for each o' us. And three for the man in the office."

"For who?" Correus kept his voice disinterested.

"For the information," Wulf said. "I dunno. The man in the office, that's what Theophanes calls him."

"You don't know his name?"

"Ziu, no. Theophanes doesn't, either." Wulf didn't care. "He sends a boat."

"Who—Theophanes?"

"No. The man in the office. What do you care?" Wulf seemed to realize through the wine haze that he shouldn't be talking.

Correus backed off. "Where have you been all this time?"

"Waiting," Wulf said.

That didn't sound promising. If Wulf was going to get out of control, Correus thought he would rather be elsewhere. "Waiting for what?"

"For *that* bastard."

The door to one of the longhouses opened, and Ennius stood framed in torchlight. He stuck his arms out and stretched, then stepped off the stoop and went around the longhouse. Behind him, the woman came into the light. She swayed, and the gold hair swam around her like water. She had on a silk gown now.

Ennius came back, and seeing her in the doorframe, he took her by one hand and tugged her toward him. She came down the step and out into the mist with him obediently.

Wulf stared after them. The woman's laughter came oddly

disembodied through the mist. It was the first sound Correus had heard her make.

Wulf made a noise that was somewhere between human and animal. Correus was still sitting on the ground when he realized that Wulf was running through the mist and that something gleamed white in his hand. Correus jumped up and ran after him, and somewhere ahead of him something screamed.

Doors flew open, and suddenly there were men and torches everywhere. The mist was spotted with them, and the salt scent of the air was full of burning pitch. There was another scream, and someone shouted, "That way!"

Wulf and Ennius were rolling on the ground by the storeroom door, and the woman stood to one side, silently watching them. Her sweet, goddess's face was expressionless, but Correus thought he saw, just for a moment, the flash of triumph in her wide blue eyes. There was a knife in Wulf's hand, and Ennius was groping frantically for his own. Wulf's other hand was at his throat. They were growling at each other like animals. It hadn't been the woman who screamed, Correus realized. That half-human sound had come from Wulf as he dove at Ennius.

Wulf had his dagger in position now, and Cerdic jumped to pull him off when Theophanes pushed him aside. He caught Wulf by both shoulders, spun, and slammed him back against the storeroom wall. Wulf leaned forward, both hands pressed against the wall behind him.

"Fighting over a woman!" Theophanes said. "No man in my camp fights another for *anything* he possesses—especially not for a gold bitch with thieves' eyes!"

Ennius struggled to his feet, his face furious. The golden woman was still silent. Correus thought she might be smiling.

Wulf snarled again. He launched himself at Ennius, and Theophanes stepped between them, knife out. He caught Wulf in the belly with it, and Wulf suddenly folded up around it. Theophanes let him fall to the ground and stood with his knife dripping, looking at Ennius.

"Go and put the signal out for Beorn."

"We don't have any cargo," Ennius said.

"Yes, we do," Theophanes said. "She is cargo." He pointed

at the blond woman. "Shut her in the slave house till Beorn comes."

"No!" Ennius had his knife out now.

Theophanes held his own knife point out. "She is cargo. Or do you want Wulf's death? She is poison, Ennius. She'll poison *you*."

Ennius looked at the blond woman and seemed to read something there that might have been confirmation. He put his knife away and turned toward the slave house. She followed him. Her blue eyes were still and lovely, but there was something about her that made Correus think of goats and the horned god, whose pipes can make a man less than human.

Theophanes turned to the rest of them. "Is there anyone who wants to dispute me?" The knife was still in his hand, and his dark eyes reflected the torchlight so that a man couldn't see into them. "Anyone else who thinks he can break my rules and stay on this side of Hades?"

A few glared back at him, but they were silent. Cerdic's fingers tapped a pattern on his hip, just beside his knife hilt. The man who fought Theophanes would fight Cerdic afterward. Correus wondered how often these two had to face down the rest. They were a wolf pack. A leader they weren't afraid of they would tear to pieces one night.

Theophanes prodded Wulf's dead body with his foot. "Put him in the bog." He picked up the silver-handled knife from the ground and stuck it through his own belt.

Two of the pirates picked up Wulf, and the others edged away, back to their hearth fires, their women, and their beer. The bog was a fast and easy burial, but it was a secret one, too. The man who angered Theophanes just now might go into the bog himself, dead or not, and no one liked to think of that cold green slime for very long.

Ranvig stopped beside Correus to watch them carry Wulf away. "A woman like that," he said. "You should just give her to your enemy and let her take him under for you. But keep her—merciful Wuotan, no. She is Earth Mother's, that one."

Correus thought of Ygerna. Ygerna had been the Mother's priestess, but she was her own woman, also. This one was *of* the Mother, part of her. She ate men. He felt sorry for Beorn, and for whoever bought her in the slave market, if Beorn got her that far.

"I knew a *man* like that once," Ranvig said. "He . . . *consumed*. Women, power, whatever came to his hand. But there was something . . . amputated . . . from him. I often wondered who he belonged to."

"You think that that kind of twist must have a god's hand behind it?" Correus asked. "Maybe you're right." Most gods had their dark side. "What happened to your man?" he asked idly.

"He died," Ranvig said shortly. "He was killed, but he managed to twist what he had touched beforehand, and left a better man than he was maimed." His expression said plainly that he wasn't going to say more than that, and Correus grew quiet and cautious. There was something there that was a key to Ranvig, he thought.

"I'm cold," Ranvig said. "I want to drink." Correus followed him back to their sleeping cubicle in the longhouse and sent Eumenes for beer. Ranvig swallowed his at a gulp. "That will be the last ship, I'm thinking. There's a gale brewing up now." The wind had begun to howl outside, and the fire wavered and danced as gusts blew in under the door. Correus could feel it bite through his clothes. "The Romans will be digging in along the river," Ranvig said, "and hoping no one starts trouble before spring."

"It looks peaceable enough to me," Correus said. He took a swallow of beer. "Is someone *thinking* of starting trouble?"

Ranvig shrugged. "There is always trouble along the Rhenus. Each new emperor comes out and tries to stop it, and then there is a war, and then it is quiet again for a while." He looked at Correus. "The Romans like to keep busy. They make their own trouble sometimes."

Correus laughed. "The emperor doesn't see it that way, I expect."

"What *does* he see?" Ranvig's tone was only mildly interested, but Correus began to get the feeling of an oyster when someone is wiggling a stick in to open it. Ranvig held his horn out to Eumenes.

"He doesn't tell me," Correus said. "I'm not the military type, you know. Someone else can go around all plated up like a tortoise and wave a stick for the empire at the barbarians. Me, I just want to go back to Italy before I freeze."

Ranvig's crooked face was pleasant but watchful. The sensation of being poked open grew stronger. Correus poked back, gently. "What the emperor does along the Rhenus won't affect the wine business in Augusta Treverorum, I shouldn't think." *In other words, if you have a blameless father in Augusta Treverorum and not a smuggling business in some Chatti village, what do you care?*

"I expect not," Ranvig said. He swirled the beer around in his horn, watching the froth it made. "Still, a war always rebounds on someone. One doesn't like to get in the way."

"Does it?" Correus said. "Yes, I suppose it does, if you're close enough. We don't get many ripples in Rome."

"Perhaps you should stay in Rome, then," Ranvig said.

"Oh, I intend to. Perhaps *you* should stay away from the Rhenus."

Ranvig laughed, his oddly set eyes genuinely amused. "Believe me, I would *like* to."

Two weeks later, winter came down in full measure, and Theophanes told Correus that his family was stalling with the ransom. If Correus wished to keep both his ears or whatever else might be cut off to prove the seriousness of his situation, then Theophanes strongly suggested that Correus write to his father again. Correus heaved a sigh of relief. He'd been afraid that Theophanes might cut first and suggest a second message later.

He took the parchment scrap Theophanes handed him and put down his plight in the most dramatic terms he could, consistent with the code he had devised with Flavius. He thought of asking Flavius if anyone on the frontier had heard of a man named Ranvig in connection with the Chatti, but that was not a question that had been planned for in the code. In any case, when he had finished with the pirates, that should take care of the Chatti's connection with them also. Time enough to send a few more scouts into Chatti lands in the spring.

Ranvig was sitting across from him in the straw, watching his efforts. *Don't do it*, Correus almost said, wishing he could show him Nyall Sigmundson's grave, and all the others who had decided to make war against the empire. *Don't take on Rome.*

It is none too easy to get a message across the Alps in midwinter, especially when it has to go through three or four hands to blur its origins. It was the start of spring in Italy when Appius Julianus took the sealed papyrus out of the woolen wrappings it had traveled in, thanked the blameless merchant who had carried it, and paid him for his trouble. He read with raised eyebrows and sent a slave into the City for Flavius.

"Take a look at this." Flavius handed Lucius Paulinus his brother's letter and a rough translation of its hidden content, scrawled in Flavius's hand on a wax slate. Lucius read it while Flavius sat and watched him with his mouth twisted into a grim expression that boded someone no good.

Lucius looked up and whistled. "Pretty damned conclusive, if you ask me. Knowledge almost to the day of ships out of Ostia, and within a week for ships out of other Roman ports and ships bound back for Rome. Have you taken this to the emperor yet? And you have cleared your slaves out of here, haven't you?"

"No, and yes," Flavius said. "First I wanted to see if your reaction tallies with mine. And my household knows better than to come within a mile of me when I tell them not to."

"All the same . . ." Lucius flicked a finger at the wax and picked up a stylus. "Mind if I scrub this out?"

"Go ahead. I'll do a formal report for the emperor. He isn't going to like the looks of it."

"*I* don't like the looks of it," Lucius said. His plain, freckled face looked a little older than usual. "I hate things I can't prove."

"I think the answer's obvious," Flavius said. "I'm going to tie that snake into knots."

Lucius was busy scraping the letters out of the wax. "Let's just hope the emperor shares your inclination," he said. "Because if he doesn't, there's not a judge in the City who's going to risk his own ass on a conviction. And if the snake gets wind of it, he's going to bite you."

VII

Theophanes

"I'M AFRAID, SIR, THAT THERE JUST AREN'T ANY OTHER POS-sibilities." Flavius stood respectfully before the emperor Titus and kept a wary eye on the emperor's brother. Domitian reclined on a couch to the side of the room, with an empty wine cup on the floor beside him. He was playing with a wooden puzzle, carefully fitting pieces through a slot.

Titus sat in a chair at his desk, a massive table loaded down with scrolls and tablets. A bronze bowl of dried figs and a miniature catapult sat at one end. He ran a hand through his hair. It looked as if he had already done that several times this morning. Titus gave his barber an hour in the morning to make him presentable and that had to last. He didn't like people hovering over him with combs.

The emperor read over Flavius's report one more time. "On the face of it, it looks as if this is our man," he said. He seemed to be waiting for an outburst from Domitian, but his brother kept silent. He rattled the pieces of his puzzle from hand to hand. Titus looked at his aide. "I have to have a name, Flavius."

"Sir, we *know* the man has access to all the shipping schedules, including cargo lists, and he gets his fastest information on the shipping out of Ostia Harbor and the Port of Rome," Flavius said. "We also know that he's making a lot of money on this, and that's going to show up. Vettius has the prefecture of the Shipping Offices and the inflow of slightly mysterious cash." He looked directly at the emperor. "He also has the ambition of another Pompey, and ambitious men need money. If you know of anyone else that all this would point to, sir, I wish you'd tell me."

"Why hasn't your brother come up with a name?" Domitian said. It appeared he had been taking notice of the conversation, after all. "He seems to have done an admirable job of digging out the rest of it."

"I doubt there's a name to be had," Flavius said. He turned back to Titus, who was the man to convince. "I would be surprised if these pirates know whom they're dealing with. That would be too much of a risk to take, even for Vettius."

"Then I don't think *we* should put a name to him," Domitian said quietly. "That constitutes slander until we *do* have some proof."

And you got him that shipping prefecture, Flavius thought. *Embarrassing for you.*

"A point I have always hoped you would keep in mind," Titus said acidly to his brother. Domitian listened avidly to each talebearer who crept into the palace. Now he looked uncomfortable. "Go and find your friend Vettius," Titus went on, "and tell him to come to me. *Don't* tell him why I want him."

"Don't you think—"

"I think that if you want to share privileged information, as befits my heir, that you had best obey me!" Titus snapped. He looked like a bull, and the muscles in his thick neck were bunched. "Push me too far, Domitian, and you may not even be able to count on that!"

Domitian rose. "As the emperor commands." He swept Titus an elaborate bow.

Titus watched his exit with an exasperated face. "He's my heir, Flavius. Don't say it."

Flavius raised one dark eyebrow and restrained himself. "Is he going to warn Vettius?"

"I don't think so," Titus said. "He's still afraid of me when I want him to be."

"I'd like to put the fear of the gods in Vettius." Flavius's hands twitched, and he picked up the purple-fringed ends of his sash to fiddle with. It was tied just above the waist around the silvered cuirass of his full dress uniform. Everyone here knew who wore a sash of office twitched at it when he wanted something to do with his hands. It was a pacifier for senior officers.

"Flavius, I want to make one thing very clear," Titus said. "I know what my brother is up to at all times. You are to make no comment about how far I choose to let him into my confidence. He won't learn to govern by being kept in total ignorance. He *may* learn from example, in time. I have no sons, and Domitian is going to sit here after me, as my father requested."

"Mithras grant it's a long way off," Flavius said.

"Flavius—"

There was a warning note in the emperor's voice, and Flavius knew enough to listen to it. "For not wanting to lose yourself, sir," he said lightly. "The gods grant you a long reign."

Titus laughed. "Your devotion is commendable. I'm young yet. By the time I die, Domitian will have a little sense of the sort that age puts into you. My father founded a dynasty, the first direct succession in the principate. As long as it continues, there will be no more civil war, and Domitian is the continuance."

"You should marry again, sir."

"I tried to," Titus said. "The Senate thought otherwise, so now they will have to take Domitian. And now you get out of here before Vettius comes. I don't want a brawl."

Marius Vettius appeared before the emperor, wearing an easy, genial smile and an air of helpfulness. His toga was of better cloth than the emperor's, and his tunic's broad senatorial stripe proclaimed a rank held by his ancestors back to somewhere just short of Romulus. Titus's father, Vespasian, had been the first emperor to come from strictly equestrian stock.

"I'm pleased to see you looking so well, sir," Vettius said. "One hopes that this year will prove less wearing than the last." Titus's accession less than two years earlier had been marked almost immediately by the explosion of Mount Vesuvius above the Bay of Neapolis, followed by an outbreak of plague in the City, and then a fire that had done great damage. Titus had personally supervised the aid and cleaning up after all three, but he found he didn't care for Vettius implying that he wasn't up to it.

"Thank you," he said dryly, "I manage to get by. Now that your concern for me is assuaged, I can tell you that it's your knowledge of shipping that prompts me to send for you." He issued no invitation to sit, and no one sat in the emperor's presence without one. He hoped Vettius was uncomfortable. The floor was marble, which grows hard very quickly, and Vettius had a bad knee.

"Some difficulty with the grain fleet?" Vettius looked concerned. "If there is any way I can help—" Rome baked her bread from grain grown elsewhere, and a full third of it, 150,000 tons a year, came from Egypt. If the grain fleet didn't sail on time, the City went hungry, and the prefect of Supply had been known barely to miss lynching.

"Thank you, no," Titus said. "The fleet made good time last year, a trip and a half each." The grain fleet shuttled continuously along the Rome-to-Alexandria run. A full round trip a year was essential. Another one-way run gave a breathing space. "We should have no problems with the grain supply, this year at least." *As you should know. I would as soon send a rabbit to weed my garden.* He looked Vettius in the eye. The senator's eyes were gray, an odd, pale color like his hair. "I'm more concerned about civilian shipping around the German coast," Titus said.

Vettius looked perplexed. "Has my office fouled up somewhere? I thought we were right on top of things. Most of our companies are doing well. There's a very good trade with the German provinces."

"Not so good as our trade with the German pirates," Titus said. He thought that Vettius looked startled, but then his face smoothed out like a wax letter scraped over. It was as pleasant and bland as ever.

"Piracy does seem to be getting worse, sir, and I'll admit our office has had complaints, but I'm afraid I don't follow you." Great respect and a hint of regretful condescension— centuries of good breeding deferring to rank.

"Let me be blunt, Vettius," Titus said. "Someone has been feeding the German pirates our shipping schedules right down to the cargo lists, and someone has been making a fortune off the death and losses of his fellow citizens, and it has been put to me that that someone is you."

Vettius let a second or two pass. "That is both scandalous and outrageous, sir."

"You deny it?" Titus's expression was not particularly pleasant.

"Of course I deny it! Who made these charges? And where's his proof?"

"At the moment the proof is highly circumstantial but close

to conclusive to my mind. Admit it and make reparations now, and you will find me considerably more reasonable than you will if I am forced to spend time digging up witnesses."

"There is nothing to admit!" Vettius's pale skin had an angry flush, and his genial mood was gone. "I am shocked and insulted that it would even be suggested! May I ask your leave to go?"

"You may not." Titus folded his arms on his desk. "You may thank the gods that I am not some of my predecessors. Until I get proof, your hide is safe. When I *do* get it, I would suggest you open a vein and spare me the trouble."

"I assure you—"

"You do not! But you can take a piece of advice in the meantime: Curb your ambition, Vettius. Better men than you have gone under from an excess of that. Also, there will be some shipping information put through your office from mine. An honest man will see no reason to question it, so you had better not. If you aren't selling knowledge to the pirates, then someone with access to your office *is*. And this is one piece of information that I *want* to reach the pirates. Do I make myself clear?"

"I believe so, sir," Vettius said stiffly.

He'll pass it on to them, Titus thought with satisfaction. Vettius would sell out the last of his kin to save his own silky hide. He would have no hesitation about selling out the pirates. He would mourn the loss of revenue, but he wouldn't risk stopping that one schedule out of all the others or stopping any of them so hard on the heels of an accusation. *And now we'll have to pull the entire Rhenus Fleet down to the coast for the rest of the spring*, Titus thought disgustedly, *or we'll be sacrificing honest men's ships for bait*. And that would leave all the lower river frontier badly guarded. He felt like a man madly shifting pieces on a game board.

Marius Vettius stalked through the emperor's outer chambers, with clerks quailing before him. No one was particularly fond of Vettius, but there were plenty who were afraid of him. As he passed through the antechamber where those who hoped to find an audience with the emperor were herded by the palace stewards, Domitian rose lazily from a bench along the wall.

"You look like you saw a Gorgon." The emperor's brother shook out the purple-bordered folds of his consul's toga. "Talking with my brother can be very wearing. I always find it so. Come and have a drink." He thought that Vettius would probably have preferred a jump in the Tiber, but if he knew what was good for him, he'd come along.

"Thank you." Vettius's finely curved mouth compressed a little, and his cold eyes took careful stock of the others in the antechamber. "I am afraid that our emperor has misunderstood a small problem in the Shipping Offices. Perhaps you would be able to reassure him." He smiled and waited while a steward bustled past. "I have always thought that perhaps you understood these things better than your brother."

It was a pity that the Fates who had allowed Titus to be born first hadn't felt the same way, Domitian thought, grinding his teeth. Titus's parting words had not been calculated to improve Domitian's temper, and it had reached boiling point when he had returned and found that the emperor had given orders that he was not to be readmitted to his presence that morning. Domitian, the emperor's brother and heir and co-consul, parked on a bench in the public antechamber, next to a fat old gentleman from Campania and a freedwoman with a petition in her hand! He had kept his temper outwardly while he sat fuming in the antechamber with the rest who came clamoring every morning for his brother's attention, but he was still furious. Domitian swept through the crowd and into the outer hall that opened onto the broad marble steps of the palace, pulling his toga to one side as he passed three Praetorian Guardsmen in red and yellow plumes, just come off duty and lounging by the doors.

"I made my opinions known to my brother," he said between his teeth as they started down the steps. He shot a glance at Vettius. "It would help if you were innocent."

"My dear consul," Vettius said smoothly, "I can quite assure you of my innocence."

"I doubt it," Domitian said, "but I don't really care. If you want to rob my brother blind, it makes no difference to me."

"Shortsighted of you," Vettius said with a smile. "You will inherit one day, you know."

"One day is too damned many days away!" Domitian snapped. "I'm tired of being treated like a lackey!"

"It's a shame that the emperor hasn't seen fit to grant you responsibilities in keeping with your abilities," Vettius said. "I expect he is afraid of being outshone. Still, I wish you would assure him of my good wishes. This accusation has made me most uncomfortable."

"You seem excessively interested in my brother's patronage," Domitian snapped. "You won't find much luck there, Vettius, not with Flavius Julianus sticking his nose into your doings."

"Julianus?" Vettius looked thoughtful. So he was the source of the emperor's suspicions. "It's a pity that young man has got so far into the emperor's trust. Do you think it's possible that Titus relies on him too much? To the exclusion of other . . . uh, wiser counselors?" There was a wine stall ahead on their left, tucked under the overhang of one of the second-floor merchants' offices that formed the upper level of the commercial district.

"Let's go have that drink now." Vettius laid a hand on Domitian's arm and steered him toward the wine stall. He would have preferred to drink in the privacy of his well-appointed house on the slopes of the Quirinal, with its serene view of water and gardens, but Domitian had a taste for public dives. "Here, let me pay." Vettius reached into the purse tucked into the front folds of his toga.

"Really, do you think it's wise of the emperor to rely so heavily on someone so inexperienced in government?" Vettius went on as they seated themselves at a table hastily cleared by the wineshop keeper. "After all, young Julianus—"

"Flavius Julianus is probably the most honest-minded aide my brother has," Domitian said. "The more fool he. He has the antiquated notion that the emperor is barely one step short of sacred. He swallows Titus's faults without batting an eye and guards him like a watchdog." He swallowed his wine and gave Vettius a sour look. "I wouldn't look for any more favors from my brother for a while. Never, maybe, if he finds out Julianus is right about you."

Vettius spread his hands in a gesture of dismay. Pale, well-cared-for hands with smooth nails, slightly too broad in the palm. "This is very upsetting. I don't know how to defend myself." Defense was essential. When Domitian stopped being mad at his brother, he would alter his views somewhat on the subject of treason. "Most distressing for me, as I'm sure you realize. I hope you'll see fit to plead my cause for me. I would, of course, be happy to pay any expenses incurred." There would be no expenses involved in Domitian arguing his case with Titus, but it was better not to offer the emperor's brother a bribe outright. It might be necessary to step up his plans a little, Vettius thought. Titus might not have the evidence he needed in the matter of the pirates, but he would watch Vettius uncomfortably closely after this and might possibly forbid Domitian to associate with him. If Domitian could be persuaded to remove his brother from this world now, it would make things immeasurably easier. "If anyone can reason with the emperor, Consul, I'm sure it's you."

Domitian scowled across the table. "It would be good if you remembered that, Vettius. A man in your position ought to keep in mind where his loyalties lie." He snapped his fingers and the wineshop keeper scurried over to pour his cup full. Vettius paid.

"Vettius? Yes, I remember him. He was a *sleek* man, like a . . . a scrubbed horse. He had a . . . fine hide." Berenice waved her hand in a gesture of looking for the right words.

"My brother-in-law called him a snake," Ygerna said. "He was mad," she added thoughtfully. "He said that Correus has risked his neck to catch this man, and now nothing will come of it." Her dark brows drew together. "It is bad enough for Correus to risk his neck, but a soldier is expected to do that. I do not care for it when nothing comes of it, though."

"My dear, if you are going to be involved in the doings of the palace, even peripherally," Berenice said, "you will find that most often nothing comes of the things that ought to. I've lived in five palaces, and that's been true of all of them. Sometimes the more important the ruler, the less he can do."

They were sitting curled on cushions in a small, pleasant room that overlooked a tiny garden like a jewel box. Spring flowers sat in neat rows along colored marble walks, and there were fruit trees growing out of small squares of emerald grass between. A fountain at one end was alive with a multitude of bright birds, and a white-domed aviary with a screen of gilded wire held more exotic specimens. The doors into the garden were open, and a spring breeze blew its perfume up the polished steps into the room.

A slave girl in an Eastern-looking gown of coral-colored cloth hovered nearby, and there was an ebony table laid with poppy-seed cakes and dishes of olives and fish and preserved fruit. Shallow two-handled bronze cups with silver linings held a rich dark wine that Ygerna drank sparingly. Too much of any drink made her head swim, but it was pleasant to sit and feel the breeze and talk with Berenice, another foreigner in the land, who didn't disapprove or poke at her or ask if she was feeling well. Wrapped in a shawl beside her, the baby lay like a caterpillar in a cocoon.

It was a girl, and since Correus hadn't been there to object, Ygerna had named her Eilenn, which was a British name and made Antonia raise her eyebrows. Then they had officially named her Flavia Agricolina, like Ygerna, and all raised their eyebrows again when Ygerna, clutching the baby to her and glowering, had made them send the wet nurse away.

It was considered an unusual virtue in a Roman lady to nurse her own children, and while Antonia had approved in principle, she had been dubious.

"My dear, you are very small, and you've had a hard time. There may not be enough milk. And don't you think you should rest?"

"*My* mother was small. She fed me." Ygerna put the baby to her breast, and old Thais, who had somehow designated herself in charge, said tartly that that was quite right. To Ygerna, it was one more perplexity of the Romans that they should think that having gone through so much to get this baby, she would now wish to give it to another woman.

Ygerna simply didn't want to think of the baby's birth. If she did, she might not be willing to do it again. The child had finally come, after two days' labor, on the night of the winter solstice, while the rest of the household was celebrating the Saturnalia. Shrieks of laughter and the high voices of Felix and Julia's and Aemelia's children came through the open windows with the moonlight.

The next morning Felix came and peered expectantly into the basket at his half sister. He would have preferred a boy, but you could play with a girl if you had to.

"Would she like my old top? Grandfather gave me a new one." Felix was prepared to do the noble thing.

"It's going to be a while before she's big enough for tops," Ygerna said. Children always seemed to think that babies were born two years old.

Felix studied the baby, red in the face, sleeping, and no bigger than Ygerna's cat. "Then what good is she?" he asked finally.

"Shame on you!" Thais said, but Ygerna was laughing.

"At the moment, not much, but she'll improve, I promise you."

Thais bustled Felix off to his own nurse and his lesson, and Ygerna sank back into the pillows, grateful for the old woman's brisk efficiency. Baucis the cat yawned and stretched on the coverlet beside her. Baucis liked nothing better than to have someone take to bed in the daytime.

Eilenn still wasn't up to Felix's standards, but she was big enough to be taken out, and Ygerna gratefully resumed her visits to Berenice, sub rosa as before. Antonia would have been shocked, Appius would have disapproved, and Flavius would have forbidden it. But Berenice fascinated her, with her worldly air and her tales of Judaea and Jerusalem and the exotic Eastern kingdoms where she had reigned. Ygerna still hadn't asked her why she never went back. She thought she knew.

Julius drove her on these excursions when he had finished with the ponies, and Cottia accompanied her. Ygerna had told them both that if they ever told anyone her trips were not to shop in the Veii market, she would make a magic they wouldn't like. Cottia believed her, and Julius was happiest when outsmarting someone, which was just as well.

She thought that maybe Berenice, who had lived among the Romans for so long, could explain things. "I thought I understood them," Ygerna said, "but then Flavius tells me what is happening, and I remember that when I was thirteen I thought that maybe Romans weren't men at all. I do not understand the way they rule themselves. The emperor has more power than a king, but if he called himself a king, they would depose him, and he always pretends that he is only doing what the Senate tells him to. Now he has a man who is committing treason, and he won't have him killed because he promised the Senate he wouldn't without evidence. What is evidence that he hasn't got now? Why does he care what the Senate says when he is emperor?"

"The Senate has more power than you would think," Berenice said, "but it's a quiet sort of power. An emperor who is wise will listen."

"Also," Ygerna said, "they will sit about like old harpers telling stories of the old days and complain that Rome should be a republic again, but they will let any man with enough soldiers take the throne and think themselves lucky if he is not as evil or as crazy as the last one."

"Soldiers are very hard to argue with," Berenice said. "That is the problem. Rome needs soldiers to contain all her provinces, but that gives too much power to the generals, so the generals make themselves emperors. Without the army, Rome could be a republic again."

"Without the army, Rome could be gone," Ygerna said. She thought of Governor Frontinus stitching a line of forts and roads back and forth across her homeland in the Silure hills until there was no corner to hide in that wasn't under Rome's eye. "Correus says that the army *is* the empire."

"That is the trouble. The only answer is to find an emperor who is strong enough to hold the other generals back. Vespasian was a man like that. Your father-in-law might have been too, if he had wanted to fight Vespasian for it. Titus is one." Berenice sighed. "But it is the same with any power. It comes to rule you in the end, if you are going to hold onto it."

"And the emperor's brother?"

Berenice's dark eyes were serious under the emerald paint on the lids. "Domitian wants the power, but he isn't willing to sacrifice his pleasures for it. It makes him vulnerable. He lets jackals trot after him if it will pay him to. Marius Vettius is one of the ones who are yipping at his heels at the moment. Don't fall foul of him. Or of Domitian."

Ygerna shrugged. "No one is interested in me."

Berenice shook her head, and the pearl drops that hung from the fillet in her hair danced gently. "In the palace everyone is interested in everyone. And Vettius is dangerous." She sighed again. "I agree, the emperor should kill him and have done with it, but he won't. And you are married to a man who is brother to the man who is making himself a nuisance to Vettius. If I were any one of your family, I would go carefully."

I will tell that to Correus, Ygerna thought solemnly. *If he isn't killed trying to trap this Vettius's tame pirates.*

"It seems you've a mommy who loves you, after all." Theophanes was smiling, a dark, unamused smile behind his badger-striped beard. His smile stretched the sickle-shaped scar on his cheek into a longer curve.

"You mean they paid?" Correus sat up, not even bothering to take offense at the pirate's tone, and shook Eumenes awake.

Eumenes came up with a start and a hand where his knife would be if the pirates had let him have one.

"Home! Eumenes, we're going home!"

Home as far as fleet headquarters on the Rhenus, Eumenes thought. *And then out on a ship again.* He fought down a cold flash of panic. He hadn't realized how deep was the fear that had come with him out of the emperor's lake until he was actually on board the merchantman with Correus and it was too late to run. *I could run now*, he thought. *I doubt he'd chase me.* He thought of Correus shaking the water out of him and changed his mind. Eumenes was a man who held his gratitude longer than most.

"We'll take you inland past the fens," Theophanes said, "with your trunks and enough coin to get you home. You've been a damned nuisance and ill luck, I'm thinking." He went off moodily.

"We can hope so," Eumenes muttered.

The pirates had found their pickings thin of late. The information continued to come, but the whole Rhenus coast was alive with Roman warships. The Romans had pulled them out of the Rhenus patrol fleet, and they would have to go back eventually or leave too much barbarian coast unguarded at their backs, but in the meantime Theophanes was in a foul temper. They couldn't catch him, and they couldn't find his camp, but they could convoy his prizes safely out of reach for as long as they could spare the ships. It was a waste of his time and theirs in the long run, from his viewpoint.

With the coast awash in Roman warships, Theophanes put Correus and Eumenes on ponies at night and sent old Commius and two others to guide them as far as the first road past the fens. They half expected blindfolds, but Commius just laughed and said that anyone who wanted to try coming back through the fens could come with his blessing. "There's more bodies than gray Wulf's in that bog."

The ground heaved underfoot with thick, sucking noises and the faint phosphorescence of decay danced just above the surface. Commius followed no visible trail as far as Correus could tell. Correus prayed fervently that Theophanes hadn't found the reason to blame them for the warships that were hugging the coast. It would be easy enough to slide him and Eumenes under that shaking, gray-green slime and let them lie forever.

At dawn they halted where Commius's trail came out of the bog onto a dirt road running south across a flat meadow. The grass was wet and still calf-high in mist. Commius repossessed the ponies, left their trunks by the side of the track, and waved a cheerful good-bye.

"Damn you!" Correus shouted. "How am I going to carry these?"

"Oh, I shouldn't think they'll be stolen before you can fetch a wagon for them," Commius said.

"I'll fetch an army and crucify every one of you!" Correus said furiously.

"Just like Julius Caesar." Commius laughed uproariously. "I'm thinking Julius Caesar must have known which end of a spear was up. Better go back to Rome, lad. It's too rough in the wilds of Germany for you!" He departed chortling.

"What are we going to do with these?" Eumenes asked.

"Leave them. I don't want them bad enough to haul two trunks down this goat track. Let the wood elves have them." Wood elves were what took spare pilum points and blankets from the quartermaster's stores in frontier posts.

Eumenes shrugged. It was a waste, but he wasn't a donkey. They set out in the growing light along the track. It was rutted with cart wheels, and only a few green sprigs of battered grass grew up between them, so it would come to a village eventually, he supposed.

The Lower Rhenus Fleet had gone back where it belonged, to its home base at Colonia Agrippinensis, and only the usual patrols plied the foggy coastal waters. And the information introduced into the Shipping Offices in Rome at the start of spring followed its accustomed path.

"Are they going to swallow that?" Eumenes was dressed in a good tunic and silver armband as befitted the servant of the fleet prefect. He looked dubiously at the paint-and-canvas superstructure that the seamen swarming all over the trireme *Justitia* were lashing to her sides. "It looks like a stage set to me. I keep expecting some fool in a blond wig to come on as Helen."

"It's only to alter the outline," Correus said in the voice of a man who has explained this to six ship's captains already. "When they get close enough to see clearly, we'll have dumped it, anyway. Watch those lashings," he added to *Justitia*'s captain. "I don't want to lose time hacking about trying to get rid of the thing so we can maneuver. They've got to come apart fast."

Beside *Justitia*, three more triremes and two big quinquiremes from the British Channel Fleet at Gesoriacum were being similarly outfitted. In the lower docks, a covey of lightweight Rhenus patrol craft were getting a new paint job in sandy tan, and the smell of the hot wax that was the medium for the pigment mingled with the usual shipyard smells of pitch and new rope and the crisp, cold scent of the Rhenus itself. Colonia Agrippinensis was governmental headquarters for the province of Lower Germany, and although the legions that had once garrisoned it had been moved to other forts along the Rhenus, the fleet had kept its headquarters there, at the naval station to the south of the city. The fleet prefect was accorded luxurious quarters in the governor's palace in Colonia. So far Correus had used them only for a few hours of exhausted sleep, which, by the time he and Eumenes had ridden into Colonia with a cavalry escort from Aduatuca, he could probably have achieved on a bed of rocks. Theophanes's men had left them fifteen miles from the nearest village, and close to a hundred from any town large enough to have a military post. His feet and

legs ached, and the cavalry nag he had ridden from Aduatuca
was a far cry from his own horse, Antaeus, who had spent the
winter fattening his gold hide in the governmental stables in
Colonia. And that, Correus thought, was another point added
to his score with Theophanes—that and the fact that no man
likes to play the fool for another. It would be a pleasure now
to revise Theophanes's opinion of him.

The only bright point had been a letter from Ygerna, waiting
for him at headquarters in Colonia, to tell him that he had a
daughter, and when could they join him, please? It would be
nice to have Ygerna to curl up with again after a winter of
Eumenes's company and a six-foot cubicle laid with straw.
Eumenes apparently felt the same. He disappeared every evening into a whorehouse on the edge of the glassworkers' quarter
in Colonia, and unless Correus sent another slave to find him,
he stayed there until morning. He was saving up, he told Correus, in case Theophanes didn't buy it and he ended up in a
bog with gray Wulf.

Now he stood with Correus on the dock, watching the wicker
frames being lashed to a quinquireme's hull and the canvas
stretched over them. A trio of sailors with paint buckets were
adding artistic touches to the canvas, and Correus shouted at
them to just paint the damned thing—if the pirates got close
enough to see painted boards and oarlocks, the artists had better
start saying prayers. Eumenes had a light tick beside his left
eye that flickered while he watched them. *He's afraid of water*,
Correus thought, and wondered what other nightmares Eumenes had carried away with him from that lake. He had considered leaving Eumenes behind in Colonia when that had
dawned on him, but Eumenes just gritted his teeth and shook
his head.

"Likely they'll send you back to the army sooner or later,"
he said. "I'll stick it till then."

Six silhouettes showed over the horizon, fat and low in the
water, with a full cargo, sails spread, working past the Rhenus
delta to Gesoriacum on the Gaulish coast.

There was a stiff breeze, but it was in the wrong quarter
and the merchantmen tacked laboriously. Theophanes grinned
behind his beard. "Slaves, and the winter tribute from the

Rhenus tribes. That should make up for our losses and give Rome a sting in the tail to boot. Our luck's on the turn." Luck mattered. Too long a stretch with no booty, and the pirates would start thinking of another leader.

Cerdic nodded. He had no particular liking for Rome, and there was a slave brand on his arm to prove it. It would be pleasant to spend Caesar's tribute for him.

"Fast stroke!" Theophanes shouted, and the oars that had been moving gently to hold the liburnian in her hiding place picked up the stroke and cut the water with a splash. She shot out from behind an outer bank of dunes, and Cerdic hoisted a signal flag above the bow. Other ships glided into place behind her. Across the water, the merchant convoy saw them and scrambled frantically to come about. Theophanes chuckled. There was no sign of the watchdog galleys that had plagued him the past months. And even if they'd had the wind, a loaded merchantman couldn't outrun his faster craft. It looked like they were going to try, though. He nodded to Cerdic, and the hammer stroke picked up to top speed.

"Here they come," *Justitia*'s captain said softly.

"Let them come a little closer," Correus said.

"We'll need time to get clear of the mess and come about again," the captain said. A dozen sailors were crouched like monkeys along the false sides, their knives out.

"You're the judge of that," Correus said, "but leave it as long as you can."

"Right." They had made an attempt to run, from the look of it, but the pirate ships were closing fast. "Now! Drop them!"

The wicker and canvas slid into the water with a splash, and sailors in the stern took poles and poked the discarded superstructures clear of the oarlocks.

"Out oars!"

The trireme swung around and pointed her lead-sheathed ram at Theophanes's ships.

"Typhon take his soul!" Theophanes saw the wicker frames drop and knew that his informer in Rome had sold him to save his own skin. The Roman decks bristled with men, and he could see the sunlight flash off armor and metal shield bosses.

"Do we fight?" Cerdic stood at his shoulder again, his legs

braced against the roll of the ship, watching the galleys boiling across the open water toward them, red oars swinging.

Theophanes thought. They ran from galleys as a matter of course. It wasn't worth a fight to take a warship, and they might not win. But he had gotten too close to these.

Cerdic shouted an order, and the oars backed in the water as the overseer on the rowing decks ordered the liburnian brought around before they were rammed. A catapult bolt whistled overhead, and the helmsman swore and flattened himself on the deck, the tiller swinging wildly. Theophanes grabbed it and kicked the helmsman up. The helmsman, praying and gibbering, flattened himself again as another bolt went by his ear, and Theophanes shouted for Cerdic. Lifting the helmsman by the arms, they flung him into the ship's wake, and Cerdic leaned hard on the tiller against the weight of the heavy steering oar. Theophanes, narrowing his eyes, watched the hunting pack of galleys bear down on them. His liburnian, Ennius's, and a few other of the fastest of his ships could outrun the Romans, he thought. With luck they could dive into the maze of the Rhenus delta and be gone before the Romans had fought their way through the slower pirate craft. Or they could engage with the Romans—but the Romans had six ships full of soldiers.

"Do we fight?" Cerdic asked again.

Theophanes shook his head. "No. We run."

"They're turning, sir!"

"So I see, Captain." Correus watched the blue-painted fleet swinging hard around. Two of them tangled their oars, crashed together, and splintered them.

"Nice of them to wait for us," *Justitia*'s catapult man said, grinning, and put a bolt through the sail as they tried to raise it. One of the triremes turned purposefully in the pirates' direction, her ram a dark shadow under the water.

The Romans were putting their catapult bolts low into the hull when they could, or sending shot and chain through the oars. One craft had been boarded now, and another holed with a ram and sunk, but the faster vessels were beginning to pull away, their blue shapes fading into blue water as they gained distance. Theophanes must have known that the loss of his slower craft was inevitable, but he would waste little time mourning them. His ship and Ennius's and a handful of others were running hard for the labyrinth of dunes and inlets that was their safeguard. They wouldn't see the little fleet of gray-brown scout ships lurking where Correus had planted them until it was too late.

Justitia closed on a blue-hulled ship that was maneuvering desperately to dodge the Roman's ram. *Justitia*'s captain snapped an order, and the trireme nosed around by one degree. Ramming was a fine art, and the window in which a successful ramming run could be made was narrow. A few seconds' delay could cost the attacking vessel her target; a few seconds too soon and the attacker could find herself rammed instead.

"Hah!" *Justitia* punched through the pirate's hull with a crash and a grinding sound as the two ships bumped together. *Justitia*'s captain slapped his helmsman on the back. The pirate began to settle almost immediately, and the sounds of terror rose from the oar deck. Correus had ordered as many of the rowers saved as possible, but most of them were chained. He was just as glad Eumenes was with the scout ships. *Justitia* backed off and looked for another target.

The water was strewn with wreckage—floating spars and listing ships. One was in flames. One of the quinquiremes had closed with the last of the pirate craft, and, as Correus watched, the quinquireme's boarding plank smashed down on the pirate's deck and the marines began to push their way along it. Amid the floating debris, a piece of wickerwork bobbed by, trailing its canvas covering behind it.

Justitia's captain looked at it and snorted. "Thought it a fair foolish idea, sir, I'm bound to say I did. But damned if it didn't work. Not but what a few got past us."

"Put her about, Captain," Correus said quietly. "We're going hunting."

"Double speed," Theophanes said. "But watch the channel. It's been shifting, and if we run aground here, they'll burn us where we sit."

The liburnian shot across a stretch of open water and into another of the myriad channels that ran among the sandbanks and sour, salt-grass islands. There were four others in her wake.

Farther behind, still unnoticed, five gray-brown shapes ran after them.

They went like rabbits into the warren that had hidden them so many times before, and Theophanes, still cursing his betrayer, got out and heaved with the rest to draw the liburnian up on the sandbar below the village and pull the screens of brushwood out to mask it. The morning mist had burned off, but it was still a gray day, the dull, flat color of a sword blade. The hunting scout ships were nearly on them before Cerdic suddenly froze and caught him by the shoulder. As he pointed, they saw, coming in behind the smaller craft, the lean, dangerous shape of a trireme.

Theophanes shouted, and they ran for the village gate, with the hope of holding it against the armored men who were pouring from the scout ships and the trireme's deck before their ships were even beached. He jammed himself into the gateway with Cerdic to one side of him. Behind him, he could hear women screaming as the men who had poured through the gate before him shouted out a warning. But there was nowhere to run, and the soldiers came up out of the trireme's hold like the warriors sown from dragon's teeth. At their head was a tall figure in a helmet and lorica, with a short sword in his left hand. On his right arm was a rectangular shield with an officer's insigne on the boss, and there was something familiar in his face.

Theophanes braced himself in the gateway, and it came to him suddenly with a shock where he had seen that face before. The ineffectual look was gone, but it was still the same face. Now the features were sharper, clearer somehow, and the brown eyes glowed with a dangerous light.

"I told you I'd be back," Correus said.

Theophanes swung his sword. Correus caught the blow on his shield and stabbed with his own sword, not Theophanes, but the man to his right. The man went down, and Theophanes tripped over his outflung arm. Cerdic beat at the Roman as Theophanes righted himself, but then the sharp-pointed head of another Roman's long pilum caught Cerdic in the throat. Theophanes swung again, high at the base of the throat, but Correus brought his shield up. "Who are you?" Theophanes shouted, but Correus hooked his shield in behind Theophane's and pulled, and his short sword slipped into the gap. If there was an answer, Theophanes never heard it.

In no more than minutes the village was burning.

Correus stood looking at the dark-haired, dark-bearded body in the gateway. The gold fillet had fallen from his hair and was lying in the dirt under one shoulder. There was blood, no longer flowing, on the bright cloth of his tunic.

Eumenes stood beside him, cleaning a sword. Eumenes was the fleet prefect's slave. He was not supposed to fight, but no one had tried to stop him.

A marine commander came up and saluted. "Pretty thin pickings, sir. It looks as if they'd already shipped out anything worth shipping. We've kept them pinned down lately. I doubt we'll find much more. There was some silver."

"What about prisoners?" Correus asked.

"We found a few slaves hiding in with the cattle," the marine said. "And the poor bastards from the oar benches—they're the lucky ones to end on dry land. Not much else. Some kids and a few women. What about them?"

"Slave market," Correus said shortly. He looked at where *Justitia*'s marines were putting up a row of crosses with the timber of a longhouse. Technically the women were accomplices, but he was damned if he would.

"No other prisoners?" Correus asked.

"None that we can find," the marine said cheerfully. "And we turned it out pretty thorough. Were you looking for someone?"

"There was a man here when I was," Correus said. "They were keeping him for ransom. I wanted to find him."

"Oh." The marine thought about it. "Likely they set him loose when the ransom came in."

"Yes, no doubt." *When the ransom came in from where?* Correus wondered. He could inquire at Augusta Treverorum, but somehow he didn't think he would get an answer he'd like.

VIII

The Mercy of Caesar

MARIUS VETTIUS SAT AT HIS DESK IN THE PRIVATE OFFICE HE kept in his town house on the slope of the Quirinal and looked out the window at his gardens. He found the view soothing, and it was necessary to be tranquil when one dealt with important matters. That was the trouble with Domitian, Vettius thought. He let himself be distracted with trivia, and then he reacted with his gut instead of his head. It made him very easy to control. Already Domitian was considering how to murder his brother. You could see it in his eyes. But Titus wouldn't see it; Titus had his heart set on a dynasty, and that meant Domitian for an heir. Vettius chuckled. If Domitian stayed in this mood, Titus would be in need of an heir sooner than he had bargained for.

Vettius spread the records pertaining to his private business dealings out on the desk before him and looked at them thoughtfully. It was necessary to raise money if his plans were to continue on course. The emperor's false bills of lading had gone through the Shipping Offices without a hitch, along with the honest ones, and the Rhenus pirates were undoubtedly dead now. That was vexatious; they had been very profitable. But there were other ways. Vettius had begun with nothing more than a very old name and no money, and he had risen so far as he had, and intended to go farther still, by having a finger in a great many pies.

Vettius clapped his hands, and a slave scurried in with a tray of wine and figs. Vettius ate a fig and examined his accounts. There were the public housing projects he had begun after the fire in the City, in partnership with old Aemilius and a few others. They were largely honest, although Vettius would turn a profit on them because he owned a large number of the building firms involved. Then there were notes—debts bought up from moneylenders, some at a discount for future profit, some for the leverage they would give him against the debtor. They were bought through middlemen mainly—too many people were wary of Vettius. As he scanned them now, a familiar name leaped out again. Vettius pulled the piece of papyrus gently from the rest. He took a fig and the note that Aemelius had signed and went to the window to look at it in the light. The fool had borrowed from a former slave—how useful of him. There was a bench under the window. Vettius curled himself up on it, ate his fig, and watched the light play across his garden. It made a pleasant pattern in the cypress trees, and the sunset gilded the reflecting pool. Old Aemelius had money, and better yet, Flavius Julianus was married to his daughter. Marius Vettius smiled. The house of Julianus owed him a debt in the matter of the Rhenus pirates. How extremely pleasant to combine revenge with profit.

"Burned!" Marbod, chieftain of the Chatti, stamped through the door of his longhouse. He was red-haired, with a drooping mustache over a long, thin mouth like a salmon's, and a nose that someone had once broken. He was in a temper.

"Burned what?" Ranvig looked up from a comfortable spot by the hearth fire. Marbod's men shouldered in behind him, and Ranvig made room.

"Theophanes's camp." Marbod put his hands to the fire. He was wearing a shaggy cloak of sheep's wool. It had been raining, and he stood steaming by the fire and smelling of wet sheep. "The Romans have burned it."

"How can you be knowing it was Romans?" Ranvig said. "When I came from there, the Romans were hunting like dogs with no trail, barking everywhere but in the right place. And there are more than Romans who would like to burn Theophanes out."

"There was nothing left but wet ashes and crosses," Marbod said. "I don't know how they found them, but that is Romans. They cut their throats and hung them on crosses."

"The mercy of Caesar," Ranvig murmured. He stared into the fire and made a swift prayer that Wuotan might look kindly on them. He doubted Marbod had bothered. "I think I know how they found them."

"I don't care if their Eagle gods picked them up and put

them there," Marbod said. "The village is gone, and the loot's gone. I *thought* Theophanes was cheating us." He seemed to feel that he had been proved right. "When Beorn didn't get a signal on time, we went to look. They were expecting a fat prize, and now that's gone, too."

"I don't think you would have wanted it," Ranvig said thoughtfully.

Marbod growled and held out his hand, and a thrall scuttled forward with a beer horn. Marbod moodily took a drink. Someone had done him out of a profitable business. Smuggling Theophanes's loot into the Free Lands had brought a pleasant flow of coins and good wool and gold drinking cups into the chieftain's hall, with less trouble than raiding for it.

Ranvig's oddly set eyes watched Marbod carefully. The Chatti chieftain had lost a good thing just when he had got used to it, and now he wanted to go and fight someone for it. He looked willing to fight Ranvig and his Semnones if nothing else presented itself.

"You said that camp was safe from anything but Donar's lightning," Marbod said. Ranvig had been the Germans' main negotiator with Theophanes, the one who breathed down the pirate captain's neck and kept him honest—for a pirate.

"Nothing is safe forever," Ranvig said. "My tribe has learned that well enough."

Marbod snorted. "Your Semnone lands are far enough from Rome. *We* have the Romans' Eagle forts across the river, with nothing but Usipi villages in between."

"I was of the Kindred of the Nicretes before I was chieftain of the Semnones," Ranvig said quietly, "and the Nicretes are a tribe that is gone with the dead leaves. The Black Forest is full of Roman forts now, and what is left of the Nicretes is joined with what is left of the Semnones. And do not you ever tell me, Marbod, that we are far enough from Rome."

Marbod looked embarrassed. The Semnones had made a great war and had almost beaten Rome, and it was a shame to the Chatti that they had not warred, too. Battle was a warrior's purpose, and if he was outnumbered, then he died and went to Valhalla, and that was better than *not* fighting and staying safe. But he couldn't fight Ranvig now, not after that reminder.

Ranvig watched the thoughts chase themselves around inside

Marbod's head. Marbod's men were glaring at him for the veiled insult and the reminder that the Semnones had fought when the Chatti had not, and Ranvig's Semnone men were glaring back at them. They were all in a bad mood from losing Theophanes's payments and seeing those crosses. Ranvig pushed the crosses out of his own mind. He had thought about telling Theophanes to put the Roman in the bog and not take chances, but he hadn't, and wishing bought no horses. His men and Marbod's would be brawling with each other if he wasn't careful; then there would be blood feuds and blood money to be paid, and his whole effort would be sidetracked into sifting out quarrels. Better that Marbod quarrel with the Romans.

"It's a long road from Rhenus Mouth to here," Ranvig said soothingly. "You will be tired, you and your men."

"A long road for a man who comes home empty-handed," Marbod snapped.

"Our packs are no fuller than yours," one of Ranvig's men said. He had a scarred ear and a reckless flyaway smile that was turned down now in a scowl. The Chatti were the first link in the trade route. From Chatti lands, a portion of the goods went east with the Semnone men to the tribes of the Albis Valley, and then east again with Dacian caravans to the markets of the Pontus Euxinus. It had been very profitable for all concerned, including "the man in the office." He had been a happy accident, a source who would deal only with Theophanes, but it had been Ranvig who had given them an outlet for too identifiable goods. Now it was stopped.

"Why didn't Beorn keep a closer watch?" Arni, the man with the scarred ear, asked.

"Beorn kept as close as he could," Marbod snapped.

"Be quiet, Arni!" Ranvig's man Steinvar said; he was a lean, scarred man with gray in his pale hair. Steinvar's daughter was Arni's wife, but Arni was too young, he thought, to be allowed a loose tongue in Marbod's hall. Arni would always be too young; he provoked a quarrel as easily as breathing.

"When the signal didn't come, Beorn sent to me," Marbod said with sarcastic patience, "because I am the chieftain, and Beorn is not. And I thought there might be trouble, so I bade him wait until we came. And I have grown to be as old as I am, and I am still chieftain, through not trusting puppies!" He turned his back on Arni and held out his beer horn to the thrall again. When it was full, he drank it and wiped his mouth on his hand. "Put a leash on that one, Ranvig."

"I will take him home instead." Ranvig laughed and shot Arni a look that said he had best not argue. "I've been gone all winter, and this matter of the Romans will have to wait until I've called council." A chieftain was judge of the tribal courts. "There are always council cases in spring. Men in winter have nothing to do but think up grievances."

"And I will have a grievance with you, Arni, if you don't keep your tongue behind your teeth," Ranvig said when they were in the saddle again. He swung around to face Arni, but he kept his voice low. The rest of his men, less the fifty he had left in Marbod's hold, rode behind them, while Steinvar, the lean, scarred council lord, trotted beside Arni on a roan horse.

"It was not work for men anyway, this trading," Arni said sulkily.

"You have rebuilt your hold with your share," Steinvar said.

"It isn't the trading; it's using bandits to fight the Romans. Now you want to use the Chatti to make a war for you. That is not for men."

"So I thought once," Ranvig said. "So we fought them with spears. I was younger then."

"You talk like an old woman."

"I'm young enough to fix you so not even Eir's priests can put you back together." Ranvig's crooked face was even-tempered. "Remember that."

"I am remembering that when Nyall Sigmundson came to the Nicretes and said 'Fight the Romans,' you spoke for him."

"And I fought for him," Ranvig said. "Three times. But we only won the first time, when the Romans were fighting themselves. We didn't know Rome so well then."

They came to a ford where the river ran through a meadow bright with water marigolds, and stopped to let the horses dip their muzzles in the cold water.

Arni kicked at a stone on the bank. "I am also remembering that when Nyall Sigmundson went to the Romans, I spoke for *you*. And brought every man of my hold to the voting."

"To be chieftain, yes," Ranvig said. "Because the northern

tribes were raiding us, and because I was the only one not dead in the battle who the Companions could agree on. The few that were left of them." Ranvig's face twisted for a moment. So many dead. "And so you and Steinvar rammed it down the Council's throat." He looked at them both. "If you've a mind to undo it, you may try."

"No." Steinvar's voice was flat, and he was fiddling with his horse's bridle, but there was a note of finality in it. Arni was only making noise. He was not the sort to undo something he had been so loud in the making of. Steinvar's hair was knotted on the side of his head, as the Semnones wore it. Arni and most of the Black Forest warriors had begun to wear theirs that way also, but Ranvig wouldn't. His pale hair hung in two braids. If they wanted him for chieftain, they would have to take him as he was. There had been some talk that the chieftainship should have gone to Steinvar, who was a birthright lord of the tribe, and not to a Black Forest man, but Steinvar didn't want it. He was too old, he said, and he didn't understand Romans. He thought Ranvig did, and he thought that was going to count—especially when it came to a fight. Ranvig would fight in the end. Rome would look too closely at the Free Lands, and then there would be no choice.

Correus lifted his head from the work on his desk in the commander's office at Colonia Naval Station and sniffed suspiciously. It was a stone building close to the docks, and the unlovely smell of bilges being cleaned came through the open window. A cloud of midges and a green grasshopper had already sailed through, and Correus got up regretfully and closed the window. It was a beautiful day for the Rhenus, warm and sunny with the gold light bathing the vineyards and the patchworked farm fields beside the river. Horses hauling their barges upriver made a gentle *clip-clop* along the towpath.

Correus was engaged in checking supply lists, an apparently unending description in his optio's finicky handwriting, of the things necessary to the proper running of Colonia Naval Station: rope, pitch, canvas, paint, wax (in bars, forty to the crate), tow for caulking, bilge pumps (portable), mousetraps, canvas needles. It was a maddening list, and it went on and on. In a month or so he could leave it to his optio, who appeared to delight in lists, judging by the number of them that crossed Correus's desk. For now it was as well to let it be known that the prefect took notice of such mattters. An army in peacetime stole from itself even more than usual.

And there *was* peace, all along the Rhenus frontier, all that season. No one in Augusta Treverorum had heard of a man who matched Ranvig's description, but the coastal shipping went unhindered now, and if anyone was cooking up a war, he was still uncommitted. The scouts reported that the Chatti were growing quarrelsome, picking disagreements at the ferries with the locals from the Roman side of the river, and pressuring the Usipi to break their treaty with Rome, but that was their nature, anyway. If it all came to anything, it wouldn't be this year. So said the scouts. Correus doubled the river patrols and sent for his wife.

Eumenes went to escort Ygerna, nurse, babies, and whatever else she saw fit to bring across the pass into Germany—including the cat. Baucis was better traveled than most of her betters and content to ride for days on a pack pony, watching the scenery go by with just her ears and eyes showing over the top of her basket.

Correus could have done without the cat, but he had their quarters in the governor's palace turned out and swept thoroughly.

Sulpicius Clarus, governor of Lower Germany, was a mild, pleasant man with the irritating habit of mislaying whatever it was that he happened to have in his hand at the moment and then sending his servants scurrying like a whirlwind through all corners of the palace to look for it. He brightened when Correus settled in, and asked hopefully if he played *latrunculi*. Correus did, and badly, which turned out to be the governor's level, too. They spent pleasant evenings together vainly attempting to improve their game, and when he heard that the prefect's wife was to join him, the governor sent his own staff to help with the cleaning and had the lady's bedroom repainted by a local artist in scenes supposedly reminiscent of her native Britain. These leaned heavily to sylvan glades and broad meandering streams, a gentler aspect than the harsh blue uplands of the Silure hills, Correus thought, but more appropriate for a bedroom.

In the meantime, Correus renewed an old acquaintance. The artist had just finished decorating a house, he said, for a lady lately come to Colonia to settle. Actually she wasn't what you'd call a lady, he added, but she must be a rich one, and her place was going to be the fanciest whorehouse in town. There followed a description that could only have matched one person, so Correus put on his parade uniform and all his medals and went to call.

Rhodope's residence occupied the same slope the governor's palace did, just west of the river wall. It was built around a courtyard with a fountain, and the two-story dining room on the east side gave onto a veranda overlooking the river. Correus gravely handed helmet and vine staff to the elderly slave who bowed him through the door.

Rhodope had adopted a few flourishes she hadn't bothered with in the days when Correus had known her. Her quarters then had been a tent of Oriental splendor, which she carried in the army's wake in a brightly painted wagon. Fancy enough for the frontier, but a pale shadow of the opulent dining chamber, awash with flowers and incense, where Rhodope's customers now reclined to make their choice of the company she offered. The floor was set with a mosaic of medallions with a Dionysian theme. In the center was the god himself, drunk and leaning on a satyr. Below him a family of satyrs displayed unusual domesticity: The mother played a double flute while the father fed grapes to his baby son. There were satyrs on donkeys, Cupid on a lion, and Pan leading a billy goat. Two parrots pulled a cart full of gardening tools, and a female leopard displayed a charming smile and a broad blue ribbon around her neck.

Correus stood in the doorway with a bemused expression, taking it all in, when Rhodope looked up from the couch where she was reaching a business agreement with a wine broker. She had a head of brilliant orange-henna'd hair, astounding against olive skin, and a red and purple gown, held at the shoulder by an emerald. There were yellow shoes on her feet, and she was nearly as broad as she was tall. She was the brightest thing in the room.

She narrowed her eyes at Correus, taking in the new gilded cuirass, the wealth of medals, and the Rhenus Fleet's trident insigne before she came to his face. Her eyes widened, and she heaved herself up from the couch.

"Correus!" A gold tooth gleamed a welcome. "Where did you spring from?"

"Up from the ground, like mine elves." He grinned at her. "You've turned respectable."

Rhodope snorted. "Certainly. And all the girls are virgins again. Here you, Leza, go and get the prefect some wine. You remember Leza, don't you?" An Ethiopian girl with a headdress of crimped curls gave him a curious stare and then a smile of recognition.

Correus bowed gallantly, and Leza giggled.

"You'll spoil her," Rhodope said. "They think enough of themselves now as it is." She looked over her shoulder at the wine broker. "Very well, Ostorius, I'll meet your price, but if any of it is soured like the last batch, you won't have any reputation left in any town from here to Augusta Raurica. Now go away and fetch the stuff."

The wine merchant gave her a much-tried look and departed, and Rhodope dragged Correus over to her couch. Leza presented him with a cup of wine and curled up at his feet. Two more half-naked girls whom he thought he remembered settled themselves beside her. He felt like an Eastern pasha.

He scanned their faces, white, black, and brown, a friendly company of whores, painted for the evening's business. "Where's Charis?"

Rhodope chuckled. "She got married. A soldier from Aquitania, just getting his time-expired pay and a nice little piece of land. He must have been fifty, but he wasn't particular, and Charis said she wasn't getting younger herself. She'd a mind to have a house and a bit of a farm and just one man to please while she still could."

"He was nice," a blue-eyed girl said wistfully.

"He had warts," Leza said.

"Enough." Rhodope rearranged her bulk on the couch. "We have customers. Why are you sitting here like a bunch of schoolgirls, ogling Correus? If he wants one of you, I will send for you."

"It's a good thing Charis isn't here," Rhodope continued as

they departed reluctantly. "She was too fond of you, that one. She would have done it for free."

Correus chuckled. "Not with you around. When did she get married?"

"Not so long ago. Just before I bought this house. It is a good house, this."

The night was warm, and from the veranda came the sound of high-pitched giggles. Below, the moon was reflected in the river and on the scales of the fish that threw their silvered forms in the air for a brief moment and disappeared into the river again with a *plop*.

"I thought you used to say you could make twice the money following an army on campaign as fighting the competition in a town," Correus said.

"That was while there was still a campaign to follow," Rhodope said. "It's been quiet since you were here last. And my bones are old. I ache, and the wagon makes it worse. It was time to settle and make a higher-class business. I endow temples now and put up public fountains, and everyone is very glad indeed to see me."

Correus laughed. "Everyone was very glad to see you in your wagon, as I recall."

Rhodope's purple bosom heaved a sigh. "Those were the days." She gave a shrewd glance to the *phalerae* strung across his chest. "You've come up in the world."

"It's been a long time," Correus said. "Two wars ago."

"And your German girl, the one that put a knife in you. What happened to her?"

"She died," Correus said.

"Ah, I am sorry." Her sharp black eyes were apologetic. She shook her head. Then she brightened. "Charis is gone, but there is Zoe, much the same type. For you I even make it for free. One time."

"You're getting soft, Rhodope. No, I am married now. My wife has told me that if I ever look at another woman, she will make a magic so that nothing will ever work again."

Rhodope's black eyes studied him, trying to decide if he was joking. "Could she?"

"Quite possibly," Correus said solemnly. "And if she

couldn't, I expect she'd take matters into her own hands and do it personally."

Rhodope laughed. "Drink your wine, Correus, and then go make an offering at the Temple of Isis that she doesn't find out you've been in a whorehouse."

"It's not as bad as that. But I had to leave her in my father's house to have her first child alone, when I came out here. I expect I owe her faithfulness, at least."

"I expect you do at that," Rhodope said. She sighed again, and the emerald rose and fell, glowing greenly in the lamplight. There was an oil lamp hung on a silver chain from the balcony of the second floor. "You never were a very good customer, Correus. You spent more time talking to the girls than you did in a bed."

"They always knew everything before the camp knew it," Correus said. He had been a very junior centurion then, with his first command and eighty legionaries twice his age in his charge. "It kept me a jump ahead of the men."

"We were all younger then," Rhodope said. She patted her orange curls sadly. "It's all gray now, under the henna. And I get fatter every year. I need this house, Correus. You tell that to the governor if he doesn't like having us on his hill. I'm too old for wagons now."

"I shouldn't worry. He's no moralist." Correus looked thoughtful. "You get a fair civilian clientele, don't you, Rhodope? This is a government town, not an army post."

"Oh yes. I've more girls than I used to have, and I've made them learn a thing or two. Zoe dances, and Leza has learned to play the flute." Rhodope's black eyes were shrewd and beady. Correus decided she wasn't as old as she was acting. "What do you want, Correus?"

"Nothing to trouble you. But there may be trouble brewing with the tribes across the frontier. The first thing they'll do is subvert the civilian populations in the Roman zone, if they can."

"They tried that twelve years ago," Rhodope said. "Colonia stayed loyal then."

"I'm not expecting to be murdered in my bed," Correus said. "But if there's rebellion being talked in Colonia, some fool will as like as not talk of it here, and I want to know about it. I've sent for my wife and my children, and I intend to have peace and quiet to enjoy them in."

"Anything I hear," Rhodope said, "it's yours. I am comfortable here, too." She patted his hand maternally. "And you are too respectable for whorehouses. It's good that you sent for your wife."

"Tomorrow. Everything is packed, and I've had all the last-minute advice I can stand without being rude. Aemelia 'doesn't know how I can think of it with two babies,' and her mother told me to be sure to take all my own linens because the frontier is always dirty." Ygerna was curled up on the cushions in Berenice's little garden room with Eilenn in her lap. The baby was blowing bubbles and catching at the pearls around Ygerna's neck. Ygerna made an amused face at her hostess. "Aemelia doesn't think Correus's new slave is safe to travel with, either. So far she has thought of forty-one things that won't be safe."

Berenice laughed. "Remember that she has only been out of Rome once. You will be more adaptable."

"I will be with Correus at any rate," Ygerna said. "And the Rhenus frontier sounds more peaceful now than my father-in-law's house. Correus's sister still is not speaking to me, his mother thinks he should divorce me, and Aemelia thinks that I am a...a—I don't know—someone from under the sea or a goblin's changeling. She keeps saying, 'But of course it must be very different where you come from.' She was in love with Correus once. Someone told me that who shouldn't have. Julius, I think."

"It will be as well for you to be away from Julius, too, you know," Berenice said. "Poor boy."

Ygerna looked embarrassed. "Yes, Correus explained that. I shouldn't have had him drive me here, I suppose, but there was no one else who wouldn't tell my father-in-law."

Berenice looked out into the little jeweled garden. The sun was low, casting a golden light on the flowers and the bright marble paving. "No, that would never do. I'm afraid you will have to go now, my dear. I am expecting another visitor— purely business, but you mustn't be compromised."

"I should have let you know I was coming, but I wanted to

say good-bye, and there wasn't much time." Ygerna picked up the baby and wrapped her in her shawl.

"You are always welcome, my dear. It is only that I can't break this . . . appointment."

Ygerna smiled. "I understand. I will miss you."

Berenice stood and kissed her on the cheek. "I will miss you too, child. But now you will be a family again. That is better." Ygerna thought she sounded wistful. "Go with God." Berenice patted her on the shoulder and turned her toward the door. Whoever was coming must be nearly due. Ygerna took the baby and went out, leaving Berenice looking out into the gold light in the garden.

She climbed into the carriage and handed Eilenn to Cottia. Julius clucked to the horses, and they set out at a trot down the dirt road that linked the little village, hidden among the trees, with the main paved road to Veii.

"You're early," Julius said.

"I have to finish packing." As a driver, Julius was somewhat short of the unquestioning attitude required of a proper servant. Ygerna had so far failed to impress this on him and had given up now that he was Diulius's pupil.

"I'm surprised you didn't stay all night," Julius said. "When you and Her Majesty get to nattering, I could die out here of old age. Thought you'd say a longer good-bye."

"She had another visitor coming," Ygerna said repressively.

"Here he comes now," Julius said. "Tuck your head in. Won't do for some hairdresser to see you keeping unsavory company."

Ygerna ducked her head back behind the carriage curtains and looked out through a narrow gap. The other carriage swept past them at a good pace. Its curtains were drawn too, but the sun shone through them from the other side, setting the occupant's face into sharp silhouette. Ygerna caught her breath. She had seen that bull-necked profile before. It was on the silver coins in her purse and one of Correus's military medals. The emperor Titus.

"Watch the road, Julius!" she hissed.

So that was Berenice's "visitor." And that was why she had looked so sad when they had talked of Ygerna's being with Correus again as a family. There would be no family life with

Titus, no time to let down one's guard, not ever, not for a woman whose love was forbidden. Not for a man with a throne at stake.

So that was the reason for the emperor's cruel edict, that no one who wished his favor should have contact with his banished woman. Berenice had traded all normal companionship, the daily round of friends and visitors, for a few infrequent hours in a hidden house.

Ygerna shivered. This was dangerous. "I want to go home as quickly as possible please, Julius," she said, and was relieved when he shook out the reins and asked no questions. Had Julius seen that backlighted profile, too? It was as well that she was leaving tomorrow. Best not to be noticed or remembered as someone who had seen the emperor Titus visiting the lover he had exiled.

"Here now, we'll be wanting that handy, not on the bottom of everything." Nurse pointed a stout finger at the leather trunk that Eumenes had just settled as the foundation point of the mountain of baggage in the back of a wagon. "Master Felix's clothes are in that one, and the baby's. It's got to be unloaded at night."

Eumenes shot her an exasperated look. Felix was dancing like a dervish on the driver's seat of the wagon, with a canvas bag of toys under one arm. "Here, stop that, you'll fall off. And why didn't you tell me that *before* I loaded it, then?"

"Don't take that tone with me." Nurse folded her arms and prepared to do battle. A cowed nurserymaid stood behind her, with Eilenn howling in a blanket and the cat beside her, howling in a basket. Cottia was piling last-minute additions on top of the luggage in the wagon, and a kitchen maid was stowing a hamper into the curtained carriage. The wagon driver, a slave of Appius's, was hitching the horses to the wagon. He tangled the traces, and one of the horses backed suddenly into the wagon.

Eumenes gave the entourage a look of disgust. "It'll take a year to get this caravan over the Alps." He glared back at Nurse. "Longer if you keep farting about with the luggage. Buzz off now, and get the children settled."

"My lady!" Nurse was growing red in the face, and Felix watched with interest.

"Mother of All, what now?" Ygerna came up. She was wearing a broad straw hat to keep the sun off her face and a plain traveling gown of brown linen.

"What I'm called upon to put up with, with this . . . this— It's too much!" Indignantly Nurse pointed at Eumenes, who was slinging the extra baggage into the wagon to suit himself.

"I was bought for a body servant," Eumenes said. "My mother didn't raise me for a damned lady's maid."

"I assume by your manners that she raised you for a pick-pocket," Ygerna said tartly. "Nurse, the wagon is loaded now; it will have to stay until we stop tonight. We will rearrange then, when we see what we need. Cottia, put Eilenn and the cat in the carriage, please. Here." She handed the baby a piece of honey cake, and she stopped howling. "We can't go on listening to that." She looked around briskly. The wagon driver had the horses hitched now, and Felix was sitting on one of them. "Get down from there, please, and go with Nurse. Eumenes, get the things strapped down, but go gently with them. That case has perfume in it."

All parties departed grumbling to do her bidding, and Ygerna passed a hand over her forehead. Eumenes grinned at her over his shoulder and gave her an army salute, and she started to laugh. "I'd sooner herd a flock of wild cows. But you are going to have to be polite to Nurse. Start now." She looked around. "Where is Julius?"

He came lounging up with a bridle over one arm. "Diulius is lookin' for me, but I thought I'd say good-bye."

Ygerna put a hand on his shoulder affectionately. "We'll miss you, Julius."

Julius looked embarrassed and muttered something unintelligible. *Poor Julius*, she thought. He had hated her when he was fifteen and she was thirteen. It was a pity he couldn't have gone on feeling that way.

"Behave yourself, Julius, or Diulius will tell Correus." She gave him a smile and turned back toward the house.

Appius and Antonia emerged and kissed her. "Good-bye, my dear. Write to us and come home soon." Flavius gave her a hug, and old Thais bustled through the door and put a little

pewter image of Vesta in her hand. "To bring you back to us."
Lucius Paulinus smiled and patted her hand and went to the
carriage to tell Felix good-bye. Helva and Julia were not to be
seen, she noted. Julia had said her good-byes to Felix already.

The wagon driver pulled the cart into line behind the carriage, and Eumenes took up the reins of the carriage horses.
Felix's pony and a gray mare with red tassels in her mane and
a red saddle were tethered behind the wagon. When they were
out of Rome, Ygerna said firmly, she would ride. If she spent
a two-month journey in a curtained carriage with Nurse, maids,
cat, baby, and Felix, she was sure to kill one of them. For now
she settled in beside Nurse and took the baby from the nurserymaid to feed her. Felix bounced gently on the cushions, his
bright green eyes wide with excitement. He opened and closed
the curtains over and over. The carriage lurched, and Eumenes
swore as the near horse stumbled on a stone and kicked.

The journey took a full two months, and it would have taken
longer if Ygerna and Eumenes, with equal determination, hadn't
pushed forward ruthlessly, to arrive in Germany before the
journey drove them mad. The paved, banked carriage road over
the Alps was awe-inspiring enough to make Ygerna gape, and
Felix immediately wanted to know how it had been built. It
was cold even in summer, a place of empty spaces and pre-
cipitous cliffs dropping into dreadful nothingness. And silent.
The rattle of the carriage wheels and the clip of the horses'
hooves were a sharp, lonely sound in the air. They occasionally
passed other traffic on the road, edging uncomfortably near the
outer bank to slip by, and once were nearly tipped over by
a loose horse dragging half a careening cart. They never did
find the cart's driver, or the rest of the cart, and after that,
Nurse drew the curtains of the carriage and refused to look
out, and Septima, the nurserymaid, was in constant, terrified
prayer from the moment they set out in the morning until
they stopped at night.

All the Alpine passes boasted imperial way stations a day
apart, for which Flavius had provided them with a pass, and
lesser inns and taverns for the common traveler. The way stations were properly heated, and no one was likely to steal the
baggage, so Ygerna thankfully passed by the taverns. Felix,

unimpressed with the engineering knowledge available from his stepmother, got a lesson in road building from the commander at one, and a guard who hadn't seen a woman all summer fell in love with Cottia.

The frontier road along the Rhenus from Augusta Raurica was nearly as intimidating to Roman eyes as the Alpine passes. It followed the broad course of the river through Argentoratum and Moguntiacum to the rapids in the wild beauty of the Rhenus Gorge below Bingium. On the Roman side, the vineyards sloped steeply from the bank, clinging to their brown shale terraces, their leaves turning to gold in the sun. Across the river, beyond a narrow band of fields, the wild lands rose up green and impenetrable. It had been a good year for wine, the innkeeper at Bingium told them—hot weather to sweeten the vintage. You could see the rock of the Ara Bacchi, the Altar of Bacchus, in the river; that was always a good sign. Below the gorge, the land softened to a gentler contour, but to Italian eyes it was still alien country, wet and wild and covered with trees—far too many trees, which undoubtedly held hidden horrors. Septima's prayers continued.

They reached Colonia in mid-September and found the city in a festival mood at the start of the fall wine-making. Ygerna blinked as a trio of sailors with drying vine leaves in their hair danced by with a blond girl among them and a wine jar under each free arm. A musician with a monkey, also with vines in its hair, was playing a little organ outside the triple temple of Jupiter, Juno, and Minerva. A workman with a slimy broom in his hand, busily clearing the drains for winter, popped up through a hole in the street and applauded them, and someone put a wine cup in his hand.

Eumenes pounded on the door of the palace, and they were ushered in with much ceremony by the governor's staff while someone sent a slave off to the naval station to fetch the prefect.

Ygerna had time to bathe and let Cottia curl her hair before they found him, and she was relaxing in the newly painted bedchamber watching the painted fish leaping in a silver stream when he came in. She threw herself at him and then backed off indignantly.

"Take that off!"

He grinned and shucked off his lorica and harness tunic,

then scooped her up and sat down with her in his lap. "I have missed you."

She gave a sigh and snuggled down into his arms. Baucis appeared from under the bed, looking suspicious, and, seeing a familiar lap, sat down in it, too.

"Damn it!" Correus dumped the cat on the floor and pulled Ygerna down on the bed. In a minute her clothes were a tangle on the floor. She shivered and put her arms around his neck, and he put his lips against the five-petaled blue-gray pattern painted indelibly between her breasts, the mark of her wild heritage underneath the Roman gown and Cottia's curling tongs.

After a while she opened her eyes again. "Correus?"

"Mmmm?"

"You haven't said hello to Felix. You haven't even *seen* the baby yet."

He started to sit up.

"No, not yet. In a while. When I've had all I want of you." She put her lips against his arm, and one hand slid along his back.

"Then why did you tell me?"

"Just so I wouldn't forget later."

He smiled and slipped a hand between her legs again. Her own smile was drowsy and full of hunger still.

"Do that some more."

"Like this?"

"Yes. You know like what. You always do."

She had thought it would be like the first time again, after so long, but it wasn't. They fitted together now, like a lock and its key, an aching pleasure that was sure and familiar and undiminished. After a moment he slipped inside her again, and she wrapped her legs around his back. They rolled entwined in the feather mattress on the bed while the sun went down and the painted fish leaped into shadow on the wall.

They emerged at dinnertime, feeling guilty, and sent for Felix, who was finally found asking Governor Clarus why the town walls were three kinds of stone and who had thought up the patterns in them. He hurled himself into his father's arms while the governor smiled at them. It was as good as making love to Ygerna, Correus decided, to hold his small son in his arms again.

Nurse brought in Eilenn, and he inspected her with pleasure and took her inexpertly into his lap with Felix. She was little, delicately boned like a bird, with her mother's white skin and a dark cap of fine hair that felt like silk under his hand. But her eyes were the same light brown as his own, not Ygerna's nearly black ones, and he thought that her features were going to be more aquiline than Ygerna's. There was something of him in her at any rate, although at first glance she was purely Ygerna's child, a dark, graceful baby who might have been a sidhe woman's changeling. She opened her eyes wide at him and giggled and kicked her tiny feet, and he was lost. *This is the next generation*, he thought. *This is the future, and I have had a hand in it.* It would be good to spend the winter with the future, watching it grow, in a peacetime posting removed from war and Rome. Felix snuggled back against his shoulder. Ygerna put an arm around them both, and the baby laughed. Governor Clarus beamed at them.

And then a slave came through the door with a military courier on his heels and whispered in the governor's ear, and the governor's face went white.

IX

Interlude

THE EMPEROR TITUS CAESAR VESPASIANUS AUGUSTUS DIED of a fever on September 13 after twenty-six months of reign, in the same country villa where his father, Vespasian, had died. On his deathbed he whispered that there was only one action of which he had need to repent, but what it was, no one ever knew. Like his father before him, Rome gave him divine honors. He was not yet forty.

The Jews, hating to the end the destroyer of their temple, called it the justice of God, but to the rest of the world he was Divus Titus, and they mourned his passing with a fervor given to no emperor since Augustus. There was no doubt as to his successor. Titus had meant Domitian to be his heir, and Domitian galloped straight from his brother's deathbed to Rome to be acclaimed as *Imperator* by the Praetorians the same day. The Senate, wanting more than anything a peaceful, orderly succession with no blood in it, made haste to confer upon him the usual powers. He counted his years of tribunician power from the following day, and by the end of the autumn had also accepted the titles of *Pontifex Maximus* and *Pater Patriae* and given his wife the appellation of *Augusta*.

While the Praetorian Guard was shouting his name, Domitian's couriers went out to the commanders of every legion in the empire and the governors of its provinces with the news of his succession and the promise of a bonus to his loyal servants and soldiers. By the time the rumors that he had had his brother poisoned had begun to circulate, there was no one with the support to oppose him, and even such detractors as Flavius Julianus and Lucius Paulinus were inclined to think the rumors untrue. An unseemly haste to leave his dying brother and ride for Rome did not necessarily argue a responsibility for the death.

Marius Vettius received the news while he was on his way to dinner. He gave a shout of laughter, sent a message of congratulations and condolence to Domitian, and went to dine, still chuckling. How immensely helpful of Titus to contract a fever while his brother was still trying to get up the nerve to kill him. Vettius was sure that Domitian hadn't done it—Domitian had been still wavering three days before, and he was not a man who could make that sort of decision without considerable prodding.

Vettius reclined on his dining couch and regarded a plate of oysters with satisfaction. Everything would be much simpler now. Domitian would allow his cronies free rein. Better yet, Domitian by his very nature would contrast unfavorably with his brother, especially if he were encouraged to be high-handed. After that it shouldn't take long to incite unrest. Vettius had a far greater goal for the long run than to be the emperor's sandal licker. He ate the last of his oysters and thoughtfully arranged the shells into a little pattern on the plate. It would prove far easier to dispose of Domitian than Titus. Given six months,

Vettius thought that half the men in Rome could be provoked into doing it for him. A slave brought in the next course, pigeon with honey and new onions. Vettius nodded approvingly. He took a pigeon from the dish, broke it in half, and considered how best to insure that Domitian aggravated as many men as possible. First there would be new appointments. . . .

If Marius Vettius regarded Domitian's accession and appointments with enthusiasm, he was the only one. For anyone even faintly connected with the government, the loss of Titus meant the exchange of the known quantity for the unknown and, possibly, the unstable. There would be new posts, new assignments, new favors conferred. There might also be some new retirements. Everyone stood nervously on one foot and waited for it to happen.

Aemelia looked wistfully around her dining chamber. There was scaffolding against the walls, and a bald man in a paint-stained tunic was carefully filling in the colors of a frieze on the top level. She had ordered the whole room repainted in honor of an event that would never be celebrated—the emperor Titus's birthday banquet. "What will you do now?"

"Back to the army, I expect," Flavius said. He was wearing an old and much-patched military tunic and had been out in the stables all morning. Flavius had been on unofficial leave since the emperor had died, because no one had thought to give him a new assignment. Or because Domitian was saving something up, but Flavius didn't tell Aemelia that. Domitian was almost totally unpredictable, so Flavius would worry about his assignment when he got it. The chances were good that he would be in the field again.

"Maybe I've been off active duty too long," he said. "A frontier tour might do me good."

He made a face when he said it, but Aemelia looked at him suspiciously. Flavius had been restless ever since Correus had gone to Germany. He hadn't used to care much for Correus, but something had happened in Britain that had pulled them together, and now they were acting like twins. Aemelia thought she preferred things as they had been. At least Flavius hadn't been talking about field commands. Aemelia closed her eyes and fought down a mental picture of Flavius being carried into her rooms and put down in her bed, with both hands black and stinking with gangrene, and raving out of his mind. He had tried to kill the physician when the poor man had suggested amputation. Correus had yelled at her and gone to get an army surgeon to treat him, then yelled at her some more because she couldn't bear to look at those hands to help clean them. The army man had saved them, and Aemelia had got used to their odd, elongated shape once they were healed, but she had never gone back to the frontier. And with Flavius on the emperor's staff it had been so pleasant, knowing all the people in the government and giving parties.

Flavius saw the distress in her face and put an arm around her. "Come along. Let's enjoy my leave while I've got it. At least you have a new dining room. We'll find a party to put in it, don't worry."

Aemelia shook her head. "I sound so selfish. It isn't that. I will miss him. He was so kind, and . . . and *nice.*"

You are selfish, my sweet, Flavius thought, *but you can't help it.* He kissed the top of her head, dodging ivory-tipped hairpins. "I will miss him, too." Flavius had sat at Titus's bed while he died, and seen all that promise and intelligence blown out like a lamp flame. Titus had been what an emperor ought to be, and Flavius mourned that as much as he mourned the man himself, but that was too complicated to explain to Aemelia.

But for good or bad, it was Domitian who was emperor now. Maybe the office would make the man. It had done it for Titus, of whom no good had been predicted at the start. But it had been there under the surface, Flavius thought. Somehow Domitian was going to have to find it, too.

"I am afraid, sir, that I will have to decline." Lucius Paulinus stood stubbornly in front of the new emperor, his plain freckled face showing as much apology as he could muster.

Domitian leaned forward in his gilded chair, his hands playing with the gold and purple folds of his toga. "Do you feel that that's wise?" he said frankly.

"Perhaps not, sir. But I am a private citizen, and I feel that it is time for me to devote myself to my writing."

"Which you were happy to neglect in the service of my father and my brother!" Domitian snapped.

Lucius was silent. There is very little that it is safe to say when one is declining to work for an emperor.

"It is my intention," Domitian said, "to restore the ancient moral values of Rome and the conduct of its citizens. To do that I need the help of men of judgment who can keep me informed."

"I'm sorry, sir," Lucius said again. He seemed to have been saying "I'm sorry, sir" all morning, and was beginning to wonder if he was a bigger fool than he had taken himself for. Would it be simpler just to work for the man? No. "I was only a sort of unofficial observer," he said, trying to slide as gracefully as possible out of the fire. "I don't think I'm the man you are looking for."

"I know what service I require!" Domitian snapped.

"What he means is, he wants a set of spies to tattle on all his other spies," Lucius said when he got home, his face set and strained. "I told him I wouldn't do it."

"*Was* that wise?" Julia asked. She had been overseeing the slaves drying fall herbs in the kitchen, and she wiped her hands on her apron in a fragrant cloud of crushed rosemary.

"Maybe not. I think we'll lie low for a while and be unobtrusive. But I know too much, Ju."

"What do you mean?"

"Well, look at Titus. I wish he hadn't been so obsessive about absolute proof—Vettius was guilty as hell, blast his sleek hide—but Titus didn't go about flinging people onto islands in exile or ordering them to commit suicide just because they once looked cross-eyed at him. Domitian's just the opposite. He goes off half-cocked on the slightest suspicion. He plays favorites, and he listens to informers."

"You aren't an informer," Julia said. Their daughter Paulilla was hanging on her skirt and repeated the word thoughtfully. Julia untied her apron and gave it to Paulilla. "Here, take this back to the kitchen, and tell Cook I said you might ask for cakes for you and Lucian."

"Lucian doesn't need cake," Paulilla said.

"Neither do you if you won't share with your brother. Now go." She turned back to Lucius. "I don't understand."

"I told you, I know too much," Lucius said. "Mildly incriminating things about a lot of people. Or just scandalous things. Things that Titus had the sense to ignore, but Domitian will blow out of proportion. He has a bee in his helmet about morals at the moment, too."

Julia snorted. "Whose?"

"Well, not his. He'll make some new laws and use them as he sees fit. I don't want to be in the position of having to either lie to the emperor or tell him things he'll overreact to. He's not stable."

"You didn't tell him that?"

"No, but I did give him a piece of advice."

"He warned me about you." In a bad mood, Domitian had an uncanny resemblance to his brother.

"Indeed?" Vettius raised his eyebrows in apparent amusement, as if to say that surely Paulinus was misinformed, but the light in his eyes wasn't pleasant.

"You and a few others." Domitian tapped his fingers, an irritable drumming on the gilded arm of his chair. "A nice post in the provinces is a license to steal if a man is inclined that way, and I am told that a number of my appointments have been exercising that inclination. I didn't appreciate it."

"I am sure that all the emperor's appointments are wise ones," Vettius said. "There may be one or two, perhaps, who have represented themselves as more honest than they are, but I am sure your judgment is good."

"How good is my judgment concerning you, Vettius?"

"Excellent," Vettius smiled. "I had hoped that I had sufficiently indicated my gratitude."

"I have a bonus to the army to make good on," Domitian said irritably. "Nothing is ever sufficient."

"I shall try to express it further." Vettius bowed and covered his annoyance as well as he could. His accession to the purple had had an unforeseen effect on Domitian: With his need for power assuaged, the new emperor was not so easily led as he had been. Sufficient money would be doubly important now.

Domitian leaned forward in his chair, one heavy hand clenched around the arm. There were three gold rings on his fingers: the seal of the *Pontifex Maximus*, his brother's seal, and the seal of the tribune of the People. "Pay attention, Vettius. It has been suggested before this, if you will remember, that you have been robbing the state blind. I don't give a damn if you are, as long as you keep in mind what you owe me. But I won't be understanding if you get caught."

"Flavius Julianus began that," Vettius said. "Your late brother's watchdog. Since he won't be at court to make a pest of himself, I am sure that the emperor's image will remain untarnished. I need hardly assure you that the emperor's appointments will remember the emperor's need for funds."

"The emperor's appointments had better remember more than that," Domitian said. "They had better remember to watch their step. If I find that an appointment has embarrassed me, the source of the embarrassment will discover that nothing is permanent. As for Flavius Julianus, you're wrong. He stays on the imperial staff."

"Why?" Vettius was startled into bluntness.

"For my skin's sake," Domitian said.

"Julianus was no friend to you when your brother was alive."

"No, but Julianus is a friend to the emperor, whoever happens to be wearing his toga. He has some old-fashioned opinions on that. It's what made him such a good watchdog."

"Do you want that watchdog watching *you*?" Vettius's expression was sarcastic. "He's no fool."

"Neither am I," Domitian said. "I'm bright enough to know I'll feel safer with one honest man on my staff. His presence may be awkward at times, but I will sleep at night."

* * *

And so I am still at court, and I will admit to a certain relief. I was never much good at a field command, and I *am* a good staff officer. At the moment my talents are occupied in smoothing out the domestic machinery and arranging for a less bothersome changeover than might otherwise have happened . . .

"That means he's stopped Domitian from sacking his brother's staff wholesale," Correus said. He leaned over Ygerna's shoulder while she continued reading Flavius's letter.

... but it appears that the emperor may make a tour of the Rhenus frontier in the spring, so I will come and visit and bounce the babies on my avuncular knee, in between inspecting the hell out of all fortifications and scaring all the commanders into fits. Beware. The emperor has never felt that our campaign to secure the Agri Decumates and build a more defensible frontier line in that sector was carried to its logical conclusion.

"Damn. That means Domitian wants a military triumph to put him on a par with his papa and his brother, and he's coming here to do it," Correus said.

"How can you tell all that?" Ygerna asked.

"You have to know how to read between Flavius's lines. There's no telling who's going to read a letter, even one that goes by imperial post. Maybe especially then. So he leaves out anything touchy. I know his style well enough to fill in the gaps."

The family are all well. Papa says to tell you that your young terror Julius is proving a fine hand with a horse and a liability in all other respects. He snuck into the City and got in a brawl with the counterman in a wineshop. He says the fellow was cheating him, and I expect he was, but it made no end of a row.

"Oh dear." Ygerna looked up at Correus.

"Don't worry, Julius always gets in rows," Correus said blithely. "Better Papa than us."

Mother sat Julius down and lectured him about it, and Diulius took a pony whip to him, so I expect he's repentant. Everyone else is thriving. Forst seems to have come out of the glooms a bit, and all else is as usual. Cook had a temperament the last time we dined there, and your mother is having her rooms repainted again. Aemelia is well and, we think, is pregnant again. I'm not sure she's pleased about it, but she'll come around. Women get these moods...

"Did you say something?"

"You heard what I said," Ygerna said. "If Aemelia wasn't so stupid, she'd slap him for a remark like that."

"Poor child." Correus put his hands on her shoulders. "You didn't have an easy time, did you?"

"No, I didn't," Ygerna said, "but you didn't go around saying 'Women get these moods.'"

"I wouldn't dare," Correus said piously. "But Flavius isn't so henpecked."

Ygerna snorted and returned to the letter.

... but in any case, she is charmed with the prospect of my staying on the imperial staff. I haven't the heart to tell her I'll probably be in Germany by spring. It is pleasant to find oneself still at the center of things, and I honestly think he needs me (or at any rate, *some* loyal body with no ax to grind).

Lucius was made a similar offer and has refused it, a choice that, of course, I didn't have. If I *had* been a civilian, I would have stayed on, however, and I think Lucius has made a mistake.

"I think he has too," Ygerna said quietly.

I tried to talk to Julia about it, but she is still in the sulks about losing Felix (I can't think why—the last time he visited us, he put tadpoles in the atrium pool, and no one noticed it until they were frogs), and all she will say is that she is sure Lucius knows what he's doing. I don't think she's paying any attention to what he's doing, and I wish she would. Lucius isn't generally a hothead, but his decision is unfortunate.

"I can decipher *that*," Ygerna said. "Lucius won't work for the emperor, and Flavius thinks that's dangerous. That's what Berenice said when Flavius tried to get the old emperor to listen about Vettius."

"*Who?*"

"Berenice. The lady who was the old emperor's lover. I met her in Veii, quite by accident, and—"

"You mean she's still in Italy? And you just struck up a *conversation* with her?" Correus came around to face her and pulled up a chair beside hers. *"Ygerna!"*

Ygerna was looking as if she wished she had kept quiet. "Yes, Correus?"

"Why didn't you tell me this?"

"I was afraid you might not like it," she said frankly.

"That's the most dangerous damned thing—"

"Correus, nobody knew about it but Cottia and Julius, and I told them I would make them more than sorry if they told *anyone*. She is a very lonely lady, and very interesting—"

"I expect so," Correus said. "She ought to be. But—Berenice! Mithras god!"

"Well, it doesn't matter now," Ygerna said. "Poor woman. I wonder how she felt when she heard. No one would come and tell her. She would have heard it in the marketplace."

"What was she doing in Italy, anyway? I would think she would have gone back to the East."

"Well, *I* know," Ygerna said, "but it wasn't a very safe secret. I found out by accident, and it scared me half to death, just knowing. That was another reason I didn't tell you."

"Titus?"

Ygerna nodded.

Correus ran a hand over his forehead. "I don't blame you for being scared. It gives me a cold sweat just thinking about his finding out you knew that."

"It was the day before I left," Ygerna said. "After that, I was ready to *run* all the way across the mountains. Well, poor man, it doesn't matter now. But what Flavius said—that is what Berenice said. That Domitian isn't . . . safe. And this Vettius person isn't, either."

"He certainly isn't, and with Domitian on the throne, he may be an absolute menace. He's already got good reason for a grudge against this family. I don't blame Lucius—I wouldn't work for Domitian that way myself. But I see what Flavius means. I hope Lucius keeps his disapproval very quiet. I wonder if Flavius thinks I have any more influence over Lucius than he does. I don't think anyone has any influence on Lucius, frankly. Except maybe Julia." Correus frowned. Lucius Paulinus was his closest friend, and Correus's sister, Julia, was very dear to him. If the emperor grew angry with them, it could be appallingly dangerous.

Ygerna had picked up Flavius's letter and was puzzling over it. "This is a very odd letter. All the chat about the family. I get the feeling it's a . . . a framework, or—no, a . . . a wrapping. I can't think of the word I want."

Correus dragged his mind away from Lucius and Julia. There were more dangers than that one in Flavius' letter. "You bet it is," he said. "And he's gone to a lot of trouble to do it. Flavius hates to write anything. He's very articulate, but it's a misery for him to put anything down on paper, much less a long, chatty letter. He doesn't write to anyone. The family's used to it. Can you pick out what it is that he thinks is worth my knowing?"

"Oh yes," Ygerna said. "Lucius. And . . . and the emperor coming here, isn't it? What you said about wanting a triumph. He's not just telling you to shape up for an inspection."

"Good girl. The emperor should put you on his staff. Flavius was out here when I was. We had our first postings in the same legion, in Argentoratum, when Vespasian decided to consolidate the Agri Decumates—the Black Forest lands, I showed you that on the map—after there was a rebellion here. That was when the Semnones, Nyall Sigmundson's people, got into it. Nyall didn't like Rome getting any closer to his own lands. If Domitian's going to push into the Agri Decumates again— we stopped short of the lines Vespasian originally planned— or worse yet, beyond it, he may precipitate more than he bargained for. The Semnones are pigheaded, but they don't have much strength; however, there are signs that another tribe, the Chatti, who are right across the Rhenus from us, *are* looking for a fight. They're the ones who worry me right now, and the emperor's been warned too, but I don't think he's listening."

"Could the Chatti win?" Ygerna said.

"No. Not in the long run. Think of your own folk, Ygerna."

Ygerna put the letter down. "So many dead, from your legion and my tribe. Why can't Domitian just stay in Rome? There is peace here now."

"I expect that's what Flavius thinks, but it doesn't sound like he's having much luck with the suggestion. Domitian's touchy about comparisons with his brother. He wants a triumph, so he'll get one, one way or another."

"There are enough wars," Ygerna said disgustedly, "without making one up. Will you tell the governor?"

Correus nodded. "Between us, maybe we can put the fear of the gods into the Chatti. And if Flavius can persuade Domitian not to push too far, we might just slide by."

"Do you think so?"

"No."

"Well, I don't, either," Ygerna said. The governor's palace was heated by a hypocaust with hot-air channels that ran under the floor, but there was a fire burning, too, in an iron brazier in the center of the room. Ygerna picked up the letter and looked inquiringly at Correus.

He nodded. "I don't want that lying around."

She dropped the papyrus into the flames, and it began to curl and blacken. "What do we do now?"

"Enjoy the winter," Correus said. "We might as well." Outside the ground was sleek with new snow. The gardener had laid the palace gardens down under a bed of straw and tied sacking over the governor's rosebushes. Correus was wearing his uniform tunic and the wool breeches and fur leggings that the army had adopted from the native dress for winter wear. He drew his chair closer to the brazier and stuck his long legs out toward it. "Where are the children?"

"Eilenn is with the Nurse, and Felix has run away again. Don't worry, he only goes as far as the pottery works. There is a foreman there who shows him how the clay is made. He made a pot for the governor yesterday and brought it home, and the governor put it on a pedestal in the atrium. He is a very kind man."

"Poor soul, I'm afraid his life is going to heat up considerably in the spring." Sulpicius Clarus, the governor of Lower Germany, was a civilian. He had held military commands, of course, all Roman officials had, but his pleasure was in a peacetime administration, with leisure to oversee the construction of public buildings and the peaceful expansion of his capital. He wasn't going to be happy that the emperor had decided to gain a military reputation on Clarus's territory.

"Come and sit in my lap before Nurse comes in or someone

finds Felix." He held out his arms, and Ygerna came over dubiously.

"Or someone starts a war?"

"You know what active duty's like. Do you really want me back in Misemum shipping sand and giraffes up to Rome and having nightmares?"

"Of course not." She sat. "Have those dreams really stopped?"

"Oddly enough, yes. It seems as if there's nothing like a nice war to put my mind at rest."

"You don't mean that. You sounded so worried."

"I am. But if I have to choose, I think I'd take a frontier war over an arena fight. The Chatti, at least, will bring it down on their own heads, and so will we, from one point of view. That's just the way things are. The arena is different. It's evil minded. A war will be such a damned waste, but I don't get bad dreams from it. I don't think I can really explain it more than that."

"Don't worry. You make sense to me." She put her arms around him affectionately. "As much as Romans will ever make sense to me."

"Good." He kissed her. She was wearing fur boots and an undershift under her woolen gown, and he began to rummage through the layers of cloth. "There's a girl in here somewhere. Shall we spend the winter in bed and let the Chatti and the emperor look out for themselves?"

"What about the governor?"

"Let him get his own girl."

X

Meeting in Colonia

IN ONE WAY OR ANOTHER, EVERYONE WHO HAD A HAND IN the matter of the Rhenus frontier came to Colonia that spring.

Domitian set out with staff, hangers-on, and almost the entire Praetorian Guard to conduct a census-taking tour of Gaul and an inspection of the German borders. It was not an unobtrusive march, and the Chatti took due note of it, especially when the emperor ordered the auxiliary units of the Rhenus augmented by forcible conscription from among the tribesmen of the Usipi on the eastern side of the river. By the time Domitian had made his leisurely way through Gaul to Augusta Treverorum and thence to Moguntiacum on the Rhenus, he might as well, as Flavius said, have been carrying a banner that read "Come out and fight."

The Usipi's treaty with Rome stipulated recruiting privileges among the tribesmen, but not involuntary conscription. The Usipi weren't strong enough to protest the change in terms, but Marbod of the Chatti sent a furious message to Sulpicius Clarus at Colonia. When, acting on a message from Domitian at Moguntiacum, Clarus responded with an invitation to come to Colonia and talk about it, Marbod clattered across the Rhenus bridge with two hundred warriors for a guard and another fifty who, he said blandly, belonged to his friend and ally the chieftain of the Semnones. The chieftain himself, representing an alliance among the peoples of the farther Free Lands, would come to Colonia when Rome agreed to negotiate with him as well. The Semnones were an added complication. Clarus agreed to include their chieftain, and sent a hasty courier message to the emperor.

Correus raised his eyebrows and did some thinking, and Ranvig, in the chieftain's hall three hundred miles away, sat and glared at Marbod's messenger until the man began to fidget.

His name was Hadden, a red-faced, big-boned man, with a gold torque around his neck and an iron ring above it. Hadden would have fought against Ranvig in a raid with no complaints, but when the chieftain merely sat and looked at him with those oddly set eyes, it made him nervous.

"I left men with Marbod because he asked it, as a sign of faith," Ranvig said after he had looked at Hadden for a while. "He did *not* ask if he might take them to the Romans and say, 'Look you, Ranvig of the Semnones wants to make a war!'"

Hadden grasped for the upper hand. He shrugged. "Ranvig of the Semnones talked of war and alliance to Marbod. Is it that he does not mean it when it comes to making good on his words?"

The men around Ranvig bristled, and a woman in a blue

dress spoke from the fireside. "Semnone men are for the Semnone lord to order, not for Marbod."

"And who is the woman who speaks for the Semnones' lord?" He made it insulting, but neither the woman nor Ranvig seemed to find him of much matter. They sat and looked at him thoughtfully again from both sides.

"I am Fiorgyn Arngunns-daughter, wife to Nyall Sigmundson, who fought the Romans while the Chatti sat by their fires and thought great thoughts, no doubt."

Hadden looked back and forth between them. They stared at him unblinking as owls, and Ranvig's council lords began to do the same while Marbod's messenger silently cursed his chieftain. Marbod had forced the issue because he thought Ranvig might leave him to fight the Romans alone, and then he had sent Hadden to tell Ranvig that.

Now the hall was very full of Ranvig's men, the younger ones who were the chieftain's Companions, and the older lords who had come from their holdings for the spring council. Each had four or five of his warriors with him, and there were several women besides: a red-haired woman with a swan's wing of gray who was Steinvar's second wife and Nyall Sigmundson's mother; a younger woman, with rose-gold hair and round blue eyes and a baby in a fur blanket, who was the chieftain's wife; and Fiorgyn Arngunns-daughter, who was Nyall Sigmundson's and whose voice might count for more than even the new chieftain's woman. Hadden sorted them out carefully. The women of the Kindred, the families from whom a tribe's chieftains were chosen, were listened to respectfully, and a chieftain's wife or mother had a place at the council. They could be more dangerous than men.

"Now the Chatti are standing alone to deal with Rome and Rome's new Caesar," Hadden said. "And the new Caesar has come with an army of his own to add to the army of the Lands-across-the-River. As Ranvig of the Semnones said he might," he added. "Now will the Semnones stand too, to push him back?" The fire in the hearth was beginning to smoke, and he coughed and stamped his foot in the new rushes on the floor. It had begun to rain, and water dripped loudly from the eaves outside.

Ranvig spoke to the thrall who sat crouched at his feet, and the slave went off through the leather flap of a door at the far end of the hall. Ranvig let his eyes run along the shields and spears that were racked along the white-plastered walls under the withy shutters that covered the high windows, waiting until the thrall came back with three more thralls carrying heavy pitchers that dripped with beer foam. They passed the beer among the council lords on their benches. Someone handed Hadden a beer horn, while the first thrall knelt down to fiddle with the fire.

"I said that the Caesar before this one might come looking at the Rhenus again," Ranvig said when all this fuss was ended. "But also that it might be made troublesome enough for him to decide not to, with Theophanes or another like him to keep the patrols busy. This is another new Caesar, and I think he is different from the last. He wants to fight someone and prove himself, like a boy at his spear-taking. If Marbod is wise, he will change his tactics with this one."

"The Chatti don't dance for the Romans!" Hadden snapped. "Already the Romans have taken men from the Usipi for their Eagle armies, against their treaty."

"And the Semnones do not dance for the Chatti! If the Chatti know only one way to fight, then let them. We will come to this council that Marbod makes with the Romans for his amusement, but let Marbod be remembering that he commands his own tribe, not mine!"

"Then let Ranvig command his, before they take him for a woman and choose another chieftain!" Hadden lost his temper, between being goaded by Ranvig and being sent to play go-between by Marbod, which was not a job for a man, anyway. He threw his beer horn to a thrall and stalked out, bumping into a priest in a white robe in the doorway. The priest gave him a black look, and Hadden made the Sign of Horns, just in case, and flung himself onto the horse he had left tethered in Ranvig's courtyard. The three warriors who had ridden with him came running from the guest hall and reined their ponies in behind. They thudded out through the courtyard gates onto the wet track that led through the village of thatched huts below the hold.

Inside, the council exploded into fifty voices, each one trying to shout his arguments above the others. When the shouting reached the point at which no one could be heard, Ranvig nodded at Barden the priest, and he stamped his staff on the floor until they stopped and listened to him.

Barden was young for a priest, his hair and beard still a light brown clay color, but a priest was never someone to argue with. He walked too close to the gods.

"Very well. The chieftain will speak his thoughts to the council, and then the council may speak theirs," Barden said. "This is no time to shout like hound puppies over a bone."

Ranvig leaned back in his chair, his pale braids hanging over his shoulders, and watched while the council settled themselves into silence. They were dressed in their best, with gold torques, arm rings, and shirts of good wool bought with the money from Theophanes's trade, but it was not the show it would once have been. There had been too little left after the last war with Rome, and most of the money had gone to weapons, cattle, and seed for replanting. There were too many missing faces and not enough young ones yet grown up to take their places. Every man of the Semnones from gray warriors like old Hauk, sitting wrapped in a wolfskin to ward off the chill of age more than the spring rain, down to boys of fourteen fresh from their spear-taking, had gone with Nyall Sigmundson to fight that war, and pitifully few of them had come back. That had been eight years ago, and now the strongest part of their fighting force was boys in their teens. There were a few of them on the council who had inherited their votes along with their fathers' holds, and they watched Ranvig with the eager eyes of children. Their fathers and older brothers had gone to fight the Roman Eagle armies and had died, and now they were grown old enough to take a fine red revenge for that. The older warriors, tall, broad men, fighting-bred, had a different look—darker, men with an old shame to erase. The Romans had beaten them, and they had limped away leaving their dead behind them. Now was the time to make up for that.

Ranvig spoke carefully. There was wounded pride to bypass here, and that was more dangerous than plain hatred. It touched on honor.

"Marbod wouldn't make peace at a treaty table with his own grandmother," Ranvig said. "He won't do it with the Romans. So now Marbod is going to learn a thing that we already know, and the knowledge has been dearly bought: No one can beat the Romans in a war if the Romans decide to put enough men into the fighting of it. There are Eagle armies in Gaul and Spain and the southern seas and all along the Danuvius. If Rome brings enough of them here, Rome will win. Nyall Sigmundson gave himself to the Romans so that Rome should *not* do that."

"Nyall Sigmundson kept his honor thereby," Hauk growled. "I am old, and I want to go to Valhalla. I am thinking that the Valkyrie will laugh and close the gates if I come with a Roman thrall collar."

Barden thumped his staff. "Your turn will come, Hauk. Be quiet. You are too old for me to send out in the rain."

There was a laugh and a spate of mutterings. When Barden scowled at them, they fell quiet again.

"We have kept Rome from looking into the Free Lands for eight years, one way and another," Ranvig said. "The old Caesar was afraid to bring enough Eagle soldiers to the river forts to take the Free Lands, for fear his own generals might turn them on him. The Romans are not above fighting each other if the chance comes. The last Caesar might have thought differently, so we began to keep him busy along the seacoast. Now there is yet another Caesar, and the seacoast is quiet, and *this* Caesar wants a name to outshine the other two."

"Now it is time to fight!" a man yelled, and the others' voices swelled behind him. "It is shame if we don't!"

"We are the Free People!"

"Nyall Sigmundson would have fought!"

"Be *quiet!*" Ranvig's voice cut through the clamor before Barden could thump his staff. "It is the privilege of the council to argue," he said sarcastically. "Let the council wait until it knows what it is arguing about. Did I say we would not fight?"

They looked at him suspiciously. "Then what is this talk of treaty tables?"

"That is good enough for the Chatti!" Arni yelled. "We are Semnones!"

"Be quiet, Arni," Barden said. "*You* I will make leave."

"No Chatti has ever sat at a treaty table longer than it takes for him to lose his temper," Ranvig said. "They will be fighting soon enough. But we will not. Not at Marbod's beckoning, and not at Rome's. We will fight when it will serve a purpose, and not only trade a life from this tribe for every Roman dead. That is the knowledge Nyall Sigmundson has bought us, and while I am chieftain, you will keep your faith with him."

They muttered warily. Keeping faith meant fighting, and if death was the end of it, it was a warrior's death, and there was a place in Valhalla for the warrior. Keeping faith by waiting was new to them, and it sounded like a Roman thing to do. But they were so few—the death of any could mean the death of the tribe, and that was a different thing.

Fiorgyn sat by the fire watching them puzzle it out, and then she stood up. She was still beautiful, with eyes the color of the sky with the sun out and pale braids that hung past her waist, but beauty counted for very little in a council meeting. She was also Nyall Sigmundson's wife, and that counted for very much. "My vote is for the chieftain."

Only Fiorgyn had called him "the chieftain" from the start, Ranvig thought. To the rest he had been "the new chieftain" for nearly a year. It was Fiorgyn who had proposed him at the council, or the tribe would never have accepted a man who was not born to them. She was kin to Ranvig, but he thought that she had done it for Nyall's sake, so that his sacrifice shouldn't be whistled down the wind by a chieftain who couldn't bring the tribe back from the brink they had sat on. Her face looked cold now, as if it were sheeted with the rain.

The woman with the red hair, Morgian, Nyall's mother, stood also. "I vote with the chieftain."

The gold-haired girl, Signy, the chieftain's wife, said nothing. Her agreement was expected, and she was uncomfortably aware that the other two women counted for more than she did. Even Ranvig seemed uninterested in her voice. She was his second wife. His first had died of a sickness, and Signy's father and brothers had died in the war, and so he had married Signy when she was old enough. She was never sure why, except that he wanted the men, such as were single, to marry— there were always too many women after a war—and it was easier to make them if he did likewise.

She pulled the fur around the baby and went out, leaving them arguing behind her. The council would do what Ranvig wanted them to—they always did. Ranvig was smarter than they were, Signy thought, in the quick, uncomfortable way that priests were smart. The rain had stopped, and she walked through the courtyard, picking the fur hem of her gown up above the mud, and sat on the broad stone lip of the well. One of her women came hurrying after her and took the baby in a shocked sort of way, although it wasn't raining. She had never had a baby before, and no one seemed to think she knew what to do with it. She curled her feet up under her on the lip of the well and looked out through the sodden hold. It was bigger and grander than her father's holding, with timbered houses heavily thatched and a green patch of garden in the middle where Barden grew his healing herbs. The streets were packed dirt, slick with mud now, and gray smoke rose above the roofs with the sharp smell of wet wood. A hound galloped by, exuberant, shaking dirty water from his coat and trailing a chewed rope from his collar. A small girl ran frantically behind him. She had wet paw prints on her dress, and her face was tear streaked. Signy got down and caught the dog as the child trotted up.

"Here. Hang onto him now." The hound fanned his tail in the mud and lolled his tongue out in a friendly way.

"I will. Th-thank you, my lady." The girl sniffled and rubbed a dirty hand across her face, smearing it further. "He will chase the other dogs, and I locked him in because there are so many here today, but he chewed his rope."

"I see. Well, take him back now before your mother finds you gone."

"Yes, my lady." The girl gave the chieftain's wife a shy smile and tugged the dog along with her.

The dog was very nearly the taller of the two, Signy thought, watching the child put an arm around the beast's shaggy neck. Signy had had a dog like that, a big brown and white hound with a flying ear, that had slept in her bed at night. He had died of old age the summer she was fourteen, just before the chieftain had sent for her. Now she was a married woman and had a baby and had to keep her hair in braids and go to council meetings where no one noticed her.

Past the wooden palisade of the chieftain's hold, past the village and the fields beyond it, the forest rose up, dark and inviting, and she could see a herd boy driving the pigs and cattle into it to forage. To the south and west it stretched away unendingly, a place with wet shadows and silent trackways through its depth. And beyond it, what? The Roman forts on the great river and the strange holds that they built, which Ranvig said were not holds at all but something entirely different, made of stone with an army kept inside, all dressed alike; or cities of stone and marble where great merchants lived and grew fat and didn't fight at all, with the Eagle soldiers to protect them. *I would like to see that*, she thought. Inside, the sound of the council meeting had risen to its usual roar and then flattened into silence, which meant that Ranvig had told them what they were going to do, and Barden had said that the sacred white horses said the same (since the sacred horses spoke only to Barden, it was hard to argue), and now they would do it. Maybe Ranvig would take her with him when he went to make a council with the Romans. It would be something to go through that forest and come out to see whatever was on the other side.

The new emperor came to Colonia shortly after Marbod, with his Praetorians behind him, resplendent in scarlet plumes to overawe the natives. The guardsmen brawled in whorehouses and ran up bills in the taverns and generally made a nuisance of themselves until Governor Clarus protested to the emperor and Flavius was sent to smooth things over. The emperor installed himself in the best wing of the governor's palace, hastily made over for him, and settled in to begin negotiations with the Germans. A messenger arrived to say that the Semnones' delegation was on its way, and the city began to fill up with people: merchants and traveling stage troupes, priests and seeresses and simple onlookers from all the towns of Upper and Lower Germany. Everyone who had any business with Domitian or any stake in the fate of the Rhenus frontier had a spy or a petitioner in Colonia that spring. It was a jumpy, exciting place to be.

The army staged cavalry sports in the emperor's honor in the arena below the north wall, and the whole town turned out to watch. The cavalry sports were as good a show as any Circus Maximus race and gaudier than an emperor's triumph. For them, the cavalry put away its regular armor and brought out the special sports armor, lovingly polished, adorning horse and rider both: silvered helmets cast in the shapes of human faces with golden hair, red-leather bridles with gilded eyeguards, gold and silver greaves and golden scale, and brilliant shields painted with famous battles. Each team carried Scythian standards with long snake's tails and wooden pilums brightly wrapped with the team colors.

The ostensible object of the games was to score a hit with the bright wooden spears on the opposing team, but the true object was just the glory of the games, the perfect precision of the charge, the interweaving columns that went at full gallop down the field, snake's tails flying, the rainbow spectacle that they made.

Almost as gaudy was the cavalcade that rode with the chieftain of the Semnones when they clattered across the bridge from the east, and the people of Colonia turned out to watch them with the same happy interest. The Germans wore little armor (indeed they often fought bare chested as a point of pride), but their horses were bright with green and scarlet saddlecloths, and their riders with gold jewelry and cloaks of the thick fur that northern winters bred.

Three spearmen swept across the bridge first, past the first Roman pickets at the eastern side. They were tall, fair-skinned men, heavy boned, bearded, with their fair hair pinned up on their heads. Behind them rode the chieftain in a gray tunic sewn with amber beads, trousers that were tucked into wolfskin boots, and a gray wolfskin cloak fastened with a gold-and-amber pin. Behind him on a white horse was a brown-haired man with a flat collar of beaten gold, the pale robes of a priest tucked up around him in the saddle, and brown boots and breeches underneath. Behind and to either side of the priest were women, riding like demons as the men were, their braided hair flying out behind them, their skirts tucked up, their bare legs clinging to the saddle leathers. Then next behind them were the chieftain's warriors. There were only a hundred of them, but they rode with the fierce grace of centaurs, with a white horsetail standard flying in their midst. A half-dozen hounds loped among the horses. The drumming of hooves echoed in the timbers of the bridge and shook the ground along the riverbank.

Correus stood with his family among the crowd that had gathered by the bridge to watch the Germans come in. His eyes widened as they neared and the chieftain's oddly crooked face swept into focus.

It was not for the emperor of Rome to stand and watch a barbarian chief ride in, but Flavius was there to see the show, standing at Correus's other side, and he took interested note of his brother's expression. The Germans drew rein at the triple arch of the river gate, and the governor and his staff stepped forward with much official grandeur to usher them through in the name of Rome.

"What are you looking at?" Flavius said in Correus's ear.

"The chieftain," Correus said. "The successor to Nyall Sigmundson." His voice had a disgusted tone. "The man I shared a six-foot cubicle with for a whole winter."

"*Him?* The pirates' other prisoner?" Flavius whistled. "Prisoner, my ass!"

Correus nodded gloomily. "To give myself credit, I did think that he might be Chatti, one of Marbod's warriors, if the Chatti were playing smuggler. The more fool I. I even heard him sing a song that Forst knows."

"I don't imagine that the Semnones are the sole tribe that knows Forst's song," Flavius said.

Correus still looked disgusted. "He even let something slip about a man he had been close to being maimed, and I didn't catch on. Worse, now I've got to tell him about Nyall." He glared at Ranvig. "When Marbod sprang it on the governor about a Semnone alliance, he did cross my mind again, but the rest just never occurred to me."

Flavius shrugged. "What good would it have done if it had?"

"Not much, I suppose. But I lied my head off to him and got his allies crucified. I rather liked the man. Now he's decided to stick his head in front of a catapult, and he won't be in much of a mood to take *my* advice."

"Germans don't take anyone's advice," Flavius said with conviction.

"Neither do Romans," Ygerna said shortly, and Flavius grinned at her because that was as close as she would come to being rude about the emperor in his presence. She still hadn't forgiven either Titus or Domitian for refusing to condemn Vettius after Correus had risked his neck to find out what was swallowing up Roman shipping. Ygerna was not a woman to

Flavius's taste, but he had a hefty respect for his brother's wife; she had stood up to their family without going mad. And there was a certain weird kinship in the fact that he had been the first Roman she had ever seen. That had been just before her uncle's allies had cut off his fingers, but that could hardly be laid at Ygerna's door. She had been nearly as scared of her uncle as he had.

Felix had been hopping up and down trying to see around a broad, bowlegged auxiliaryman who was part of the honor guard lining the gateway. Correus stooped down and put Felix on his shoulders. The baggage wagons, which had come across at a more sedate pace, were just beginning to pass by, and Felix peered at them interestedly.

"What is in there?"

"Clothes, I expect," Correus said.

"What else?"

"Jewelry," Ygerna said in the voice of one who had learned that Felix never left a question until all possible information had been extracted, "to dress up for the council. Spare pony bridles, in case they break one. Things for the priest to cast omens with; I don't know what kind of things. The chieftain's spare riding boots. Presents for the Chatti and the emperor."

"Why is he giving the emperor presents? I thought he didn't like us."

"They always give presents," Correus said.

"Why?"

"It's part of the game. The bigger the present, the higher you score."

"Like giving bigger banquets," Felix said thoughtfully.

"Precisely."

Everyone gave everyone else a present, wildly valuable and useless as gifts of state were apt to be—gold bridles and drinking cups set with uncut gems. The citizens of Colonia watched the show like theatergoers enjoying the action as long as the canvas-armored armies of Greece and Troy stayed on the stage and out of the audience. The more enterprising among them sold souvenir glass and pottery with the likeness of the emperor.

The German chieftains and their attendants were housed in Colonia's inns, and after much negotiating it was agreed that their warriors would be billeted on a farmstead three miles to the west. The farm's German owner protested loudly that he was a Roman citizen and didn't have to put up with that, and Flavius was sent to calm him down as well.

By evening a field command was beginning to look good. Flavius fled the emperor's wing of the palace and hid himself in his brother's private office. He had cajoled, sympathized, argued, and pulled rank all day long to sort out the myriad crises that had risen like bubbles in a pot.

"And the worst of it is, nothing is going to come of these talks. They're a fancy dance while both sides get ready for war. The emperor has already given orders to pull detachments out of all four of our British legions and the Twenty-first from Bonna, and ship 'em up to Moguntiacum to 'await events.' And he's called out Velius Rufus to take charge of 'em. That old buzzard eats a pilum every morning at breakfast just to keep his spirits up. And Marbod looks to me like a man with the temper of a pig."

Correus groaned. "He'll frighten our German interpreters silly, just like Nyall did. The interpreters' farms are all too close to this war. I mentioned that to the governor, and now I'm assigned to the talks as a 'German expert,' which only means I speak the language fluently enough to be rude in it. I hate interpreting."

Flavius chuckled. "Unfortunately, it's a talent of yours. Well, it'll give you a chance to look Ranvig in the eye."

"I'm not sure I want to. I'd hate to get to liking the man again. There's no way he's going to come out of this with his skin if he decides to fight Rome."

"It's a mystery to me why you wanted an army career," Flavius said seriously. "You can't spend your life weeping for the enemy, Correus."

"I've thought that one over, believe me. I wanted an army career because it's what I'm good at and because Rome does something valuable out here. This was forest and bog before we came. Wasteland. We cleared it and drained it and built on it. Now it's productive and safe. A free man can live on it without sleeping with a knife under his pillow. Civilization— the progress of man. That's our justification." He thought for a minute. "What's the emperor's, Flavius?"

"Oh, no," Flavius said. "I've argued that one with Lucius,

and I'm not going to argue it with you. He's the emperor and I'm his servant, and that is that. I'll provide what influence I can, but I won't oppose him."

"No one expects you to, although I imagine the local farmers would be grateful. It's likely to be their land that gets fought over. There was a good chance of keeping the peace out here before Domitian arrived. He provoked this war, and you know it. And if it's to buy him popularity in Rome, Flavius, I wouldn't bet on it working. I've heard nothing good about the emperor's standing at home, and a great deal that's so bad I'm afraid to repeat it." He waited for an argument from Flavius, but there wasn't one. His brother was too loyal to agree and too honest to deny it.

In Rome, Marius Vettius read the sentiment in the wind with pleasure. Domitian didn't have to be encouraged to alienate the Senate. He was doing it naturally, Vettius thought, amused, by grasping for every penny he could gain and allowing his appointees to do the same as long as the appearance of respectability was preserved—and as long as some of it came home to Domitian's treasury. Thus the Senate grew disgruntled, the emperor grew nervous, and his ear became more open to the whispers of informers.

These days, there were few men in Rome who didn't fear a midnight knock at the door. It wouldn't be long before they began to think of defending themselves. Marius Vettius had insured that that idea was put carefully into a number of ears, and he had a spy in nearly every great house in Rome. When someone took the bait, he would know about it. Already old Gentilius Paulinus, who had once been in the service of Domitian's father, Vespasian, was beginning to make rumbling noises. Vettius chuckled. Gentilius Paulinus was Lucius Paulinus's uncle. It would be pleasant to pull the nephew into the net and settle a score. There was a tidiness that appealed to Vettius about tricking his enemies into doing murder for him and then executing them for it.

The war that Domitian was stirring up in Germany was to be encouraged, Vettius decided. It was easy for an emperor to be killed on the frontier. Easier still for a new one to be made there. When the time came, Vettius would put himself in the right place, but there was no hurry. He had business to conclude in Rome, and Domitian would never leave Germany until he had his triumph. Vettius clapped his hands for a slave to bring him his accounts book. Only money would keep him in Domitian's favor in the meantime, and there was still the matter of contriving to call in that note from old Aemelius. Vettius would give himself the present pleasure of settling that much of his score with the house of Julianus.

In Colonia, the emperor made an offer of peace that no one believed in, from a dais in the Hall of Justice in the Colonia Basilica. He sat on a gold chair with his Praetorians behind him, plumed and gilded and arrogant, and presented his terms to Marbod of the Chatti. Ranvig he treated as a disinterested representative of the outlying barbarians whose territory lay beyond the proposed boundaries of Roman control. Ranvig responded in kind, but Correus said afterward that he would have eaten his horse if Ranvig believed a word of it. Domitian would go as far as he could to match his brother's triumphs.

Marbod of the Chatti listened grimly, his hand where his sword would have been if he hadn't finally, furiously, agreed to the protocol that forbade it in the emperor's presence. There were signs that Domitian was also going to demand from the Germans presenting themselves to him the sort of emperor worship that could sometimes be got away with in the East. Fortunately Flavius managed to persuade him of the unwisdom of that. Marbod would no more have been willing to prostrate himself before another chieftain than he would have to put on a dress and pick flowers.

The sun had come out, and the Basilica was overly warm with the press of bodies. Domitian leaned comfortably in his chair with a page boy to fan him, and presented his terms.

"The emperor says," the interpreter began nervously, watching Marbod's thin mouth clamp down as if he were biting something, "that he will allot to the Chatti the lands that they now hold, in the forests called the Taunus, to be held henceforth by the emperor's favor, with due taxes to be paid for their protection from the barbarians to the east and the upkeep of the roads in their district. In addition," he went on hurriedly as Marbod appeared to boil over, "there will be three cohorts due in a draft to the auxiliaries of the empire every third year and a double tribute on every fifth year for the upkeep of the frontier."

"By what right?" Marbod shouted furiously. "By what right does the chieftain of Rome *allow* the Chatti to keep the lands that are ours and ask tribute in exchange?"

"By right of the fact that the Chatti have become a danger to the peace," Domitian said, "and to the tribes that are Rome's allies. If Marbod of the Chatti will agree to the terms, then he will also be allowed to keep his chieftainship so long as there is no further interference with any other tribe in alliance with Rome, and no further fostering of piracy against Rome's commerce."

Correus was watching Ranvig. Marbod's reaction was plain to anyone, but Ranvig's crooked face was only thoughtful. He had come to the council with the young priest who had ridden with him and two of the women, and now they all sat quietly and listened to Domitian's lazy voice, the nervous stutter of the translator, and Marbod's angry answers. Correus turned his eyes to the women. They would have some importance among the Semnones or they wouldn't be here. One was middle-aged, with a beautiful lined face and with red hair going gray. Correus wondered sadly if she could be Nyall Sigmundson's mother. There was very little other red hair among the Semnones. The other woman was younger, with an ivory white face and pale blond hair, like wheat. Her only color was in her lips and in the sky-colored eyes that reflected the blue of her gown. He noticed that Flavius, seated to one side of the emperor on the dais, was looking at her, too. She wasn't Ranvig's wife; the chieftain's lady had been pointed out to him earlier, a beautiful child with rose-gold hair and a slightly sulky look, shopping with her women in the perfume market.

"Let the chieftain of Rome remember, while his towns are burning, the insult he has put on the Chatti." Marbod had stopped shouting, and his words were clipped off, short and menacing. He had not come to the council with any intention of making peace with Caesar, but Domitian's lazy ultimatum had forestalled his own. "We have seen the 'peace' that Rome has made with the Usipi and how Rome has broken it by raiding like a thief for its Eagle army. I will put your 'peace' to my council, Caesar, because that is their right, but I will tell you now that we will burn your frontier for you and put your peace down your throat before we will be whistled to Rome's heel!"

He spat on the Basilica floor and turned his back on the emperor. The Praetorians put their hands on their swords. Flavius shook his head at them. When, after a second or two, Domitian did too, they sank back into their places. Domitian was furious, almost out of control, but to let the Praetorians hack Marbod to pieces here in the Basilica would stain his reputation forever. And Marbod's two hundred men would loot the farmhouse where they were billeted, and the villages around it, in a vengeful rampage, and then Domitian would have an angry countryside at his back as well as ahead. Marbod walked out of the Basilica untouched, with his attending warriors behind him.

Ranvig sat, apparently unmoved, and watched the emperor trying to get his temper back. Domitian's teeth were clenched, and his face was red with anger. His staff shifted warily in their seats. The aide who crossed the emperor today might find a very short career ahead. Ranvig spoke in a low voice to the fair-haired woman and then to the interpreter who appeared to be scared witless and was still trying to translate Marbod's last speech in terms that wouldn't anger the emperor further. The emperor wasn't listening to the interpreter, and the interpreter wasn't listening to Ranvig. Ranvig apparently didn't feel inclined to speak personally to the emperor, although his heavily accented Latin was good enough.

Correus sighed and stood up. He walked over to the polished oak table where the Semnone delegation sat and stood for a moment to let Ranvig take notice of him. He wasn't sure whether the Semnone chieftain had recognized him among the crowd of Romans in the room, but it appeared that he had.

Ranvig smiled a slanted smile and said in Latin, "I see you reached home safely, Julianus. Or is that your name?"

"Oh, it's my name, all right. I was relieved to find that you had been . . . uh, ransomed as well, when we went back to the camp. I would have hated to have crucified you."

"Is that what you did with Theophanes's other prisoners?" Ranvig made a shocked face.

"Certainly not," Correus said. "And you were no more a prisoner than I am the great god Wuotan."

"I thought," Ranvig said, "of telling Theophanes to put you in the bog. I am not sure now why I didn't."

"Theophanes should not have taken on Rome," Correus said pointedly. "Someone would have come along to hang him up soon enough. If you wish an interpreter," he added in German, "I am to translate for you. Marbod has given our local interpreter a stomachache."

Ranvig showed only mild surprise at Correus's sudden ability to speak German. "He will give the emperor one. The Chatti are quarrelsome by nature, but their warriors obey without question. They fight like Romans." Most German war hosts were unmanageable once launched at the enemy, each man fighting for the place of honor at the fore, dangerous but undisciplined. "Marbod won't make any threats he can't carry out."

"And you?" Correus asked.

"I haven't made any," Ranvig said. "Yet."

Correus shrugged and told the frightened interpreter to sit down. He bowed to the emperor and began to translate.

Domitian presented his terms to the Semnone delegation with assurances that Semnone lands lay outside the territory that Rome wished to incorporate. Rome wanted only peace with the Semnones and old wars to be forgotten.

The Semnones wished exactly that, Ranvig agreed gravely.

But—Rome needed to be assured that the tribes outside her borders would make no threat to her frontier. And there was the matter of fostering piracy, an unfortunate break of the agreement between the Semnones and the emperor's father. It was time perhaps to renegotiate the old treaty. A stronger alliance . . .

Ranvig leaned back in his chair. It was ebony, elaborately carved and slatted in keeping with the chieftain's dignity. His long-fingered hands moved in graceful explanation: The Semnones would have to discuss that in a council of their own. The chieftain had come, it was understood, merely to advise on the Caesar's dealings with the Chatti. . . .

Unfortunately, Rome needed an answer now. Domitian was

still playing at politeness, but there was a thin edge of iron in his voice that needed no translation.

Ranvig bowed to the emperor's wishes. But there were many details to work out, and a chieftain did not possess the powers of an emperor. Perhaps in two days' time?

The room was overpoweringly hot, and everyone was lying. Correus breathed a sigh of relief when the emperor raised a ringed hand and announced that he would spend two days in sacrifice to the gods, and the chieftain of the Semnones might use them to make his council.

The Germans rose and bowed, and Correus was out of the hall almost on their heels. He planted himself in front of Ranvig in the Basilica's antechamber.

"Before the chieftain goes back to Caesar, there is something the chieftain should know about Nyall Sigmundson."

The bedchamber allotted to Signy in the Inn of the Roses had a flower garden painted on the walls and a picture of a woman and a swan in colored stones on the floor. The swan was one of the Romans' gods, Barden had told her. Signy puzzled over the picture silently while her women brushed out her hair and the murmur of voices came from the adjoining chamber. The rooms opened into each other as well as onto the colonnade that ran the length of the inn. Ranvig had come back from the great hall in the center of the city and brought a Roman with him, a tall man with brown eyes and a harsh, aquiline face like a hawk's, and gone into the other chamber without sending for her. She knew better than to go in unbidden, but he had taken Fiorgyn with him. He had taken Fiorgyn to talk with the Caesar in the great hall, too. Signy he had sent out to see the city with her women and amuse herself, but it wasn't as much fun without someone to talk to about it afterward, and the city frightened her. There was too much of it, and it was too alien. There was a fire under the building that heated the floors, and the water came from miles away in tunnels under the ground. There were holes in the street that led down to them. To Signy it was a place of subterranean horrors.

It was full of soldiers in red tunics and iron plates, and one of them had tried to put his arm around her in the market. She had screamed, and the soldier's lord, who was another soldier in even more armor and a scarlet cloak, had snapped an order and the man had backed away. No German would have put even a hand on a chieftain's wife and expected to keep the hand. There was a nervous excitement about being in the Romans' city, but it had begun to frighten her to be left alone in it. She listened to the voices beyond the door. Maybe Ranvig would come back soon, and there would be time for him to talk to her without Fiorgyn and Morgian and Barden at his heels.

"He is dead," Correus said flatly. "He died because he fought Rome."

"No," Ranvig said. "He died because Rome won."

"It will be the same thing in the end," Correus said. "Rome always wins." He was sitting in a chamber of the chieftain's rooms in the Inn of the Roses, with Ranvig and the blond woman with the sky-blue eyes. Correus wanted to scream with frustration, to take Ranvig by the shoulders and shake him until he believed—believed that Rome would win, would always win, that there would be nothing left if he tried to fight again.

Ranvig didn't ask why the prefect of the fleet had come to him privately to tell him that Nyall was dead. They had spent a winter in Theophanes's village drinking together and growing wary of each other, and an odd companionship had come of it. The prefect didn't want to see him dead on a battlefield or in a bed with his own knife in his throat. Ranvig didn't want to see the prefect that way, either. Each would put the other there if he had to.

"No one has made a war yet," Ranvig said lightly, to give Fiorgyn time. She was sitting very straight in her chair, her sky-colored eyes looking off through the painted wall into some other place. There was a tangle of bright thread from Morgian's sewing box on an ebony table, and she picked it up and began to straighten it, not looking at it.

"Rome is just as dangerous at a treaty table as with her army in the field," Correus said. "Remember that, Chieftain, when the emperor grows polite."

"I will be remembering. Can you tell me that your so polite emperor does not want my land? That he has not come here to *start* a war?"

"No," Correus said frankly. "I cannot answer for the emperor. But the Senate has some say in this. Agree to the emperor's terms, and you will only pay tribute. There will be no burning of villages and no slaves sold."

"No," Ranvig said agreeably. "Only half my young men taken for the auxiliaries. A pleasant bargain."

"I don't think it would come to that," Correus said.

"Can you promise?"

"No. But I think the emperor will leave Semnone lands as a client state and draw the frontier line when he has consolidated the rest of the Agri Decumates. He is right when he says that should have been done in the last war."

"He may be right," Ranvig said. "We were too weak then to fight anymore. But now . . . it may be he has waited too long. His father should not have been so afraid of his own armies, perhaps." Domitian's father, Vespasian, had never been willing to put enough troops along the Rhenus, remembering what a short march it was from the Rhenus to Rome. He had remembered too well that Vitellius, the man who had fought him for the throne, had gathered his army from the German legions.

But now there were troops. And Ranvig would go the way Nyall had gone if Correus couldn't convince him otherwise, even if he called in every man of the Chatti and the Semnones. Whatever the emperor thought, Correus knew there was no truth in Ranvig's pious agreements to negotiate. And he thought also that Ranvig believed the things that Correus had told him. So why? Correus looked at Ranvig, trying to understand. Ranvig was not like Nyall. There was no hard, bright flame at the core, no touch of the gods such as Nyall had had. Nyall Sigmundson had died twisted and bitter, but he went that road for his tribe, because it was his destiny. There was no god's hand on Ranvig.

"No, Prefect," Ranvig said, seemingly reading his thoughts, "there is no mark on me. It may be that I will win because of that."

"From a clearer vision?" Correus shook his head. "No. Not unless you can see Rome as it is."

Ranvig's face turned very thoughtful at that, and Correus thought he was about to speak. Apparently he changed his mind. He was silent for a moment, and when he did speak,

Correus thought that it was something different from what he had been going to say.

"My thanks to you for telling us what has happened in Rome with Nyall Sigmundson. We will mourn him. And it may be that you have given me the chieftainship, truly, now that he is dead."

"No," Fiorgyn said, coming back from wherever she had ＿. "He is only buried now, may they take him in Valhalla." Her eyes were dry as if her tears had all been shed years ago when a twisted leg had turned her husband into some other man. "My thanks also, Prefect." She put down the handful of bright thread and went out.

"That is Nyall's widow, Prefect," Ranvig said.

"I am sorry," Correus said. "I didn't know." He looked after her unhappily.

Ranvig shook his head. "It is as well. She has been a widow for eight years now. It may be that now she can be a wife again."

Correus stood up. "If you leave her anyone to marry, Chieftain."

XI

The Lamp Flame

"AND THEN THERE IS THE MATTER OF THE SEATING AND THE number of men who will come with me. It is not thinkable that the chieftain of the Semnones should come before Caesar like a village elder with a petition to read." Ranvig leaned back on the couch and swung his feet up onto it, not as a Roman would recline, leaning on one elbow, but with his head against the padded cushion at the end and his legs stretched out in front of him. He was eating a rib of broiled meat from a platter on the table, and a red hound waited expectantly for the bone, his tail thumping on the tiles.

Flavius was beginning to be aggravated. He suspected that Ranvig was setting himself to be aggravating. "The chieftain made no such demands at the first meeting," he said. He was dressed in silvered cuirass and purple sash, the emperor's messenger. The chieftain's wife was curled on the end of the couch, playing with a string of beads. Her round blue eyes and child's face watched him as if he were something come up out of the Otherworld.

"We came only to advise, at the other meeting," Ranvig said. "If it is a matter of treaties . . ." He smiled, but there was no cooperation in it. Treaties were a matter of protocol, a careful balance of rank and recognition.

Stiff-necked bastard, Flavius thought. He smiled, also. "Of course, Chieftain. We have already allowed your men to be moved back into the city, now that there is more space—a place for them to stay, you understand." Flavius's German was not as good as his brother's, but he was fluent enough to make conversation with only occasional stumbles. Ranvig seemed disinclined to bestir himself to speak Latin.

"Now that Marbod is gone to make war on you, yes, I understand," Ranvig said, chewing at the rib bone. "But it is a matter of the meeting itself, you see. Unlike the emperor, I have a council to answer to."

"The emperor answers to the Senate," Flavius said.

"Oh? Yes, the prefect has told me this also, but I do not see it." Ranvig flung the bone to the dog, who caught it in midair. He held out his hand and a thrall put a beer horn in it. "Still, *my* council will not permit that I go before your emperor as less than an equal."

"I assure you, Chieftain, it is only a matter of the space in the hall."

"Then let the emperor bring less men," Ranvig said. "I do not find it pleasant to have his guard looking down at me when I speak."

"There will be more men posted outside this inn!" a voice said angrily from the doorway. "And they will be allowed more weapons!"

Flavius turned to see Fiorgyn standing in the open door, hands on hips. "That is the second time!" She had a knife in her belt, as most of the German women did, and she looked as if she would like to use it. He could hear a girl crying in the next chamber. Fiorgyn slammed the door shut so that the iron bolt rattled. "Your Eagle soldiers will start a war before your emperor does. The first time it was the chieftain's wife, and one of your officers called the man off. This time a soldier has bothered one of my women, and there was no one to pull him away. A shopkeeper shouted that his captain was coming and so he ran away, or I would have put a knife in him. Her dress is half torn off."

"My lady, I am very sorry." Flavius stumbled through an apology. The more he looked at her, somehow the more tangled his words grew. "I will see that the man is disciplined."

"Thank you, Centurion." Her face had grown less angry as he spoke. She drew up a chair and sat, and the thrall handed her a beer horn and put another plate of food in front of her. There was a vat of beer somewhere in the next chamber, and Flavius was beginning to be afraid that its supply was unending. He was nursing a horn of his own, slowly because he hated beer and if he drank it and set it down, they would only fill it again. He was interested to note that she had got his title right since his dress uniform was much like a tribune's. Centurion covered a lot of ranks, from lowly juniors with one century in their charge and their first command, up through the primus pilus of a legion, second-in-command to the general, but they were all called centurion.

"It will spoil the talks, Centurion, if one of your men rapes one of my women."

Flavius cursed under his breath, wishing the emperor's Praetorians were in Tartarus. The emperor was reluctant to discipline them properly since their loyalty to his person was his best shield against assassination, and as a result they were unmanageable.

"My lady, I will speak to the emperor personally."

Ranvig gave him a look that had teeth in it. "If the emperor wants a treaty at all, he had best call his hounds to heel!"

"We will have to make some concessions, especially now that his precious guard have made asses of themselves."

The emperor's chief clerk sighed and studied the wax tablets littering his desk. "Very well, but he's not going to agree to meet this barbarian as an equal."

"I know," Flavius said. "But we're going to have to come

closer than this." He gestured at the tablets with their shorthand notes on protocol and seating. "And keep the damned Guard in line."

The clerk sniffed. "The barbarians should keep a better watch on their women. *I* saw them ride in, with their skirts up around their asses! I wouldn't be surprised if the woman put her maid up to it, to make trouble."

Flavius put both hands on the clerk's desk and leaned over him until the clerk scooted his chair back nervously. "That is not a possibility."

"Then what is she doing running around loose and putting her nose into politics?" the clerk said sulkily. "The Germans are supposed to be so touchy about their women."

"She is the widow of the old chieftain and has a standing probably only slightly below that of the new chieftain," Flavius said. "You don't understand about German women, so keep your tongue between your teeth." He wasn't sure why he was getting so mad, but he stood and glowered at the clerk until the man sniffed again and went back to his tablets.

"I came to convey the emperor's personal apologies to the chieftain's lady and to your maid." Flavius stood in the inn colonnade, helmet tucked under his arm, and held out a box wrapped in red silk. The emperor hadn't made any such apology, and Fiorgyn looked like she knew it.

"That is kind of you, Centurion," she said gravely. She took the box. "The chieftain and his lady and Lady Morgian have gone to the theater, but come in, and I will ask for some wine for you."

She had seen him making a face into his beer horn then, Flavius thought. He chuckled. "My brother drinks beer, but I have never been able to make myself like it, even after two tours on the Rhenus and one in Britain." He followed her into the room, and she called to one of her women. A freckled child who looked even younger than the chieftain's wife hurried across the tile.

"Go and ask the innkeeper for wine for the centurion." The girl pattered away down the colonnade. Fiorgyn unwrapped the red silk. There were four gold bracelets in it, shaped in graceful swirls, with carnelian clasps.

"One is for you," Flavius said, embarrassed. "And one for the chieftain's wife and Lady Morgian. The other is for your maid."

Fiorgyn slipped one on and smiled, and Flavius felt most of his good sense slide quietly away.

"That is very kind of you. Here, child." She gave the rest to the girl as she came back with the wine. "Take two of these and put them away carefully. The other is for you, because the emperor is sorry for the way his soldier acted."

The girl's eyes widened, and she put the bracelet on one freckled arm. "Thank you!" She took the others into the next room, carefully as if she were carrying eggs.

"You paid for those, didn't you, Centurion?"

"Yes."

There was sunlight coming through the window from the courtyard at the center of the inn, and it lit her hair to a heightened gold, and somehow her face seemed to be more brightly colored than before, startlingly blue eyes and berry-red mouth against ivory skin. The longer he looked at her, the less inclined he felt to give the emperor credit for the gift.

At first Fiorgyn had thought that he was much like his brother the fleet prefect; the resemblance was strong. But now she began to see differences. The emperor's aide had darker hair, nearly black, in tight curls that fell over his forehead. His back had the same spear-straight carriage that all the Roman soldiers had, but he was a little shorter than his brother. When he had stood, Fiorgyn had looked directly into his face. And there was something wrong with his hands. She looked closely and made a shocked sound in her throat.

"I'm sorry," Flavius said. "I'll put them out of sight if they bother you." He folded his hands in his lap so that the missing fingers didn't show.

"No," Fiorgyn said. "I'm not a fool."

Aemelia had got sick when she first saw them, he remembered, but they hadn't been healed then.

"What happened to them?" Fiorgyn asked. Her interest seemed more personal than ghoulish, and he bit back his usual short retort and looked self-conscious.

"Someone . . . cut them off. A British chieftain. I . . . uh, knew something he wanted to know." At least it hadn't been a German, he thought, and then he laughed silently at the silliness of that. "And in any case, the man who did it is dead now, and I'm not. He was an ally of King Bendigeid of the Silures, so it's all very much in the family. My brother ended up by marrying Bendigeid's niece."

"The dark-haired woman with the blond boy," Fiorgyn said. "I have seen her in the market."

Flavius nodded. "The boy is my brother's son by his first wife. She was German." *What are you trying to do?* a voice in his head said. *Use Freita to ingratiate yourself with this woman whose husband has just cut his throat because of us? It was you and Father who kept Correus from marrying her.* Now that she was dead, everyone tactfully referred to Freita as Correus's wife, but she hadn't been.

"Does your brother get married every time he gets a new post?" Fiorgyn inquired gravely.

Flavius chuckled and decided to examine his conscience later. "So far, but I think Ygerna will put an end to that trend. This is good wine. You must be high in the innkeeper's favor." He smiled at her over the cup.

"We pay in gold," Fiorgyn said, "unlike the emperor's men." There was still a bite in her voice at that, but she was finding it hard to extend her dislike to the emperor's aide who had bought her a gold bracelet for an apology because his emperor wouldn't make one. This man had served in the campaign that had crippled Nyall, but it was hard to hold onto that bitterness now. It was all such a long time ago. She had mourned Nyall with the terrible grief of youth when she had first known that he was lost to her. She felt too tired to do it again.

"How do you like Colonia?" the emperor's aide was saying. "You should have gone to the theater with the others. They are doing one of Terentius's comedies, *The Maiden of Andros.* Cheerier stuff than the tragedies they've been giving us."

"I don't know enough Latin. None of us do except Ranvig, but Signy wanted to see it. Latin is an appalling language. It makes no sense to me at all."

"Latin's a very straightforward language," Flavius said. "German's enough to make someone crazy." They looked at each other and laughed.

"Morgian decided to go with them," Fiorgyn said. "I think

she is trying not to think about what the fleet prefect told us. Nyall was the last of her children, and her grandson died in the last war."

"He was your husband," Flavius said. "I am sorry that it came to that."

"She had him longer," Fiorgyn said. "I did my mourning a long time ago. I think she finds it hard to see that. So when they all went out and Barden went to talk about healing herbs with some man he met in the market, who looks like a spider, I was glad enough to stay by myself."

Flavius put his wine cup down. "I am intruding."

"No. I don't know why I don't think so, but you are not."

Flavius picked up his cup again. He was finding it a strain to keep up the talk in his shaky German, but he didn't want to leave. *It's odd*, the back of his mind thought. *I don't like women like this. Correus does.* Flavius kept his life neatly compartmented. Fiorgyn would never stay in a compartment. He looked at her sideways and caught her sky-colored eyes watching him uncertainly. *I don't need this*, he thought desperately.

"I have a wife in Rome," he said, not quite knowing why.

"I see."

Fiorgyn's women had all gone into the next chamber, apparently thinking him no threat. She made as if to call them back.

"No. Don't."

There was something in the air, a feeling like the spark from rubbing a hand on wool on a dry day.

"I am a Semnone. We will be at war soon, I think," she said in the same tone in which Flavius had said "I have a wife."

Her face seemed to him to shimmer like a lamp flame, and her hands were perfectly still in her lap, as if she were afraid to move them.

He leaned forward in his chair, put down his wine cup, and placed his hands on her shoulders. The warmth of her skin came through the soft wool. She moved her hands then and put one on his arm, and he bent his head and kissed her, while something in the back of his mind screamed *Don't!*

Fiorgyn's lips quivered under his. Then they parted, and she turned her head a little to fit the two of them closer together, and her other hand came up and rested along the back of his neck. She never made a sound but her body leaned into his, against the silvered figures on his cuirass. Aemelia always sat still under his kisses, affectionate and obliging, but Fiorgyn was like a flame in his arms, and he knew with a horrible certainty that he was going to burn himself at it.

There was a sound from the next chamber, sharp in the taut silence, and they sat back at the same time, looking at each other desperately.

"I didn't mean to," Flavius said.

"No, Centurion. Neither did I." Her voice was low but not a whisper.

"Don't call me centurion. My name is Flavius."

She nodded silently.

He stood up. "I will go."

She nodded again, watching him.

"If you want to, I will be at the path that goes by the northwest tower, day after tomorrow, in the morning."

"That is not possible," Correus said, translating Ranvig's speech. "Hear now the, uh, alternative proposals of the chieftain." The German interpreters weren't fast enough with their Latin to suit the emperor, and Correus, to his dismay, had been appointed to the job. It was frustrating enough to watch the Semnones bring their own doom down on their heads, and he didn't much want to translate while they did it. And he didn't like to think about what the fleet was doing; although he had given his second-in-command a hefty chunk of extra authority in his absence, a unit that was short its regular commander could go to Hades on a horse in a week.

"The tribes of the Free Lands are free people. It is not possible that they should pay tribute to the emperor of Rome," Correus translated.

"Do the Semnones speak for all the tribes of the barbarian lands?" Domitian interrupted. There were several other tribes whose lands lay between the Semnones and the Rhenus, or to one side. Most of them had cooperated informally with Rome, at least off and on.

"Yes. There is agreement among us that the chieftain of the Semnones shall speak for all," Correus translated. He thought

Ranvig was lying, at least about the tribes nearest the Rhenus, but he would tell the emperor that later. He could hardly say so now, with Ranvig listening. "The tribes of the Free Lands will agree to the following terms. . . ."

Flavius listened to Correus's voice droning on, listing an interminable set of arrangements that were not quite so outrageous as to anger the emperor, but clearly unacceptable to Rome. The chieftain had unbent slightly from his previous proposal, but if Domitian hoped to make a client state of the Semnones, these negotiations could go on forever.

The emperor's clerk had finally achieved an arrangement agreeable to both sides, and Ranvig sat now in his ebony chair, widthwise across the hall from the emperor, with his councillors at the polished oak table behind him and fifty guards leaning on spears ringed on three sides of them. The spears were ceremonial weapons with collars of white heron's feathers, but their iron blades were perfectly functional and they represented the major concession on the emperor's part. To make up for the spears, Ranvig wore only a jeweled silver-hilted dagger in his belt. An equal number of the emperor's Praetorians, fully armed, stood behind Domitian, and the emperor's gilded chair was set facing Ranvig on a dais. The dais raised it only six inches from the floor, but there was at least two feet of significance in that six inches. Rome did *not* sit on level ground with a barbarian. Between the two of them Correus stood in his parade kit and all his medals, looking like a man who wished he were elsewhere.

Flavius listened with half his mind to Correus wading through a complication of water and timber rights, road taxes and guarantees of privilege, and tried not to look at Fiorgyn. She sat with Morgian and Barden at the graceful thin-legged table behind the chieftain's chair. There were carved animal heads on the bow of the table legs, fanciful faces with wild, protruding tongues and unlikely appendages sprouting behind their ears, which ended in a single splayed foot at the base of each leg. Flavius studied them with an absorbed expression when Fiorgyn looked across at him. Then helplessly he felt his eyes slide back to her face. In the bright white light reflected from the Basilica walls, she had a cold, snowy beauty again, her braided hair shining nearly silver and her eyes and lips pale at this distance. She was wearing another blue gown, with a shorter gown over it in the German fashion. All her clothes seemed to be blue. Flavius thought that she might have more vanity than she showed. Her looks were at their best in blue. *She is like me*, he thought ruefully. *She cares what she looks like. And cares that no one should think so.* He found the idea unnerving that a woman should be like himself. It let her too close to the bone. There was a thin silver torque around her neck, and she was wearing the arm ring with the carnelian clasp, although Lady Morgian, he noted, was not. He wished suddenly that he had bought silver instead. It would have suited her better.

"I must discuss that with my council," Ranvig said again, maddeningly, for what seemed like the fiftieth time. So far he had conceded one point to the emperor, on the matter of trade between the Free Lands and the empire, but it was enough to make Domitian hopeful. Soon he would have to put troops in the field against Marbod, and in the unconsolidated parts of the Agri Decumates too, if he didn't wish to have them threatening his back. If he could bring the Semnones into the Roman fold as a client state, it would be a double victory; client states had a way of becoming provinces when Rome got a foot in the door.

"Subject to an emergency, the emperor Domitian grants the chieftain the time he asks," Correus said tiredly.

The northwest tower loomed over Colonia's gray stone walls, an immense circular bastion, the top of which could be seen rising above the morning mist, if one were a bird. From below, it dwarfed the scattered huts that lay outside the walls and the wet darkness of the woods that grew nearly in its shadow. The stone was still damp with dew, and Flavius could see clearly the patterns that were set in it, beginning just above his head— rosettes, half-rosettes, triangles, and bands of lozenge-shaped stones, some given color by blocks of red sandstone and limestone. They soared away above him until the mist that still hung thick in the air obscured his vision. A hundred feet away a path ran out of the sparse jumble of huts and into the wood beyond.

The mist had nearly burned off by the time she came, and

a thin band of sunlight flowed over the top of the tower. Flavius was standing in the shadow of the wall where anyone passing was less likely to notice him and wonder why the emperor's aide was spending the morning here, twisting the fringed ends of his sash of office around his fingers. The purple sash looked as if it had been chewed. He hoped alternately that she would come and that she would have more sense than he had, and wouldn't.

She came around the tower quickly, holding her skirts up out of the dirt, and stopped suddenly when she saw him. The sun made her hair a pale aureole around her head. "I was hoping you wouldn't be here," she said.

"Oh, no." Flavius shook his head. "I said I would. I was hoping you wouldn't come."

"Now that I have, what shall we do?"

"Go for a walk." He held out his arm, and she laid hers across it gravely. The bracelet was a bright band across pale skin.

The path through the woods was cool and inviting, splotched with sunlight through the newly leaved trees and only slightly clammy. There was a furious rustling in the undergrowth and a half-grown pig looked out at them, startled, with a twist of wild blackberry hanging across its snout.

"How did the chieftain and his wife enjoy the theater?" Flavius asked, making conversation.

"Signy liked it," Fiorgyn said. "None of our poets do things that are meant to be acted out like that. The chieftain explained things as they went along. It was something for Signy to see. It is tiresome for her, with nothing to do."

"Lady Signy is very young," Flavius said.

"Yes, poor thing. Ranvig married her because there was no one to take care of her, and she is so pretty, but I don't think he really wanted another woman after his first wife died. It hasn't been easy for her."

"Or for you," Flavius said. "Why have you let them do that to you? Ranvig carries you before him like a figurehead on a ship. The great Nyall Sigmundson's wife. I'm willing to bet he uses you to keep his council in line."

"When I give advice it is listened to," Fiorgyn said, "and not just for my husband's sake. Ranvig was the best choice for chieftain. They are my people, Flavius, and my responsibility, and that is not something I will argue with you."

"No, I suppose not. I'm surprised you are willing to talk to me at all." He halted and stood looking into her face, while the forest murmured to itself around them, a sound that was birds and insects and just the noise of the trees themselves. A squirrel swayed on the end of an oak branch over their heads, squawked at them, and ran back.

"I wasn't going to come," Fiorgyn said. "I told myself until I went out the door this morning that I wasn't going to." A dry leaf, caught in a branch since the winter, fluttered down and clung in her hair. He pulled it out gently and stroked her pale head.

"If I kissed you again, would I be able to stop?" he said huskily.

"I don't know."

She didn't say not to, and he realized that Fiorgyn had no more control over this compulsion than he had. That frightened him, and he backed away a step.

"I am not sure there is even a choice to make," she said softly.

This time it was Fiorgyn who reached out for him, with a low sound in her throat, and then he was pulling her hard against him, and her arms were around him. A desire that was stronger than anything he had ever encountered shook him from head to foot while he kissed her. It was like floating on the current of a river, the direction inevitable but no longer in his control. When he stood back finally, his skin felt hot and the forest air sharp and cold against it. He didn't know how long they had stood there.

Fiorgyn drew in a long shuddering breath. He could see her breasts, achingly close, rise and fall under the loose overgown. Her hair was ruffled at the back where one of his hands had been. Suddenly, more even than he wanted to hold the body under the gown, he wanted to pull the braiding from that pale hair and see it ripple down her back.

A sound rustled in the forest, and an old German came stumping down the path, with a trio of yapping hound puppies and an older dog, wise in the ways of the hunting trail, that stopped and cuffed the puppies when they ran into the undergrowth.

They stood silently while he passed, and the mood that had nearly let him make love to her here on the ground passed with it. It was growing late, and they would be missed. He gave her his arm, and by mutual consent they turned back toward the city. But he knew with a certainty that needed no questioning that she would come to him by the tower again in the morning, and that from that point there would be no turning back.

Fiorgyn's hair lay spread on the rough, unbleached cloth of the pillow. The braiding had left crimps in it, so that it rippled like a little sea.

Outside were the sounds of voices and laughter, and then someone swearing, but neither of them looked toward the door. It was barred, and the inn was clean and respectable, but it was in the glassworkers' quarter. No one would come to seek them there, and they had shut out Rome and the Semnones both when they had barred the door.

The bed was only a straw mattress on a low platform, and Flavius, in his tunic, sat beside it on the floor with his arms around his knees and just looked at her. She wore an old gown and overgown that could have belonged to any glassblower's wife, and Flavius wore an old military tunic and a scarlet centurion's cloak, much patched, which he kept for hunting. The innkeeper had paid them no mind when Flavius had taken the room. Soldiers weren't allowed to marry, but plenty of them did anyway and brought their women with them. Or the officer could have been romancing some merchant's wife. The keeper of the Dolphin didn't care.

Flavius put out a hand, slowly, the way a man warms himself at a fire. She rolled into his arms, and he got up onto the bed with her, stroking her, trying to find his way through what suddenly seemed like innumerable layers of clothing. The Rhenus was a colder climate than Italy, even in summer, and the double gowns were of a heavier cloth than the fashionable nothings that Aemelia wore, and all the fastenings were in different places. In any case, he had never undressed his wife.

Her maids did that and left her in her night shift before he came to bed.

He found the clasp of Fiorgyn's girdle, which was made of flat bronze squares linked together and worn low on the hips, and fumbled with it until it came open, only to discover that there was another above it, around her waist. It was leather, and buckled, and he undid it, too. There were more fastenings at the sleeveless shoulders of the overgown, and he thought Fiorgyn was laughing at him.

She struggled up in the soft mattress and pulled the overgown off over her head. When her face reappeared she was grinning like a naughty child, and Flavius started to laugh, too. He pushed her back down and kissed her while he wrestled with the fastenings of the undergown. It came off finally to reveal a white shift underneath.

Flavius groaned. "Oh, no. I don't think there's anyone under there at all. It's just clothes, all the way through!"

She shook out the ripples of her hair and took his hand and put it against her breast. The shift was a fine, thin wool, as thin as silk. His hands cupped her breasts hungrily. She wriggled out of the shift, and his laughter turned to an aching longing and a sense of distance from the world that made the plain, whitewashed bedchamber a far country of their own.

She lay and looked at him while he pulled off his own tunic, the rippled hair tangled under her and one white knee drawn up. She stroked a hand across his chest as he bent over her, and he felt the calluses on the palm and fingertips. Among the Semnones, even a chieftain's lady had known her share of labor in the last eight years. But she was beautiful, with a skin like milk, and the color glowing from her eyes and lips. Her breasts were rose-tipped against the whiteness.

She gasped as he put a hand on the flat of her belly and drew it slowly downward. There was a look on his face that she hadn't seen before, and the look in the dark eyes fixed on her own was almost triumphant. They were a part of each other now, no matter what, even if this was the only time they ever had together. She wanted to laugh with joy at that, and then to weep with pity for them both. She had been wed to Nyall because he was the chieftain of the Semnones and because there had been another man who wanted her whom she *didn't* want to wed and it was the one or the other. She had come to love him and had mourned him honestly, but Nyall was not, she knew clearly, the one who could have been the other half of her soul. She had found him in the dark man who bent over her now, and to her utter horror he was a Roman.

It had been so long since a man had touched her. Flavius put his lips to her breast, and the sadness faded away, out of their private country. There would be time enough for sadness when there was no more time here. Like any warrior, he had old scars on his body, pale against the olive skin. She buried her face against his shoulder so she wouldn't see them and wonder who had been killed in getting them.

"You are mad! What is wrong with you?" Ranvig's face was honestly horrified.

"How *dare* you spy on me?" Fiorgyn's eyes snapped.

"No one spied on you. I gave Signy some silver to spend in the glassblowers' shops. She wanted one of those little bottles shaped like birds."

"And so she came running back to tell you what *I* was doing. She's a better informer than Wuotan's ravens!"

"Did you expect she wouldn't?" Ranvig said. "She saw you coming out of an inn with that Roman, dressed up in an old gown like a village wife. Did she draw the wrong conclusion?"

There were bright spots of color in Fiorgyn's face. "That is not something I will talk to you about, Ranvig."

"What is *wrong* with you?" Ranvig said again.

"Loneliness," Fiorgyn said between her teeth. "You had such great care that all the widows should marry again, Ranvig. But not me. Me you made into a shrine to Nyall Sigmundson."

"You loved him!"

"It's been eight years! I lost Nyall the day that leg was maimed. The man I got back after that battle was someone I didn't even know!"

Ranvig sat down, his anger fading into puzzlement.

Fiorgyn stood against the arching rose branch painted on the wall, her back straight and her hand on the bracelet on the other arm. "It was between him and me. It changes nothing, not for either one of us. You have no right."

"No right! You are a kinswoman to me. I have every right when you throw your honor into the mud with a Roman."

Fiorgyn took two steps across the tile and hit him, hard. He grabbed her hand and flung it away from him. She stood, eyes blazing, and glared down at him. "And I suppose you have discussed my *honor* with Signy and Morgian and Barden!"

"No, I told Signy to hold her tongue," Ranvig said. "I have no wish to make a scandal in the council."

"Then hold your own tongue!" Fiorgyn snapped. "What has my precious honor bought me so far but eight years alone?"

"You could marry now," Ranvig said. "Any man of the tribe that you wanted." His oddly slanted face had lost its anger now, as hers had grown. "I do not understand."

"It's too late," Fiorgyn said stiffly. "And I do not belong to you, Ranvig. If I want to trade my honor that you are so careful of, for a few weeks to be happy in, then that is my right!"

"It is not your right with a Roman," Ranvig said.

"Do you think I will betray my people, Ranvig?" Fiorgyn's expression was dangerous.

"No."

"Then let me alone."

"I only think that you are a fool and will be hurt."

"That much *is* my right. Let me alone, Ranvig."

The treaty council proceeded, an elaborate round of protocol and small concessions, while in the background of the forests of the Taunus, Marbod gathered in a war host. Couriers rode almost nonstop between General Velius Rufus in Moguntiacum and the emperor in Colonia with plans for a two-pronged push across the frontier. And Ranvig, baffled and in no good mood, held a secret meeting with Correus.

"Have you gone mad?" Correus unknowingly echoed the chieftain.

"I expect so."

Correus contemplated his brother with horror. "Flavius, I don't ordinarily interfere in your affairs, but this is insane. She won't leave her tribe for you, and you couldn't take her to Rome if she would."

Flavius just smiled and shook his head and said, "Yes, I know." He had been saying that ever since Correus had tracked him down in the emperor's wing of the palace and dragged him back to his own apartments to be talked to in privacy.

"I couldn't take a mistress back to Aemelia," Flavius said. "It wouldn't be fair."

"You love Aemelia," Correus said accusingly.

Flavius said, "Yes, I know."

Ygerna sat in the next room and listened to the conversation go around in a circle again. She would not have been shocked if Flavius had taken a Roman mistress, or even a slave, the way his father had. But no good was going to come of this. She picked up Eilenn, who was poking her fingers into Ygerna's paint pots on the dressing table, and combed her dark hair while she eavesdropped. Correus wouldn't mind. But Correus wasn't going to be able to talk his brother out of anything. Ygerna recognized that polite, stubborn tone. It was the same one Correus himself used when he had thought out all the objections to something and had made his mind up anyway.

"You're worrying for nothing," Flavius said. "Fiorgyn won't leave her people."

"Worrying for nothing! That worries me almost as much as if she would. Flavius, what happens when a war starts?"

"Then that will end it," Flavius said. "We are not fools."

"No?"

"Not in that respect."

"You're sticking your hand in the fire, Flavius. You're going to get it burned."

"Yes, I know."

Correus made an exasperated noise and paced the room, while Flavius rested his elbows on his knees and put his chin in his hands. He didn't blame Correus. Correus had always been the impractical one. It must be a shock to come suddenly upon that part of his nature in his brother. It had also shocked Flavius, but he felt as if he were sleepwalking, that all his well-controlled emotions and his neat compartments had stayed somewhere behind.

Correus was right about the ending of it. He could never take Fiorgyn to Rome, or even with him when he moved on to the next posting, not even if her people lost the war and she had no tribe to hold her. His father, Appius, had done that, and Flavius didn't think much of it, although for Appius it could at least be said that he was in love with neither wife nor mistress, nor were either in love with him, and so no wounded hearts had come of it. But Aemelia was different, and Appius's behavior didn't enter into it. Appius was the last generation, Fiorgyn was no slave girl to be contented with a second place, and Aemelia was no marriage of convenience.

There was everything in the world, he thought, against himself and Fiorgyn coming within a spear's length of each other, and nothing in their favor. Nothing except the fact that they couldn't stop it.

XII

Cavalry Canter

APPIUS JULIANUS RAISED HIS BLACK EYEBROWS INTERESTEDLY as he broke the purple imperial seal and read the message inside the folded sheet of heavy papyrus. An army courier stood at attention before him, trying to look incurious. Appius Julianus had been a famous man in his day, and his military reputation was still unfaded. More important, he had just got a courier message with a "priority" on it, from the emperor himself.

This was an odd retreat to retire to, the courier thought, sneaking a look around the old general's study. Plain buff walls, a black marble floor, and no furniture to speak of except the big, dark, polished desk and the shelves that covered most of the walls. The shelves were a bit more interesting. In between the scrolls and bound works were a collection of souvenirs, no doubt from the general's campaigns: weapons mostly—an odd-looking little bow, a big spear with a collar of white feathers, and a bronze knife that looked evil somehow, although it was perfectly plain except for some markings down the blade.

The general took a thin wooden tablet from a compartment in the desk and scratched on the wax surface with a stylus. He closed the leaves and held a sealing stick over the flame of a dog-headed lamp that sat on the end of the desk. When it was softened he smeared the end across the folded leaves and stamped his ring into it.

A slave tapped cautiously on the door and poked his head around it. "My lord, the senator Aemelius is wishing to see you."

"Very well, send him in." Appius handed his tablet to the courier. "I am the emperor's servant, as always," he said, but the interested expression was still on his face as the courier saluted and left. So the emperor had a need for horses . . . enough of a need to send for them personally, instead of waiting for the army to acquire them and ship them on. The rumors of a new campaign in Germany didn't lie, it appeared.

There was the soft scuff of sandals outside the door, and it opened again. "Ah, come in, my friend."

Aemelius's round blue eyes flicked nervously about the room, and his plump face was troubled. He pulled up the one visitor's chair, which sat beside Appius's desk, and hunched himself into it.

"My dear friend, you are distressed." Appius gave him a quick, questioning look and called back the slave who had escorted him. "Bring us some wine and something to eat, and then see that we're not interrupted."

"It's good of you to see me," Aemelius said with a heavy sigh.

"*Roma Dea*, man, you're a neighbor and my son's father-in-law. What's happened?"

"I'm being robbed!" Aemelius said with a flash of anger. "Robbed by a thieving snake who's a disgrace to his family name! Marius Vettius has taken me to court."

"Vettius?" Appius looked concerned. Law-court thievery was all too prevalent and difficult to stop if the judge was corrupt. "How did he get his hooks in you?"

Aemelius's dejected mood returned. "It was after the fire." The great fire of the first year of Titus's reign had consumed the Augustan Library, Pompey's Theater, and the temple of Jupiter Capitolinus, as well as a large portion of the City's housing. Rebuilding was still continuing in the wake of the destruction. "I agreed to invest in new housing—some land that was going cheap."

"With Vettius? I'd sooner put my money into ice in Egypt."

Aemelius nodded gloomily, and the slave came back with the wine, a pitcher of water to mix it with, a silver tray full of figs, and a light bread with nuts in it, the master's usual noon meal. He had a folding table under one arm. Appius motioned to him to set it up and leave.

"Of course that's hindsight," Appius said. "One always has a clearer view after one has *made* the mistake. What happened?"

"Well, the investment appeared to be going well," Aemelius said, "although now I don't think I'll see the money back; he'll find some way to bury it in the accounts. But anything I *do* make isn't due me for four months yet under the agreement, and Vettius has got hold of a note I took out elsewhere that falls due this month, and he's demanding payment on it. And the damned thing is forged, and I can't prove it!" Aemelius's hands shook as Appius handed him a wine cup. He took a swallow and seemed to be trying to get them under control. When the cup was half-empty, he set it down carefully and began to explain.

It became clear to Appius that Marius Vettius had set out to trap his victim from the start. Some time ago Aemelius had taken out a small loan from a former slave of his, now a freedman with a thriving interest in the wine trade, in order to make some improvements in the farming of his estate that would more than pay for themselves in a few years. As was often done, the freedman sold the note to raise cash for a venture of his own, and the purchaser had apparently sold it yet again, this time to Vettius, who now produced a note for twenty times the value of the original. The forgery was expert, and the only witnesses whom Aemelius could produce to testify in his behalf were the first purchaser and his own freedman. The purchaser proved to be Vettius's man and was lying. And under Roman law the testimony of a freedman in favor of his former owner was unacceptable on the grounds of probable prejudice. It was Aemelius's word against Vettius's, and Vettius had a forged signature to back him up.

"All my cash went into the building scheme," Aemelius said miserably. "It wouldn't have been enough to pay off the amount he's claiming, but it would have helped. If he gets a judgment against me, they'll sell everything I own."

And for far less than it was worth, Appius thought. If Vettius got the court on his side, some man of his would buy the land up and leave Aemelius with nothing. And then let him try to get his money back out of the building scheme. He never would.

"Well, we mustn't let it come to that," Appius said, endeavoring to sound encouraging. "I'll do everything I can, starting with talking to the courts to try to get your freedman's testimony admitted. And maybe Flavius can persuade the emperor to take a hand. Titus wouldn't have tolerated this for a minute."

"Aemelia has already written to Flavius to tell him what is happening," Aemelius said. "She and my wife are taking this hard. But I'm afraid. . . . Vettius seems to be a pet of the emperor's, and it was no secret that Flavius was after Vettius's blood before Titus died. Vettius would be glad to ruin me to settle that score. I'm afraid I don't have much faith in Domitian's putting a stop to it."

"We aren't lost yet," Appius said. "I still know a few men with a reasonable amount of influence, and a lot more who would call it a civic benefit to get Vettius convicted of fraud. Try to keep your wife from fretting, and I'll start working on it."

"I . . . I wouldn't want to involve you too deeply," Aemelius said hesitantly. "Vettius isn't a safe enemy to have."

Appius raised his eyebrows at that. "There's no such thing as a safe enemy. But this is my business, too. He'll set his sights on my land next if it's Flavius he's trying to get to. In any case, I wouldn't think much of myself if I sat back and watched him rob you. Go home and rest, and I'll send a slave in a day or two to tell you if I've made any progress."

Aemelius put his wine cup down and straightened his toga restlessly. His plump hands made little jabs at the folds. Appius came around from behind the desk and called for a slave to escort him. There would be one in the colonnade outside, making sure that no one disturbed them. "No interruptions" was an order that Appius's staff had learned to take literally.

When Aemelius had gone off down the corridor, the bounce and self-importance that generally imbued his bearing gone from his walk, Appius went back to his desk. He wondered if it were possible simply to have Vettius killed, and decided against it. More than likely, Aemelius would catch the blame. He took another tablet out of the desk and picked up the stylus again. It was nearly evening when he called in his slave.

"I want you to go to all the men on this list and tell them that I request the favor of an interview with them. I will come to them at their convenience. Except for Lucius Paulinus. He's my son-in-law, he can damned well come here. And send Forst to me as soon as you can find him."

If Domitian wanted horses in a hurry, he could have them. The local purchase officer for the cavalry wasn't going to like having horses sold out from under his nose, but he wasn't an emperor. This was a good time to keep Domitian happy.

In the City, the innumerable officials who made up the government of Rome appeared to feel the same way. It was a summer of games and festivals piled endlessly one upon the other, and there was talk of increasing the grain dole. The emperor Domitian wished the people of Rome to know that their welfare was ever closest to his heart. . . . So said the aedile who opened the games. Of all the things an emperor feared most, a City mob was high on the list, and Domitian's unpopularity was growing alarmingly.

The day that Forst went into Rome to pick up some breeding stock, Arab mares that had come by ship, there was a wild animal show in the Circus Maximus—not a mere slaughter, but a performing act with ponies that danced on their hind legs, leopards that carried saddles, and other exotic attractions. He installed Emer and a burly slave to guard her in good seats in the public section, and went off to the docks to inspect his horses.

They were unnerved from the voyage, their little ears swiveling in all directions at the confusion of the dockside. One of them snorted in surprise as a crane swung a crate over her head. She reared and came down on Forst's foot.

"Here, get off!" He leaned into her shoulder with his own, and she danced skittishly away from him. It wouldn't be much use to put them through their paces now. The horse dealer he had contracted with for them could always be found later if he had lied, Forst decided. He had brought two stablemen with him, enough to handle six mares, so he sent them back to the farm, the long way around to skirt the City traffic, and went back to the Circus to watch the dancing ponies with Emer.

"You should have stayed," she said when he appeared beside her. "There were elephants, Forst! One of them wore a toga, and two more ate breakfast at a table, and there was one that played the cymbals!"

Forst smiled at her. "No expense spared." That was what they always said on the signs that advertised the show. The emperor wasn't there, of course, but one of his officials, a sleek, fair man named Vettius, was in the imperial box, throwing coins and little wooden balls into the crowd. The balls had tickets that were redeemable for wine or gold or new clothes. Some of the senators were scrambling for them as avidly as the common people, and Vettius was amusing himself by throwing the balls between two men and watching them squabble over them.

Three tumblers with horns ran out onto the sand, flipped themselves into the air, and blew a fanfare as they landed. One of the gates by the track opened, and six little chariots came out, drawn by ponies and driven by furry brown monkeys wearing the colors of the four factions that traditionally raced in the Circus Maximus—red, white, blue, and leek green— as well as the two new ones recently added by the emperor, gold and purple. They trotted around the track with the monkeys grasping the chariot sides with their feet, tails curled up over their heads, and clinging to the reins for dear life with their hands. They wore little tunics in their team colors, and the chariots were painted to match. They were somewhat better mannered than the human drivers, being careful not to crash their chariots into each other.

Emer giggled. "Julius should see this."

When the monkeys had gone round and disappeared back into the gate under the stands, a pair of leopards came out wearing blue leather saddles and collars with reins attached. A small, solemn boy and girl sat in the saddles with a beaming dark-skinned man walking beside them. Emer thought they were probably the trainer's children. They waved proudly to the crowd, and the women in the front rows cooed and threw money to them. An older boy in a loincloth and a red jacket ran behind them and scooped the coins up in his cap.

Next was another boy in a loincloth, who wrestled with a tiger, and then the inevitable dancing ponies, and a slim girl in a red costume with glass beads sewn on it who danced on the broad back of a hippopotamus. A trainer walking ahead of it threw it cabbages.

The crowd was in a good mood, and Emer sat happily eating a box of sticky sweets and licking the honey off her fingers. There was another fanfare, this time from a military trumpet, and a gate swung open at one end as the animals disappeared back to their stalls at the other. A gold cart came out, drawn by white horses with gilded hooves and purple ribbon in their manes. It was loaded with every conceivable example of Rome's conquests: gold vessels from the temple in Jerusalem, silver bowls full of pearls from the waters of Britain, dark furs from Germany, grain from Egypt, wine in red-glazed amphorae from Gaul, bolts of bright silk, and even twenty pairs of slaves, each matched for height and coloring.

Vettius rose and beamed, and a slave beside him held up an enormous silver bowl full of more little balls, these made of gold and silver with the emperor's name stamped into them. These were the special prizes, the people's share of the booty and Domitian's proof of the breadth of his rule. The fact that the conquests were his father's was not mentioned, and the people didn't care. Vettius flung the little balls into the crowd, and they scrambled for them with a savagery that was soon appalling. Slaves in the imperial livery were throwing others all through the tiers. There was another trumpet fanfare, and while Vettius continued to toss his prizes with an aim that grew steadily more evil-minded, a garlanded box behind the imperial one began to fill up. The occupants were pointed at eagerly by the crowd, and ignored by Vettius and the aedile beside him, who was supposed to be running the show. They were a display for the crowd only, the same foreign "residents" who had sat with Nyall Sigmundson in their special box in the new amphitheater. They rated no extra courtesies from the imperial box as they sat to watch the spoils of their former territories tossed to the crowd.

Forst shifted uncomfortably in his seat. "Are you ready to go?"

Emer shook her head. "There will be animals again later." A little silver ball dropped from the air, and she shot a hand out and snatched it, laughing, while a bald man with a wrinkled chin glared at her from the seats in front of them. "Look!" She twisted the ball open eagerly and shook the little bronze ticket out into her hand.

"What do you need with a pair of fancy slaves?" Forst said sourly.

"No, look, it's a pearl necklace!" Emer sat looking at the ticket with greed. Never in her life had she owned anything like a pearl necklace. If it was long enough, she could take two of the pearls off and make pins for her hair, too. She caught Forst's expression. "And don't say I mayn't have it! I'll take Quartus and collect it myself if you won't!"

"I didn't say you couldn't have it," Forst said. "I reckon that would be too much to ask. But Quartus can fetch it without you." He glanced at the burly slave sitting next to her. Quartus belonged to Appius Julianus, and he was big enough to defend a pearl necklace. "And without me." He looked at Vettius with distaste. "I'm damned if I'll take that toad's dole with a ticket in my hand."

It was late when they came back to the farm. Forst left Emer alternately holding the pearl necklace against herself in front of a bronze mirror, and trying to get two pearls off the ends to put in her red hair. The mares were settled in a paddock of their own and seemed to be less twitchy, and a barefoot urchin who belonged to the master's household was sitting on the paddock rail waiting for him.

"Clear off," Forst said automatically. "You'll scare them."

"I won't," the boy said. "And I'm not your slave. They aren't your horses," he added as an afterthought.

"Close enough," Forst said. He raised a hand, and the boy hopped off the fence, out of reach.

"Master wants you," he said. "Maybe you're in trouble. They've been looking for you all day." He stuck his tongue out and ran.

"How many mounts have we got," Appius said almost as

Forst came through the door, "that are ready to go into the line?"

Lucius Paulinus was with him, sitting in the chair by the general's desk. He gave Forst a friendly greeting, but his face was angry.

Forst thought. Most of the horses ready for the sale ring were only broken to saddle. They would go to a cavalry training camp to be schooled with the recruits who would ride them. Horses with enough training to go straight into the field were fewer. "None," Forst said after he'd reviewed the stock on hand. "Not enough to do any good. A dozen maybe. That's not counting the three hundred head we just sold to that Spanish officer."

"Have they been delivered?" Appius asked.

"Not yet. But he's paid. Or at least I have an army treasury chit for them."

"Give it back," Appius said.

Forst whistled. "He's going to be mad."

"I imagine. But the horses are going to the Rhenus."

Forst's hands stiffened, and he spent a moment carefully relaxing them. "Is there a war there, sir?"

"I have not been informed of one," Appius said. "But the emperor has requested all the remounts we can give him, delivered to him personally, so you can draw your own conclusions, like the rest of us." He shot Forst an ironic look. "You will be in an admirable position to find out, Forst. You are going to take them to him."

"Me?"

"You." Appius's face turned serious. "You're the only person I've got to send with them. Unless you think that old Alan can make an Alps crossing at his age?" He paused. "Or that I can't trust you in Germany?"

Forst flinched, but it was a fair question. "No," he said slowly. "I'll be taking them for you. And you can trust me." Forst hoped he was right.

As he left he heard the talk start up again behind him. Lucius Paulinus was speaking loudly, in a black, angry voice.

"You can bribe the emperor with three hundred horses if you want to, Appius, but he won't put a leash on Vettius. And don't tell me he doesn't know what Vettius is doing."

"I have no intention of telling you that," Appius said grimly.

"Do you want to ask me again why I wouldn't work for him?" Lucius said.

*   *   *

My dearest Flavius,

   The most awful thing has happened since you left and poor Papa is just prostrated by it and so depressed and only mopes about the garden instead of business, and Mama has gone to bed, and I simply don't know what to do, you must talk to the emperor. Your father told Papa that he might be able to help, but I do think that you could do so much more, don't you, since you *are* on his staff?

Flavius blinked his eyes and read the first few lines of Aemelia's letter again. He held it sideways, as if it might make more sense that way, and peered at it. It was wound on a wooden pin, and it seemed to go on without end. He turned it around again and plunged on.

   If you can't, we are just going to be *ruined,* and there *is* another baby on the way, but now I don't know what to *do*! It is such a disgrace, and all because of that terrible man that you never liked, poor Papa should never have got involved with him, but of course he didn't *know*. But now he can see that Marius Vettius is the worst kind of a thief and all the judges seem to be eating out of his hand and of course all the evidence is forged and Pausanias is only a freedman.

Vettius. Flavius grasped the name and held onto it. Who Pausanias was, he had no idea. And it appeared that Aemelia was pregnant again, which always seemed to render her hysterical. He revised that thought guiltily. The last time she had lost the baby in her fourth month, so no wonder she was upset. But something besides the baby had reduced her to a state of total unintelligibility.

He read on and gradually began to sift the details from the letter. His mouth had a furious set to it by the time he had finished.

*   *   *

"My dear Julianus, I never interfere with the law." Domitian was stretched out on a couch having his back rubbed by a blond slave with a pretty face and bowed legs like a frog's. He talked to Flavius over his shoulder. He looked like he was half-asleep.

"It would appear that the law has already been interfered with, sir," Flavius said. He felt like a fool standing at attention talking to a man who was lying face down. He expected Domitian knew it.

Domitian made a clucking noise with his tongue. "Then I am sure that the courts will put things to rights. I never tolerate dishonesty, you know. But I really can't run around personally arguing lawsuits; it isn't dignified."

Flavius sighed. He really hadn't expected much more. The emperor was setting a high record for spending money, and some of it was certainly coming from Vettius. Looked at one way, Domitian was being remarkably tactful. He might have simply confiscated the disputed estate and let both claimants whistle for their money. Flavius hoped he wouldn't think of that.

"Do let me know how it all comes out, Julianus," Domitian said as he left. The slave poured a sweet oil between the emperor's shoulder blades and rubbed it in with the heels of his hands. "I do hate to see you troubled."

Forst sat on a rock that looked down into the horrifying gorge that fell sheer from the side of the road. The horses were being given their morning ration by the team of stableboys he had taken with him. It took too long and left too much time to think. The last time he had crossed the great barrier of the Alps, he had walked, with a rope around his neck, in the company of a hundred other hopeless and captive souls and a guard commanded by a soldier who spoke no German and made his wishes known with a stick.

It was all a long time ago, and it had all been buried under the neat layers of a pleasant life that were built up in Emer, the horses, and the small whitewashed house with a garden that Appius Julianus had given them. He hadn't even wanted to go back to Germany, not for years, not since he had married

Emer. Now suddenly all the layers were stripped away again, and he felt naked under them, going back to Germany with Nyall's ghost by his side and three hundred head of horses to be used to fight his own people.

Even the horses were part German, many of them, bred from a German stud that Correus had brought back from the Rhenus seven years ago. It might be no bad thing to be a horse, Forst thought, and not know the difference.

One of the stableboys shouted to him, and he picked himself up and dusted the dirt and gravel off the seat of his breeches. The ground was cold, even through his boots. He swung himself into the saddle, grateful for the horse's warmth against his legs.

The loose horses were boxed in between the riders, and they went slowly, hoping to meet no traffic in the opposite direction. One spooked horse on this road could panic the lot of them. Forst was grateful that they were all cavalry-trained. It made them more unflappable. They were weapons, Forst thought. He might as well be shipping a load of new pilums to the Rhenus forts.

That thought had been coming into his mind more often with every day on the road. And every night it had been replaced by sad, disjointed dreams in which he rode side by side again with Nyall and Kari and the rest. But the dreams always ended with a fight against the Romans, and at the end Nyall and Kari would be dead, and Forst would look down at himself and find he was wearing Roman armor.

One of the stableboys was whistling. Forst recognized the tune and gritted his teeth.

Oh, we're going to fight the heathen in the
    wilds of German-ee,
On a tall horse, a black horse, a
    horse named Victor-ee!

It was an old cavalry canter song that Alan used to sing. Alan had served in the auxiliaries when Claudius was emperor. Now they were fighting in Germany again, maybe fighting the last sad remnants of Forst's own folk. The cavalry canter tune went maddeningly, insistently through his head, and last night's dreams came up in his mind's eye in cadence with it. The

Germans had never had enough horses—only the lords could ride into battle.

Such thoughts were dubious companions for a man with nothing but a grief to keep him company. It may have been small wonder that by the time they were on the downward side of the trail, into Augusta Raurica, Forst was no longer sure to whom he was taking those horses—or himself.

XIII

The Shadow of the Hawk

THE RHENUS LOOKED PEACEFUL ENOUGH: FAT FIELDS CHECK-ered and sleeping under the August sun, and here and there the lean shape of a patrol galley slipping by along the river. Fields on the eastern bank had been taken under the plow as well, Forst saw, and much of the timber cleared. This was the Agri Decumates, the triangle of land between the upper reaches of the Rhenus and the Danuvius that the Romans had moved into ten years ago, and the lands nearest the river had become as Roman as the old colonies on the western bank. But there was a dark forest smell to the air all the same, which Forst could feel almost like a cloud blowing out of the wild lands beyond the neat fields.

They passed Argentoratum under the shadow of its gray stone walls. Forst's hands began to shake on the reins, and his horse jibbed and fidgeted under him. Argentoratum had been timber built twelve years ago, and when Forst had seen it then, it had been burning. One of the last desperate defenders in that fort had slashed a short sword into Forst's thigh so that he had fallen and his horse's hoof had come down on him just above the ear. When he woke up he had been tied to a stake in the ground, and an irritable-looking man with what Forst thought now must have been the staff of Aesculapius, the Romans' healer god, on his belt buckle, had been pouring wine into the wound. The ragtag camp of the beleaguered Romans hadn't been far from the Rhenus, but for Forst the Free Lands across the river had suddenly become as distant as Valhalla above the rainbow bridge.

Now there was Argentoratum Bridge, stretching solidly across the shining sweep of the river, broad enough to carry three hundred horses and one bad conscience. It would be so easy to turn them and cross over into the Free Lands. Forst was a warrior, or he had been one, and like most of his kind he had never thought overmuch about his honor. Honor was there, it was part of a man, like his head. He did not go against it, ever. There was not much more to it than that. But now the question had got tangled. There was his honor as a man of the Semnones, a debt to Nyall's ghost, maybe. And there was the honor that he had sworn to Appius Julianus to take his horses to the Roman emperor.

They rode past Argentoratum Bridge while Forst thought it out with very little conclusion except that there would be more bridges before Moguntiacum.

Beyond Argentoratum and the city that circled the fortress, the road grew bare of civilian traffic. A farmer in a field by the road was hurriedly cutting hay, in the manner of a man who shutters up a house before a storm, as if he knew that war was coming and wanted his hay in before it was ridden over. He watched them with nervous eyes as they passed. It was the first sign that Forst had seen of the frightened scurrying that a war casts over the villages in its path. The stableboys seemed not to notice. They had been born in Rome, where wars did not come. But Forst could feel it, the way an animal in the field feels a hawk overhead. The horses' shoes made a harsh rumble on the road like moving thunder.

But they weren't at war here, that was the odd thing. The west bank of the Rhenus was well into the Roman zone, with the river and the new forts of the Agri Decumates for a buffer. He was still puzzling over that when the farmer threw himself flat in his hay like a rabbit. A stableboy screamed a warning that ended in a choke of terror.

Forst's first thought was: *Where did they come from?* Then he saw the old grove of oaks with the thick woodland on either side that ran nearly down to the river. Oaks were sacred to the Mother. They would have left them alone when the land was cleared. The wood was no more than two acres, but it was older than the Roman-kind, thick virgin forest deep enough to have hidden the thirty men who now seemed to rise up out of the earth at his horse's feet.

They had been waiting for him. He thought furiously: *Why didn't they give us an escort at Argentoratum?* He had his sword out now, hacking desperately at the spear points rushing at him. Because he hadn't stopped at Argentoratum to *ask* for an escort. Because he had had it in his mind to take the horses over the next bridge to whoever ruled now in Nyall's place. Forst's sword knocked a spear shaft to splinters, and the man rushed in, pulling his own sword. His tunic and breeches were gray-green like the oak grove.

Forst slashed his sword into the other man's ribs, and he twisted and yelped. It was the first sound they had made, and it ended in a choke as Forst drew his sword back and stabbed with it, through the throat. The man's head flew back open-mouthed, and Forst saw with a furious recognition that the pale hair was knotted on one side of his head. But the man was young, and the face behind the beard was not one that he knew. The smell of death was in the air, fear and sweat and his own anger, but there was something wrong with this strange, silent fight. Germans went loudly into battle, shouting curses at the enemy. And they should have cut him down by now. There were more than enough to do it. He swung his sword, breaking another spear, and risked a look around.

Most of the attackers were fanning out, catching loose horses to ride. It was the horses they wanted. The stableboys were a panicked huddle at the center of the herd.

At least the question of honor had been answered for him. To forswear his word to Appius and take the horses across the river might have been something he could do. To let them be taken from him with an ambush for an excuse to hide behind was not. He kicked his heels hard into his horse's flanks and dropped the reins long enough to put two fingers in his mouth and whistle.

The horses threw up their heads in confusion. The whistle mimicked the notes of the cavalry Advance, but they were riderless. The smell of blood began to spread fear inward through the herd like a ripple. They bucked and snorted. Forst whistled again, and they panicked. They galloped back and forth along the road and into the wood and the plowed fields. A few plunged into the shallows of the river. Forst rode for the nearest of the attackers and caught him from behind as he swung himself onto a rearing horse. The horse screamed and trampled the man under him, slipping in the blood on the paved road.

Ten or twelve others had caught horses, but they were bridleless and would be hard to control. Forst managed to get one more German before there were too many of them mounted and riding for him to fight. He pulled his horse around and ran for Argentoratum.

Four of the boys were ahead of him, one of them bleeding from a gashed leg. And one was back in the road with a spear through his back. Forst had recognized him: the plump, puppy-faced boy who had whistled the cavalry canter song.

There was chaos at the gate. A troop of cavalry were coming through, and the boys were still huddled together while the cavalry commander snapped questions at them. The cavalry troopers saw Forst's hair and nearly rode him down before he shouted at them.

"And why in the name of Mithras's holy bull weren't you riding with an escort?" the cavalry commander snapped when they had sorted themselves out and the troopers and a decurion had gone off down the road after the Germans.

"No one said I'd be needing one," Forst snarled. "We rode right under your damned walls. Don't your sentries have enough sense to say 'Look out' unless someone asks them first?"

The cavalry commander slapped his riding crop into the palm of his hand. "Don't *you* have enough sense not to ride through a war zone dangling a whole great herd of horseflesh out for bait?"

"And no one was mentioning it was a war zone," Forst said. "You Romans have been squatting like toads on this bank of the Rhenus for years."

"And who in Hades's name are *you*?" The cavalry commander said. "And if it comes to that, where'd you get the horses?"

Forst shoved his pass under the man's nose, and they stood and glared at each other. "Well, the emperor's going to be pissed," the cavalry man said finally, when he had read it. "We need those horses."

"Oh, I can get the horses back," Forst said. "If your troopers haven't scattered them clear to Hel's domain."

"All my troopers'll scatter are your thieving countrymen," the cavalry commander said. "If I were you, I wouldn't wear my hair that way. This province is jumpy enough to put a pilum in you first and ask for your pass afterward."

Forst snorted. "*Pax Romana*. Three hundred head of horses in broad daylight. Are you that undermanned?"

"If you'd gone with a patrol they mightn't have tried it. That's the idea—tie up the civilian traffic till no one can move, and give the locals something to complain about. The emperor's talking peace with the Semnones in Colonia and building up an army in Moguntiacum to chase the Chatti with, and meanwhile they're jumping out of trees like trolls in this neck of the woods. The frontier scouts say it isn't Chatti tribesmen, and the chieftain of the Semnones says it isn't *his* men, perish the thought, but *someone's* been cutting bridges and setting fires and picking on the civilians and any patrols that don't keep their heads swiveling around like owls. And any time a civilian gets killed or gets his shipments stolen, someone comes crying to us for not protecting his precious ass for him."

"Then I'll be taking a patrol," Forst said, "the rest of the way. The one that's off chasing your will-o'-the-wisps will do. After I've whistled up the horses. And buried the boy." He turned to the rest of the stableboys. "Go and get him," he said gently. "The Germans will be gone now."

"Like enough in the next province," the cavalry commander said disgustedly. "Or down whatever hole they popped out of."

"Are they Chatti after all, then?" Forst asked.

The cavalry man made a noise through his nose. "What do you think?"

"I wouldn't be knowing," Forst said. The men he had seen were Semnones. He thought the cavalry commander knew it.

They buried the boy among the civilian graves that lined the road southward from Argentoratum, and Forst said a prayer for him to the Roman gods, and then to the gods of the Semnones because it had been Semnones who had killed him.

They got the horses to Moguntiacum with no further incident. As Forst had told the cavalry commander, the horses came to his whistle. All the stock from the farm did that; it was a useful measure of proof if one was stolen. They only lost sixteen, counting the ones the German raiders had ridden off with, and the cavalry commander looked suitably impressed after that.

At Moguntiacum he gave them into the charge of the horsemaster there and stood by while the emperor's general, Velius Rufus, inspected them personally. Velius Rufus was a frog-faced little man with an improbably thick shock of hair brushed down over his forehead. Rumor said it was a wig. When he was drunk, which he usually was when he wasn't fighting, he let people pull on it to prove that it wasn't. He stalked through the herd, prodding and shoving, with his optios edging nervously behind him, and came out on the other side looking pleased.

"They'll do," he said to Forst, flicking horse hair off the white and gold fringes of his harness tunic. "They're overpriced, but we'll pay it. Tell Julianus I said he's still a thief."

"Yes, sir," Forst said. He towered over the general, but Rufus didn't seem to mind. He gave a barking laugh.

"You look like you might. I hear you had to fight the wood elves for them."

"They were large for elves," Forst said.

Rufus barked again. "That's army slang, son. Means the local scavengers. Not quite accurate here, I don't expect, but we don't want to frighten the civilians. Go and pick up a chit for the horses from my office. You don't want to be carrying gold over the Alps. You can cash it in Rome if the emperor's cronies have left anything in the treasury while his back's been turned."

The horsemaster and the stableboys took the horses off to the cavalry barns to have the army brand put on them, and Forst was left standing in an empty parade field. He followed the general's retreating back past the great cenotaph of Drusus, stepson of the Deified Augustus and conqueror of Germany, through the gates of the camp proper. Moguntiacum was newly built in stone after the rebellion that had followed the civil wars, and now it was full to bursting. Domitian's army was gathering here, detachments from all the British legions and the legions of Upper Germany, and the camp was full of the noise of war. A steady *thunk-thunk-thunk* came from somewhere that must be the armorer's shed, and carts rumbled past, laden with dismantled catapults and bundles of new spears. An army courier trotted past on a sweating horse, and men laying tile were clambering over the roof of a new barracks building.

Headquarters was a monstrous stone-built Principia, with a portico and balustrade carved with German captives chained in pairs. One of Rufus's optios had hung back to wait for him, and he pointed to it proudly.

"That's a wood carving from Drusus's day, done over in stone. Moguntiacum's always been Drusus's camp. Some of the locals even pray to him, though they're not supposed to. They salvaged some of the old carvings after the fire, and the general found 'em in a storage shed and ordered 'em done new in stone and put up, for luck."

Inside the Principia Forst collected his chit from the purser's office, a cubbyhole stuck away at the far end of a vast antechamber, and wandered out again, this time unescorted. The antechamber and the portico were full of men from all the army's services and civilians come for payment for the grain and meat the army was buying. The stableboys had come back and were waiting for him in a corner of the portico. Forst handed one of them the purser's chit.

"Be careful of this on the road. It's in the master's name so no one will try to steal it from you, but just see you don't lose it."

The boy looked startled. "Aren't you going to take it?"

"No."

"Aren't you coming?"

Forst gave him a pouch. "This is the rest of the travel money. It'll get you back to Rome safely enough. I'm . . . going to stay a little. I—tell my wife I will write to her and explain." He went away quickly, through the throng of soldiers and supply wagons.

"Appius, can't you do anything for Aemelius?" Antonia's face was worried, and the lines in it showed sharply as she tugged her cushioned wicker chair forward into a pool of sun. "I'm always cold these days. Valeria Lucilla came to see me yesterday, Appius. Poor woman, she never did have much strength, but now—"

"She's a puddle," Appius said. He raised his hand as Antonia started to reprove him for this lack of feeling. "I know. I saw her. She's close to the edge, but hysterical fits aren't going to help her husband. Aemelius is facing enough trouble."

"Isn't there anyone else you can talk to?"

"My dear, I have talked to people until my throat is sore." The door opened, and a slave brought in a breakfast tray: bread and honey, eggs and olives and wine in a silver service, with roses from the garden in a blue and yellow pot that matched the room's walls. Appius picked up an egg and stared at it as if it might hatch a dragon. "Has Cook been careful with these?"

"Oh yes, sir. They're fresh today."

"Good." He bit into the egg and waited until the girl had gone. "I'm getting old, my dear. All my influence is with old comrades, and they are old, too. Senile, some of them, I think. We've all retired to potter on our farms and let the power go to younger men. Vespasian might have listened to me. Titus would have listened to Flavius. Now not even Domitian's judges will hear me out."

"That is ridiculous," Antonia said crisply. "You have a great deal of influence, Appius. But Domitian has let thieves like Marius Vettius line their purses with enough money to bribe anyone short of the Fates."

"Perhaps you're right, but the end result is the same. Influence can very rarely compete successfully with greed. I've done everything I can, and so has Lucius, who has enough money to put in a few bribes of his own, but Aemelius is still going to lose that lawsuit. The judges simply won't admit his freedman's testimony. I think Vettius probably has fear on his side as well. He's too powerful to cross."

"I wish Flavius had thought of that," Antonia said. "I'm afraid it's Flavius that he's aiming at."

"Flavius could hardly have known that Titus was going to die. And he's too smart to let Vettius get his hooks in him. But poor Aemelius—"

"What will they do?"

"There will be enough left to live on," Appius said. "Carefully. Aemelius is too proud to be anyone's client."

"To live like peasants!" Antonia said. "My son's father-in-law! It's disgraceful!"

Appius spread honey on his bread and looked thoughtful. "Are you suggesting a divorce?" Aemelius's endangered lands bordered Appius's, and the marriage had been arranged to join them.

Antonia sighed. "No. We couldn't, that would be disgraceful, too."

"You had best assure Aemelia of that," Appius said. "Or no, it would be better from Flavius. Has he written to her?"

"Yes, but all he told her was what he told you—that Domitian won't do anything. I have no patience with Domitian. He is not the man his father was. I am not sure that it is worth letting a dynasty begin, just to have a stable succession."

"You wouldn't go back to the wars?"

"Never!" Antonia shuddered. "There wasn't once that whole year that I wasn't afraid. But there must be a better way. If Domitian isn't careful, someone will take it in his own hands, and we will have wars again."

"Dear gods, I hope not," Appius said.

They were silent for a moment, then Antonia stood up and wrapped a shawl around her. "This does no good for Aemelius. I am going to go and see his wife and try to make her be practical. And then I am going to see Aemelia. Flavius's letter was very distant and odd, she said. I am not going to wait for him to remember that he'd best reassure the child that losing her inheritance isn't going to cost her her husband."

Appius looked up from his bread and honey. "If I were you, Antonia, I would let Flavius do that. Especially if his letters are odd."

Forst tightened the bags behind his saddle and laid his cloak over them. There was little enough to pack. He had sold the silver arm rings he had been wearing for enough money to buy his meals out of the common pot in the taverns along the Rhenus road. He had spent a month drifting from one to the next and fetched up finally last night in Colonia. The inn he had bought a bed at was not a place where a wise man would leave so much as a spare cloak in his absence. But the new chieftain of the Semnones was in Colonia, meeting with the new emperor of Rome, and Forst knew that his wanderings had ended here because of that. Maybe when he had seen the man who sat in

Nyall's place, he would know if he was going home again—and where home was. He would find a job at one of the pottery kilns and take time to think and make up his mind. And maybe, he thought desperately, just maybe this new chieftain would make a peace and there wouldn't *be* any war. Then Forst wouldn't have to decide between Rome and Emer or a ghost and a losing fight. He realized that he knew already that it would be a losing fight.

He got on the horse and threaded his way through the traffic in the streets toward the Basilica. Oh, aye, the innkeeper had said, they were meeting today. They met every day, and when they'd spent four hours on such fancy points as who got the bigger chair to sit in, they had another hour to work out their treaty in. Or so said his daughter, whose husband had a little wineshop across from the Basilica.

Forst was in time to see the Germans as they crossed the square, and he searched their faces with a sort of fear, but there were only two he knew: Morgian, Nyall Sigmundson's mother; and a brown-bearded man in a white robe, whom he decided after a moment's thought must be Barden. Barden, who was only a year or two older than Forst, had gone to study the healer's craft in another hold the year of his spear-taking. Now he wore a flat gold collar over his robe and carried a staff with the gold disk of the sun on the top. The other two were a pale woman in a blue gown and a thin man with a cat's walk and braided hair. He had a strange, crooked face and the heavy gold torque of a chieftain around his neck.

The Roman delegation was coming now, behind the emperor in a gold litter carried by four matched slaves. Forst bent his head and fiddled with the strings that held his bags behind the saddle. He knew the two slim figures walking beside the emperor's litter, and the sons of Appius Julianus knew him. He should have known that they would also recognize a horse bred from their father's gray German stallion. The beast had four white boots and a wide blaze like a splash of whitewash down its bay head. Correus had been there when it was foaled, Forst remembered, cursing himself as he heard his name called.

"Forst! I thought you would have been back to Rome by now. Father wrote he was shipping horses, but I thought they were for Moguntiacum." Correus put a hand on the bay's white nose and gave it a pat.

Forst straightened up in the saddle, resigned to confrontation, and saw that Flavius was ambling over, also. "They've been delivered," he said. "This is my country, or close to it. I wanted to see it again."

"Thinking of staying?" Correus said softly.

Forst didn't answer, and Flavius came up on his other side. Forst began to feel foolish, sitting there on the horse while they looked up at him and seemed to know what he had been doing.

"Father freed you," Correus said. "I can't do anything about it. But think before you try to jump back into something that may not be there anymore. Ranvig isn't Nyall."

"Is that his name?" Forst said. "He is a Black Forest lord, isn't he?" His mouth twisted. "Couldn't they have found *one* man of the Semnones to lead them?"

"I expect they took what was . . . left," Flavius said. "Nyall's widow spoke for him."

At that, Correus gave his brother a look that Forst couldn't quite read.

"I have not said I was staying," Forst said. "As you say, your father has freed me."

"Twelve years is a long time to try to find old tracks across," Flavius said. "We will win—and I don't want to fight you."

Forst picked up the reins. "Nor I you. I have no grudge against your house. But this is my land, and you are making a war in it."

"Not us. We are holding a frontier."

"It comes to the same thing."

Flavius gave up. "Let us know what you are going to do, before you do it. I would rather it wasn't me that put a spear in you."

Correus put a hand on the rein just in front of Forst's. "If you stay here, Forst, you will write to Emer and tell her why, and let her divorce you." The words had teeth in them. "If you don't, I will find you."

Forst gave him a level look and took Correus's hand off the rein. Correus and Emer had been occasional bedmates before Correus had gone to the Centuriate. "I have written to Emer to say that I am staying on a while, only to see the land again.

I will tell her otherwise if I need to. Do not you be doing it for me first."

He turned the horse's head away and put his heel to the bay's flank. Behind him he heard Correus's voice snapping at his heels: "There are some things the Fates don't permit, Forst!"

"Damned fool," Flavius said irritably, watching Forst's tall, broad back ride away.

Correus snorted. "And you," he said. "I'm not sure you have more brains than he does."

"What are you going to do about little Emer if the fool does it?" Flavius said, ignoring him. "You can't take her under *your* wing."

"I don't intend to!" Correus snapped.

"No? You've been busy enough about everyone else's welfare!"

"And you've been acting like a damned stallion!" They were squabbling because Flavius had been making love to Nyall Sigmundson's widow all summer.

They stood and glared at each other until an optio came scouting through the crowd for them. The optio saluted. "They've been looking for you."

"We're coming." Correus put a hand on his brother's shoulder in apology. "It's just that I hate to see a man stretch himself out on a cross and wait for someone to string him up. You *or* Forst."

"I know. But I honestly don't think I can do anything about it," Flavius said. "I won't have much of her, Correus. Let me take what I can."

"And what happens when you lose her?"

Flavius's face was set. "I live with it."

He asked himself the same question at the end of the day, when he found another letter from Aemelia waiting in his quarters. His life seemed to be tangling itself around his feet until the only way clear was to kick it to pieces and start over.

He slumped down on a couch to read the letter. He knew what was going to be in it before he started. Aemelius had lost his lawsuit and retired in prideful, genteel obscurity to the one house left to him. Valeria Lucilla had taken to her bed with an undefined ailment. And Aemelia, left alone in her own big house to fret, was afraid of her shadow. Vettius had become for her a sort of night goblin out of a nursery tale, a dark presence that might turn its malevolence on her next. Flavius *must* be able to make the emperor do something. Maybe if she wrote to Domitian herself? Flavius was heartless not to have done something before now. He must not love her now that she had lost her inheritance.

The illogic of this last statement was not something he felt up to explaining to her. Flavius put the letter down and flipped over on his back, staring at the pale green plaster on the ceiling. Did he love her? Yes, but Fiorgyn was his heart-mate. And now there was no way he could keep her, even if he had gone momentarily mad enough to think that he might. To leave his wife for love of another woman was something that the world, if not the wife, would not forgive. To leave her now, when the marriage had lost its financial advantage, would gain him a reputation he didn't want to live with. And it would be crueler than he had the heart to be.

"Run along now." The emperor patted the little slave on the cheek and put a sweet from the gold bowl beside him into his hand.

Domitian was collecting boys again, Flavius thought with more disgust than he generally permitted himself with regard to the emperor's affairs. That might be all right out here, but it was going to upset the conservative faction in Rome.

"Ah, Julianus," Domitian said pleasantly when the slave had trotted off. He waved a hand at the other couch and at the bowl. It was full of some sweet, repellent concoction. "Do relax."

Flavius sat on the edge of the couch and ignored the bowl.

"Do you have news for me?" Domitian looked inquiring.

"Uh, no. I'm afraid I've come to ask you again if there isn't something that can be done for my father-in-law."

"The suit went against him." Domitian didn't make it a question.

"Yes, sir. I hesitate to cast accusations on anyone, and it may well have been the middle buyer who tampered with the note, but I know my father-in-law. He is much too prudent to borrow an amount like that and squander it. And too honest to lie about it afterward."

"Well, *someone* is lying," Domitian said in pained tones.

"Yes, sir."

"Now see here, Julianus. I've told you that I must leave it for the courts to decide." He sounded aggrieved. "I simply can't interfere in matters like this, especially when I have no firsthand knowledge. I have more important matters to consider just now, you know."

"Yes, sir. It is only that justice—"

"Justice is what I have appointed judges to deal with. I would be very irritated if I found that a member of my staff was taking it upon himself." Domitian's voice had grown sharper. "I do hope I'm understood."

"Yes, sir," Flavius said stiffly. "I will see that you are not troubled again."

"Good." Domitian nodded approvingly. "I've always thought that you were a sensible fellow. I wouldn't like to be disappointed in you."

Flavius picked up a pen and stared at the papyrus sheet in front of him. He loathed writing letters, but this one had to be managed somehow. Aemelia was carrying his child again. He couldn't let her go through that thinking he didn't love her. More important, he had to make sure that she didn't do anything as unwise as she had hinted at in her own letter. Domitian's warning had been quite plain.

Flavius dipped the pen in the ink, assured his wife that he loved her, and forbade her to write to the emperor directly. Aemelia had been able to charm Titus, but Domitian was not Titus. *And you ought to be able to see that.* The pen snagged and splattered ink, and he slammed it down on the table in aggravation.

"I understand about courts," Fiorgyn said. "Ours are much the same, but it is the chieftain who makes the judgment. Sometimes a chieftain will take bribes. Not often."

Flavius chuckled. "Almost always a judge will take bribes. Your chieftains are more honest."

"No, it is only that the council that made a chieftain can

unmake him. It has been done. Your emperor rules the judges, and the only way to unmake him is to kill him."

"That has been done, too," Flavius said, "but it's dangerous to remember it." They were sitting on a bank that ran down to an old dry ditch among the trees, the ancient fortifications of one of Drusus's marching camps. There were vines growing into it now. He put an arm around her and laid his head against hers and sat looking down into the ditch. Rotten wood poked up through the vines at the bottom. "Lilies" maybe, the little sharp stakes the Romans set into dry moats. The Rhenus had been new territory then. He shouldn't have told Fiorgyn about the lawsuit, Flavius thought. She saw too many things too clearly, and he was desperately trying to keep what was between them separate from the rest. That way, there would be fewer gut-wrenching memories later. But she was no longer merely a dangerous liaison; she had become a retreat for him. And despite his intentions, a great many griefs and questions that he would have hesitated to tell Correus, and shielded entirely from Aemelia, he had laid in her lap.

A squirrel with something in its mouth wriggled through the vines and up the trunk of a beech tree.

"It will be winter soon," Fiorgyn said.

Flavius tightened his grip on her. Domitian would go to Moguntiacum soon, with Flavius behind him, no matter what the results of Ranvig's peace talks. If they *were* peace talks. Flavius, like his brother, doubted that entirely. But there was an unspoken pact with Fiorgyn not to ask her the things that she couldn't tell him. She turned her face and kissed him, a kiss with coming separation in it. The dim light of the woods was green under the canopy of the trees, and it gave her pale skin and hair an otherwordly cast. There was a German song about a chieftain's son who met an elf girl in the wood and vanished away into her world. The chieftain's son hadn't had a Roman wife and an army oath and a world of his own that didn't permit things like that, Flavius thought savagely.

He stood up and tugged her insistently to her feet. Then he caught her against him until he could feel the shape of her through the blue gown and smell her hair in his face.

"How can I give you up?"

"Flavius, don't. There is no choice for either of us. There never has been a choice."

He bit back his reply. It wasn't fair to put the burden of keeping an eye on reality entirely on her. Not when he knew the same things she knew, and knew that he could not have taken her with him or gone with her, if *she* had been the one to ask.

"I am sorry," he said into her hair. "And I am ashamed. You are behaving better than I am. I will accept what I can have, and not do that again." She was shaking in his arms. It was wrong to play at things that were not possible, pretending that they might be. He kissed her hair. "I have paid for a room."

They went by the path that led past the old ditch, out of the wood into a road that skirted a farmer's hayfield, cut to stubble now, with the hay standing in neat shocks. In the dusty sunlight her skin and hair were white and gold again, not green and silver like the elfin girl's. She wore her old gown, but she walked with her head up, as if it were her right to go to an inn with her lover, and no man's right to question it. She slipped an arm through his, and he forgot his misery in the sharp shock of the desire that the mere thought of her could stir in him.

The shadow of a hawk went by on the ground, and the rustle of something in the stubble of the hay field froze into stillness. Along the Rhenus people had frozen too, tense, silent, waiting for the war that would surely come with spring, praying for the talons to pass them by.

XIV

"...In the Interests of Justice"

"HELLO, NEPHEW. DON'T YOU KNOW THAT IF YOU STAY IN there too long, the water will leak through your skin and you'll drown?"

Lucius Paulinus opened an eye to find his uncle Gentilius

beaming genially down at him, a towel wrapped around his ample middle, and a slave with hot tongs trying to finish curling his hair as Gentilius made his rounds along the edge of the swimming bath.

Lucius, who had been floating on his back, flipped upright and paddled to stay afloat. He shook the wet hair out of his eyes. "You have more skin to let the water in than I do. It will take me longer, I should think."

He paddled to the edge of the pool, and his uncle squatted down on the marble tiles, ignoring the slave—slaves were expected to get on with it as best they could; that was what they were for. Gentilius adjusted his towel. "Came back to town, I see."

Lucius hooked his elbows over the edge, dripping on the red and green squares. "Why, yes," he said innocently. "I thought I would."

"As long as the cat's gone to Germany, the mouse can go bathing, eh?"

"I can bathe at home," Lucius said. "But it's more interesting here." The public baths in Rome were more than a place to get clean or practice one's backstroke. Appointments were kept, marriages arranged, and fortunes changed hands in the baths. A bather could buy sausage and cakes from the vendors who shouted their wares through the crowd, a rubdown in the massage rooms, and quite possibly a country estate from a down-on-his-luck acquaintance who needed to raise cash in a hurry. Beyond the swimming bath were the warm room, the steam bath, the cold plunge, and, finally, the entrance hall with the ticket taker's booth. There were beauty parlors for the women, ball courts and exercise rooms, and lead weights for the muscle builders. A hardy soul was grunting his way through a bout with these a few feet away, and a shouting and scuffle from the direction of the changing room announced that one of the pickpockets who also worked the baths was being hauled away. A pleasant fog of steam and rubbing oil hung in the air.

"That poor fool Aemelius's land comes up for sale today," Gentilius said. "I'm surprised you aren't there. He's a relative of yours."

"Only in a complicated sort of way," Lucius said. "I've done everything I can."

"I heard you were spreading silver around the law courts," his uncle said.

Lucius lost his lazy expression, and his eyes snapped open. "Oh, you did?"

"Oh, don't worry. You were wonderfully discreet. I just happened to find out that *someone* was, and Appius is well enough off but he doesn't have that kind of money, especially now that young Flavius's expectations don't include his father-in-law's land. So I assumed it was you. Your mother left you more money than is good for you."

"My mother's money came from the same inheritance that yours did," Lucius pointed out. "I suppose you mean that it would have been better if you had had it all."

"Certainly," Gentilius said. "I am older than you and have more sense. Just take your recent refusal of the emperor's favor, for instance."

"It seems to me," Lucius said, "that I heard—oh, just in the marketplace—that *you* had retired." Gentilius had served the old emperor, Vespasian, and had kept his hand in for Titus's benefit as well; Lucius was nearly sure of that.

"I have the weight of my years to lend plausibility to that," his uncle said. "My health has not been good."

Lucius gave his uncle a disapproving eye. "There is nothing wrong with your health but the weight of your stomach. You should go on a diet of bread and vegetables."

Gentilius shuddered. "I would rather be dead." He sat down on the wet tile and put his head nearer his nephew's. The slave, seeing his chance, went to reheat the curling tongs. "I expect you were right all the same," Gentilius said quietly. "The rumor that runs in the marketplace is not something I would care to give Domitian to make charges out of, and you always did have entirely too good an ear for it."

"Too good for whom?"

A chubby youth, still wet from the cold plunge, dropped a clammy towel on the tile beside them and heaved himself into the swimming bath. A mountainous wave of water shot up around him, and he surfaced spouting a fine spray. Gentilius glared at him, and he paddled off to a group of cronies who were tossing a ball at the far end of the pool. Gentilius poked the wet towel away from him with distaste. "Puppy." He considered his nephew speculatively. "The baths are not a particularly good place to talk."

Lucius waited to see what was coming. He thought his uncle hadn't found him by accident.

"You might dine with me," Gentilius said.

"I might."

"A gentleman's dinner, to discuss philosophy perhaps, and, uh, the nature of things. Don't bring Julia."

"Julia will be consoling Aemelia, I expect," Lucius said.

"Quite."

"The nature of things being what it is just now."

"Yes." Gentilius heaved himself to his feet as the slave trotted up with the reheated tongs. "Perhaps we'll discuss that. Tonight then. It will be a small party." He went off, clutching his towel, while the slave scurried behind him with the tongs.

Shortly after nightfall, Lucius stopped in the pool of light cast by the gate lamps of his uncle's house and adjusted the folds of his toga.

"I'll just be waiting for you," the man beside him said.

Lucius gave him a bland look. "That's hardly necessary, Tullius. This is my uncle's house, you know, not a robbers' den."

"I'm not so sure," Tullius said. "That old robber inside never said a straight speech in his life."

"All the same, I won't need a strong-arm man." Tullius was an exlegionary with the physique of a gorilla and the firm conviction that his employer needed protection at all times. "You may come back for me in four or five hours, but I won't have you hanging about the place like a watchdog. You know you don't get on with my uncle's staff."

"I get on all right with Cook," Tullius said hopefully. "She's not so fine haired as that fancy houseboy. I'll just wait in the kitchens and have a bite."

Lucius gave up. "All right then, but see that you stay there and behave. My uncle won't like it if he sees you lurking about." He gave him a firm look. "The conversation at dinner is going to be private."

"Got something up his sleeve, I expect," Tullius said. "You just watch yourself."

Lucius's face was suddenly serious and a good deal older

in the lamplight. "I've got an idea I already know," he said. "So stay away, or I'll be the one protecting you."

He pushed open the iron gate and crossed the narrow strip of yard to the great house, which sat inside. It turned a blank face to the street; like most Roman houses, all its windows faced inward on the courtyard around which it was built, a little world drawn in on itself to shield its master from the dirt and traffic of the City outside. An elderly majordomo with a prim face and a carefully curled fringe of hair around his ears met them at the door. He ushered Lucius in and held out his hands for the younger man's mantle. He gave Tullius a look of finicky distaste.

"Tullius will go around and wait for me in the kitchens," Paulinus said firmly. He gave Tullius a push on his way before either of them could protest. The majordomo gave Tullius a sniff of disapproval.

Uncle Gentilius's dining room was on the far side of the house, and they crossed between neat, clipped borders of box-wood in the open central court to get to it. A fountain splashed in the moonlight at the center, and a marble naiad poised on tiptoe above it. The air was warm and thick with the scent of rosemary and bay trees. The dining room also had a fountain, which murmured pleasantly as a backdrop to dinner conversation. Flowers adorned the marble busts of Gentilius's ancestors in their niches along the walls, and the table was set with the sort of cooking by which Gentilius had acquired his stomach, a girth he hadn't carried with him in his army days. But the usual array of musicians and dancers and impoverished poets invited to sing for their supper was conspicuously absent. Lucius noted that his uncle and his guests were serving themselves.

As Gentilius had said, it was a small party. Besides his host, there were only two other men reclining on the couches around the table. Lucius recognized one of them: a dark restless man named Faustus Sulla, who was a distant kinsman of the great Republican dictator and one of this year's *triumviri capitales*. He blinked with surprise when Gentilius introduced the second: Roscius Celsus, a spidery young man with pale, shortsighted eyes, whose father had been the head of the Oil and Wine Importers' Guild, and a power in almost every other trade guild in the City. He had died in the plague two years ago, and Roscius Celsus was now one of the richest young men in Rome. But he was an odd addition to Uncle Gentilius's dinner party. Lucius's expression grew wary as he took his place on a couch beside Faustus Sulla's. Roscius Celsus reclined on the third couch beside his host.

"I'm delighted to see you, Lucius," Uncle Gentilius said. "We were discussing poor Aemelius's, uh, misfortune."

Faustus Sulla looked at Paulinus and added bluntly, "The emperor could have stopped that, you know."

Lucius let his gaze wander over his uncle's company before he replied. Dinner-party conversation was generally confined to scientific questions and other people's amorous affairs, with politics an almost forbidden subject. Otherwise one was likely to discover later that one's dinner partner had the emperor's ear. Lucius could think of no reason why his uncle should lay traps for him. "Unfortunately Marius Vettius picked a time when the emperor was not in Rome," he said.

Faustus Sulla made a face. "And so found it convenient not to interfere."

"I'm afraid so. My brother-in-law—Flavius Julianus, I mean—did try. He's on Domitian's staff, you know, but I don't think he thought he was going to have much hope from the start. His wife is taking it very badly. She's Aemelius's daughter."

"We were aware of the connection," Sulla said.

I'll bet you were, Lucius thought. He contemplated a plate of lettuces before him. Beyond them were lobsters in shells, with a cracking tool and a bowl of herb butter to dip the meat in, a round cake with nut meats in it, oysters, snails, eggs, the roasted ribs of a kid, and a stew of fruit with wine, honey, and spices. Lucius picked up an egg and apparently addressed his remarks to it. "Flavius Julianus is a loyal man."

"You will note that I have not invited Flavius Julianus to dine," his uncle said.

Lucius bit into the egg. "Am I insulted?"

"Not at all," Gentilius said briskly. "Don't play the fool with me, Lucius."

"I wouldn't dream of it," Lucius murmured.

"Flavius's loyalty is to the person of the emperor," Uncle

Gentilius said. "Whatever man happens to fill his sandals at the moment. Some men feel that loyalty should have a wider scope than that. To the empire itself, you might say. The emperor should serve the empire and not the other way round. That sort of idea. What do you think?"

"I think this is dangerous water." Lucius appeared to be talking to his egg again. "You might meet a shark."

"On the contrary," Gentilius said. "We were thinking of fishing for one."

"This is ridiculous!" Faustus Sulla exploded. "You're tiptoeing around this like a lot of maidens in a barn full of spiders. We're all here because each of us has a grievance with Domitian, and you've been invited, Lucius, because we think you do, too."

"Well, that's to the point at any rate." Lucius finished his egg and looked around the table at them. Sulla was fuming darkly. Uncle Gentilius wore his usual careful, mildly amused expression and was cracking lobster claws with brisk efficiency. Roscius Celsus sat folding his napkin into careful shapes. "What's your quarrel, Sulla?"

"If you'd ever had the faintest interest in holding public office, you wouldn't have to ask!" Sulla said. "Half the men in Rome's prisons haven't done anything worse than fall foul of Domitian or one of his tame thieves like Marius Vettius! 'Somebody said that another man said that a third man spoke against the emperor.'" He pounded his fist on the wooden armrest of his couch. "Two days later they're all *three* up in front of a judge, and five minutes after that they're in *my* charge." The *triumviri capitales* inquired into crimes and had command of the prisons but no power to pass or alter sentences. "I go home at night with a conscience I don't think I can live with much longer." He slammed his fist into the armrest again.

"You'll break my couch," Gentilius said mildly. "But he's right, Lucius. You've been hiding at home, and you haven't seen it, but matters are getting worse. If something isn't done, there may be rebellion."

Lucius raised his eyebrows. "Odd, but I had the impression that that was what *you* were advocating."

Gentilius raised his hand in oratorial style before Sulla could burst out again. "Sometimes it is best to substitute a controlled event for one that might otherwise be, uh, unsupervised."

"I see," Lucius said. "Sulla would like Domitian removed in the interests of justice, and you want to do it before someone else does."

"I do not want civil war again, Lucius, let me put it that way," Gentilius said. "None of my generation does. Neither do we wish to spend our old age wondering when Domitian's eye will light on *our* estates."

"Or when someone will tell him we have been talking treason," Sulla said.

"Which they may now do with perfect truth," Lucius pointed out. He looked at Roscius Celsus, who was still fiddling unhappily with his napkin. "What is your stake in this?"

Celsus looked uncomfortable, a man in unfamiliar territory, but he put the napkin down and squinted to focus across the table on Lucius. "The merchants, all of us, will be ruined if the emperor continues to allow men like Marius Vettius a free rein. There are toughs now who work the waterfront offices and threaten us if we don't give them a percentage to go away. And half the officials in the Shipping Offices are demanding a cut, too. We made up a delegation, myself and a few others of those with the largest trade, and went to complain to Vettius. He shrugged one shoulder and ate a bowl of olives while we talked to him, and after we left, a man from his office came to demand another three percent to give us our port clearances."

"They leave the grain fleet alone," Gentilius said, "but every other ship coming in or out of harbor has been shaken down to the point that they're losing money."

"Old Cornelius Suffuscus tried to raise a stink about it, and now he's gone to prison, and we don't even know on what charges," Celsus said. "His physician says he has a bad heart, and it's not likely he'll survive his term."

"Even if someone doesn't help him along," Sulla said. "Old Suffuscus has a warehouse full of spices."

"They will confiscate it, you see," Celsus said. "It may not be long before they will do the same to the rest of us and not wait until we provoke it."

"Is there no way the merchants can fight this?"

"I am fighting," Roscius Celsus said quietly. "That is why

I am here. For the rest, no. They will either pay up, or they will try to argue and go the way Cornelius Suffuscus did."

Lucius sighed. "I had the feeling when you invited me, Uncle, that I should have stayed home."

"Then go home," Gentilius said. "And contrive to forget the conversation."

"And let the three of you fight my fight for me?" Lucius asked. "That *is* what it amounts to. I'm not immune from Domitian's informers, either. Far otherwise, I expect."

"Just so," Gentilius said.

"Now that we are agreed, perhaps we could cease to pussy-foot!" Sulla snapped.

"I never pussyfoot," Gentilius said.

"Balls. You could teach a shadow to slink."

"I take it you do have some plan in mind." Lucius looked at his uncle. "For, uh, afterward?"

"Oh, no," Gentilius said sarcastically. "We were just going to run up and stab Domitian and shout, 'For the empire!'"

"Without being rude," Lucius said, "it has been done." Faustus Sulla looked like a man who would take that approach.

"And that's just what will happen if we *don't* do it," Gentilius said. "Or it will be someone with an eye to the purple himself and a rabble in back of him to enforce it."

"It must be a man who is . . . acceptable," Celsus said. "An admirable man whom the Senate will not quarrel with and whom the merchants will trust."

"And whom the army will support," Lucius said. "If they don't support our man, they will put up one of their own." It gave him a shock to find that he had accepted the lethal idea of assassination—lethal for more people than Domitian. But his uncle was right. Someone else would eventually do it if they didn't, and the aftermath would be deadly. And the voice of justice that spoke from Sulla and Celsus was not something that Lucius could ignore. "Very well, Uncle. Who is the paragon you propose to give the purple to?"

"Grattius Benacus."

Lucius whistled. "He agreed?"

"Not exactly," Gentilius said.

"Not at all," Sulla said. "But he's the right man. He's got the Fourteenth Legion in Upper Germany just now—"

"Right under Domitian's nose," Lucius said.

"That is not a bad thing. Benacus is popular with the army, and if he's proclaimed emperor, they'll back him. He comes from a good, old family entirely acceptable to the Senate. And he once held the post that Marius Vettius is making free with now."

"The trade guilds remember him kindly." Roscius Celsus's face showed a half smile that took some of the nervous look away. "Especially in contrast."

"It's not going to work," Lucius said flatly. "Grattius Benacus is no sword-made emperor. He won't do it."

"That's why he's the right man," Gentilius said. "He doesn't want the power, so he won't abuse it if he gets it. But he *will* take it if it's handed to him. If the alternative is chaos, Benacus will do what will keep the empire stable."

"How do you know?" Lucius looked suspicious.

"Because he's much like Vespasian," Gentilius said. "And it worked on Vespasian."

"Vespasian told me once that he had been pushed to the purple," Lucius said. "Do I detect your hand shoving, Uncle?"

"Mine and Appius Julianus's, and one or two others."

Lucius saw Faustus Sulla and Roscius Celsus listening with interest. That hadn't been common knowledge. "Is Appius in on this?"

"No," Gentilius said. "Appius would stop short of regicide, whatever his views on the situation otherwise. And, in any case, it would be unwise, knowing Flavius's stand. I do not wish to set father plotting against son."

"But you're perfectly willing to set *me* plotting against my brother-in-law," Lucius said. "Damn it, Uncle, this could get Flavius killed, too. He'll fight for Domitian."

"It is not our intention that it should come to fighting." Gentilius contemplated his ancestors in their niches along the walls. "And certainly not that any move should be made when Flavius is at hand."

"'Not your intention.'" Lucius looked unimpressed, and he pointed a finger at his uncle across the table. "That isn't good enough, Uncle. I want an assurance that Flavius will be kept absolutely out of it."

"Assurances like that can be difficult to make good on," Gentilius said. "You're asking a lot, Lucius."

"So are you." Lucius's plain face looked weary just now in this circle of treason, and the lamplight showed up lines around his mouth and eyes. "You're asking me to risk my hide calling in favors from old connections for you, and I assume you want money. You won't buy the Praetorian Guard without money, before *or* after."

Roscius Celsus nodded. Money was the major contribution from his kind as well.

"Very well, then. Give me an assurance about Flavius, or you don't get any of it."

"And if we can't?" Gentilius asked.

"Then I'll warn Flavius myself to stay clear. And to hell with your plots if he decides to warn Domitian."

"That would be . . . unwise." There was a fair amount of menace in his uncle's voice, but Lucius looked back at him steadily.

"Then you'll have to kill me. If you think you can."

His usually unassuming face had a dangerous expression that Gentilius was not such a fool as to underestimate. "You add an unnecessary complication, Lucius," he said irritably.

"Not from my point of view. I am reasonably fond of Flavius, and his sister is my wife. Swear it, Uncle, or I am leaving right now. You may try to stop me if you wish. Incidentally, Tullius is in the kitchens."

"I am not going to murder my own nephew at the dinner table in front of witnesses," Gentilius said. "Don't be an ass." He glared at Lucius. "All right, then. I will swear that Flavius Julianus stays uninvolved. I expect we can arrange for him to be elsewhere."

"Thank you. Sulla?"

"I don't want *any* innocent blood in this. That is why we are doing this. I agree."

"I, also," Roscius Celsus said. "Although I doubt that I could affect the outcome one way or the other." He smiled. "The money is my province. That and support for the new man in the City." The trade guilds had a fair amount of influence with the plebeian class through the price of their goods. Cheap wine is a powerful vote getter.

Uncle Gentilius cracked another lobster claw and reached a large hand across the table for the butter. "Then if all consciences have been salved, perhaps we could get to specifics."

It was odd how fast matters went, Lucius thought later, once they had all admitted that they were going to kill the emperor. A fast, dangerous slide down a mountain, with only one right way to land. Within three days he was involved in a network of bargains and assignations so convoluted he could not have disentangled himself had he wanted to. The largest of the possible stumbling blocks was the short, bowlegged figure of Velius Rufus, the emperor's general at Moguntiacum. Grattius Benacus's legion, the Fourteenth Gemina, was part of his army. Although no one had the nerve to approach Rufus directly, it was decided after much debate that he would likely make no trouble over Benacus's candidacy once the thing was done. Velius Rufus lacked the connections and the family lineage to make him as acceptable a candidate as Benacus, and he was outspoken enough to have a good stock of enemies in the Senate. Also he had never shown any sign of wanting more power than he had now, so likely he would let well enough alone.

The other problem of course was Grattius Benacus himself, who would never countenance a revolution in his name. Gentilius Paulinus and his cronies would have to push him into it, as apparently they had pushed Vespasian. He would accept it. They were sure of that. A man like Grattius Benacus had too much conscience to let a war start when he could make peace with his acceptance. And unlike Vespasian, he had no sons, a blessing in itself. Having pushed a man to the purple, it was very difficult to control him thereafter, and Vespasian's desire to found a dynasty had been a good idea only so long as Titus had lived.

And if Grattius Benacus was essential to the plan, so too was its timing. Domitian would have to be killed while he was in Germany, and Benacus acclaimed by his own troops and the other German legions, with the emperor's Praetorians to lend their weight to the matter before the Senate could question the succession and give time for another candidate to step in.

It all took, Lucius discovered, endless careful planning. Each step had to be mapped out and plans made to deal with each possible failure along the way. Each possibility had to be thought of, and solutions that might never be needed made certain in advance. In the end, whose hand actually would hold the knife became less important than how it would be made possible and the assurance that all would go as planned afterward.

Secrets like these are hard to keep. The more problems that arose and were dealt with, the more paths crossed in the network. Julia was still mourning Felix, hugging her own children to her in compensation, and her days were bounded by the nursery and the garden. She gave Aemelia what comfort she could, but mostly the other woman's talk washed over her unheard, and when her husband ceased to tell her what he was doing with his days, she seemed not to notice.

There were other ears pricked for rumor in the wind. And because a man who will work for a cause for money may talk about it elsewhere for more money, it was not long before the men who were attuned to the political undercurrent and rumors of the City knew that something was in the offing.

"I don't like this. It gives me an unpleasant crawling sensation on the back of my neck. There are too many hands in this." Lucius was sitting in the sunny library where he worked on his *History*, with Gentilius beside him, ostensibly come to give his opinion of his nephew's latest work.

"It is all very well for four high-minded souls to plan an assassination," Gentilius said bluntly. "To put it into action is another matter. The stock of men willing to risk their hides for the good of the empire is not particularly large. We have no choice but to deal with the people we need on their own terms."

"There are too many of them. There are people involved in this now that I don't even know."

"Consider that a blessing," Gentilius said. "That way, they don't know you."

Lucius looked dubious. "Too many men with an eye to the main chance is dangerous. All it takes is one who finds informing a better proposition."

"I doubt it," Gentilius said. "Once you've put your hand to treason, it's very difficult to get it unsticky again. Informing would shed more light than the informer would care for."

* * *

They concentrated on that thought as each new man was admitted to the plot, and in the end it was that thought that let disaster in the door, because no one remembered that there were worse things to fear than discovery—most particularly not the man who sat chewing the end of his pen in one of the innumerable shipping offices belonging to Roscius Celsus. He was only a very small cog in the wheel, a matter of delaying those ships on the grain run if a certain message came from Germany. He hedged cautiously with the man across the desk from him.

"I don't know what you've been hearing, but I think you must have it wrong."

"No, I don't, either," the man said. He had introduced himself as Tetricus Fulminatus, and he was also a small cog in another works, those of Marius Vettius's domain. "What's more, I want in on it. A man has to think about his future, and Vettius is on shaky ground. And you need me. I know better than anyone what my man's likely to be doing, and you don't want *him* getting wind of your doings."

"*If* I were doing anything, I shouldn't care to have Vettius take notice," Celsus's cargo master said. "But the same could be said of any man in trade in Rome these days. Your boss has a long arm."

"And a long thirst for money," Fulminatus said. He grinned. "*If* there was to be a . . . change in the government, I'm betting I know who else would be out of a job if the trade guilds had anything to say about it. I expect they do."

The cargo master remained silent.

"That wouldn't be so good for me, now, you see," Fulminatus went on. "Not unless I had some friends I could count on. Friends who owed me for some help, say."

"In other words, you think Vettius is going to go down if the emperor does, and you want to jump ship first." Celsus's cargo master looked disgusted.

"You bet I do. I was hoping you'd see it my way. Of course if you don't," Fulminatus added thoughtfully, "I expect I could make enough trouble while my boss is still in office that *this* office couldn't move a ship in or out of harbor for months."

He favored the cargo master with an unpleasant look, and the cargo master knew that this was no idle threat.

"Oh, they bit, all right. I'm in, and my job's to keep tabs on you." Fulminatus exhibited a cocky smile and hooked his thumbs into his tunic belt. "'Course if anything goes wrong, I'm in deep water. I'll be counting on you to take care o' that."

Marius Vettius laid his stylus down and gave his subordinate a long look. "Stand up straight. You aren't a dock thief. If anything goes wrong, I will tell the emperor that you joined the plot on my orders, to find the ringleaders. Does that satisfy you?"

"That and the farm you promised me. I've a mind to retire like a gentleman."

"Not even I am capable of turning you into that," Vettius said acidly. "But you shall have what I've promised, so long as you behave yourself."

"What I can't figure is why you're helpin' this along." Fulminatus perched himself chattily on the end of Vettius's desk. "Seems to me, like, if they dump Domitian, they ain't goin' to be sendin' you any love letters."

"Get off!"

Fulminatus stood up, looking aggrieved.

"You are not required to understand," Vettius said icily. "You are required to do your job and keep your mouth shut, and if you are not capable of that, I can find a replacement for you." His eyes were as cold as the waters in the Tiber, and Fulminatus backed off. "Permanently."

When he was alone, Marius Vettius sat looking thoughtfully at the reports spread out on his desk. They were beginning to grow. This was his third contact with the plotters. Soon he would be so enmeshed in the organization of their scheme that they wouldn't be able to cut him out of it, even when they discovered his unwanted assistance. But Fulminatus had been a bad choice. Fulminatus was going to have to go, just as soon as Marius Vettius had the emperor's purple securely enough about his own shoulders that he could spare him.

XV
Marius Vettius

IT WAS COLD THAT WINTER, AS COLD AS HEL'S DOMAIN, AND
the Rhenus froze—a smooth and glassy ice road, and an endless
bridge between the barbarians and the Roman zone. Marbod
of the Chatti came across it, sword in hand, leaving the Roman
outposts on the eastern bank burning like beacon fires behind
him. Velius Rufus took his army out of Moguntiacum to meet
him, swathed in furs and leggings, grasping their pilum shafts
with icy hands.

Blood on snow has a sickly beauty, and by the time the
Romans had pushed Marbod's warriors back across the Rhenus,
the white ground was wet with it. It had been no more than a
skirmish, a testing, and that frozen river was a deadly open
door. Velius Rufus sent an emergency message to the emperor
in Colonia and set about strengthening his defenses. Then he
looked at the Dead List and began to swear in disbelief.

"Did you hear?" Flavius's face was shocked. "Grattius Benacus was killed!"

"I heard." Correus was slinging tunics and winter leggings
into a trunk. "The whole palace has been running around all
morning like apes in a circus. They just handed me this." He
shoved a wooden tablet with a broken purple seal across the
bed at Flavius.

In the next room Flavius could see Ygerna and her maid
carrying armfuls of clothes about, and he had met Nurse towing
Eilenn and Felix across the courtyard as he came in. He looked
at the tablet and whistled. "Primus pilus to the Fourteenth!
Congratulations. That's Benacus's legion. What happened to
the primus pilus they had? Did they give him command?"

"Far otherwise," Correus said. He slammed the trunk lid
down and sat on it. "They cashiered him, and from what Governor Clarus said, he was lucky to get out alive. I don't know

what happened exactly, but Velius Rufus held him to blame for Benacus."

"You mean he thinks he deliberately set his commander up to be killed?"

"That's what Rufus thinks, but he can't figure out who would want Benacus dead, so he let him off with a Dishonorable for negligence." He pushed the pin of the trunk latch home and shouted for Eumenes.

"And they gave the post to you? Quite a decoration." Correus's last legionary posting had been as centurion of an Eighth Cohort. Promotion to primus pilus, commander of the First, was an unusual jump, even with a major fleet command in between.

Correus snorted. "I'm not so sure. I get a demoralized legion to hold together until a new legate gets here. Fun, that, in the middle of a war."

"At least it's dry land, sir," Eumenes said cheerfully. "The horses are all ready, and the wagon's loaded except for this and the lady's things." He shouldered the trunk and balanced it carefully through the door.

"Ygerna! How are you doing?"

Ygerna appeared in the doorway with a night shift and a wooden rabbit in her hand. "I am going mad, as you can see. Good morning, Flavius."

"D'you want me to send a slave around to help?" Flavius asked.

"No, thank you. I have too many slaves as it is. Septima packs the children's things, and then Nurse says she has done it wrong and packs them again in a trunk that Cottia has been putting my gowns in, and now everything is mixed, and instead of my winter boots I have a rabbit."

Flavius laughed. "Why don't you sit tight here and let Correus send for you when he's settled in?"

"That is what Governor Clarus said, but I know what will happen. Correus won't settle in; he will go off with the army, and then they will say I can't travel unescorted in a war zone, and I will sit here until the war is over. No, we will go to Moguntiacum, thank you. At least there I will know what is happening." She would know if Correus were killed was what she meant, but she wasn't going to ask ill luck and say it. Two-year-old Eilenn slipped up and clutched her mother's skirts, her brown eyes as wide as pools.

"Mama!" Felix's voice wailed somewhere in the background. "I've lost Eilenn!"

Ygerna scooped the baby up. "Try to stay put, poppet. Correus, tell Eumenes he may take the two trunks that are fastened, before Nurse and Cottia begin to dig in them again."

Flavius watched the baby wistfully. His own second child, a boy, had been stillborn in the fall, not long after his father-in-law's trial. He owed Vettius another debt for that, he thought savagely, and then twitched guiltily because no doubt he had been in Fiorgyn's bed when it had happened. "I had better take myself off," he said. "We'll be on the road today, too. The whole town looks like an anthill. Even old Rhodope has changed her mind and bought herself a new wagon."

"Well, so much for the emperor's peace treaty," Correus said, silently cursing Ranvig along with Marbod of the Chatti. There would be war on two fronts now, no doubt. The peace talks had produced nothing more than a season's respite.

"No," Flavius said, and Correus could hear a sort of desperate relief in his voice. "The delegation from the Semnones has been invited to join us."

"What!"

"It's not such a bad idea," Flavius said defensively. "They will travel with the emperor's camp, and they may see for themselves what happens to the Chatti and the ones who have been making trouble on the Upper Rhenus."

"The ones who have been making trouble on the Upper Rhenus belong to Ranvig!" Correus said.

"The chieftain says not."

"The chieftain is lying, and you are not such a fool that you don't know it!" Correus snapped. "The *emperor* knows it."

"The emperor also hopes that Ranvig will see the error of his ways when he sees our army in action. We aren't undermanned the way we were the last time. If the damned river hadn't frozen and given Marbod a place to cross and surprise us, we'd have gone over in the spring and wiped the ground with Marbod. As it is, we'll do it soon enough."

"I expect we will," Correus said. "But I don't expect Ranvig to take a lesson from it." He picked up an old pair of army-issue saddlebags and began moodily stuffing a change of clothes into them. "I wish he would," he said sadly.

"You like him."

"I have a good healthy respect for him. I—yes, I do like him. He's not like Nyall. There's something more human and crafty about Ranvig. But if he thinks he can outsmart Rome, he's wrong. He'll end up just like Nyall, and it makes me furious to watch it."

"Not if he makes a treaty with Rome," Flavius said.

Correus shook his head. "He isn't *going* to make a treaty with Rome. We'll have to fight him eventually, and it'll cost us more men to do it and gain us less land because we can't hold anything beyond the Agri Decumates unless it's friendly. But it will cost Ranvig his tribe to prove it. You know I'm right, Flavius. You said the same thing to Forst."

Flavius made a noise that might have been a laugh, but he didn't look like he was laughing. "A fine trio we are, you and me and Forst. Trailing about after Ranvig and the emperor, all hoping it isn't going to come to a war, and all knowing damned well that it is."

"I was hoping Forst would take himself home when the Alps passes opened."

Flavius shook his head. "Poor man, he doesn't know where home is, I expect. He just sort of . . . goes on, and hopes he won't have to decide."

Correus looked at his brother helplessly. He found Flavius as pathetic as Forst, turning a blind eye to the realities of war and a wife he would have to go back to, to snatch a few more days with Fiorgyn in some private world they had built up between them. Flavius would be more unhappy than most men who did that, because when he wasn't with Fiorgyn, he would see the real world all too clearly from a seat beside the emperor.

Correus looked about the room to see if he had left anything and decided if he had, it probably wouldn't be anything he would have a crying need for in Moguntiacum, with five thousand unnerved legionaries to keep him busy. The common legionary was used to his commanders changing, but not in the way the Fourteenth Gemina's had done. Correus had no illusions about this posting. His own abilities had no doubt had a lot to do with it—no one was going to hand a legion over to an incompetent—but so had the fact that he was handy. With the legate and primus pilus both gone, someone was needed to take over immediately, and a fleet commander wasn't a lot of use cooling his heels in Colonia waiting for his river to unfreeze.

He ran a hand through his hair and jammed his helmet down over it. Eumenes went by and reappeared with Ygerna's trunk, and Correus sat on the bed and tried to buckle his greaves himself. They were parade armor, heavily silvered and embossed, with fidgety, intricate buckles that were almost impossible to fasten oneself without sticking one leg up in the air like a cat.

"Here, let me do that." Flavius knelt down and poked the tongue through the buckle. "There, you look more yourself."

There were very few differences between the uniform of a cohort commander and a commander of Marines, insignia mainly, but Flavius knew that his brother's attachment to the legions, the Eagles, bordered on obsession. Correus had taken time to drag out all his old insignia and refit it, down to the Second Augusta belt buckle with the same Capricorn badge the Fourteenth Gemina carried. Both legions had been raised by Augustus and carried his natal sign for a badge. A good omen, maybe.

Correus twitched his gold and scarlet cloak into place and gave his brother a quick grin and a thumbs-up sign. There were little flames of excitement in his brown eyes. Correus could complain all he wanted to. He looked the way he had the day he got his centurion's insigne. He shouted restlessly for Ygerna again. Flavius wondered how Ygerna was going to take it all, and then remembered that she had traveled with Governor Frontinus's army for most of the campaign for West Britain.

A palace slave scurried in and bobbed a respectful obeisance in all directions. "The governor has lost the speech he was going to make, and has anyone seen it? And the emperor is looking for you, sir, and the centurion's escort is ready."

"No, we haven't seen it, tell the emperor I will be along directly, and the centurion thanks you," Flavius said gravely. Things were starting to move. He found himself catching some of Correus's excitement.

* * *

Half of Colonia turned out when the emperor left for Moguntiacum, and if one didn't look too closely, it might have been a festival. Laden carts rumbled by, the Praetorian Guard lined the way in their showy uniforms and then fell in behind the emperor's carriage, street singers added their dubious talents to the noise, and tumblers flip-flopped in the snowy road, hoping to attract the emperor's eye and largesse. Everyone who had come to Colonia in the previous spring made ready to move out again to wherever things would be happening now. Even Rhodope, complaining about her bones, joined the cavalcade at a respectful distance in a wagon even more splendid than her old one.

Correus waved at her as she sat imposingly beside the wagon driver, in a saffron-colored gown and a green hood with a hat over it, and got a glare from Ygerna in her own carriage. He laughed and made the Sign of Horns at her as if he thought she might curse him for waving at a whore, and she laughed back but kept her eye on him. Rhodope's girls were peering interestedly at the soldiers from behind their curtains, and Correus saw with a small shock that there was a new one among them—a blond woman with a pale, virgin's face and wide blue eyes. She rested one white hand on the rim of the carriage and watched the men outside. The last time Correus had seen her had been in Theophanes's camp when a man had died for her. He made the Sign of Horns in earnest now. Correus was generally unimpressed with curses and bad omens and the like, but that woman made his skin crawl. He would warn Rhodope, he thought, when he got the chance. How the woman had come into Rhodope's keeping, he had no idea, but she would be trouble to someone if she stayed.

He turned his mind back to his family. On a primus pilus's pay he could afford a good house in Moguntiacum, and Ygerna was going to stay in it, whatever she thought, until he was sure that wherever the Gemina was sent would be safe for her. She could keep Eumenes with her. Correus had looked after himself before; he was not so great a man now that he couldn't do it again. He looked back and saw the big-boned men of the German delegation beginning to ride out also. Flavius would be with them, on some pretext, he thought, unless Ranvig sent him about his business. He hoped Ranvig wouldn't decide to stick a knife in Flavius when he had finished his talks with the emperor.

The cavalcade moved on, taking the excitement with it, and when they had gone, Colonia seemed empty, hollow, bereft of the throngs that had flocked there in the emperor's wake. There was only a small guard left under Governor Clarus's command, enough to hold the city walls if the Chatti got that far, which seemed unlikely. Opinion in Colonia was that Marbod had made a mistake attacking the Romans, and no one had shown any inclination to join him in it.

"Dunno why you're goin'," the foreman of the glassworks said irritably. "Now that that lot's left, we can get down to proper business and leave off these finicky little portrait plates and things."

"You'll do less business, too," Forst said, "and someone will have to go. It might as well be me." He laid his leather apron over the end of his workbench.

"I could turn loose four of those useless layabouts and keep you," the foreman said, "and still come out ahead." He gave a disgusted look at the boys trotting back and forth with stacks of molds at the end of the open hall. While he watched, one of them tripped over a loose board in the flooring and dropped his molds. "At least you can walk a straight line, and you have a fair amount of tálent in yer hands." He shook his fist at the culprit. "All right, sweep it up, and it comes out o' yer pay, mind!"

"Nah, it is time I went," Forst said obstinately.

"Whatever for? You got a girl with those heathen Germans?"

"I'm a German, too," Forst said. "So are you."

The foreman shook his head. "My dad and mother was Germans. *I'm* a Roman, and I know what side my bread's buttered on. Those tribes came snoopin' around Colonia in the last war with a lot of large talk about freedom and Roman oppression, and we gave 'em the boot same as we done this time. Don't you go get mixed up in that, or you'll have a slave ring around yer neck again sooner than you can say 'Mercury help me.'" He shrugged. "Well, I suppose if you're goin', I can't stop you. You can collect yer pay at the office, but they'll short you for the day you didn't finish out."

Forst nodded and poked a finger at the mold he had been carving. "This is done." It was a ribbed bowl with a chariot race going around the side, carved to factory standard from a pattern.

The foreman picked it up. "You should stay. I could give you more pay, maybe." He thought of a parting shot. "If you're fool enough to go somewhere, then go back to Rome. Moguntiacum's not goin' to be healthy."

Forst paid the landlord of the dingy room he had taken and got his horse out of the stable where it had been eating up half his pay. It left him little enough to travel on. He had sent most of the rest to Emer with a letter full of lame excuses. He had so far been unable either to turn his back on Germany or to break his faith for good with Emer. The quickest road to Rome went through Moguntiacum. He would decide there . . . maybe. He pointed the horse's nose for Moguntiacum, wishing for a hand to come down out of the sky and point the way.

Lucius Paulinus sat at his desk with a shocked, panicked look on his face. Grattius Benacus, the "right man" who was to have pulled the empire back from the downhill course that Domitian had set it on, was dead. The plans for Domitian's death were made, a long and complicated chain of events already put into action. And now there was no one to replace him, no man to replace Grattius Benacus in judgment or honor or acceptability to Senate and people. Only a handful of sharks to tear the government to pieces when Domitian died. It would have to be stopped, all of it, the whole chain, link by link, without Domitian learning that it had existed. Lucius, Gentilius, Sulla, and Roscius Celsus were to meet that morning to decide how best to do it.

That was when they found out that they couldn't.

"*No.*" Faustus Sulla stood stubbornly in Gentilius's library, an airy, open room with tall windows to let in the light. It would be difficult to be overheard here, but Tullius stood guard in the doorway, just in case. "No. We have come this far. If we stop now, Domitian will find out eventually, and then there will be more deaths than you can count."

"If we don't stop now, there will be civil war," Gentilius

said. "We didn't invite you here to debate that, Sulla. It is not a matter of *if* but *how*."

Sulla's dark face was obstinate. "There are more men involved than you, Gentilius. And a lot among them who agree with me."

"Oh? Are you trying to threaten me, Sulla?"

"No, but I will do what I have to, to see that there are no more prisons full of condemned men whose only crime has been having property worth confiscating or falling afoul of the informers the emperor gives his ear to."

"There will be war again then," Gentilius said grimly. "Is that what you want, Sulla? Roman fighting Roman?"

"Of course not. We will put up Velius Rufus instead."

"The Senate won't accept Velius Rufus. And he doesn't have Benacus's reputation. Someone will fight him for it."

There was a murmuring at the door, and Tullius admitted Roscius Celsus. He was clutching his toga awkwardly with one hand, and a wax tablet with the other, and his shortsighted eyes were worried.

"What about you, Celsus?" Gentilius said as he came in. "Are your tradesmen fool enough to think we can go on now?"

"I don't know," Celsus said unhappily. "I am not, and I have some influence. But they are afraid. We have gone so deep. If we stop now, they are afraid that what they have done will catch up to them later."

"*That* is the truth!" Sulla exploded. "No man who has come within a mile of this will be able to sleep at night for the rest of his life."

Lucius sat up on his couch and looked Sulla in the eye. "If there is civil war, we won't be sleeping at night, either. In fact, I'm not sure we'd be safe from Velius Rufus if we *did* bring that off. Rufus could take it into his head to track us all down just to prove he had nothing to do with it, especially if the Senate is kicking about his confirmation. You're leaving too many *ifs*, Sulla."

"Then we should not have hung this on one man!" Sulla said. "Men get killed when they fight a war, or didn't you think of that?"

"Legionary legates don't get killed," Lucius said quietly.

"Not as a rule, not in a minor skirmish. Rufus has cashiered the primus pilus. Stop and think about *that*."

"What do you mean?"

"I mean that somebody wanted Benacus dead," Lucius said levelly. "Now who was he so important to, besides us? I smell something here, and I don't like it. It makes me inclined to pull back in my hole and stay there."

"That's your usual style, Lucius," Sulla snapped.

"And thus have I lived so long," Lucius said.

"Stop it!" Gentilius said with a voice he had developed on the parade ground and which had not entirely left him. "I begin to wonder myself if we can halt this thing with hotheads like you, Sulla, running loose in it. Celsus, you've been staying out of our squabbles like a gentleman. I want your opinion."

Celsus had sat down on the edge of one of the leather couches and appeared to be trying to arrange his words to provoke neither side. At the far end of the room a gilt cage full of ornamental birds could be heard squawking in the silence. "A number of our men feel as Faustus Sulla does, I am afraid," he said at last. "There is bad feeling against Domitian, and it goes deep. Also, we have had to use many men who have come to us only because they expect a reward at the end of it. If we stop now, they may seek their profit elsewhere, with Domitian."

"That is a danger also," Gentilius admitted. "It may be that we will have to spend some money, but I think that they can be dealt with."

"You'll just invite them to blackmail you over again when they decide they want more," Sulla said.

"I didn't necessarily mean to pay them off with silver," Gentilius said. "Not if they prove awkward." There was a calm menace in his voice that the others duly noted.

Sulla gave him an angry look. "And how many men can you have killed to keep a secret, Gentilius?"

"There is also one other matter," Roscius Celsus said unhappily. He held out the wax tablet. "This." He was holding it toward Lucius, gingerly, as if it were dangerous.

Lucius took it with an interested expression that changed to pure fury when he opened it. Roscius Celsus looked guilty, and Uncle Gentilius gave him a raised eyebrow of curiosity. Lucius rarely got mad, and when he did, someone had generally better watch out.

"Have you read this?" Lucius asked.

Roscius Celsus nodded. "It was sent to me, you see, through the cargo master in one of my shipping offices, with instructions to pass it on to you. I'm afraid I can trace the trail through my cargo master."

"Whose trail?" Uncle Gentilius said.

"Marius Vettius," Lucius said reluctantly. He read: "Marius Vettius wishes the enterprise well and would like to see Lucius Paulinus to discuss how he may best assist in its completion."

"Dear gods," Gentilius said.

"I do not recall, Paulinus, requesting that you bring your uncle with you." Marius Vettius reclined elegantly on his couch. He propped himself up on one elbow. "Or your dog." He turned his sleek, fair head to the doorway where Tullius stood, looking surly.

"I don't recall asking your permission for my doings," Lucius said. "I got a very cryptic message from you, and when you are cryptic, Vettius, I always bring reinforcements."

"I thought perhaps it would be as well to be cryptic. Don't you?"

"Depends on what you're being cryptic about," Gentilius said. "Vettius, you're boring me. What do you want?"

"Why, only to help. I understand that funeral arrangements will shortly be in order, and I thought I might be of use."

"I can't imagine at what," Lucius said. "No one's died."

"Ah, but someone's going to."

"No."

Vettius arranged his tunic into a slightly more perfect fold and snapped his fingers. A slave pushed in past Tullius. "Bring something for my guests." He gave Lucius a charming smile. "No? I think you're mistaken. And I'm afraid a great many of your, uh, comrades agree with me."

Lucius could feel his temper rising and pushed it firmly down. A cold knot of panic came and sat in his stomach instead. "What's your stake in this?" There wasn't much sense in continuing the pretense that he didn't know what Vettius was talking about.

Vettius gave him another pleasant smile. "Why, the good of the empire. Isn't that yours?"

"The good of the empire now requires that the emperor Domitian live long and safely," Gentilius said.

"Oh, I disagree. And I am afraid that it's out of your hands now, you know. As I said, too many of your people feel I am right."

"I take it the fox has been busy persuading the chickens to come home with him," Gentilius said.

"Not at all." The slave came in with a tray, and Vettius made a hospitable gesture while the two of them sat and glared at him. "I merely thought you had conceived an admirable idea and that it would be a shame to stop now."

"The emperor would hate to hear that," Lucius said.

"I do trust you weren't thinking of telling him, Paulinus." Vettius poured himself some wine and filled the other two cups in a friendly fashion. "It would be a shame to cut your own throat."

"I do hope I misconstrue you, Vettius."

"Oh, I shouldn't think you do." Vettius sipped his wine. "You see, I can do you so much more damage than you can do me. It just wouldn't be a contest. Shall I be blunt? I suppose I had better. This little plot you have hatched is going to go ahead. If it doesn't, the emperor is going to find out about it, and you will wish you *had* gone on, at least until your execution."

Lucius gritted his teeth and gave Vettius a bland look. "Which should take place shortly after your own."

Vettius shook his head. "Oh, no. The emperor trusts me. Or at least he thinks he can control me. You, on the other hand—you haven't been particularly obliging. I don't think we can expect Domitian to favor your viewpoint."

"He didn't when I warned him about you," Lucius said.

"Quite."

"Benacus is dead, Vettius." Gentilius gave him a thoughtful eye.

"Yes, so I had heard."

"Whom would you suggest putting in his place?"

"Oh, I expect Velius Rufus will do to go on with," Vettius

said. "Perhaps someone else will occur to me. When I get to Germany."

"Get to Germany?" Lucius's eyes narrowed.

"Yes, didn't I mention it? The emperor has been good enough to give me command of the Fourteenth Gemina. I've been wanting to get back into harness. A civilian post has its disadvantages, I find." He smiled at Lucius over his wine cup.

XVI
The Bridge

"SO YOU ARE GOING TO GERMANY!" JULIA GAVE HER HUSBAND a scathing look. "To try to stop what you put in motion yourself! How *dare* you, Lucius!"

"How dare I what?" Lucius said tiredly. "Go to Germany or try to keep what happened with Nero from happening again?"

"Any of it! All of it! You have jeopardized me and the children along with yourself, and you had no *right*! You weren't appointed to save the world!"

"I thought maybe someone should try," Lucius said. "Look, Ju, I am sorry. We did something that we thought was necessary."

"Murder." Julia turned her back on him. "I am ashamed of you."

"Now, just a minute. You knew what I did when you married me."

"Yes, you worked for the emperor. Now you are planning to kill him—"

"I am planning that he *not* be killed!"

"You are planning to kill him, and if he finds out, he will kill *you*. And probably me. And the *children*."

"It won't come to that," Lucius said desperately. "You can divorce me," he added. His voice was thick with unhappiness.

Julia turned around. "What do you think I am? You're my *husband*. I married you *confarreatio*. They wouldn't give me a divorce if I asked for one." *Confarreatio* was the old religious form of marriage, before the Pontifex Maximus.

"I could arrange it," Lucius said grimly.

"Well, I don't want one! You're horrible!"

"You aren't being very logical," Lucius said.

"I don't intend trying to be." Julia started to cry, and he put his arms around her. "This is horrible. I don't want to divorce you, I'm just afraid something awful will happen."

"It won't touch you or the children, I promise you," he whispered into her hair. But that wasn't the truth. If he were executed for treason, there was no certainty that his family wouldn't follow him. Domitian was vengeful, and Marius Vettius was worse.

"I don't want to lose *you!*" Julia sobbed. "Lucius, how did this happen?"

"My own foolishness," Lucius said wearily. "I expect it comes to that in the end. It will be all right," he said with more confidence than he felt. "Stay here, and sit tight. If anyone wants to know where I am, just tell them I haven't been well, and my physician has sent me to the seacoast for the summer."

Julia wiped her face with the end of her mantle. "What about Papa—and Aemelia? And your uncle Gentilius?"

"My uncle knows where I'm going. You'll have to lie to your father. Don't tell Aemelia anything if you can help it."

"All right." Julia laid her head against his chest. "I am sorry I yelled at you. I'll pray to Juno and Isis to send you back to me."

He held her for a moment and then pulled away reluctantly. "It's time, Ju. Tullius is waiting for me."

When he had gone, she went and got the children. She pulled her mantle over her head and took them with her to pray.

Correus dropped onto a couch in the green-tiled atrium of the house he had taken in the *vicus*, the civil settlement, outside Moguntiacum Fortress, and pulled his helmet off. He misjudged the distance to the floor, and it dropped the last few inches with a clatter that would probably dent it, he thought, companion to the dent he would like to put in the collective skull of the Fourteenth Legion Gemina. As he had predicted, they were a demoralized mess, and even the pleasure of his promotion didn't always provide him with the patience to put up with them. In their defense it could be said that the death of their legate in a border skirmish and the subsequent accusation of responsibility against their primus pilus was enough to render any legion nervous. Correus told himself this three times a morning when they fell over themselves at drill. They would be better when they had a legate again. Or so he thought until the post was announced. Now he thought that a legion with no legate at all would be better off than a legion with Marius Vettius. Especially for its primus pilus.

Correus ran a hand through his hair, which left it standing wildly upright, and slumped back on the couch. He expected his cuirass was scratching the upholstery.

Eumenes came in, and Correus sat up again and let him unbuckle it and strip off his greaves. Ygerna was behind him, shooing a slave before her with a cup of wine.

"You look surly," she said, inspecting him.

Correus took the wine and drank it. "Observant of you."

"I am not in your legion, Commander."

"No, darling, you are not. I am sorry. Come and sit with me."

Eumenes gathered up the armor and departed with it, pushing the other slave ahead of him. If she couldn't tell when the master and mistress were best left alone, he could.

"Marius Vettius will be here tomorrow," Ygerna said, sitting down next to him. "I heard in the camp market." Correus's leather harness tunic was damp with sweat, but she cuddled up to him anyway. "Will that help or make things worse?"

"I don't know," Correus said. "It may help the legion to have a legate again."

"And you?"

"That depends on whether he thinks I named him to Domitian for dealing with pirates, along with Flavius. And if he cares. I may be too small a fish for him to bother with."

"I don't like this," Ygerna said. "That man is dangerous. That general Rufus would have kept him in line."

The emperor had split his army. He had sent the four British detachments and the Twenty-first Rapax under Velius Rufus to show Marbod of the Chatti the error of his ways. The Upper

German legions would move the other way, to take in the last of the Agri Decumates lands, and box Marbod in between them and Rufus.

"There may be a bright note," Correus said. "Julius Frontinus is coming out too, as chief of Engineers under Domitian. Not much gets by him."

"No." Ygerna gave him a thoughtful smile. "What a long time ago it all was, Correus. Could we ask him to dine, do you think?" Julius Frontinus had been governor of Britain when they had last seen him.

Correus laughed suddenly. "Yes, why not? He'd like to see you again, I should think. And Felix is his namesake. It wouldn't hurt to have old Frontinus on our side."

Sextus Julius Frontinus, former governor of Britain, and Marius Vettius, new legate of the Fourteenth Legion Gemina, arrived in Moguntiacum almost side by side. Correus paid his respects to Vettius and formally turned over the legion to him. The new legate greeted him with sleek charm and disappeared in the direction of the emperor's headquarters. Julius Frontinus snorted and gave the disappearing back a look of dislike. Correus pushed through the crowd of legionaries still wrestling with the mountain of baggage belonging to Vettius and the more modest accoutrements of Julius Frontinus, and invited the chief of Engineers to dinner.

"You'd do better to save it for your commander," Frontinus said. "Though I expect you'll be seeing more of him than you'll want to. What's Domitian about, to put that horse's rear in charge of a legion?"

"He's a good enough commander, or so I've heard," Correus said noncommittally.

Frontinus snorted. He was an angular man, with heavy, callused hands. He inspected Correus. "You've done well for yourself, Julianus. I'm glad to see it. Keep an eye on Vettius. That's an honest warning. We're into tricky times."

"Yes, sir. Now, will you dine with us? My wife wants to see you."

"I heard you'd married that Silure child," Frontinus said. "I'll be interested. Can you promise she won't put poison in my dinner?"

"Nothing of the sort. It was her idea, frankly. I think she wants to show off."

Frontinus gave a bark of laughter. "I wouldn't doubt it!" When he had known Ygerna, she had been a hostage in his keeping. She had been strong-minded then, at fifteen. Ygerna grown up might be something to see. "I'll bring her a present. For old times' sake."

They would be on the march in two days. Ygerna's dinner party became a farewell-and-good-luck offering for her, an effort to so charm Sextus Julius Frontinus that he would somehow keep his hand over Correus before Vettius could do him an evil. Something about Vettius made her hackles rise. In her mind Frontinus was a shield against him. Frontinus must have a dinner set before him that would make him remember them with kindness. With an unshakable determination, she turned the *vicus* outside Moguntiacum upside down for the delicacies she had learned that Romans liked at dinner. She set Cottia and Septima to haunting the markets at opening time, and sent Eumenes with a piece of silver to bribe the cook in the officers' mess in the fort for an amphora of better wine than the *vicus* shops offered. She brushed and washed Felix within an inch of his life and threatened him with horrible retaliation if he put so much as a foot wrong during his presentation to their guest. She changed her own gown three times before the party.

Correus bowed before the whirlwind and went obediently to find fresh lettuce. He didn't think Julius Frontinus needed bribing with lettuces, but if Ygerna thought it would help, he wouldn't deny her the solace of her efforts. She had developed an obsession about Vettius. He wondered uneasily if she had the Sight. She had always said she didn't, but he had heard that one could possess it in many forms.

Moguntiacum marketplace produced no lettuces that would have met Ygerna's standards, and on a last chance he went where the best food in town was reputed to be—the palatial house near Nero's Column that Rhodope had hired for her brood to await the new campaign. He wanted to tell her about the blond woman, anyway. She was still there, or so he had heard. There had been a knife fight two days ago, and he knew without asking that it had been over her.

Rhodope provided him with new lettuces and a clay pot of snails into the bargain when he told her about Ygerna's relentless preparations.

"You take her these," she said, her gold tooth glinting. "Tell her it's a present from a friend. Maybe better not tell her which one."

"You are a jewel among women, Rhodope," Correus said solemnly. "It was all my life was worth to go back without lettuces." He took her by the arm and led her away from the cluster of girls who had gathered around them, into the shadowed corner at the end of the atrium. "I'll give you a warning in return. I should have come sooner."

"Not that the emperor is passing laws on whores again?" Rhodope looked annoyed. "He is a fine one to make noise, that one."

"No, no. It's one of your women. The new one. I've seen her before."

"The one with Earth Mother in her eyes," Rhodope said. She nodded. "I know, I saw it, too. She takes men, that one, right down to the soul. I made her leave when there was the knife fight. But she has gone with one of your officers."

"You mean a man in my legion, or just an officer from Moguntiacum?"

Rhodope snorted majestically. "One who should be a man who knows better. Your new legate."

Mithras, Correus thought. If there was anything to make Vettius a more chancy commander than he was, it was that pale, golden woman with the hungry eyes. "How did you get her?" he asked Rhodope.

Rhodope shrugged. "She came. She had manumission papers, but no money. She said her master had freed her, but when I asked why, she never said. He didn't give her any money."

Some man had run for his life, Correus thought. And now she had Marius Vettius. He paid Rhodope for the lettuces, and she bustled away to put the coin in some secret hoard. She had new shoes, he noted: scarlet with purple laces.

When he got home, Lucius Paulinus was waiting for him, and with a puzzled look Ygerna took the lettuces.

"I have sent for Flavius," she said. "He says I am to tell

no one else but you that he's here. He is up to something, I think."

"What's he doing in Germany at all?" Correus muttered, unpinning his cloak. Faces that ought to be elsewhere seemed to be springing up in his path like mushrooms. The day had begun to take on a sort of mad quality with his quest for lettuce, and Lucius's appearance, sub rosa, heightened the effect. "Here." He gave Ygerna the snails, and she wrinkled her nose at them. "You bake them," he said. "With butter and herbs." He went to find Lucius, leaving her peering dubiously into the pot.

Flavius appeared, practically on his heels, swearing because Eumenes had fetched him out of his bath, and they found Lucius sitting miserably in the room that Correus had commandeered for his office. Tullius was with him, and Lucius told him irritably to go away with Eumenes, that he wasn't a mother hen.

Correus took one look at his brother-in-law, pulled up a chair, and said, "What have you done, Lucius?"

For so grave a matter it didn't take very long to tell. Two or three minutes, no more, until Flavius sat looking at him with a pale, shocked face, and Correus was cursing a blue streak and trying desperately to think, think of something besides what would happen to his brother-in-law and his sister if so much as a word were whispered in Domitian's ear. Or worse, what would happen if the plan that Lucius and the rest of those poor high-minded fools had started couldn't be stopped again. It wasn't Lucius's plan anymore; it had a life of its own. And it wouldn't benefit anyone but Marius Vettius. . . . Marius Vettius, who had had his predecessor murdered by his own primus pilus, to pave his own path to the purple.

Flavius licked his lips and looked from Lucius to his brother. "Go away," he said finally to Lucius. "Go and lie low until we can do something about this." There was no point in arguing the rights and wrongs of it now, but he didn't want to see Lucius for a while.

"I came here to stop Marius Vettius," Lucius said. "Not to hide while you two stick your necks out."

"And Marius Vettius will take one look at your face and

know just what you're after," Flavius said. "And us. He's Correus's commander, you miserable fool."

Correus glared at Flavius to shut up and put his hand on Lucius's shoulder. Lucius Paulinus was no fool, but he looked just now like a man at the end of his rope. "Go to the kitchen and have Eumenes show you the guest rooms. Take Tullius with you. And Flavius is right about one thing: Lie low, for Mithras's sake. We have Julius Frontinus coming to dinner."

Flavius stood up.

"Go and unobtrusively put some extra bodies around the emperor," Correus said to him. "But I don't think they'll try anything until we're in the field." He looked at Lucius. "Will they?"

"No."

"And not until Vettius has had a chance to settle in and get on the right foot with the army." Flavius gave a short laugh with not much amusement in it. "There'll be bonuses all around, I expect."

Dinner was a mad affair with a strong undertone of hysteria that Julius Frontinus fortunately seemed not to notice. Maybe it was all in his own mind, Correus thought. Ygerna presented them with lettuces and the snails, which were rubbery but passable, and broiled fish from the river, and a dish of spiced raw lamb with fish sauce, and set herself to charm the chief of Engineers.

Julius Frontinus patted her hand. "I think I did well, my dear, to make a Roman of you. This is for the one I wouldn't let you carry in my camp." He put a little dagger with a silver handle in her hand.

Ygerna grinned at him. "Thank you, Governor."

"I'm not a governor now," Frontinus said placidly. "Just an engineer. On the emperor's service like the rest."

"A chief of Engineers," Ygerna said. "You're the one who makes the roads and bridges for the emperor. It seems to me that that is better than being a governor."

Frontinus laughed and dipped his fingers in the bowl of snails. "Of more lasting use, certainly. Treaties come unstuck. A road is forever."

In an odd way it was a family party. Julius Frontinus and

Ygerna, come together again in the no-man's-land of Germany, took to each other happily. Before the last course, she had Nurse bring Felix in, and he eyed the chief of Engineers with the greatest admiration.

"You build things," he said. "I built an aqueduct once, in the garden, but it fell down."

"Ah," Frontinus said. "And do you know the principles of construction of the arch?"

Felix shook his head.

"That would be your problem."

"Will you teach me?" His green eyes rested on the engineer hopefully.

"Well, I'm afraid there isn't time before we leave Moguntiacum," Frontinus said. "But this winter, maybe—you never know. Would you like to see a bridge built? We'll be doing a lot of that this season."

"May I help?"

"Not this war," Frontinus said. "But I wouldn't be surprised if you grew up to build a few of your own. When you're ready, you come to me. I was there when you were born, you know. A sad affair, but a happy outcome. You are named for me. And they swaddled you in one of my old cloaks."

"Frontinus Appius Julianus," Felix said. "But mostly they call me Felix. Grandfather has the cloak, at home in Rome. He says when I am grown up, maybe I can wear it. It's purple," he added thoughtfully, "so I expect I'd have to be very grown up."

"It's a military governor's cloak," Frontinus said. "I wouldn't be surprised if you got there."

Felix smiled at him. "This winter you can teach me to build an aqueduct. That would be a start, I should think." He seemed to feel that the chief of Engineers would regard this as a high treat. Nurse took his hand, and he went with her obediently. "I am pleased to have met you, sir," he added when Nurse prodded him.

"You have made a conquest," Ygerna said.

"Well." Frontinus looked pleased. "It's no bad thing to be a hero in someone's eyes. You're raising an engineer, I think. This winter I'll show him what he wants to know."

"He didn't tell you," Ygerna said, "that when he built the

aqueduct, he built it in his grandfather's rose garden with tiles he pried up from around the pool."

The evening passed on a convivial note, and Julius Frontinus seemed inclined to stay. If Ygerna had set to charm him, Correus thought, she and Felix had done the job. But Lucius was still in the guest room, and Correus wished the chief engineer would go home. When Frontinus eventually took his leave, it was late, and they said farewell in the portico under a scattering of stars in a black sky.

"That was nice," Ygerna said sleepily as Frontinus walked back toward his quarters in Moguntiacum Fortress.

"It will be less nice when I have to get up in the morning," Correus said. "And I've got to talk to you about Lucius." He was plainly worried.

Ygerna settled herself on the couch in the atrium and looked suddenly wide awake. "I was afraid something bad was happening when we couldn't tell Julius Frontinus that Lucius was here. What is it?"

It took no longer to tell Ygerna than it had for Lucius to tell his brothers-in-law, but she looked less shocked than they had, apparently considering the matter solely from the angle of its effect on her husband. Ygerna had no great love for Domitian, and she had grown up under the ruthless wing of her uncle Bendigeid, who had been willing to throw first Ygerna and then himself to the wolves if it would buy security for his tribe.

"Lucius will have to stay here with me when the army goes," she said. "If it is safe enough for us to follow you, what then?"

"I don't know," Correus said. "We'll worry about that then. It will be a few weeks before I can send for you, after we see how much resistance we meet. Maybe I can think of something by then." He didn't sound as if he thought he could. His face looked lined and tired. He couldn't shake off a vision of executions, a flood of blood. Lucius, Julia, the children . . .

"Go to bed," Ygerna said. "You have parade in the morning. I'll be there in a minute."

When he had gone, she slipped into the room he used for an office and rummaged in the desk for the writing implements she knew were there. Writing was something new to Ygerna, or it had been when she had first met the Romans. Tribal history and the descent of kings were memorized by the bards; the Britons used their runic letters only to make magics with. But the Romans wrote down everything. It had unnerved her at first, but she had doggedly learned it when they had made her into a Roman. She pulled out a sheet of papyrus—this was going to be too complicated to scribble in wax—and sat down to think it out.

Berenice had grown up with palace intrigue in the tangle of the old Judaean court and had waded through it unscathed in her husbands' and her brother's courts. And she knew Domitian. She would know the best way to stop something like this.

Ygerna had a suspicion that Correus wouldn't care for her telling their dangerous secret to Berenice; after all, he didn't know her. So it seemed simpler not to fight over it, and just do it. If Berenice had any help to offer, Ygerna could tell him then. The only problem was telling Berenice without telling the world. Ygerna chewed on the end of the reed pen, and then dipped it in the ink.

I hope that you are well. . . . It is very cold and boring here, and when it snowed this winter, I used to sit and remember how nice it was to have lunch with you in the room that looks onto the garden and tell each other stories. So I thought that I would send you one in a letter, and maybe you can send me one back. This one is about my family.

When I was in Britain, there was a king who should not have been made king, perhaps, and there were many men who thought that. One of them was married to my sister. They decided, foolishly, that they would kill him and put in his place another man who had the god's hand on him to be king, they thought. But the other man was killed in a cattle raid, and then they found that their plan had grown by so many men that it could not be stopped, and one of the men—a sleek, slippery man that was not such a one as men trust—insisted that they do murder on the king anyway, thinking to be king himself when it was done. If they would not agree, he said, he would tell the king about their treason, and then there would be more innocent blood spilled than anyone had ever seen.

In this story, they couldn't stop him, and the king died, and the sleek man became king after him, and then used the others' treason to make the council put them to death afterward. I have always thought that it should not have happened that way, but such a plan is a hard thing to stop. What do you think?

Will you tell me a story now? I hope that you are well, and that I can visit again when we come back to Rome. . . .

Ygerna read the papyrus over one more time. She didn't have a sister, and Berenice knew it. And knew also, she thought, that no such event had enlivened Ygerna's childhood. She took the guttering lamp, poked a sealing stick in it, and daubed it on the folded sheet. She folded a second around it the other way and sealed that, too. It was risky, but as long as Marius Vettius didn't know that Lucius was in Germany, he would have no reason for suspicion. Some spy along the way might read her letter just on principle, but it was unlikely that he would get much out of it. A pair of bored women amusing themselves with silly tales.

She tiptoed into their bedchamber. Correus was asleep with the cat on his chest, and Ygerna slipped the letter into her sewing basket. In the morning when Correus was on parade she would find some trader or one of the civilian posts to carry it.

She climbed into bed beside Correus and said a quick prayer to the goddess whose priestess she once had been. Killing a king was a dark magic, so maybe the Goddess would intervene. But she wasn't sure if Earth Mother would care whether a Roman emperor were killed or not, so she prayed to Jupiter, and Juno, too, for good measure, and to the Eastern god that Correus worshiped. Mithras didn't admit women to his service, but maybe he would listen to her anyway.

Domitian's army marched out two mornings later in the cold air, their breath making little clouds before them, like the mist that drifted ankle-deep along the ground. Domitian was in command, with Julius Frontinus as chief of Engineers, and the bulk of four legions: the Fourteenth Gemina, the First Adiutrix, the Eleventh Claudia, and the Eighth Augusta, in which Correus and Flavius had held their first commands. The senior officers of the Augusta were all changed over now, promoted to other legions, but Correus recognized a junior centurion whose promotion he had recommended from the ranks in the first war for the Agri Decumates. Centurion Quintus blinked when the primus pilus of the Gemina rode by and nodded to him, then recognized Correus and raised his vine staff in salute.

The German delegation from the barbarian lands rode in the emperor's train, and Correus saw Fiorgyn, riding with the same easy grace that the German warriors had. Ranvig was on one side of her and the brown-bearded priest on the other, and at least Flavius was showing enough sense to keep away. Or maybe he was only keeping his eye on the emperor. Correus could see his brother's straight back under a purple cloak among the generals in Domitian's train. Marius Vettius was there also, in a helmet with the eagle-feather crest of a legionary legate, and he seemed content to leave his primus pilus to ride in his place at the head of the Gemina, under the shadow of the great gilded Eagle of the legion. It soared above him, its silver wings stretched back, its claws grasping the golden thunderbolts, above the staff that carried the legion's wreaths of honor. Last night as every night, Correus had made his prayers before it in the Chapel of the Standards with the rest of his men, but he could never see the Eagle without feeling something clutch at his heart. It was the life and the honor of a legion, and it embodied his love for the army in a way he couldn't put into words. He shot Vettius a look of pure dislike. The man was a thief and a danger, but in some ways it was worse to Correus that he had no caring for his legion. It was only a stepping-stone, an appointment charmed out of an unwary emperor to further his own ambitions. As Flavius had predicted, the new legate had made a handsome bonus to every man in the legion, but he would leave the on-the-march command of it to Correus. Vettius didn't waste his time when there was no glory to be had.

The blond woman had come with him. Correus had seen her with Vettius the day before in the market stalls of the Moguntiacum *vicus*, under the column with the bronze Jupiter, once dedicated to Nero. The name of that unstable prince had been chipped off in ruthless fashion after his death, but the memorial remained, dedicated by the citizens of Moguntiacum as a mark of their tie with Rome. The woman had been looking at a pearl necklace, and Vettius had had an arm around her shoulders like a hound shielding his bone from the reach of another dog. Her gold hair spilled down over his hand and rippled the way a wheat field does, and her movements were slow and languid. The pearls were good ones, from Alexandria, a little opalescent fortune, and she held them up so that their luster shone against her skin. She had been wearing them when Correus had passed her this morning, riding in her own litter among the baggage wagons.

His optio came up beside him and told him they were on the march, and Correus nodded, feeling the excitement that nothing else quite matched run through him.

They crossed the Rhenus and moved south into the Nicer Valley. They halted at Lopodunum to set up a headquarters there, and Correus decided he could send for Ygerna to come that far forward, at least. Lopodunum was still well within the Roman zone. He didn't bother to ask his commander's permission. If the legate could have his doxy in camp, Correus thought irritably, he could have his wife.

"You will stay here and see that he doesn't put his nose outside this door," Ygerna said to Tullius. She gave Lucius Paulinus a firm eye. "Correus and his brother are with this Vettius. They will be doing what they can. It won't help if you try to take a hand."

Lucius nodded glumly. He was used to dealing with matters himself, not hiding in a burrow while someone did it for him.

"I'll see he don't twitch," Tullius said, looking down at Ygerna genially. He was nearly two feet taller than she was and twice as broad. He could have put her in his hand. He liked the little mistress. She was a woman who made up her mind.

"Good." Ygerna pulled her heavy brown traveling cloak around her and checked to see that the children had theirs and the fur boots that were still needed in late spring. Eumenes,

Nurse, and Cottia were going with them. Septima would stay to keep the house up because it seemed likely that they would be back at Moguntiacum with the fall, and Ygerna didn't rate Tullius high as a housekeeper. They had all been threatened with the copper mines or any other unpleasantness Ygerna could devise if so much as a peep escaped their lips about Lucius's presence. Even Felix, who generally told everyone everything, seemed to understand the importance of that. Eilenn, who was only two and a half, didn't say enough yet to be dangerous.

One of the cavalry patrols that ranged through the Roman zone across the river was making the sweep back toward Lopodunum, and they would ride with that. The cavalry commander gave them the look of a man much tried and told them to fall in with the supply train he was shepherding south to the emperor's camp.

"Don't see what he's got to complain about," Eumenes said. "He's got those lumbering great wagons to slow him down, anyway. We're a sight faster than they are."

They were on horseback, all of them, except for Nurse, whose bulk was wedged in beside the army driver assigned to their wagon. Cottia, determined that if her mistress could ride a horse then so could she, swayed only slightly in her saddle, and Felix was on his pony, with a lead line handy in case Eumenes thought he needed it. Eilenn was in the saddle in front of her mother, and Baucis the cat was in her usual basket in the wagon. Ygerna had tried to leave her behind in Moguntiacum, but the cat jumped into the wagon and sat on a trunk with her ears flattened out, and Ygerna gave up. The cavalry patrol was split before and behind the wagons as they crossed Moguntiacum Bridge into the Agri Decumates.

They turned south almost immediately to parallel the broad blue sweep of the river to where the Moenus River emptied into it. Here was another bridge, narrower than Moguntiacum Bridge, and built on wooden pilings sunk into the riverbed and braced against the current. The cavalry horses clattered onto it, their iron shoes ringing hollowly against the planks.

"Mama." Eilenn turned her head around and tugged at the front of Ygerna's cloak.

Ygerna kissed the top of her head through the baby's traveling hood. "That's right, sweetheart. Can you say 'horsie'?"

She patted the gray mare's shoulder with the baby's hand.

Eilenn's brown eyes looked up at her from under the edge of her hood. "Bidge," she said emphatically. "Bidge fall down."

"No, darling, it's a nice bridge." Ygerna patted her soothingly. "You didn't mind the last one. We have to cross it if we're going to see Papa."

"Bidge!" Eilenn wailed. "Bidge fall down!"

"No, darling, see—it's just fine."

"*Bidge!*" The child's face was terrified now, and she was screaming and hiccuping.

"What's the matter with little miss?" Eumenes said.

"I don't know. She's scared of the bridge. I—" Ygerna leaned down and took another look at the little girl's face, and something cold crawled into the back of her mind. Eilenn was still screaming with fear. Ygerna kicked her mare into a gallop and pulled her up sharp at the head of the bridge where the cavalry commander sat watching his men go by.

"Call them back!" Ygerna said, holding the screaming child with one hand and grabbing at the mare's reins with the other.

"What?"

"Call them back! That bridge is going to go!"

"Looks fine to me," the cavalry commander said. "You an engineer?"

"No, but I know!" Ygerna said desperately. "When the wagons hit it—"

"*Bidge!*" Eilenn shrieked.

"Take that kid back to the wagons!" the cavalry commander snapped.

"Call them back off that bridge!" Ygerna said.

"Who in Hades are you to tell me my business? You," he shouted at Eumenes, "get this damned-fool woman back to the wagons!"

Eumenes appeared to have been stricken deaf.

Ygerna pushed back her hood and gave the commander a look that made him a little nervous. "I am Flavia Agricolina," she said evenly. "I am the wife of Correus Julianus, who is primus pilus of the Fourteenth Legion. I am not a fool. Call your men back off the bridge. It will break when the wagons hit it." She made her voice stay calm.

The commander looked at her dubiously as the lead wagon rumbled by onto the bridge. She had eyes like wide black pools set into a pale face, and two bright spots of color on her cheeks now. She didn't look more than fourteen. But her husband was a senior officer. And there was something in those dark eyes that the cavalry commander found himself unsure he wanted to tangle with. He fidgeted as she lifted her head and glared at him. The child had stopped screaming now and sat hiccuping softly in the crook of her mother's arm. He supposed the woman could have seen something. . . . There was a creak and a sigh as the wagons rolled past, and he shouted suddenly, "Back 'em up!"

The nearest wagon driver gave him an inquiring look.

"Back 'em up, damn it!" the commander shouted. "Here, you, get on up there and turn those wagons back!"

A cavalry trooper clattered onto the bridge past the halted wagon to the head of the column. They could hear him shouting to back up. The lead riders were nearly across. They too turned and came back, and the bridge gave another groan.

"You should have let the horses go on," Ygerna said. "They were nearly over."

"I didn't *tell* 'em to come back," the commander said irritably. What was he doing, pulling a whole column off the bridge because this fool woman thought she knew something?

The bridge was too narrow to turn the wagons, and they backed laboriously off it with much swearing and shoving. The mules flattened their ears and bit at each other. The drivers looked as if they were going to ask questions, and the commander gave them a look that said they'd better not.

Ygerna's wagon had halted this side of the bridge, and Eumenes came up now and addressed himself to her. He took no orders from the cavalry commander. "Is there trouble with the bridge?"

"I—" Out of the corner of her eye Ygerna saw the cavalry commander watching her. "Yes," she said firmly. "Go and help these men to check the bridge. It will be weakened somewhere. Rot or sabotage; I don't know."

The cavalry commander swung around. "You mean you didn't actually see—?" He clamped his mouth shut again. He'd look a fine ass now if he put them back on the bridge without checking. "Go and look at it," he said curtly to the trooper he had sent to pull the wagons off.

Eumenes gritted his teeth and followed him. He shucked his clothes on the bank with the cavalry troopers. They weren't making much effort not to shock the ladies, he noticed, and grinned in spite of himself. The mistress didn't shock, not that easy, but old Nurse would have something to shake her up. It would do her good. The current was still fast and cold with the melting snow from the mountains, and they swore as they paddled their way along the row of pilings on either side of the bridge to peer upward at the underside. Eumenes's teeth were chattering, and the current was strong enough that a man who stopped swimming had best keep a good grasp on the bridge while he looked. *You have swum in worse for the fun of it*, he told himself firmly. But not lately, not since the mock battle on the emperor's lake in Rome. The air was dank and shadowed and smelled of waterweeds under the bridge.

Halfway across they found it, five of the horizontal supports cut nearly in two with an ax. It could have been done at night from a boat moored to the upstream pilings.

The cavalry commander swore when they came back, shivering, to tell him, and he left a pair of troopers at the bridgehead to warn anyone else away until it could be repaired. He made two others swim across to the far side to keep watch there. Then he turned the column around with an uneasy look at Ygerna and took them back through Moguntiacum and down the west bank of the Rhenus to the next bridge.

Ygerna looked long and thoughtfully at the baby, who now sat happily playing with the tassels in the gray mare's mane.

"She has the Sight." Ygerna glanced from her husband to the open doorway that separated her room from the children's at the inn in Lopodunum.

"So it would seem. It's a pity we can't send her out with the army for a watchdog. They got another bridge last week, and that one went down with a whole century on it."

"Correus, this is not a joke. It is a terrible gift, the Sight." It came through her line, Ygerna thought, from the sidhe folk, the Dark People of the hills.

"Neither is the sabotage a joke," Correus said. "It's getting worse, and we're beginning to feel the losses from it. It's come to outright raids occasionally." He looked at his wife's worried face. "My dear, there is nothing we can do about it if she does have it. You can't make it go away."

"No. But you didn't see her, Correus. She *saw* that bridge collapse and the wagons fall and the men all drown. What happens when she is older and sees things like that and knows what they mean and can't stop them?"

Correus looked through the doorway to the children's room. "Poor little Cassandra."

"Who is Cassandra?"

He put his arm around his wife. "Never mind. And you stopped that bridge from falling, so it may not be like that." He tightened his grip on her. "We're lucky that she *did* see it. Maybe I shouldn't have sent for you. These attacks are getting worse."

"We will be safe enough in Lopodunum. Is it the Chatti?"

"No, the Chatti are busy fighting with Velius Rufus. It's Ranvig's men, despite what he says, and the emperor knows it, but he still thinks Ranvig will get good sense when he's seen our army in the field."

"Do you think so?"

"No. He's seen our army. He doesn't have to see it fight to know what we can do. But the emperor still believes he can make the Semnones come over as a client kingdom and put another leaf in his laurel wreath without working for it. Or maybe he's just amusing himself by letting Ranvig play with these raids. His mind is like that sometimes." Correus's voice was suddenly savage. "But it's costing us men! And it won't change things in the long run. We'll take what we've set out to, and that will be the end of it, except for the men who needn't have died!"

XVII
A Matter of Money

"IT'S MONEY THAT HOLDS THAT THIEF TOGETHER," FLAVIUS said. There was nothing any of them could do about Domitian's war except fight it as ordered, and a family council had gathered to attack the more pressing problem of doing something about Marius Vettius. "Aemelius's money, pirate money, whatever he's extorted one way or another—it all goes to keep Domitian smiling on him and to buy the army. No money, no Vettius. A pity we can't separate him from it."

"I do not understand this matter of buying an army," Ygerna said.

Flavius chuckled. "That's because you haven't read enough Roman history, child."

"That's not true," Correus said. "That is the black side, but it's not always true."

"Mithras forbid I should insult the army in my brother's presence," Flavius said piously, "but it *is* true. The army holds the empire together, and it makes the emperors as often as not, and soldiers who don't get paid don't stay loyal very long. Vettius is passing out some fat bonuses and spending a lot more on gladiators and the like to keep the troops amused. 'This week's entertainment sponsored by the unlimited generosity of Marius Vettius, friend of the soldier.' If we could stop that, we might stop him."

"I begin to see," Ygerna said. She looked disgusted. "Is that why the horse race?"

"What horse race?"

"There was a notice put up in the market. The sort they announce the arena shows with. I always read them for the practice. This one was for a horse race, with chariots, at the end of the summer. Vettius is paying for it. Or no, I think it said Vettius will hold the bets. I don't quite understand that."

"I do, the thieving son of a bitch," Correus said. "If Vettius holds the bets, he expects to win. If that race isn't fixed, I'll eat my saddle."

"Well, it's certainly his style," Flavius said. "He gives the troops some fun and cheats them at the same time. Why Domitian can't see through him is a mystery fourteen augurs couldn't explain."

"I don't expect the emperor *cares* if Vettius cheats the soldiers," Ygerna said practically. "He didn't care if he cheated your father-in-law."

Correus was looking thoughtful. "When is this race?"

"The notice said at the end of summer, when the army reaches the Moenus. For a reward. There will be gladiators too, in the emperor's honor. That is horrid, but I would like to see the horse race."

"I expect you can," Correus said. "We'll dig in at the Moenus for a while and put up a permanent fort." Ygerna didn't like being left in Lopodunum, but he couldn't take her and the children out with the road-building crews. He was still thinking. If all went well, they would halt at the Moenus to build a bridge and meet with Velius Rufus, with most of the Agri Decumates under control. The emperor would be there, and all the hangers-on who trailed in the army's wake would come with him. A big enough population to serve Vettius's purpose. And maybe theirs. He looked up at Flavius. "D'you think we could liven up his horse race for him?"

Three hundred miles to the east, in Steinvarshold on the Semnones' home ground, Lady Morgian's husband sat looking at a visitor who had ridden in that morning. The remains of a feast were scattered on the table top, and a thrall was sweeping spilled food into her apron. Steinvar leaned back in his chair, one thin hand wrapped around a beer horn, and the other feeding pieces of meat from the table to a red hound bitch by his feet. His scarred face was creased into a smile. Steinvar liked the man who was sitting at the table with him. His name was Decebalus, and he was a prince of Dacia, the country that bordered the Roman province of Moesia along the Danuvius.

Decebalus was younger than Steinvar, with curling brown hair and beard, and a heavy mouth half-hidden under a mustache. He had a heavy straight nose and a square jaw, and brown, thick-lidded eyes. He looked like a man who was used to arranging the world to suit him. Decebalus wore a shirt and breeches much like Steinvar's, and a felt cap with a rounded point pulled forward and pinned down over the forehead. He stretched and belched appreciatively. "That was good."

"Not so good as your father's house," Steinvar said. "But you won't starve among us. That is enough. Go on, go!" He shooed the thrall away.

The thrall shrugged and left. They had eaten enough for four men, and the table was still littered with it, but Lord Steinvar was not particular about the housekeeping when Lady Morgian wasn't there.

"My father is a petty king." The younger man dismissed his father's house. "When I am done, my father's house will be a cattle shed to mine."

"The Romans won't like that," Steinvar said.

Decebalus grinned at him across the table. "Isn't that why I am here?" They spoke a rough mixture of the Germanic tongue of the Semnones and Decebalus's Dacian, and they understood each other well enough.

Steinvar laughed. "I thought it was because the trade had stopped between across-the-Rhenus and your caravans."

"It was a good trade," Decebalus said. "Later it will be better. Where is Ranvig?" He didn't call the lord of the Semnones "the chieftain." Decebalus was going to be a great king, and he saw no need.

"Keeping the emperor of the Romans at bay," Steinvar said. "I speak for him."

"That was not an insult," Decebalus said. "I know you do. But if he can hold the Romans thus, why does he need me?"

"Because large talk will not be holding them forever," Steinvar said, serious now. "Not for us, and not for you."

Decebalus nodded and drank his beer. "Then we must give the Romans something more than talk, to worry them. Now tell me—what is this plan that Ranvig is so sure will work?"

It never ceased to catch him by surprise, Flavius thought, how deeply the woman had grown into his soul. Fiorgyn sat with her back half to him, combing her hair. Her gown was still down around her waist where he had left it, and he could see the tip of one breast, achingly familiar now, behind the curtain of her hair. She was sitting on a rock under the low overhang of a tree. Lopodunum wasn't big enough to hold an inconspicuous inn, not for the emperor's aide and a woman of the Semnones, and they had come of necessity to the final indignity and found a place in the woods for themselves. Flavius didn't think he cared about his dignity anymore anyway, not with Fiorgyn.

She looked over her shoulder and smiled at him. He came and knelt before her with his face against her breast. She sat still for a long time, just holding him to her, so still that a rabbit ran out from the undergrowth and sat up and watched them. She put the comb down and brushed her lips through his dark hair.

"You've hardly spoken today. Is there something troubling you?"

"Yes." Flavius sounded tired, his voice on the edge of cracking.

"Is it something you can tell to me?"

"No."

She nodded. So many things they couldn't tell each other. She couldn't tell him that Ranvig had had a message from Steinvar yesterday. She had stormed at Ranvig and made him tell her what was in it when he hadn't wanted to, and he had admitted, grudgingly, that she was not some Roman officer's doxy who would run to him with everything she heard like so many of the women in Lopodunum. Almost, she wished she were.

Flavius sighed, lifted his head, kissed her, and pinned her gown back on her shoulders. He couldn't tell her that there was a plan in motion to kill the emperor. Never. Not even if they weren't at war. And he had no illusions about the war. It was going on now, even if Ranvig and Fiorgyn weren't fighting in it. Before and behind them, wherever the main army wasn't, the attacks went on. Slowly the Agri Decumates was being strangled as Julius Frontinus's net of forts and roads was laid down on it, but the Germans were a presence felt in cornered patrols and burned-out watchtowers. Lately they had taken to setting fields alight so that the Romans couldn't forage and so the local folk would be left for the emperor to feed along with his soldiers. It was costing the Romans dear, but still it was only a matter of time until the Agri Decumates fell. And then Flavius would lose Fiorgyn. The realization left him tongue-tied and panicked today. That and the fact that unless they could stop it, the emperor would lose his life, and along with him, Lucius Paulinus and Julia and whatever other poor fools had got in the way. Together he and Correus had thought of a scheme that *might* curb Vettius. Correus had sent a letter to Rome for the help they needed, but it was chancy. Everything was chancy that summer, thin and insubstantial like a marsh light, dangerous as a knife in the dark.

He put his hands in Fiorgyn's hair before she could rebraid it, and kissed her one last time, burying his face against hers.

"Sir, they were out without their armor on. They're lucky the Germans didn't get them. I think three days' punishment drill is entirely merited." Correus stood at attention before his legate, feeling helpless and steadily more furious. The emperor was still at Lopodunum, but his army was in the field, sweating under Julius Frontinus, laying road northward from the Nicer River to the eastern end of the first great loop of the Moenus. And the legate of the Fourteenth Gemina was busy spoiling his troops, banking away their goodwill like the gold he was stockpiling, against the day he could make his bid for the purple. When Correus gave a punishment, Vettius countermanded it. The legion was a mess, and it would serve them right if the Germans ate them whole.

Vettius gave him a smile and a shrug of the shoulders. "It's hot work, Centurion, laying road. We must make some allowances, don't you think?"

"I think they won't hold in the field, sir, when it comes to a fight, if they aren't straightened up now." Correus stood stiffly and tried to keep his temper out of his voice. "The legionary thinks only in here-and-now. They're just happy to be let off punishment, but they'll get used to it and not think what shedding their armor could cost them if the Germans show up. And if they lose their discipline there, it isn't going to stick anyplace else. And neither will my orders, sir, if you countermand them."

Vettius gave him a wave of his hand. "Go on with your road, Centurion, and allow me to decide that. If you don't give such ill-advised orders, I won't find it necessary to reverse them."

Correus banged his fist into his breastplate in salute and stalked out. Vettius had been just charmed to have that order to countermand. It made Correus the villain, and Marius Vettius the friend of the common soldier, and Correus would still be around to blame things on if the legion disgraced itself. And it was going to if he couldn't knock some sense into them when Vettius wasn't looking.

Correus stood irritably in the dirt road outside the principia tent and squinted northward. It would be another month maybe before they reached the Moenus, and there they would stop to build a bridge. If nothing happened before then, he might be able to solve Paulinus's problem and his own—if his father got his message, if Julius got there in time, and if nobody killed Domitian in the meanwhile.

The road moved on. The Roman army were the builders of the empire, and they carried pick and shovel as well as sword and shield. Where they had been, the road stretched out behind. Their marching camps became permanent outposts along the river valley, and signal towers sprang up between. They worked like mine slaves, and Julius Frontinus seemed to be everywhere among them, surveying, measuring, and watching his road grow. He was an engineer by nature, and almost as happy with a pick in his hand as an officer's staff. Under Frontinus's watchful eye even Marius Vettius found he had less time to relax; as long as the emperor was in Lopodunum, Frontinus was in command.

There were no real battles fought for the valley, only a series of skirmishes, ambushes, and night raids—exhausting, bloody, maddening, but more a trouble than a danger to eventual conquest. They were a threat, Correus thought, a promise that wherever the Romans pushed, they would have to push through burned fields and dead bodies in the water, making their progress slow and wearisome. The men were growing quarrelsome from it, and Frontinus personally knocked some heads together, summoned Marius Vettius to his tent, and informed him that his legion was the worst of the lot.

"Get out of that blond whore's bed and out into a ditch with your legion, and they'll come along some better," he said briskly.

"It is my privilege to have a woman with me," Vettius said. "Don't threaten me, Frontinus, or I'll make your little command a burden to you."

Julius Frontinus looked irritated. He would have liked to have connected his sandal with the legate's rear, but he expected his emperor wouldn't like it. "No threat involved," he said. "But they won't go on loving you if they get cut up in a fight because you've been coddling them. Mull it over. You're dismissed."

Vettius pressed his knuckles to his gilt-and-silver breastplate, even more elaborate than the one Frontinus wore, and strolled out, keeping the pleasant, slightly bored expression on his face with difficulty. He wondered if Julianus had been sniveling to the chief of Engineers behind his back. Probably not. Old Appius's bastard didn't have enough sense to get ahead by climbing over his commanders. And the Fourteenth Legion *was* getting out of hand. But their greed for the next promised bonus was growing daily. They would put him on the emperor's throne, and then their next commander could straighten them out. Or disband them; Vettius didn't much care.

The woman was waiting for him in his tent when he got there, curled on the bed while one of the legate's household slaves brushed her hair. Her name was Gwenhwyfar and she was Gaulish, or so she had told him. He thought she had probably had a lot of names. She hadn't told him how she had come to be in a whorehouse in Moguntiacum, and he hadn't asked. Likely she would have lied. She stood up now and stretched and wrapped her arms around him, paying no attention to the slave, and he saw again the hungry look that lay under the innocent face. It was what had attracted him to her in the first place—a woman with a hunger to match his own. He pushed the slave out of the tent.

She twisted herself around him. "When we reach the Moenus, then there will be a house to live in, and I will have clothes to wear."

"You are not dressed in rags now."

"I am not dressed as a great man's woman should be." She put her mouth against his ear and smiled when she felt his fingers tighten on her. "When we reach the Moenus, I will need more clothes."

"There won't be anything at the Moenus until we build it."

"Then you can build me a house."

"That will take money."

She tilted her head back and smiled at him, eyes heavy-lidded. "Then you will have to have more money. Won't you?"

He kissed her and felt her mouth open under his. When they had made love—an odd, consuming passion that made him feel it had been almost a contest to see who should master the other—she opened her eyes and smiled again, drowsily. "Your commander—the tall one who builds the roads—he has been watching me. Maybe I will go with him."

"He doesn't like you," Vettius said. "Don't try it." He grasped her wrist hard. "I won't fight him for you, and he won't give you anything." But there was something in the languid eyes that made him a little cold in spite of himself. Almost more than money, she liked blood.

Ygerna sat down on the bed at the inn in Lopodunum and hastily pulled the seals off her letter. Berenice *had* written. Now if the older woman had only understood what it was that she was asking . . .

My dear child,
   I am grateful for your letter. I am very lonely too these days, and court news passes me by, and I read your story with much interest. It had a very sad ending. It would be such a shame for that to happen. Very dangerous, too, of course, to stop it and then leave loose ends lying about. We have had a fire here, and the whole kitchen wing is gone. The slaves were going to put out the fire when it was only half-burned, but I told them to let it go right down to the ground. It is always better to start fresh, my dear, don't you think, than to try to clean everything up when a mess is left. One always finds things that aren't properly understood, and that makes trouble. A good fire is a cleansing, I always say.

The rest was small talk and good wishes. Ygerna went back

and read the beginning, her dark brows creased together. Then she saw it. Berenice couldn't solve the problem. Correus's scheme was going to have to do that, if it could. But Berenice had seen the danger in the aftermath. Ygerna folded the letter and pushed it down into the bottom of her sewing box.

Berenice, daughter of Herod Agrippa, once a queen, once an emperor's mistress, sat placidly on a milestone by the road that ran past her country house and watched her kitchen burn. The big slave beside her gave her a puzzled look, but he knew better than to question his mistress when she wished to be uncommunicative. She had said to let it burn, so they were letting it burn. But she had set the fire herself, and he'd seen her do it.

Berenice raised her mantle to her mouth and coughed as the smoke drifted in their direction. There was a half smile on her face under the mantle. Her cook had been asking for a new kitchen. Now he could have one. And no one who might read her letter in its journey north would wonder why she would lie about a kitchen fire. It was always as well to cover one's tracks. She had lived in too many palaces not to have learned that. So many palaces, she thought, and all such a long time ago. What was it that kept her in Italy now that Titus was dead? Pride, maybe. If she went back to her brother Agrippa now, it would make another scandal, and they would look so foolish, at their age.

But with Titus gone, and Ygerna gone, too, to be with her soldier husband in Germany, she was so lonely. Maybe it would be better to make her peace with the priests and be old in Palestine among her own kind. She could make her peace with God too, she thought. It was probably time for that.

Frontinus's army reached the Moenus, with the road stretched out behind it, studded with eleven turf-and-timber forts, and another piece of the Agri Decumates was locked into the control of Rome. The Germans were still loose in it, in the pocket between the new boundary and the Rhenus, and the Chatti were across the Moenus, but it was safe enough along the road, so Correus sent for Ygerna. They would halt to raise a fortified bridge to join them with the army of Velius Rufus, which was driving its own road of forts southward from the Taunus Mountains and pushing the Chatti ahead of it. It was at that juncture, named Castra Mattiacorum for the hapless tribe of the Mattiaci in whose territory it lay, where Domitian planned to set up new headquarters. The innumerable folk who were making a living in the army's wake began to pack their baggage again. The road that ran from Moguntiacum along the Moenus River to Castra Mattiacorum was jammed with carts and wagons.

Julius, having traveled from Rome with two mud-spattered ponies hitched to the front of a wagon, and two more, biting each other, tied on behind, took a look at the conglomeration of army supply carts, *baa*'ing herds of sheep, and a troupe of traveling actors on muleback, and said a quick prayer to Poseidon Horse-Father. There was a goat in the back of the wagon, bleating conversationally to itself, and Julius shot it a look of hatred. He gritted his teeth and edged the ponies out onto the road. An old woman trundling a crate of chickens on a handcart pushed past them, and the ponies snorted and started trying to kick in the front of the wagon.

Julius jumped off the seat onto the near pony's back and grabbed an ear. "You're a foul beast. Bide still. You can still be a pony-hide rug tonight." He whispered his threats in loving tones, and the pony blew down its nose and stopped kicking. Julius looked over his shoulder at the other two. They were behaving no worse than usual. The goat was nibbling thoughtfully at Julius's spare cloak, and one of the tethered ponies whickered softly and rubbed its nose against the goat's curving horns. Julius sighed and kicked the lead pony. "All right, then, get moving, you bastard son of a milk cow."

It had been, as he told Correus when he finally nursed the ponies and cart into Castra Mattiacorum, a proper bitch of a trip, and the next time Correus wanted a team of chariot ponies dragged across the Alps, Correus could let him do it the right way, on lead lines, with a spare groom, or he could do it himself. With the goat.

Correus grinned. Julius had filled out some and grown another half an inch, he thought. He was still thin, but he was tough and wiry, and his arms and shoulders were muscular. His character seemed to have undergone no change. "Where have you put them?"

"They're tethered up in the civilian quarter, like you said, with all the other riffraff." The *vicus*, the civil settlement that grew outside an army post, had mushroomed almost overnight at Castra Mattiacorum. The fort was built just beyond the drab huts of an unprepossessing native settlement, and the *vicus* had swallowed the native village whole. Most of the village had been abandoned when the Romans came anyway, and now the entrepreneurs who had flocked from Moguntiacum had adapted it to their uses.

"That's fine," Correus said. "Keep 'em there, and keep 'em looking like cart horses."

"Well, they don't," Julius said. "Not to anyone who knows a horse from his hind end. Not that any carter would have them," he added glumly. "They kicked in the wagon twice. They wouldn't pull it at all until Diulius thought of putting the goat in with 'em." He sounded as if he wished Diulius hadn't. "The goat's the mascot. Diulius uses it to keep the race ponies happy when he ships 'em. Have you ever slept with a goat?"

"No, but I'm afraid you're going to have to go on doing it. We can't leave them alone, and *I* don't intend to sleep with them. Keep 'em out of sight as much as you can. Nobody'll look close as long as they're muddied up. The man we're after doesn't take his amusements in the *vicus*, anyway."

"What are you up to? I saw all the notices for a race. They were pinned up in Moguntiacum, and they're all over the *vicus*."

"The ponies are a substitute entry," Correus said, "but this isn't going to work if anyone gets a look at them."

Julius gave him a baleful look. "When *I* entered a substitute horse, Forst said he'd beat me." He sounded aggrieved.

"You weren't riding your own horse," Correus pointed out. "And the stakes are a lot higher this time."

"All right," Julius said grudgingly. He turned in the tent doorway. "They had better be. I wouldn't sleep with a goat for the fun of it."

When Julius had gone, Correus set his helmet on his head, picked up his vine staff, and went to find Rhodope. The Mattiacorum *vicus* was a hodgepodge of dog kennels, stables, wine stalls, and temples to every god worshiped between the Tiber and the Nile. There were tents, native huts, and timber-built houses constructed of the leavings from the fort and the work that was progressing on the bridge a mile away. Correus had commandeered a reasonably serviceable native house on the outskirts for Ygerna and the children, and installed them in it with Eumenes for a watchdog. A few other officers' wives had arrived, and those of the camp followers who hadn't found other occupations could make a living either by building living quarters for officers' families and Ranvig's delegation, which had arrived in the emperor's train, or by working on the bridge itself. There was a raw look to it, but Castra Mattiacorum was a town already.

Rhodope's tent was pitched at the center of things, and she was ensconced in a padded armchair in front of it, surveying the prospective clientele. The tent was waterproof leather outside, hitched at one end to the red-and-green wagon it traveled in. Inside, striped silk hangings and beaded curtains gave it an air of Eastern splendor, and the pegged wooden floor, which could be taken apart and put together again without nails, was covered with cushions and thick rugs. Rhodope's olive face broadened into a smile when she saw Correus, and she ushered him inside and sent one of the girls to get some wine. They wore old gowns with scarves tied over their hair, cleaning house for the evening's company. Rhodope settled herself in a chair beside a folding table that bore an incense burner and a little bronze statue of a couple in an acrobatic position. Correus took a chair beside her and stretched out his legs. The air was heavy with incense, and the bronze girl appeared to wink at him over her partner's left foot.

"I thought your bones were too old for wagons."

Rhodope chuckled. The gold tooth gleamed at him. "I am also too old to stop eating. Moguntiacum is as dead as Colonia now that the emperor has come here."

"How is business?"

"Ah, very good. Come tonight, and you will see."

"My wife is here."

"You are too respectable, Correus. It will make you dull."

He laughed. "I want a favor, Rhodope."

She became businesslike. "Of what sort?"

"I will give you a piece of useful information. Profitable

information. I just want you and your girls to see that it gets passed on."

Rhodope looked interested, but wary. "And this useful information that I suspect could get me in trouble?"

"Only a tip on a horse race," he said lightly. "Not dangerous."

"Your legate is holding the bets for this horse race," Rhodope said. "And *he* is dangerous."

"Not to you. If you want to make some money, you can put your bets on the team entered by Centurion Quintus."

"That is a long shot." Rhodope, as he thought, appeared to have the odds in her head. Very few things having to do with money passed her by.

"Not so long a shot as Tribune Petreius's team."

"That is the favorite. The odds are even on."

Correus shrugged. "Vettius wouldn't like having to pay that."

"Stop being subtle with me, Correus," Rhodope said. "Has your thief of a legate fixed this race?"

"Yes." He was certain of it now. Eumenes had been making cronies among the other officers' slaves, and Tribune Petreius's driver proved talkative when he had a head full of wine.

"And he means for this Quintus's team to win?"

"Not exactly. His own team is the best horseflesh entered, barring Petreius's."

"But you tell me Quintus. I have seen Quintus's team. They do not look so fine to me."

"Then don't bet," Correus said. "All I ask is to put the word out and say to keep it quiet."

Rhodope chuckled. "That should spread it faster than a fire." She gave him a long, thoughtful look while he pretended to study the bronze couple on the table. "Your father raises horses, doesn't he? I think I will bet."

The bridge was halfway across the river. Julius Frontinus, his tunic tucked up into his sash of office and his legs wet from the knees down, stood on the bank, going over calculations with a junior engineer. A log barge was moored beyond the end of the bridge, and the crack of the pile driver's lead weight sounded sharply across the water. Felix, who appeared each morning as soon as work began, tugged at Frontinus's elbow.

"Can I ride on that?"

Frontinus looked down, amused. "Certainly not."

"Why not?"

"Because you would fall off and drown." He checked the calculations again and ran a hand through his graying hair. His helmet was on the bank, with his sandals and greaves. "That should do very well." The engineer went away, shouting something at another man with a surveyor's tripod, who stood on the completed planking partway out. Frontinus looked down at Felix. "You can ride in a boat with me if you like. Would that do?"

"Yes, please." Felix smiled sunnily. "I have brought my lunch so I can stay all day." He would have spent the night on the bridge, too, if anyone would let him.

Eumenes, sitting astride a log they were bracing between the upstream and downstream pilings, saw Felix's small form trotting after the chief of Engineers and gave a sigh of relief. He should be safe enough with Julius Frontinus. Eumenes had been sent out to work on the bridge—Frontinus was commandeering any help he could get—not to nursemaid his master's son, but if the little devil fell in the water, his mother was not going to think that was an excuse. He gave a final yank to the cording that secured his end of the log and started to splice in the cord end. Beyond him on the pile driver's barge the ratchets clicked as the weight rose to the top of its trough. Eumenes winced as it slammed down again.

"Gets into your ears, don't it?" a soldier said. He was standing in a boat moored to the pilings. He grinned up at Eumenes astride the log. "I'll buy you a drink to chase the headache with if you'll do me a favor. I want a bet put on for the legate's race, and I'm confined to quarters." He made a rueful face. "Drew three days for bein' out after hours last night, but it was worth it. Old Rhodope's got a girl who knows more positions than a snake."

Eumenes laughed. "What's your bet?"

The soldier looked over his shoulder and back to Eumenes. "Centurion Quintus's team. Word's out that they're hotter than they look. I want to get in before the odds change. Put some on for yourself if you want to, but don't spread it around."

"I'll keep it quiet," Eumenes said. He chuckled and swung himself off the log. Those whores were better than a town crier.

"What have you been doing? You'll out-clever yourself."

Tribune Petreius looked at Vettius uncomprehendingly. "I haven't been doing anything."

"No? Well, if you weren't the one who was stupid enough to try to sweeten the odds, who was?" Vettius looked as if he thought Tribune Petreius was plenty stupid enough, and Petreius bristled.

"I told you, I haven't done anything, and I don't care for your tone."

"Well, someone," Vettius explained patiently, "has been touting Centurion Quintus's team as a hot bet, and there's been a lot of money laid on."

"But, that's all to the good, isn't it?" Petreius said. "I mean, Quintus's nags are a long shot. They couldn't take your team."

"Then why is every soldier in this fort scrambling to bet on them?" Vettius inquired icily. "They have *stopped* betting on your team, I might add, which was supposed to be the point of our arrangement."

"What's the difference?" Petreius took a peach from the bowl of fruit on the legate's desk and tossed it from hand to hand. It was pleasantly cool in the legate's tent, and Petreius was disinclined to worry. "They aren't going to win."

"The difference is, they aren't guaranteed to lose," Vettius snapped, "and when that sort of rumor gets going and I didn't start it, I get suspicious."

"You're always suspicious."

"It has paid so far."

"Well, Quintus's team doesn't look like much to me, but if you're that worried, then have someone take care of them. He's just a junior, and a through-the-ranks man at that. What can he do?"

"Admirable," Vettius said sarcastically. "And then I will have to give back all the money that's been bet on them if they're scratched. And since no one seems inclined to bet on *your* team now, we seem to have lost the purpose of this race."

"Oh." Petreius looked thoughtful. "I know someone who might be interested in holding a second book. We could always bet on your nags with him."

"You show signs of intelligence," Vettius said. "That is useful. I'll shorten the odds on Quintus, and maybe the fools will decide he's not such a prospect, after all. But put the money down with your man, because if they don't take the bait, I'm going to scratch Quintus."

Tribune Petreius departed, eating his peach, and Marius Vettius looked after him nervously. Petreius was not the only backer involved in this race. A number of useful men had been included in the money-making here, and if anything went wrong, they were not going to be understanding.

"I took a look at Vettius's team. Them and their driver," Julius said, shuddering. "No offense, sir, but it's a good thing you sent for the bays."

"We thought so, too," Flavius said, "when *we* looked at them." Flavius kept his own chariot team, for his amusement, but one look at Marius Vettius's golden-hided beasts had told him that his own hadn't a prayer. Petreius's team was even better, but they weren't competition.

"That little horror who's driving them is even worse," Julius said. Vettius's chariot boy was a subhuman menace with the temperament of a crocodile and was popularly believed to have had an ape for a mother. "I want to keep well ahead of him."

"Now just a minute," Correus said. "You aren't going to drive."

Julius sat up straight, indignant. "I didn't nursemaid those nags clear from Rome to watch *you* drive 'em! And you weigh too much!"

"I weigh enough to sit on you," Correus said. "Now look, Diulius says you have promise. He didn't say you're invincible. And you're not a better driver than I am—not yet."

Julius was outraged. "I drove in the Circus Maximus last year! In a *real* race. And I won." He glared. "What have *you* been doing?"

"Getting old," Flavius said. "But not so old that we can't deal with you."

They stood side by side and looked down at him. "I'm still a better driver than you are," Correus said. "Keep arguing and we'll shut you up in the stables."

Julius looked disgusted, but he gave up. Flavius turned to his brother. "Now that we've settled that point," he said lazily, "are you going to try to tell me you're a better driver than *I* am?"

"Not you, too!" Correus said. "I cooked up this scheme. You aren't going to risk your hide on it!"

"You had help," Flavius said. "And Aemelius is *my* kin."

"And I suppose you'll say that Julia's only *half* sister to me, so she and Lucius don't count!"

"Don't be an ass," Flavius said. "The man's your legate. He can boot you from here to a hole in Syria, and you never did like desert."

"Not if we win," Correus said.

They stood stubbornly confronting each other, and Julius watched them with interest.

"There's more at stake than this race," Correus said. "And the man we don't want suspicious is the emperor. You're on his staff."

"He already knows I have a quarrel with Vettius," Flavius said.

"He also told you to let it alone. If you want to be around when we've finished with Vettius, you'd better not show your face in this quite so publicly. Domitian doesn't like being crossed."

"Right," Flavius said sarcastically. "He's going to swallow a tale that Quintus really owns those bays, once he's seen them race. Quintus couldn't afford those ponies if he put his whole year's pay into them."

"He'll believe they're *my* ponies," Correus said, "and I stepped in for friendship's sake. Quintus and I go back a ways."

Flavius snorted. "Quintus was a menace. He went Unlawful Absent and punched a sentry. And you got him a promotion. He owes *you.*"

"He straightened up when he got it, too," Correus said. "He just used to get bored when there was nothing to do. Anyway, none of this makes any difference. Domitian doesn't know that, and he hasn't ordered *me* to keep *my* hands off Vettius. And there's something else you haven't thought of." He looked hesitant.

"What's that?"

"*Your* hands."

Flavius held them up. Long hands, four-fingered. He didn't seem to be offended, but his stubborn expression didn't change. "They haven't slowed me down yet."

"You haven't driven in a race that mattered this much yet. Can you say for sure that it might not matter?"

Flavius sat down and spread his hands out on the white skirt of his harness tunic. "Damn you, Correus. No, I can't say for sure." He looked up at his brother, and there was a lazy, dangerous light in his eyes. "All right, you can drive the bays."

"And you'll stay out of it." Correus looked suspicious. He didn't trust his brother an inch farther than he could have tossed the horses.

Flavius stood up again and smiled. "I told you, you can drive the bays."

When race day dawned a week later, Correus was still suspicious, but so far his brother hadn't tried to have him doped or tied up, which Correus wouldn't have put past him. Correus passed up the dubious cooking of the officers' mess, to which duty generally drove him, and had breakfast with his family. He was halfway through the light meal that was all he was going to allow himself, when Julius found him. After he had listened to Julius, he had worse things to worry about than what Flavius might do.

XVIII

The Race and the Rose
of Italy

"DOPED!" JULIUS SAID INDIGNANTLY. "DOPED IN THEIR STALLS, Centurion Quintus's poor nags that weren't even going to run! The centurion's some mad, I can tell you. He thinks he may lose one of them—the bastard overdid the dose!"

Correus tried not to look unnerved. They had done what they set out to do and ruined the betting, and now Vettius was afraid. A frightened man was unpredictable.

"He is a bad man," Felix said. "The chief of Engineers got mad and shouted at him." He seemed to have no doubts as to whom Julius meant.

Ygerna put a hand over his mouth. Felix was entirely too clever. "You are not to repeat that, ever," she said. "Now eat your breakfast." Felix wrapped his feet around the legs of his chair and returned to his bread and honey, but he kept his ears open. Eilenn sat next to him, eating her own bread and honey, with Nurse washing her between bites. "Nurse, leave us, please," Ygerna said. "You can wash the whole child when she has done. It will be simpler." She poured Felix a cup of very watered wine and pushed the bowl of olives at him. "Eat some of these and be quiet, or I will make you leave, too."

"Go and find the cavalry vet from the Eleventh Claudia, and have him look at Quintus's horses," Correus told Julius. "He's the best we've got. Tell him I asked."

"Correus, this is beginning to frighten me," Ygerna said when they were alone with the children. "That man will try to do you an evil."

"Well, now, we knew that when we started," Correus said.

"I didn't think he would show his hand so openly. I wish now—"

"You wish I could back out," Correus said. "Well, I can't.

And I wouldn't if I could. This is my *family*." His voice suddenly lost its note of forced placidity. She saw both hands clench into fists. "*No one* does what this man has done to us and gets away free. And if I don't do it, Flavius will, and I have a better chance, whatever he thinks."

"Maybe Julius Frontinus could have done something," Ygerna said doubtfully.

Correus shook his head. "We've been through that. We can't tell Julius Frontinus that Lucius has tied himself up with treason. Not even if Frontinus would understand. No, this is for us to do."

Ygerna gave up and sat poking raisins into her bread and honey, making a pattern. She didn't feel much like eating. *One day I will understand them,* she thought. This was her first experience with a family so tightly knit that even though they squabbled among themselves, they would close ranks like a locking door against the outside world when one of their own was threatened. Her own family, notably her uncle Bendigeid, would have each cheerfully sold the rest straight into Annwn if it had seemed propitious. Except her mother maybe, and even she had gone to live with the holy women on Mona to escape from Bendigeid, and left Ygerna behind.

She sat and watched her husband eat breakfast. He was drinking from the children's pitcher, which had more water than wine. For him, or for either of the children, she would kill. That was natural. But she had married into a more far-reaching bond than that, it seemed.

When he had finished eating, Correus went off to the hovel where he and Julius had been hiding his father's ponies. Ygerna called Nurse back in and told her to get the children ready. If Felix was forbidden to watch the race, he would only run away and watch it anyway.

Nearly everyone in Castra Mattiacorum had turned out for the legate's race. Ygerna settled herself in the stands above the track with Eilenn in her lap and Eumenes beside her, to keep a grip on Felix and to make it clear to the crowd that his mistress was an officer's lady and not to be annoyed. Ygerna looked nervously at Eilenn, but no dark visions clouded the child's face this morning. *Maybe it will be all right.* But that wasn't much to go on. The Sight only came when whatever god had given it saw fit to send it once again.

The arena was a natural hollow with wooden planks set into it for seats on three sides, and the course marked out below. The *spina* was a makeshift barrier of sawhorses and lumber from the bridge, draped with scarlet cloth and garlanded with greenery. A pole with the Capricorn badge of the Fourteenth Gemina and the personal emblem of its legate rose at one end. A reviewing box had been built opposite the open side where the horses would come in, and it too was draped in scarlet and hung with garlands of pine and oak branches.

The emperor was in the reviewing box, looking bored, but Ygerna couldn't see Flavius. Vettius was there, with his optio beside him. His sleek face showed a bit of a smile at the corners of his mouth. Tribune Petreius lounged on a bench nearby, with a slave holding an oiled canvas parasol in case it should rain on the tribune's armor. A fat man with oily dark hair and gold rings on the pudgy hands clasped across his paunch sat beside Petreius, with another slave arranging a rug across his lap. The benches everywhere were crowded to overflowing with soldiers and all the civilians of the *vicus*. Rhodope was there, like a fat, jeweled hen, with all her painted chicks around her. The German delegation turned out in wolfskin shirts and gold torques. Vettius's woman sat eating sweetmeats on the other side of the reviewing box, and a little farther on was Julius Frontinus in his purple cloak. It was a festival hiatus in the middle of an irksome campaign, and the crowd was set to enjoy itself. For a provincial race, a great deal of money was on the books.

The army trumpeter beside the reviewing box raised his horn, and the crowd settled in expectantly. Beside him, a race keeper with a wooden slate called out a name. The first team, a showy set of sorrels, swept through the opening at the end of the track. The driver, a blond, red-faced decurion named Rabirius, drew rein in front of the reviewing box, saluted the emperor, and took his place along the starting line chalked in the damp earth.

The next name was Quintus, and Vettius permitted himself a slight smile as it was called. Centurion Quintus was sitting in the stands and looking surly. Vettius waited for him to stand

and say his team was scratched, but Quintus didn't twitch. The sound of ponies' hooves made Vettius snap his head around.

The bays frisked and swished their black tails as they came around the track to the box, and Correus held them well in. Like the other drivers, his reins were lashed around his waist, and there was a knife in his belt to cut them if necessary. He wore breeches and shirt to block the cold, which had a sharp edge in a moving chariot, and an old army-issue helmet without insignia. He saluted the emperor as he halted, and gave Vettius an evil grin. Vettius looked back, a long, cold look like a snake's, and Correus saw his hand clench on the box rail. The race keeper announced the next entry from his slate.

The third team was Tribune Petreius's, four white half-Arab ponies with little pricked ears and fine-boned heads. The driver, Musa, might have been Arab too, a swarthy beak-nosed boy with a gentle hand on the reins. He lined his team up beside Correus's bays, scanning them with a startled look.

"Fine day for a race," Correus said cheerfully. The Arab driver didn't answer. The first team, on his other side, Correus gave no more than a glance. The sorrels didn't have much to them. Even in the pole position, they wouldn't be dangerous. But Vettius hadn't bothered to fix the draw for position, and Correus had got lucky—he had the number-two spot. Next up were Vettius's, a sleek, gold team that reminded Correus unnervingly of their owner. Their driver, Tubero, the reputed half ape, lined them up in a businesslike fashion, saluted the emperor, and shot a look to the Arab boy Musa that said he had better remember instructions. Then the ape gave a baleful stare at Correus. Behind Tubero and the gold ponies came a team of blacks belonging to the legate of the Claudia, with his personal slave, Brygus, driving. That was it, Correus thought. Five entries. He tightened his grip on the reins, and the bay ponies began to dance sideways. The trumpet sounded its raucous announcement a sixth time.

Correus jerked his head up and narrowed his eyes across the track at the team coming in. Seeing their silky white hides, their red harness making a cheery splash of color, he didn't need to hear the race keeper to know whose horses those were. The slim, straight figure driving them was a mirror image to his own—except that Flavius was wearing full dress kit, embossed cuirass, and white harness tunic. Flavius never looked at him. He saluted, turned his ponies into the outside position that a last-minute entry had to be satisfied with, and settled his helmet forward so that the ridge would cut the sun.

Pigheaded ass! Correus shot the thought in his brother's direction as he gathered his reins, and Flavius laughed suddenly as if he had heard him. The trumpet sounded a last fanfare, the sorrel ponies to his left jumped and reared, and the emperor's hand dropped a white handerchief over the edge of the box.

The bay ponies were shooting forward as it fell, and Correus held them carefully in place. It was a short track, but the race was for eight full laps. The driver who was fool enough to give his horses their head now would have them limping home dead last at the end. Rabirius's sorrels had taken the lead, and now Correus discounted them completely; they could take that pace for no more than three laps. On his other side, Petreius's Arab driver, Musa, was neck and neck with him, with Tubero and Vettius's gold beasts on his flank. Brygus and the legate's black team had fallen slightly behind them, and out of the corner of his eye Correus saw Flavius's ponies pull past the blacks and begin edging closer to the inside, trying to cut them off.

They swept around the first turn and came into the straight with the sorrels still in the lead and Correus, Petreius's team, and the gold ponies dead even. Brygus and the blacks were half a length back, still holding Flavius on the outside. The track was wet, and the ponies' hooves were beginning to send up clods of mud. Correus could feel the cold bite into him even through the heavy woolen shirt. Flavius must be freezing. It would serve him right for peacocking about in his dress uniform, although Correus had to admit that if Flavius had wanted a rig to unnerve the other drivers, he had hit on it. He and his ponies looked expensive enough to have driven straight from the Circus Maximus in Rome. Only Correus knew that Flavius's white team couldn't have taken Marius Vettius's ponies on the best day they ever had. But then Flavius wasn't planning to win. Correus settled down to drive, and his irritation with Flavius faded when he saw Vettius's monkey-faced driver flick his whip out: As it came back over his head, it caught Brygus full in the face and laid open his brow. If Flavius had decided to risk the emperor's temper to give Correus an ally on the track, it was because Flavius thought his brother was going to need one.

They careened past the reviewing box in a thunder of noise and mud, and the race keeper tugged on a rope. A bronze ball rose up to the top of the pole beside him: one lap down. The vibration came through the floorboards of the chariot like the shiver before an earthquake. In the stands, Ygerna thought that the chariots looked flimsy enough to shatter at a touch. They were not the whippy leather and wicker two-horse chariots of her home hills, built for the rough rolling roads of Britain, but thin, featherlight contraptions made for a smooth track, with the least weight possible. A child's toy, meant to pull a doll in, not something to drive at a dead gallop against a man trying to kill you. *Epona of the horses, let him win.*

As the third bronze ball went up, Rabirius's sorrels pushed to their limits, began to slacken quickly, as Correus had thought. Correus began to edge his own team closer to the *spina*. As they nosed past the sorrels, he could see Vettius's driver, Tubero, begin to pull away from Petreius's Arabs. Correus risked just one quick look at Musa's face, saw his mouth set in a grim line, and noted the angle of his hands and arms. He was pulling his horses. Vettius's team would be in front of him and hanging on Correus's flank in another minute. Correus gave the bays their heads, and they pulled past the flagging sorrels into the slot nearest the *spina*.

Tubero slashed his whip across the white Arabs' noses in a fury because Musa hadn't pulled them back fast enough, and then he was beside Correus, with his whip back over his head again. It was blatant cheating, but it is very hard to see from the stands what is happening in the center of a flying pack of chariots and horses in a rain of spattered mud. Correus let go the reins, and the bays shot out almost out of control as he turned and tried to catch the end of the whip, aimed at him this time. It hurt like Hades, but he got hold of it a third of the way from the end and yanked on it hard. Tubero had also dropped his reins, and his ponies thundered beside Correus's dangerously close. Correus pulled his knife and cut the whip rather than wrestle for it. Tubero stumbled a little, snarling as it came back in his hand. Correus looked at his piece and threw it into the *spina*. There had been a metal ring tied onto the end, and it had torn a gash in his hand. He grabbed the reins, gritting his teeth as the leather rubbed his torn hand, and fought with the bays until they were back under control.

The fourth ball went up the pole. The pack began to sort itself out: Correus closest to the *spina*, with Rabirius's sorrels behind him now, tiring fast; Tubero and Vettius's gold ponies ran beside him. Tubero turned his whip in his hand and struck at Correus with the handle. Musa and Petreius's Arabs galloped behind them, caught between the sorrels and Brygus's blacks— as good a place as any for a man with orders not to win. Correus had seen the look on Musa's face as he had reined his horses in, though. The Arab boy had followed his orders, but he hadn't liked it. Beyond the blacks, Flavius's white ponies had pulled ahead and were angling across in front of the blacks' noses to hang on Tubero's flank.

They held that pattern as they careened through the fifth lap. Then Correus shook out his reins and began the familiar singsong croon that all of Appius's ponies had learned meant the last few laps of a race and the last burst of speed. The bays flew into the curve with their black tails streaming out behind them like smoke, and the gold ponies racing beside them, so close that a man could have jumped from one to the next. Too close. The *spina* flashed by on the left, the scarlet cloth rippling as the far-left pony brushed it as he passed. Tubero edged the gold ponies closer, deliberately pushing Correus's team in on the *spina*. The blunt ends of a tangle of sawhorses and old lumber showed ominously through the scarlet cloth.

"Keep off!" Correus shouted furiously.

Tubero swung his ponies hard into Correus's. The right-hand bay screamed and bit at the gold pony, one of the center bays stumbled and righted itself, and the chariot rocked. Correus grabbed his own whip and slashed at Tubero with it, but they kept coming, pushing relentlessly. As they went into the straight, the bays were beginning to lose their stride, unnerved by the crowding. Rabirius's sorrels were well behind, at the tail of the pack now, and Musa and the Arabs were running along the *spina* behind Correus. Correus looked frantically over his shoulder. He would have to chance it. They swept past the reviewing box again, and the sixth ball went up. Only two laps to go. At the next curve Correus deliberately overshot, turning wide, to put more room between himself and the *spina*, pushing Tubero's gold team out with him. He was too busy watching the gold ponies and the curve to look back again, but as they swept into the straight with a team's width between them and the *spina* now, he saw that Musa was still pulling his horses, ignoring the chance to push up beside Correus and box him in. Tubero shouted back at the Arabs' driver, but the boy raised his hand and made an obscene gesture. Tubero would get no more help from him. Correus looked back at the gold team just in time. The driver had gathered all his reins into one hand and was perched like a monkey on the front rim of his chariot. He jumped and landed on the flying gold back of the pony on the left. Correus saw that he had his dagger out, and the look on his broad, ugly face said that he meant to use it.

Correus swore and swung his whip at him, but it missed, and Tubero leaned over and grabbed at the rein of the bay pony running at his side. There was the dull gleam from the blade, and the rein snapped. The bay was running free, still hitched by the traces to the chariot. Tubero leaned down and reached for the traces.

As the reviewing stand flashed by again, Correus wondered how Vettius and his tame ape were going to explain to the emperor the cutting of another driver's traces. Maybe they wouldn't have to explain it. The emperor probably wouldn't care if he won the money. With the team unbalanced, it would be easy to run the bays in on the *spina*, and then Correus likely wouldn't be around to complain. He pulled his own knife out and cut the reins that were knotted about his waist. He looped them through a ring in the chariot rim instead, the short end of the severed rein whipping in his face. There was only one way to control a pony running loose, and that was from his back. Uncontrolled, they would all be on the *spina* in seconds. The jagged lumber of the makeshift *spina* would be death if they hit it at this speed.

Poseidon help me. He pulled himself up on the rim and hung there. He could see the ground falling sickeningly away below him through a tangle of legs and iron-shod hooves. Julius was right. He weighed too much. Half again as much maybe as Vettius's agile driver. But it was jump or go into the *spina* as soon as the right-hand pony was loose. He jumped.

He landed on the bay's back and grabbed frantically at the bridle with one hand and pushed awkwardly at Tubero with the other, his right. The knife flashed again, and the bay pony stumbled as Tubero caught the trace and held on. Both teams lost their stride and drifted in on the *spina* again.

Someone shouted something Correus couldn't understand over the pounding hooves, and then as he turned to wrestle with Tubero again, he saw the white team coming up like ghosts on the other side. Not Musa's ponies this time, but Flavius's, with the red harness a bright splotch against their hide. They ran mouths open and nostrils wide, foam spattering from their bits as Flavius pushed them past the limits of their strength to catch the gold team. *He'll break their wind*, Correus thought in the second before Flavius yanked on the reins and slued them around so that his chariot slammed hard into Tubero's empty one. It rocked, and there was the sound of splintering wood as a piece flew out of the wheel. The gold ponies stumbled, and the right-hand one went down with a frantic scream. The two in the middle reared in panic, and in the next instant they were all down. Tubero disappeared with a shriek under the thrashing hooves. Flavius's chariot also bounced on a broken wheel as he stood fighting to pull his ponies in.

Correus looked down at the traces. The right-hand one was almost cut through. He grabbed for the next pony's bridle with his left hand and held the one he rode with his right. Out of the corner of his eye he could see Brygus's blacks dodging past the wreckage to come up on their right. "Run, friend," Correus crooned into the bay's ears, and felt a small jolt as the trace snapped in two. "Run and hold together." With Correus on his back, the loose pony stretched out his legs and kept pace with his mates, and the eighth bronze ball rose on the pole as the finish line flashed by.

Now how do I stop them? That hadn't occurred to him. He could have managed the pony he was riding easily enough, but if he let go of the other three, they would probably run until they overturned the chariot. He remembered old Alan teaching him to ride: "Be remembering first that the horse is a creature of small brain." *Sound advice*, he thought grimly. He tugged experimentally on the bridle in his left hand, and the pony slowed. His teammates slackened with him. Correus leaned out and tugged a little harder, forcing himself not to look at the ground rushing away under him. Ahead of him, the crowd that had poured out onto the track to cheer the winner saw him coming and dived back into the seats on the slope. Behind him the race keeper and his crew were pulling Vettius's broken chariot away, with the gold ponies limping after it. Tubero was a still form in the mud, with a legionary surgeon bending over him.

It took Correus a whole circuit of the track to get the bays down to a walk, and by that time the crowd had surged out around them again, yelling his name. Julius pushed his way through and hopped into the chariot to grab the reins. The race keeper came up with a sober look and Flavius at his shoulder. His eyes widened when he saw the cut trace.

Correus had a short, sharp explanation prepared to account for the wreckage of his commander's chariot, but no one asked for it. Flavius had got there first, and Marius Vettius was frantically denouncing Tubero's conduct to the emperor, who wasn't listening. Tubero was dead with a broken skull. Correus slid down from the bay's back, hoping he wasn't going to make a fool of himself by falling. His knees felt like soup. He stumbled, and Flavius stepped up and let him lean on him. Flavius's cuirass and face were black with mud, but there was a satisfied look in his eyes.

"Your ponies?" Correus asked. The white team were his brother's pets. Correus hoped they weren't wind broken.

"They're all right," Flavius said. "I think. I hope. The groom's walking them."

"Good." Correus thought of Vettius's gold ponies, ruined and limping for their owner's greed. He should feel as guilty about Tubero, he supposed, but he didn't, much. The dead driver had been trying to kill him. He thought about the jump onto that loose horse, and his stomach turned over again.

Centurion Quintus came up and pounded him on the back, grinning. Quintus seemed to have no regrets for Tubero, who had probably been the one who had doped his horses. The trumpet screeched again, trying to make a dent in the din of the crowd, and the emperor stepped to the front of the box and dropped the victory wreath down with a perfunctory gesture of congratulations. The race keeper gave it to Quintus, and Quintus hung it over the neck of the pony Correus had ridden. The pony snorted at the evergreen scent in his nose. When Correus looked up again at the box, it was empty and Domitian was stalking away up the aisle through the emptying seats, with his slaves and his staff scurrying after him. If he had bet on Vettius's ponies on Vettius's say-so, he would be in a temper.

Everyone else came crowding up with loud congratulations. They had got their money's worth for excitement, and those who had bet on Centurion Quintus's team were going to have their faith repaid at twenty-to-one. Brygus pushed through the crowd with his master, the legate of the Claudia, behind him.

"That was a fine fight," Brygus said appreciatively. "And he was no loss to the world, that one." His face was still bleeding from the cut over his brow, and Correus remembered the iron ring on the end of Tubero's whip. The legate of the Claudia looked as if he would cheerfully see Vettius in Hades.

Next to the *spina*, Petreius's Arab driver, Musa, was walking the tribune's ponies cool, with the tribune arguing furiously at his side. "You said to pull 'em, sir," Correus heard the stubborn voice faintly over the crowd, "and I pulled 'em."

"Be quiet, you fool!" Petreius snapped. Tubero's blood had sunk into the mud of the track, but the ponies smelled it and shied. Petreius backed out of the way. Up on the slope the fat man with the dark curls sat smiling benignly. He had taken Petreius's bets, and now the tribune owed him a great deal of money, more money than the tribune wanted to pay. Petreius looked thoughtfully at the tall, graceful figure of Marius Vettius, looking down his nose at the fat man, while the fat man just smiled and shrugged. Vettius would owe him money too, probably more than he had, after he covered the bets on Quintus. Petreius found that insufficient vengeance for his own losses, but he was too afraid of Vettius to cross him. Still, there had been other backers to this race, promised a sure thing by Vettius for mysterious reasons of his own, and they wouldn't be so hesitant. *They'll turn on him*, Petreius thought. *He's not going to come out of this*. He went back to Musa and promised him a gold piece not to tell any soul on this earth that Tribune Petreius had come within ten feet of Marius Vettius, ever.

The milling crowd pushed around the winners. Eumenes came down the slope, with Felix on his shoulders. Felix beamed sunnily at his father.

"That was exciting! Can I ride like that, Papa?"

"Certainly not."

Felix didn't bother to argue. "Certainly not" was what people mostly said to him when he wanted to do something, he had found. Eumenes set him on the ground, and he climbed into the chariot with Julius to see what he could see from there. Ygerna and Eilenn were still sitting on the slope waiting for them to come back, and on the other side, Felix could see his uncle Flavius in his mud-spattered armor, walking up toward the blond woman who was the German chieftain's widow. Papa wouldn't like that, he thought shrewdly, but he didn't say anything. It wasn't something he was supposed to know about.

Flavius felt good. A little bouncy. Drunk maybe. He rocked back on his heels and looked up at the place where Fiorgyn was sitting. He caught her eye, and she rose, turning her back on Signy, who put out her hand and said something, and Ranvig, who just glared at her. Maybe he should adopt that tactic, Flavius thought, instead of trying to explain to all the well-meaning people who gave him reasons why he shouldn't see her. Right now he didn't care. Vettius was never going to be a threat to the emperor again, and Julia and that treasonous idiot Lucius Paulinus were safe. Vettius had lost his own money and a lot that belonged to his backers, and they weren't going to forgive that. He'd be lucky if they didn't hunt him down. Flavius felt avenged. For his father-in-law, for his stillborn baby, for Aemelia.

So now that you have made your wife happy, you will go off like a tomcat in the woods with another woman, something said. His conscience, maybe. He didn't want to listen to it, so he didn't. He'd pay his penance for Fiorgyn soon enough.

She was smiling as he came up to her, her sky-colored eyes bright against snowy skin. "I am glad you have a whole hide still," she said gravely.

"My brother's the one who nearly got his split open," Flavius said. "No nicks on me, but I think I'll stay out of the emperor's way for the afternoon. Just till he sees the light of reason."

"And now you have your vengeance on Vettius. That will

make your wife happy." Startled, he wondered if she knew what he had been thinking. She usually didn't mention his wife, the way he usually didn't mention Ranvig.

"Yes." He was standing carefully distant from her, here in the open.

She watched his eyes and saw hunger blaze up in them like fire. She only said, "We shouldn't go together," and turned and walked away, holding her blue gown above the mud. At the rim of the hollow she went south, toward the woods. After a moment he followed her.

Correus pulled Felix down from the chariot and handed him to Eumenes. He looked around him for Flavius.

"He has gone with my kinswoman," a voice said in his ear. He turned to find Ranvig beside him, his eyes annoyed. He stood hands on hips and looked accusingly at Correus.

"Typhon take them!" Correus said. "Why didn't you stop her?"

"Why didn't you stop your brother?" Ranvig said. "I couldn't stop Fiorgyn unless I locked her up, and that is beneath her dignity and mine both."

"Are you under the impression I can lock up my brother?" Correus asked. He wondered if he looked as surly as he felt. He pulled his helmet off and ran a hand through his damp hair, making it stand up wildly in the front. *Damn Flavius!*

"It is an idea," Ranvig said sourly. "Before I think of another one."

"Put a knife in my brother, Ranvig, and I'll put one in you," Correus said, "treaty or no treaty." He glanced around him. They were speaking German, but this place was about as private as the Forum at Rome, and everyone was looking interested. "This is not the time."

"Agreed." Ranvig's oddly set eyes were considering. "There is a stall that has good beer in the village outside your fort. We might as well drink and curse them there."

Correus thought. "We might at that." Maybe Ranvig would have something useful to say. Maybe he just felt like drowning his wrath at his kinswoman in a beer pot. He gave the ponies to Julius, and he and Ranvig shouldered their way together through the crowd, companions in indignation. People slapped

Correus on the back as he went, but most gave a wide berth to Ranvig's slim figure in his wolf's-hide shirt.

The *vicus* was thick with wine stalls, but there was one that had native beer of a better brew than most. They ducked under the precariously balanced board above the door that proclaimed its name as The Rose of Italy, and found a bench at the back. The Rose of Italy had a floor of German mud, thinly overlaid with straw. Correus scraped his boots clean against the table leg before he sat down. As an afterthought he pulled off his neck scarf and rubbed the mud off his face, too. That would do, he thought. The Rose of Italy's customers weren't overly particular. By the counter at the front a pair of Asturian cavalry troopers were arguing in their native tongue about horse liniment, and the only other occupant was a legionary in the corner who had been brooding into his wine cup. He gave them a mournful glance and pulled his cloak up around his ears further to contemplate whatever ailed him.

The proprietor, a burly German with what looked like an old pair of breeches tied around his waist for an apron, came over and looked inquiring. Correus passed up the wine, which he doubted was palatable, for a pot of beer. It was a heavy, dark brew and fairly cold from sitting in kegs in the river. He emptied the first pot practically in one swallow and held it out for more. Since the start of the race, his throat had been dry as an old riverbed. He wiped his mouth on the back of his hand.

"My brother appears to have lost his mind," he said flatly. "Don't think I haven't told him so."

Ranvig stretched his legs out in front of him, in breeches of fine, warm brown wool and wolf's-hide boots. Around his neck there was a heavy collar of beautifully worked gold that ended in the smiling heads of doglike beasts. His pale braids were knotted with leather thongs with gold caps on the ends, and there was gold on his wrists and in a thin fillet in his hair. Gold off Roman ships, Correus thought, that came through Theophanes's camp into Semnone land. Ranvig drank his beer with the frustrated expression of the ant who has tried to preach good sense to a grasshopper. "The world is full of fools," he said.

The legionary in the corner, who appeared to speak some German, looked up. "Thash right," he said sadly. "Fools everywhere you turn. Like . . . like rabbitsh." He heaved a sigh and stuck his nose back in his wine cup.

Correus's mouth twitched, but he thought of Lucius Paulinus and the fools who had let Marius Vettius wriggle into their plot. And the emperor, who was in a temper because he had bet on a horse race that Marius Vettius had staged to give him enough money to buy the emperor's guard when he was dead. And Forst, who was in Castra Mattiacorum working on Frontinus's bridge and trying to decide where he belonged. And Ranvig and his whole tribe. The fools seemed to be thick on the ground just now. "You will swell their company if you don't leave the Agri Decumates alone," he said and drank his beer.

"Isn't that why I am meeting with your emperor?" Ranvig said politely.

Correus made a rude noise in his throat. "And picking off patrols and throwing dead horses in the river."

"If we are to be truthful," Ranvig said, "yes. Wouldn't it be simpler if *you* left the Free Lands alone?"

"We can't afford to," Correus said shortly. "The Agri Decumates is a weak spot. It's got to be shored up. And Marbod's tribe has been trouble from Day One. Marbod asked for it. You won't stop us. Don't think you can. But we'll stop the frontier line short of your lands if you'll use your head."

"Rome has said something of the sort before," Ranvig said. "About stopping at the Rhenus." He gave Correus a smile, like that of the beasts' heads on his torque. Maybe they were snarling.

Correus set his beer down with a thump on the table. "Until the Germans came sword in hand over the Rhenus when we let our guard down!"

"There were enough grievances to warrant that," Ranvig said. "I rode with that war host. I remember."

"The *last* chieftain of the Semnones dreamed up that excuse," Correus said. "Mithras! Why do we argue this? How many times have we had this conversation, you and I?"

"Since Colonia?" Ranvig said. "Too many." He drummed his empty cup on the table for more, and the proprietor put a pitcher down. Correus moodily poured his own cup full.

"It's the same talk we made in Theophanes's camp," Ranvig

said. He drank his beer and appeared to be in a truth-telling mood. "Only without the fancy stories. I never did think you were as stupid as you looked."

"I'm not," Correus said.

"Tell me. Since you say that Rome will win no matter what the Semnones do, why does it matter to you what we do? We came to talk about my kinswoman and your brother," he added.

"So we did. We can talk about them until you have a beard as long as Wuotan's, and nothing will change."

"I know what Rome is, Centurion," Ranvig said, "and nothing will change that, either."

"Then why are you trying to go the way Nyall Sigmundson went?" Correus said, exasperated.

"I asked you, why do you care?"

Correus glared at him. "Because I think it's a pity you aren't a Roman. Because I don't want to meet you from behind a shield. Because I don't want to fill in your grave."

"Nor I yours," Ranvig said softly. "It may not come to that, you know."

"And snakes may sprout wings."

"Assuredly. But I am thinking that this may be the last chance we have to drink together, you and I," Ranvig said. "Your general has almost finished his bridge." He waved his hand, and the proprietor put another pitcher down. The legionary in the corner was singing softly to himself now, an old marching song from the last war here. Ranvig poured both cups very full.

Somehow, it was nearly sunset when they left. They stood in the long shadows that the wine stall's doorposts cast on the muddy street, and looked at each other. They were both a little drunk.

Finally Ranvig said, "May the gods watch over you, Centurion," and went south along the street to the timber house that had been built for him. Correus went the other way into the fort.

XIX

A Box Full of Blood

WHEN CORREUS GOT TO HIS OFFICE IN HIS TENT AT THE END of the First Cohort barracks row, Eumenes was there with Centurion Quintus. Quintus was sitting in the chair by Correus's desk, leaning his arms on his knees and poking at the plank floor with his vine staff. He looked up with relief when Correus came in.

"Glad you turned up, sir. I'm not sure, but I think we've got trouble."

Correus sighed. Trouble seemed to follow him like a faithful slave lately. "What?"

"They hauled me off the parade ground this afternoon, up to the Praetorium. Bit of a surprise." The days when Quintus was regularly getting hauled before his commander were long gone. "The emperor was lookin' like a kettle that's just on the boil, and he wanted to know what you were doin' in the race, under my name. I guess they couldn't find you."

Oh, Lord, Correus thought. And he'd spent the afternoon drinking beer with the chief of the Semnones. "They didn't look in the right wineshop," he said. "Sorry." And a good thing, too.

"I told him you offered me your team after we found mine drugged this mornin', and the cavalry vet you sent round can vouch for it, praise be, but the emperor was hopping mad, and your legate was there, and it looked like they'd been arguing."

"Did you say who'd done the drugging?"

"I don't know, do I? Not to prove it. I said there'd been some heavy betting laid on my team, and the emperor knows enough to know who wouldn't like *that*, if they should win. He drew his own conclusions, and then he said to send for Tribune Petreius, and they sent me packing."

"Well, Petreius can put the finger on Vettius," Correus said cheerfully. "Not that Domitian doesn't already know the race was fixed. He should—he bet on it. He's mad because we upset things."

"That's not what worries me," Quintus said. "It's Vettius. *He's* going to put the finger on someone. He said so. And it wasn't about the race. They hustled me out before I heard any more. He wouldn't have said that much if he hadn't been in a temper, either. Like a pair of kids they were, squabbling."

Correus groped for his chair and sat down. He hadn't thought of that. Stupid, he thought with mounting horror, not to have allowed for Vettius's spite. *I'm the fool.* He felt cold.

"Look here, sir," Quintus said, "I never asked why you wanted to set Vettius up like that, and I ain't goin' to ask now. But whatever it is, he's got the goods on somebody, and he was sayin' he'd go and get 'em when they threw me out."

Vettius's records, Correus thought frantically. His hoard of secrets, carefully collected. Enough to cut the throat of everybody connected with the plot, starting with Lucius and Julia. It wouldn't save Vettius's hide for him, but it would give him company in Hades. He'd be looking for Quintus, too, if he realized Quintus had heard. "Where did you go when you left the Praetorium?"

"Straight here," Quintus said, "and lay low."

"Good." Where would Vettius keep his secrets? Moguntiacum. It would have to be Moguntiacum. A tent in a marching camp would be too dangerous. He turned to Eumenes. "Go and find my brother. He'll be back by now. Tell him to meet me on the west road as soon as it's dark and to stay out of sight until then. Then go get my horse saddled and take him out there."

"Mine's in the cavalry lines," Quintus said. "The big dun with three black boots."

"You'll get your tail chewed, Quintus," Correus said, "if you don't show for parade in the morning."

"It's happened before," Quintus said philosophically. "I don't know what you're doing, but I want a hand in it. That bastard killed my horse."

"Correus?" Ygerna pushed open the back door and looked at him suspiciously as he slipped through it out of the dusk, with Quintus behind him. "Where have you been?"

"Drinking beer with Ranvig," Correus said.

"Mother of All! The emperor has been sending for you every five minutes, and you've been getting drunk with a German."

"Not so drunk now," Correus said. "And it's a good thing. The next time they come looking for me, tell them I'm at Rhodope's, or that you think I am. Act furious."

"That will be easy. Since you wouldn't tell me if you *were* having dinner with whores, where *are* you going?"

"Moguntiacum. Vettius has something incriminating there, and he's about to go after it."

"I have been thinking that that might happen," Ygerna said. "Here." She dug in the bottom of the sewing basket that sat on the floor by her chair. She must have been working while she waited for him.

Correus took the twice-folded papyrus and opened it up. It was a hand he didn't recognize. "What is this?"

"A letter from Queen Berenice," Ygerna said. "I wrote to her because she knows the sort of thing your emperor may do."

"You—" Correus swallowed whatever he had been going to say. There wasn't much point in it now, and Quintus had popped his eyes wide open at the name.

"Not the—"

"Of course not," Correus said. "She has left Rome. You must have heard wrong. In fact, you aren't even here."

Quintus subsided.

"Ygerna, will you get us something to eat? Something we can carry in saddlebags. You, please, not the slaves."

"Nurse and Cottia are with the children, but it's a small house, so keep quiet then." Ygerna disappeared through the pantry door. "Read the letter while I am gone," she said over her shoulder.

Correus held the sheet next to the lamp. It appeared to contain no deadly secrets. The woman had had a fire, and she went on and on about it. Ygerna came back with food wrapped in a napkin. "This doesn't make any sense," he complained.

"You *are* drunk," Ygerna said. "Think." She took the letter and held the corner in the lamp flame, and then set the burning papyrus in a dish that sat on a table with the household gods. She noted Centurion Quintus's interested face and gave Correus an exasperated look. "She thought that Vettius would do this," she said shortly. "She is telling you what to do about it."

Correus went over the words in his head. He looked at the ashes thoughtfully, and a certain amount of light appeared. There could be no half measures when they found Vettius's evidence. *Anything* left behind could be deadly. He went into the bedchamber, pulling his muddy shirt off over his head, and they heard him rummaging in a chest for the hunting clothes he kept there. When he emerged he had on a clean shirt and breeches, with more clothes tucked under his arm. He tossed some of them to Quintus. "Go and put these on."

"They'll never let you through the lines in that," Ygerna said.

"We aren't going through the lines," Correus said. "I don't want to be known to have been within a day's march of Moguntiacum. I just hope to Hades he hasn't got the stuff in the fort itself."

"Wouldn't he?"

"I don't think so. Not with the place thronging with busy little optios. Too risky. I'm betting it's in his private house with a couple of his own people to sit on it."

Quintus went into the bedchamber to shed his armor and his officer's scarlet for the gray shirt and brown breeches. Correus kissed Ygerna and held her close for a moment. "After we've gone, send one of the slaves for Julius, tell him what's up, and tell him to stay here with you. I've left a message for my second that I've gone hunting with Flavius. I've got leave coming. When he finds it, they'll think I spent the night carousing at Rhodope's or somewhere in the *vicus*, and left in the morning."

"No one will swallow that," Ygerna said.

"They may. Rhodope always covers for her customers, and they know that. They'd have to take the place apart to be sure I wasn't there, and they won't do that. It's Vettius's blood the emperor's after just now. I think. He just wants me to come and tell him if Vettius cheated him on purpose or not. And in any case, it's the best I can think of." If they got caught, it wasn't going to matter anyway.

Quintus came back in the hunting breeches that belonged to Eumenes. Correus picked up the roll of his own clothes for

Flavius. Ygerna let them out the back again and watched as they slipped through the neglected bean patch behind the house, into the shadow of a hedge. Correus vanished first. She could see Quintus long after Correus was only another patch of dark against the thorns of the hedge. Correus had done this before, she thought, but never against his own kind. If the Roman patrols caught them, it wouldn't be good.

She closed the door and poured some sweet oil on top of the ashes of Berenice's letter and lit it for the household gods. Then she lit the fire that was laid in the hearth and sat down to stare into it. There had been a time when she could have made a magic with the red heart of the fire, a singing magic to call him back safe to her, but that time had gone with the dead leaves of—how many winters? She put her hands out to it, but nothing ran up through them but the heat of the fire. There was a voice and a knock from the front of the house. *I am a Roman now,* she thought. *I must do this like a Roman.* She called for Cottia. "Go and see who that is, and then get Julius from the stables. Tell him I want him here. The master isn't back yet, and he has Eumenes with him, most likely. I am not going to spend the night in this thieves' village with nothing but women."

She made her voice loud enough for the man at the door to hear, and he came in with an apologetic expression. He had come four times that day already. Ygerna met him with fire in her eyes, but he stood his ground.

"I'm sorry, my lady, but has there been any word from the primus pilus?"

"He is not here! He is as not here as he was the last time you came, and the time before that! I do not know where he is, and I do not care!" She glared at him. "Likely he has gone with his brother somewhere, to tell each other how clever they have been to risk their necks in that silly horse race. Probably to that—that fat whore with the orange hair in a tent, that your army should not allow to be here!"

The optio looked embarrassed. "We checked there already," he mumbled.

"Then check again, if you want him. Maybe he has gone drinking. Maybe he has been carried off by eagles. Maybe if he is lucky, you will find him before I do!"

"Uh, yes," the optio said. They must have had a fight, he figured. He looked at Ygerna's small, furious face. If he'd been the primus pilus, he'd have ducked out, too.

"Get out!" Ygerna said.

It was fifty miles to Moguntiacum by the Roman road. Longer to ride around it and dodge the patrols. Flavius and Eumenes were waiting with the horses when Correus and Quintus slipped up out of the ditch beside the road, beyond the *vicus*.

"We'll never make it before someone gets wise," Flavius said. It was not an argument, only a comment.

"I've tried to cover our tracks a bit," Correus said. He tossed Flavius the clothes.

"I was hoping you'd think of that. My rooms are too close to the emperor's to lift a pin out quietly." Flavius was still wearing his white harness tunic and cuirass, and if he had cleaned the mud off it earlier, he must have put it back on. The gilt and silver were splotched to a dull gray in the moonlight. But by day, or close up, it would still be as conspicuous as the emperor's purple cloak. He slid down and pulled it off, tying it on behind the saddle, and put on the shirt and breeches. He tied the cloak over his cuirass to hide it.

The moon was up, hanging low over the timber walls of the fort behind them. Correus stared at it, trying to think how long they would have its light to ride by. And worse, how long till sunlight.

"You have gone too far this time," Domitian said flatly. He stood up, tugging the skirt of his tunic into place. He was wearing a gilded breastplate over it, with a cloak of gold and Tyrian purple over that. In this light he looked uncannily like his late brother.

"Believe me, the emperor is making a mistake," Vettius said. He stood, too. At this point it seemed as well to be respectful, but his handsome face was composed and smiling.

"I doubt it," Domitian said. "You see, I have talked to Tribune Petreius, and I never saw such a frightened man."

"Petreius sees ghosts over his shoulder," Vettius said. "I'm afraid he isn't suited to an army post. I have been meaning to talk to you about that."

"Petreius has one foot in a tar pit," Domitian said, "and he knows it. I gave him the choice of a rope to pull him out or a shove to push him in, and he split open like an old fruit. I don't think he feels very kindly toward you."

"Oh, come, sir, you must have had your suspicions about that race. I did promise you a sure thing, and that implies some . . . uh, manipulation. I am sorry that it came unstuck, but—"

"You have lost me a great deal of money," Domitian said, "but you've scared Petreius witless, and it would take more than getting caught cheating on a horse race to do that."

Vettius felt a faint movement at his back and realized that there were guards in the room. "And just what has the tribune had to say?" he inquired softly.

"The tribune doesn't know," Domitian said. "The tribune is very sorry he ever met you. The tribune thinks you stood to win more on this race than anybody knew, and he wonders what you were going to do with it." Domitian's voice was low, and there was an edge of menace in it. "The tribune now regrets that he didn't tell me this sooner."

Vettius got a grip on himself and kept his hands from twitching at his sash. "Perhaps I have been lax also, sir. There are certain matters of which I wished to inform you, but not until there was proof available. Grave matters, I am afraid."

"I am beginning to be afraid so, too," Domitian said. He nodded his head once, looking past Vettius. "You should have kept quiet about your documents."

"If I have your leave to depart, I will fetch the documents in question," Vettius said. "I am sure that the emperor will understand then that I have been working for his welfare." Domitian didn't answer. Vettius heard a step behind him and spun around as a guard pulled the legate's sword and dagger out of their sheaths.

"I feel much more comfortable with you unarmed, Vettius," Domitian said.

Vettius began to feel the night close in on him. "Sir, if you will only listen—"

"Where are these documents, Vettius?" Domitian said.

"I am afraid they are not accessible to anyone but myself, sir. They would be difficult for anyone to find—"

"Don't bet on it," Domitian said. "A man looking hard enough can find anything, including treason."

"I assure you, sir, I was going to inform you—"

Domitian looked right through him, to the guards behind. "Go and find them. Start with the legate's headquarters here, and then Moguntiacum. Has Flavius Julianus turned up yet?"

"No, sir. Apparently he's gone off drinking with his brother. His brother's wife was in a fit over it."

Domitian considered, then shrugged. "Just as well perhaps. Flavius doesn't like you, Vettius. I do wish to be fair about this." He gave the legate a half smile that was no smile at all and looked at the guard again. "You are personally responsible for the documents. Anything you find is to be brought to me unread. When you have finished with the legate's chambers here, you may put the legate in them, and see that he stays there."

"And leave the Fourteenth without a commander?" Vettius made a last effort, looking worried for his legion, but there was the beginning of panic in his eyes.

"From what I understand from Julius Frontinus, with whom I spoke since you and I last chatted, Vettius, the Fourteenth hasn't *had* a commander since I gave you this post." Domitian's eyes narrowed, and his heavy face was flushed with anger. "Frontinus described them as a 'menace.' Even if you should prove innocent of treason, which I doubt, if anything goes wrong with this campaign, I will give you to the Germans to hang up on a tree for their gods. You've overreached yourself, Vettius. I want this victory and a triumph to go with it. You should have known that."

The farmstead was still, spread out along the river's edge, with the checkered pattern of its fields behind it. An unshuttered window spilled out a dim glow of light, but there was no movement in the yard between the hayricks and the house.

"Will they have a boat, d'you think?" Quintus whispered.

"No one lives along a river without owning a boat," Correus said.

"A boat and a dog, most likely," Eumenes said.

They were crouched in the trees on a little slope above the farm's hayfields, with the horses tethered behind them. They had pushed them hard for almost twenty miles through the woods south of the Moenus, praying against rabbit holes.

"It'll have to do," Correus said. "This is where you leave us, Quintus."

"Sir—"

"Somebody's got to take the horses back," Correus said. "You'll get marked Unlawful Absent if you don't get back, and they'll pull your rank for it."

"What about you?"

"I've got more rank than you do, and so does Flavius." Junior centurions had very little more freedom than the men they commanded. "And in any case, this is our fight. Leave the horses in the spot we picked with enough grain for a day, and then go tell Julius where they are. We'll just have to hope the wood elves don't find them before he gets there."

Quintus looked mutinous, and Flavius slipped up and dropped down beside them. "Do what he says," he said under his breath. "If anyone connects you up with us, we haven't Persephone's hope in Hades of getting away with this."

Quintus swore, but he stood up and unhitched the horses' reins. "I was fond of that race pony," he said. "I've had him since he was old enough to leave his dam. He used to eat cake out of my hand." He settled himself in the saddle and gathered up the lead reins. "I'll go along back and look innocent, but if you don't come in on time—"

"If we don't come in on time, you'll sit still and behave yourself," Correus said. "Now get those horses out of here before they smell the farm animals and make a noise."

The moon was still up, running in and out of the clouds, and they picked their way carefully down the slope, feeling for loose stones. At the edge of the hayfield, they went around the long way, downwind of the farm, to the riverbank, and then slowly back upstream.

"There it is." Flavius laid a hand on his brother's and pointed. A shallow boat was moored to a post in the riverbank, swinging gently with the current.

"Let's hope he's left the paddles in it." A tangled clump of trees and vine blocked their way, and they splashed out into the shallows around it. To their left the river flowed by, whispering to itself over the rocks in the shallows. To the right, the bank sloped up to the farmstead, and there were steps cut into it, set with stones that showed faintly silver in the moonlight. The farmyard was still quiet, but any noise from the men on the riverbank would be bound to wake something. A thief's life was easier in the city, Eumenes thought, where the night was a constant noise, and people kept their dogs decently indoors. They reached the boat, and he steadied it while Correus and Flavius climbed in.

"Here're the paddles," Correus murmured, feeling in the bottom. "He's a trusting soul."

Eumenes gripped the side of the boat and swung one leg over. There was moss on the stones under the water. His other foot slipped, and he fell back in the river with a splash.

There was instant chaos from the farmyard above. A dog barked wildly, and a furious honking proclaimed that the farmer kept geese. A door banged open, and shouting voices came from the house.

"Get in, damn it!" Flavius held out a hand, and Eumenes picked himself out of the water and dove for the side of the boat. He struggled over it as the little craft tipped dangerously, and Correus cut the rope. Above them was more shouting and the sound of running feet.

"Push off!" Correus jammed his paddle against the bank, and the boat moved into the river as a spear sang past his left ear. Something hurled itself out of the darkness, fangs bared, and he swung the paddle at it. The blade caught the dog across the muzzle, and it fell back with a yelp as the farmer came down the path. He had thrown his spear, but there was a hayfork in the other hand and two more men behind him with spears. A woman was screaming in the farmyard, and the geese were honking in a wild cacophony that would have waked the dead in Erebus.

"Merciful Athena," Flavius said. He ducked his head down, and they angled the boat into the middle of the river and let the current take it. Eumenes was spitting out water in the bottom. Another spear splashed in the river behind them, and then the noise receded into the darkness. They raised their heads cautiously.

"I hate geese," Eumenes said, his teeth chattering.

"We were lucky," Correus said shortly. "They're living in the middle of a war here. It makes them jumpy. Look around and see if there's anything to bail with. You brought half the river in with you." He and Flavius swung their paddles out again and the boat shot forward. Eumenes found a bronze pot and began to bail with it.

They kept to the middle of the river where the moon would show up any rocks that broke the silvered surface of the water, although Eumenes thought that that would likely only give them a few seconds' warning that they were going to drown. This was a boat made for the shallows, not the fast-running current at the center. A black and jagged shape rose up, and Correus and Flavius veered the boat. The rock slid by on the side, and Eumenes gritted his teeth, telling himself that he wasn't drowned yet. He crouched in the bottom of the boat and watched the dark banks glide by.

He lost track of the time he spent huddled wet and shivering in the bottom of the boat, but they hit no rocks, and it was still black night when Correus and Flavius eased carefully through the pilings of the bridge that spanned the river close above Moguntiacum. There were patrols on the bridge, but the moon had gone, so they kept their heads down and prayed. Below the bridge the river flowed around an island into the waters of the Rhenus: It would be dangerous working their way across to the west bank, with the current of the Rhenus pulling them down toward Moguntiacum Bridge in the shadow of the fort itself.

"We'll never make it," Correus hissed. "We'll come up smack on their feet." There would be pickets at either end of Moguntiacum Bridge. "We'll have to go past."

Flavius nodded, and they aimed the light boat carefully between the cutwaters of the bridge and then kept their paddles still as the current swept them under it like a shadow on the water. Correus let out his breath as they came out on the far side, and they began to angle the boat carefully for the west bank. Above to their left were the scattered pinpoints of light that marked the Moguntiacum *vicus*: a night patrol's lanterns and a wineshop or two. The rest would be dark. They grounded the boat on the sandy edge of the river and left it there, scrambling up the slope in the darkness.

The Moguntiacum *vicus* was an old one, a fair-sized city now, with Roman-style houses and a basilica to house its civil business. Correus and Flavius slipped through it quietly, trying to look like honest men, with Eumenes squelching miserably behind them. They tapped at the door of the house that Correus had rented there and where Lucius Paulinus was still staying. They were going to need him.

Septima let them in and went to fetch Lucius, who came out with a worried frown tightening his face. A midnight visit never boded any good.

When Correus had told him what Marius Vettius was threatening, the frown deepened and Lucius put one hand in the other to keep them both from shaking. "We should have known," he said wearily. "I should have just killed him."

"Mithras god, a lot of good that would have done!" Flavius snapped. "His precious packet of papers still would have come boiling up out of his grave. We've got to get to those tonight, and you're going to help because you know what he's got."

"I don't know all of it," Lucius said grimly, "and neither do you. You may not like what we find."

"We'll chance it," Correus said.

"Yes." There was very little choice in the matter, Lucius thought, cursing himself again for pulling his family and his friends into this catastrophe with him.

Lucius was right, Correus thought. There were some things it was undeniably safer not to know. But he could live with the knowledge better than he could live with Lucius's death—and Julia's. And he was a soldier. Like his father before him, he would usually be too far from Rome for unpleasant secrets to be a danger.

Lucius wrapped a nondescript cloak around his tunic. His servant Tullius was still asleep, and Lucius decided against waking him. There were already four of them, and he would as soon not bring Tullius into it. If they failed, which was entirely possible, there might be just a faint chance that Tullius could still get out with a whole hide. *Someone* ought to survive, Lucius thought grimly.

* * *

The private house that Marius Vettius had taken for his off-
duty hours was an L-shaped building with a roofed portico
forming the other two sides of a rectangle and enclosing a
formal garden at the center. It stood conveniently near the
fortress, between Drusus's cenotaph and the theater. Too near
the fortress, Correus thought, standing in the shadow of the
house across the street. One noise would bring down more
guards than the farmer's geese had done.

A thick hedge nearly five feet high was planted along the
edge of the portico to screen the garden from the street. There
was a gate set into it, opposite the main wing of the house. A
lantern hung from a post above the gate, with its flame guttering
out. Correus looked at the sky, trying to gauge the time, but
the cloud cover had blown in more thickly, and it was hard to
tell. He thought there was a faint shading of light to the east,
but it was still nearly pitch black except for the lantern. As
they watched, the flame sank and rose, and then died out
completely. Correus breathed a sigh of relief. He would rather
rely on the night sight that the dark ride down the river had
given them than have that lantern illuminate them like moths
at a lamp flame.

"Come on."

They ran for the gate, tried it, and it opened with a shrieking
of old hinges. Correus jerked his hand back. "Typhon! It would
have been better to climb it." The gate was open only a few
inches, and he drew it back experimentally. It closed without
protest. He latched it and pulled himself over the top, landing
catfooted on the other side. Flavius came down after him with
slightly more noise, then Eumenes and Lucius behind him in
perfect silence. Correus gave them an approving look and decided not to ask either where he'd learned that.

The main door was barred, as they could have predicted.
They would have to risk a noise now, but at least they were
screened from the street. Correus pounded his fist on the door
and waited for a reaction. He pulled his cloak around him to
cover the shirt and breeches, and motioned the other three out
of sight into the shadows. On the third knock there were sounds
of stirring in the house, and the rattle of a bar being pulled
back. A burly man with a nose that looked as if it had been

broken lifted a lamp and gave Correus a suspicious eye through a six-inch gap.

"Master's not home."

Correus recognized him as one of Vettius's personal toughs and said a swift silent prayer of thanks to the God of Soldiers that it hadn't been a man of his legion. "Of course he's not, you fool," he said, pushing on the door. "I've got orders from him to fetch you and the rest of the house up to the Moenus. He's closing this one down."

"At this time o' night?" The man shifted the lamp. "Who in Erebus are you?"

Correus made an exasperated noise. "Here, it's all written out. Can you read?" He stepped forward as he spoke and brought a hand from under his cloak. There was a dagger in it.

The man at the door had just enough time to see the lamplight on the blade but no more. He made a gagging sound at the back of his throat and fell, spitting up blood. Correus pushed him back from the doorway, wincing as the lamp clattered on the tile. He closed the door as soon as the others were through, and bolted it. Eumenes crouched by the man on the floor with his knife out, but he was dead already.

"We're in," Correus said. He kept his dagger out. "It'll be in his office."

"Is there anyone else in the house?" Eumenes whispered.

"We'll hope not," Correus said grimly.

The bronze lamp had spilled when it had fallen, and there was a little pool of oil burning on the tile floor. Lucius stamped it out gingerly and picked up the lamp. They left the dead guard in the darkness and moved on through the shadows of the house, opening doors cautiously, daggers in hand.

They found the office on the third try, a red and blue room with painted gardens on the walls and an ornate desk in front of a pair of carved scroll shelves.

"No!" Correus said as Eumenes put a hand to the shelves. "This is for Lucius and Flavius and me. Go and guard the door, but don't come in."

Eumenes backed out again, and Correus began pulling everything from the desk while Lucius held up the lamp. Flavius started on the scrolls. He unrolled the first, which proved to be pictures, gave it a revolted look, and dropped it on the floor. "If this is his entertainment," he said, "he has unpleasant tastes."

"It won't be in the—wait!" Correus pulled an iron box with a lock on it from the desk. "This may be it." There was very little use in looking for the key. No man locks a box and leaves the key beside it. He jammed his dagger in the lock and wrenched it sideways. The blade snapped, but the lock came open, and he pushed the lid back. Flavius snatched the top sheet from the pile inside, scanned it, and his mouth came open a little in sheer horror. Correus looked at first one scrap of papyrus and then the next, his own horror growing. They were letters mostly, deadly letters, some to Vettius, some not, gathered by clandestine means: promises of aid, commitments to treason, a handful of pleas against exposure. There was a list of names in Vettius's hand that made Correus cold to read it. The evidence against Lucius Paulinus was there, but the rest of the box was enough to ruin half the families in Rome, guilty and innocent together: men who had begun this conspiracy in a sense of pious outrage, men who had been sucked into it later or terrorized into it by Marius Vettius or simply framed by him to give him a hold over them when he should need it. What Domitian would do with this box full of death was unspeakable.

Flavius looked up, with slips of papyrus clutched in both hands and real fear in his eyes. "I feel like I'm standing knee-deep in blood," he whispered.

"I told you," Lucius said. He didn't move to inspect the box himself. He must have known most of what it contained already. Correus thought he didn't want to touch it.

"We can't leave this," Correus said.

"This may not be all." Flavius looked around the dark room. There might be more deadly hoards.

"He'll have copies somewhere else in the house," Lucius said. "Bet on it."

There was a sharp movement at the door. "Someone's coming!" Eumenes hissed.

Correus grabbed the lamp from Lucius and lit the papyrus in his hand with it. He dropped it back in the box, and it blazed up like a live thing, twisting into blackness. He poured the lamp oil over the desk and the scrolls in their shelves. Queen

Berenice had spoken literally when she had talked of burning. Burn the whole plot to the ground, he thought savagely, and take the chance that Vettius would go free, to save the other poor fools who had put their feet in this tar. The desk was old wood, and it was blazing now, too. He kicked the side in and pulled one of the legs free with the fire licking at the end of it. There was shouting in the corridor. Swiftly he touched the flame to anything in the room that would burn and ran for the door. Flavius was behind him, sword in hand. Correus saw as he looked over his shoulder that Lucius had his dagger out, a thin, plain-hilted blade that looked oddly at home in his brother-in-law's hand.

In the corridor Eumenes was crouched with his back to a corner as three men tried to get past his dagger to him. Correus put his torch in his right hand and drew his sword. A dark-faced man spun around to face him. He had a long curving knife that gleamed evilly in the flames, and he slashed at Correus with it. Correus scrambled backward, waving the burning wood in the other man's face. The dark man hacked at the wood, while Correus tried to knock the knife away with his sword. The room behind them was blazing now. He could feel the heat at his back. The other man came in again, crouched to slash with the curved knife that had a longer reach than Correus's short stabbing sword. Correus feinted with his sword and then swung the torch at the man's hair as the knife came up to block his sword thrust. The man screamed and stepped back with his hair on fire. Correus's sword opened up a deep gash across the thigh, and the dark man fell, clutching at his hair. Correus drove the sword in through his chest.

The flames had caught the hangings in the corridor now. Correus looked frantically through the heat and the hellish light for the other three. Lucius, who had always claimed he couldn't fight, had somehow killed a sword-armed man with that plain, murderous-looking dagger. Flavius was pulling the third man off Eumenes. The man turned to fight Flavius, and Eumenes, bleeding from a gash in his shoulder, put his knife into the man's back as the whole corridor exploded into flames.

"Run!" Correus yelled. They held their breath and dived through the smoke-filled corridor into the atrium beyond. Flavius's cloak had caught fire, and he threw himself onto the tile floor and rolled on it, then pushed his arm into the atrium pool up to the shoulder.

"Are you all right?"

"Burned," Flavius said, with gritted teeth. He pulled himself back from the pool. Correus set the torch upright in a bronze urn and peered into the pool, looking for the drain. He reached in and pried it out with the tip of his sword. His dagger was back in the holocaust of Vettius's office.

"What're you doing?"

"No point in making them a present of water." The pool had begun to empty. Correus picked up the torch again, singeing his hands, and touched it to the atrium hangings and furniture. There was a shattering sound as window glass broke from the heat. The flames rose with a roar as the night air rushed in.

"Get out!" Lucius yelled. "These walls are timber!" He pulled the torch out of Correus's hands and pushed him at the door.

The painted plaster was beginning to crack, and there was another explosion of flame as the doorway from the corridor collapsed. They dragged the bar from the main door, pulled it open, and stumbled choking into the garden.

"You did a mite too good a job," Eumenes said, coughing. He could feel the blood running down his arm from the wound in his shoulder, and he stopped to wrap his cloak around it. Above him the house had begun to fall in, in a hellish boiling of smoke and flame, and he backed away from the heat. He would never be afraid of water again, he thought.

Shouting from the house across the street and running footsteps in the distance sent them racing for the gate. Correus wrenched it open and turned to look at the house as Lucius, Flavius, and Eumenes stumbled through. "Burn," he said with harsh satisfaction in his voice. *"Burn!"* He turned and raced after them into the dark, empty streets, with the sounds of the hunt growing behind them.

XX

A Roman Way to Think

"LET US IN!" THEY HAMMERED ON THE DOOR OF CORREUS'S house in the *vicus*.

Septima gave a little screech at the ragged, burned men in the doorway, and Tullius appeared behind her with a menacing expression.

Correus pushed past Septima. She recognized him and screeched again while Tullius helped the others in. "Quit squawking and go get some water and bandages." Tullius pulled the cloak away from Eumenes's shoulder and peered at it professionally.

Septima gave Correus a look of nervous apology. "You did give me a turn, sir." She hurried out.

The atrium was gray with the dawn light, and Correus could still hear yelling in the distance. "I think we lost them, but we'd better get out of sight." He herded the rest through the back of the house into the kitchen and gave Eumenes's shoulder a worried look. "Is that going to need a surgeon?"

"No, you got lucky." Tullius was a time-expired legionary, and, among other things, he had been a surgeon's orderly. "It looks nastier than it is." Septima brought him the bandages, and he cleaned the gash and tied a clean bandage around it while Eumenes grimaced.

Flavius was inspecting his burned arm in the pale light from the kitchen window. "Go and find me some salve for this." Septima scurried out again, looking scared.

Lucius Paulinus perched himself on a kitchen table, and Tullius gave his master a long look of disapproval. "What in Typhon's name have you been doing? And is that you they're chasing out there?"

Lucius nodded wearily. "I doubt they'll come here. No one saw our faces."

No one who's still alive, Correus thought. He leaned against the scrubbed wooden table and looked at the other man. "You're clear, Lucius."

Paulinus's face flushed. "I'm ashamed," he said in a low voice, "that you had to take that risk."

"Don't be," Flavius said. "Not for that. We owed him an evil ourselves. But you can be ashamed you ever began this, Lucius, and there's a price on tonight. You are to make your peace with Domitian."

Lucius nodded. "Yes, I expect I owe you that."

Flavius made a satisfied noise and began smearing salve on his arm, gritting his teeth.

"That's Flavius's price," Correus said. "Mine is that you make my sister make her peace with my wife."

Lucius gave a ragged chuckle. "That may be harder."

"I expect you'll manage," Correus said. "Don't think I'm not grateful to Julia, and to you, because I am. But it's my fault, not Ygerna's, that Julia got to thinking Felix was hers. Felix has settled down very well, and I won't have it all started up again." He braced himself against the table. "I think I could sleep for a week."

"You'd better," Tullius said. "You look like a fresh corpse." He glared at Paulinus. "I won't tell you what I've been thinking since I found out you was gone. Put your head in a noose it won't come out of one of these days, I expect."

"You may continue to keep your thoughts to yourself," Lucius said. He turned back to Correus. "He's right about sleep, though. Can you lie low here for a day?"

Correus shook his head. "We told a large tale about a hunting trip to get us here, and it wasn't very plausible then. If we don't get back fast to Castra Mattiacorum, it'll smell like old fish. We need horses. Beasts that can't be tied to this house."

Tullius considered this necessity. "There's a nice little livery stable down by the ferry," he said finally. "Be a bit quieterlike, crossing on the ferry."

"And the stableman to say where we went," Eumenes said sarcastically. "*And* identify the three of us."

"Oh, I don't think so," Tullius said. "I'll meet you there. Give me a quarter hour's start." He departed purposefully, and Eumenes raised his eyebrows. The gap between slave and free,

master and servant, had been bridged in that burning house.
"What's he going to do?"

Paulinus chuckled, this time in genuine amusement. "Don't
ask. I never do."

Correus knotted the reins around the dun horse's saddle
horns and gave it a smack on the rump. It began to trot wearily
back the way they had come. It might even get back before
the stableman woke up in his feed bin and shouted for someone
to come and untie him. He picked up Antaeus's reins and leaned
wearily against the gold neck for a moment. They would make
it. If they didn't pass out on the trail back. Flavius and Eumenes
looked ready to drop.

Julius gave them an appraising look. "You might just get
away with it. There's the grandmother of all rows going on up
at the fort. The ghosts of Carthage and all their elephants
could've come through there and I doubt anyone would've
stopped arguing to notice 'em." He hopped up into the saddle.
He was riding Ygerna's mare. "Give me a bit of a start. It
won't do to come in together. There's a deer under a pile of
rocks to keep the wolves off, by that big twisty pine west of
the town. Not much of a deer, but I wasn't after one that could
fight back."

It was nearly dusk when they found the deer as promised,
pulled it out from under the cairn of rocks, and tied it on the
back of Eumenes's horse. It looked as bedraggled as they did,
Correus thought.

They trotted through the dirty streets of the *vicus* to leave
the deer at a butcher's stall to be dressed, and rode smack into
Julius Frontinus striding purposefully in the other direction.

"Julianus." He gave Correus a suspicious eye, which then
roved over Flavius and Eumenes as well. "I've been looking
for you."

Correus laughed. "Don't tell me *you* lost money on that
race, too! If I'd known it would cause such a stink, I wouldn't
have entered. But poor Quintus—someone doped his horses,
you know," he added helpfully.

"Hmmm." Frontinus did not look impressed. "Where have
you been?"

"Hunting." Correus pointed a finger at the deer.

Frontinus inspected it. "It looks like you beat it to death with clubs. It looks worse than you do. What happened to that man's shoulder?"

"It turned and tried to gore me, sir," Eumenes said. He pulled his cloak over the bandage.

"A courageous beast," Frontinus said. The deer's horns were three inches long. "What about you?" He directed his gaze at Flavius's forearm. A twist of bandage showed under his shirt-sleeve.

"Burned it in the campfire," Flavius said shortly.

"I see." Frontinus considered. "Well, I came to tell you that your commander's under house arrest," he said grimly to Correus. "So you'd better get to that legion before they riot. They're shaky enough. You won't be hunting again for a while."

"The town patrol was putting out the fire when I got there, sir." The guard pulled himself to attention before the emperor and fought off the desire to curl up and sleep on the floor. He had ridden to Moguntiacum and back at full gallop, commandeering a fresh horse from each fort on the road.

"And his household staff?" Domitian's voice was level, but his face was splotched with furious color. Julius Frontinus picked up his sheaf of plans and eyed the emperor warily.

"There were four bodies in the mess, sir," the guard said. "They were too far burned to say much more than that."

Domitian's fist clenched. "He should have been better watched. I'll decide later who's to blame for that. Dismissed."

The guard departed in haste, and Domitian swung around to confront Frontinus. "I made a mistake with Vettius," he said levelly. "I do not wish anyone else to be telling me that. I trust that's clear."

"Certainly, sir," Frontinus said. Domitian did not like his mistakes to be remarked upon, a natural enough preference for an emperor.

"What do you think, Frontinus?" Domitian said suddenly. "Did Vettius have that fire set?"

Frontinus paused. "I think he's capable of it, sir, certainly," he said cautiously. "And capable of having his staff's throats slit to shut their mouths, too. Unless we catch the, uh, man who did it, I don't expect it will be proven."

"The man who did it is fifty miles from Moguntiacum by now!" Domitian said.

"Uh, yes. I rather think he is," Julius Frontinus said. He thought about the men who would likely have been ruined by Marius Vettius's secrets and decided to keep any further thoughts to himself.

"I want that legion got into shape *now*," Domitian said. "Marius Vettius is relieved of his command. See to that for me, will you?"

Julius Frontinus saluted.

"And make a list of his creditors," Domitian went on. "He's in over his head, and I want his estates sold to pay it. You may put my name at the top of the list."

"Yes, sir. I'll have your staff begin immediately. To what figure is he in debt to you?"

"I will have to check the accounts," Domitian said. "You may leave that unspecified for the moment."

Frontinus's mouth twitched. The emperor would see that the most influential of Vettius's creditors were paid off, and then he'd claim the rest. He expected Vettius owed it to him at that. "Flavius Julianus is one, sir," he ventured. "He bet on his brother in the race."

Domitian gave a sudden sharp bark of laughter. "Yes, see that *he* gets paid. That will be my penance for not listening to his advice. He can buy back his father-in-law's land with it. Maybe the old fool will stay clear of shark waters in the future."

"Yes, sir. Will there be anything else?"

"Yes. Tribune Petreius is also relieved of his rank. Boot him back to Rome."

"And Marius Vettius?"

Domitian gave the chief of Engineers a wintry smile. "Vettius is also free to go. If he can get out fast enough."

Marius Vettius watched Frontinus's square form stalk away into the dusk. It had begun to rain, and he pulled the door closed with a shiver. The room was strewn with the wreckage of overturned trunks and broken furniture. He hadn't bothered to set it to rights since the guards had pushed him in when they were through with it and posted one of their number outside the door. The woman Gwenhwyfar hadn't seemed to care, either. She had tipped a couch back upright and curled herself on its split cushions to watch him pace. Now he slumped against the doorpost.

"Where will you go?" Gwenhwyfar said.

He knew, as clearly as he knew that he had lost and it was over, that Domitian would never let it rest that easily. "I wouldn't get far." Maybe not even as far as the Rhenus before the emperor's messenger caught him.

"I see." Her voice was low, with an odd excitement in it. The wide blue eyes glittered, like polished stones. "What will you do?"

He looked at her bleakly. "Take you with me, maybe." He took a step toward her, and she got up and backed away. "Julius Frontinus was right. I should have kept you out of my bed. I might have seen this coming."

There was another knock at the door, and a guard came in without waiting for an answer. He gave Vettius a wax tablet and a thin thing wrapped in a cloth. "You have an hour," he said, his face expressionless, and went out again. Vettius opened the door after him and looked out. The guard was standing beside it looking the other way. Vettius unwrapped the cloth and turned the dagger over in his hand. He looked at the woman again as she crouched behind the couch.

"I don't think you're worth it," he said. "Let some other man have you." He gave a dull laugh. "My gift to Castra Mattiacorum. I wish I could think it would be Domitian."

She stood up and moved lazily to the couch again, knowing that he wouldn't kill her now. "If I could have had the emperor, I would never have taken you."

"No." He turned a chair upright and sat down in it, holding the knife.

She ran her tongue over her lips and watched him intently. "What are you going to do?"

"Die like a gentleman. It is preferable to having my head cut off."

"I will stay with you."

He looked into the blue eyes fixed hungrily on his. "No," he said thickly. "Get out. Get out, or I'll put the knife in you."

She went reluctantly and stood outside the door while the guard stared stiffly ahead under his helmet crest. After a minute or two she went back in. Marius Vettius was slumped forward in the chair with the knife between his hands, driven into the breast. The sleek, fair hair looked grayer than before in the dim light, and there was blood under the knife and at the corner of his mouth. She stood looking at him for a moment with an odd look, almost of satisfaction, on her face. Then she began to pick out her clothes and jewelry from the wreckage of the room.

"There will be a new legate as soon as may be," Correus said. He stood, irritably tapping his vine staff against his left greave, before the assembled Fourteenth Legion Gemina. "It will not be too soon for me, but in the meantime, I am not willing to hand you over as you are." He glared at them implacably. "You appall me. There will be an extra hour's parade every morning until you can drill without putting a pilum into the man in front of you by mistake." They stirred and muttered at that, and Correus hefted the vine staff and pointed it at them accusingly. "Before we march, this legion is going to be fit for it, if I have to put every man in it on report between now and then. And if it's *not*—my recommendation to the emperor is going to be that he break this legion. I don't think you will care for the freedom, if he does it."

The legionaries looked surly at that, but Correus was gratified to see that the cohort centurions and their juniors wore a uniform expression of earnestness. *Yes, sir!* The cohort commanders, paraded before him, snapped a salute. A soldier from a disbanded legion might get another posting, but he would never, not in all his life, get another promotion.

Correus nodded grimly and spoke to the officers. "We understand each other. I am aware of where the fault lies, but you are the ones who will have to correct it. The world is most unfair." He raised his voice again and addressed the legion as a whole. "You have two hours to make sacrifice for the shade of Marius Vettius. Then we are going to march until you look like a legion of the Eagles again. When you do, your Eagle will be given back to you."

He nodded to the standard-bearer beside him, and the standard-bearer lowered his staff until Correus could reach the gilded Eagle at the top. There was a gasp from officers as well as men as he reached out and unpinned the standard from its staff. "You aren't worth an Eagle just now," he said. He stalked off the parade ground, cradling the golden form and silvered wings in the crook of one arm, leaving the standard-bearer behind him, looking miserably out from under his lionskin hood, under an empty staff.

It rained that afternoon, but Correus took them out anyway, first onto the parade ground and then out on the road that ran between Castra Mattiacorum and the Nicer Valley. When they had realized that each new complaint got them another mile on the march (and, of course, another mile back) they ceased to grumble and merely trudged along through the mud, footsore and eyes front. He turned them back finally and sent them to their dinner, too late to bathe and too tired to make trouble. The next morning they did it again, and by the end of the third day they had become nearly as attentive as proper soldiers should be and with a grudging admiration for the primus pilus who had made every single march with them.

"You will kill yourself," Ygerna said, rubbing the burning muscles of his calves while he lay stretched on a couch by the hearth.

He grunted as a muscle tightened up and cramped. "It won't work if I'm not with them. The Fourteenth has lost too many commanders. As it is, they're beginning to come around. They want their Eagle back." The Eagle was on a post in the Chapel of the Standards, but they were forbidden to touch it. "One of my men caught a man from the Claudia writing 'Wingless Fourteenth' on a tent flap with a piece of charcoal, and there was a row and a fight, and they're both in the guardhouse."

"That is good?"

"Absolutely. The other legions are going to make their lives a burden to them until they get their Eagle back. It's improving their frame of mind no end." He rolled over. "Thank you. I think I will be able to walk tomorrow. Did Julius get on the road this morning?"

"Yes," Ygerna said, amused. "Grumbling every step of the way, ponies, goat, and all. He wanted to stay."

"Those are expensive ponies. I can't keep them on the frontier with a fight coming. I'm lucky I got them out of that race in one piece."

"Is there a fight coming? A real one, I mean. A battle?"

"Oh, yes." Correus looked gloomy. "We'll tie up with Rufus, and I expect Ranvig will go to the Chatti. Then we'll try to finish them off. That's why I'm worried about that legion full of summer soldiers that Vettius created."

Ygerna's small white face was serious. "Are we going to lose? If your legion doesn't hold?"

"No. I don't think so. They'll hold by the time I get through with them." He yawned. The fire felt good. He could feel the cold beginning to creep out of his toes. "I hope," he added. "Want you well back, though." His eyes began to close.

"Correus, you can't sleep here." Ygerna prodded him with one hand. He hadn't slept for the whole of the night and day spent on that mad ride to burn down Vettius's house in Moguntiacum, and not much since.

"Mmm." He turned his face into the crook of one arm.

Ygerna prodded him again, but he didn't move. She got his cloak and pulled its gold and scarlet folds up over him. At least he had taken his armor off.

He woke midway through the night to find Ygerna wrapped in a cloak, poking at the fire. "That is what we have slaves for," he said sleepily.

"I wasn't tired. And Eumenes is in worse shape than you are. I wanted to send him to the camp to have the surgeon see to that arm, but he wouldn't."

"He can't. It would draw too much notice. And it's healing all right. I checked. Otherwise I would have sent him somewhere else to have it done. Typhon, I feel like I've been sleeping on bricks."

"I tried to make you move."

"Did you? I don't even remember."

"You were dreaming again."

He remembered them: strange, mad, half-lucid conversations in which he argued unendingly over something he couldn't remember now, with Flavius, with Ranvig, with Forst, with the surly, slovenly ranks of the Fourteenth Legion. Huddled in his cloak, he sat up and put his hands out to the fire. The room was icily cold and dark except for the saffron glow of the fire. It was a German house, and the villages east of the Rhenus had never adopted Roman principles of heating.

"Was it bad?" Ygerna cocked her head to consider his face. Her black hair was unpinned for the night and hung in two long plaits over her shoulders. Her dark winged brows drew together as she looked at him. "You will make yourself sick, Correus. You are trying to put your hand on things that are not your business."

He smiled. "Did you make a magic in the fire to see that? Or was I talking in my sleep?"

"I do not need a magic to see when you are bone tired. Or when you have been tearing yourself apart because you can't make other men see things your way. Your brother, Flavius, for instance. Or the chieftain of the Semnones. Or that fool Forst, who is still here on the frontier trying to decide if he is a German or not. You get angry when their good sense is not as good as yours, and then you have dreams. You cannot save the world, Correus. You are not the great god Jupiter."

He smiled at that, ruefully. "My delusions do not run that high."

"No? Then why do you fight with Ranvig in your sleep? A man must know what he can change and what is in the gods' hands or in another man's Fate. That is what the Druids say."

"Don't quote the Druids to me, Ygerna. That is what the Druids say when they don't want their own concerns meddled with."

"All the same, they are right about that. You are going against What-Will-Be, and that never works. Lucius, yes. And your legion, yes." Ygerna looked at him solemnly. "But Flavius will get burned by this woman if he chooses. He doesn't *want* you to stop him. Forst will have to find out for himself where his road goes. And you can't change Ranvig from what he is, any more than you could have changed Nyall Sigmundson."

"Nyall was different. I see no god's hand on Ranvig."

"Even so, you won't change Ranvig. Content yourself with being a fear to your soldiers. I watched them march. They looked like a centipede that is fighting with itself."

He banked the fire and made sure that the stone hearth around it was free of kindling in case it spat. "This is a useless conversation. Come to bed."

She got up and followed him. Too much conscience, she

thought. More than she had, or his brother, Flavius, or Lucius Paulinus. Enough to be a burden.

He was up before light in the morning and waited for his legion on the drill field in case they should think that their commander grew tired of the pace he had set. It was clear that morning, but it had rained all through the night, and the roads were sloppy with it. There was already traffic in the *vicus* streets. Somehow everyone knew without being told that there would be fighting soon. Velius Rufus's army was camped on the other side of the bridge, with the lands that had once been Marbod of the Chatti's behind them, dark with blood and burned steadings; and with Marbod caught between Rufus and Domitian. The hangers-on would leave now, the nervous among them, lest the blood should come closer. A carriage splashed by, the mules' hooves and the iron-rimmed wheels spraying muddy water. The sun was out for the first time in days, and the curtains were only half-drawn. Correus could see Vettius's woman leaning out, her body curled like a cat on the cushions and her wide blue eyes watching the wet timber buildings of the *vicus* as they passed. A fat man with dark curling hair rested one pudgy hand on her shoulder as if in possession. Correus remembered where he had seen him before: with Marius Vettius after the race, making claim on a debt that Vettius hadn't been able to pay. Maybe he was going to Rome, to be there when Vettius's land was sold.

Roscius Celsus stood on the edge of the crowd and squinted his eyes, trying to see the men gathered around the emperor's procurator as he called the next lot. His agent had instructions to bid on one of the farms, but Celsus was staying prudently out of the procurator's sight. He was a wealthy man and had no desire to drive up the price with his presence.

"It is done," a voice said at his elbow, and Celsus turned to find Faustus Sulla beside him. "Done, and the vultures have come for him." Sulla nodded his head at Gentilius Paulinus standing a little way off. Others of the men who had been part of the ill-fated plot were scattered through the crowd.

"They have every right," Celsus said mildly. "You are here yourself."

"And Domitian is still wearing the purple," Sulla said blackly under his breath. "If it hadn't been for Vettius, we might have done it! But to make a profit—"

"At least Vettius is no longer with us, and he was one of our quarrels with the emperor," Celsus said. "And the better price I get, the less profit the emperor will make."

"The docks are clear of Vettius's thugs now, but nothing else has changed." Sulla's eyes were darkly angry. "The prisons are still full, and there are more informers than there are toads in the spring. Your friend Suffuscus died, did you know that?"

"Yes, I know," Celsus said. "This is a most unwise conversation." Men around them were beginning to look their way. "There is nothing to be done now, not for a long time. You will have to swallow that, or you will make it worse."

Sulla bit back his retort and pushed his way through the white togas of the crowd. He was a born assassin, Celsus thought, a tyrant hater with too hot a head. Someone would kill Domitian eventually, but if Sulla showed signs of doing it now, they would have to do something about him. Celsus edged his way through the crowd toward Gentilius Paulinus, wondering if he would ever be entirely free again of this brush with murder.

The emperor Caesar Domitianus Augustus sat leaning on his elbows over the map spread out on the tabletop. All this summer's forts were marked in brown ink, while the campaign of his father, Vespasian, was in black. The projected frontier was a wiggly line of cross-hatchings that followed a path from the Rhenus just above Bonna through Chatti lands and the Taunus Mountains to take in the territory of the Mattiaci (who were still afraid of Marbod and wavering between the Chatti and Rome). After that it crossed the Moenus at Castra Mattiacorum and drove south along the Nicer, then east to end at the current Danuvius frontier, west of Castra Regina. It had the practicality of being more easily defensible than the old lines and the satisfaction of completing a task left unconcluded by his father and ignored by his brother. When it was done, he would add "Germanicus" to his name, Domitian thought, pleased.

A footstep touched the floor behind him, and he tensed. He made himself relax and turn slowly.

Flavius held out a stack of thin wooden sheets. "The troop counts you asked for, sir."

"Thank you. Has Velius Rufus come in yet?"

"Yes, sir. He's on his way." Flavius laid the wooden tablets on the table.

"Good." Domitian tapped them with the air of a man making up his mind. "Send for Julius Frontinus, as well, and make sure someone brings us dinner. Then go and find me the chieftain of the Semnones. He will give his oath to a treaty at midday tomorrow, or we are at war. This has gone on long enough."

"Yes, sir." Flavius saluted briskly, but there was a hunted look in his eyes. Midday tomorrow. Only one day left.

The emperor reached for the wooden tally slates, and the stack spilled over. Flavius put a hand out to catch them, and the emperor's eyes narrowed as the mark of a healing burn showed on the inside of his aide's arm. He opened his mouth to speak, considered, and closed it again. "Dismissed, Julianus."

Domitian sat looking thoughtful for a long while after Flavius had gone. Was that burned arm what had had him so nervy lately? And if he had burned it where Domitian thought he had, why? Flavius Julianus was utterly, completely loyal, incapable of being otherwise. If Flavius had covered up treason, he had done it to pull someone else out of danger. And Domitian would never find out who that someone was from Flavius. Domitian decided that he didn't want to know, not this time. Whatever had been afoot, it was ended for now, buried with Marius Vettius, who had thought he could make himself emperor.

It wasn't the first time rumors of assassination had surfaced; they were the constant companions of any man who held the purple. For the rest of his life Domitian would tense at the sound of a footstep behind him, but with Flavius Julianus on his staff, he had a better watchdog than most men had. He was not yet foolish enough to trade that security for vengeance for a plot already dead. Domitian carefully turned the map so that his back was no longer to the door and went back to his work.

*   *   *

The sense of urgency in and around Castra Mattiacorum
was growing. Forst could feel it hanging in the thin dawn like
the portentous stillness before an earthquake or a summer storm.
In the wine stall where he had found a cheap lodging, he shook
the straw off his cloak and stumbled out in the half-light past
the sleeping forms of the shopkeeper and the thin, cowed girl
who served the wine and lay with the customers in the storeroom at the back. He ducked under the door flap and stuck his
head in the rain barrel outside. The dirty streets and raw timbered buildings shook themselves into activity as the wake-up
sounded from the bugler's post inside the fort.

A supply wagon rumbled past, loaded and on the road already. At the end of the street two sentries from the patrol that
kept the peace in the *vicus* by night were trudging back to
camp, quarreling over some long-gone dice game. Behind him,
the shopkeeper stirred and kicked the girl awake. Forst shook
the water from his hair and went slowly, then faster as the
urgency in the street began to catch him, toward the house
where Ranvig and his people were lodged. The Germans were
awake, too: There were thralls coming and going from the
house, and a knot of warriors standing lordlywise in the street
and watching them work. Forst knew Ranvig and Fiorgyn by
sight now, and Barden and Lady Morgian across the long, sad
gulf of years, although he had never let himself get close enough
for them to see him for fear that that would make his decision
for him then and there. But these men were none that he knew.
They stared back at him blankly, an unknown man with his
hair in a Semnone knot and a desperate indecision in his face.

"Hai! You!"

Forst spun around. A wiry blond man trotted across the
street, and Forst recognized the Macedonian that Correus Julianus had pulled out of the arena.

"This came in with the army post last night," Eumenes said.
"Master turned me out this morning to go and find you." He
held out a wooden tablet with leaves sealed with a blotch of
wax. Forst read Correus's name and then his own in laborious
Latin letters across the front. He clutched it and stood staring
at it with a cold unease. Emer could write, but she did it badly.
He could see her in his mind, scratching those characters across
the wood, with a thin reed pen.

"Can you read?" Eumenes asked.

"What? Oh. Yes, I can read. As . . . as well as she can write." He still stared at it.

"Well, if I was you then, I'd read it," Eumenes advised. "It'll have to be important for the old general to have wangled it into the military post for her."

Forst looked at the Semnone warriors again, and they looked back at him blankly as at some oddity that had no bearing on their world. He went back to the wineshop and shut himself in the storeroom with the wooden tablet:

> You have a child. A girl, if that will make a difference to you. She was born at the end of April. I had thought not to tell you, thinking that you must make up your own mind to come back or not. But now there is another man, and he will marry me if you do not come.

Forst leaned his head against the cool clay of the storeroom wall and stared miserably at the straggling letters.

> I do not love him, but he will be good to us, and I need a man, and the child needs a father.

It was stark, a statement of fact, not as she would have spoken it, but Emer didn't write well, and it was not a thing she would have been willing to speak to a scribe.

> So now you will have to decide. I am sorry, but the man will not wait, and I will not either, anymore. You have had enough time.

It was a bitter, proud letter. He could see her image, superimposed on the straw bins and their wine jars, drawing each awkward character, her face set, her red hair pulled up in a knot on her head and coming loose to curl in fine tendrils around her face. There was a splash of freckles across her nose and cheeks, infinitely dear, and remembered with an aching clarity. He stared at the wine jars as if the image could speak and somehow make all other things clear to him, too. The clamor in the street outside rose to a confusion of screams and angry voices before he heard it. He ran for the storeroom door as the face across the wine jars faded out.

The street was full of Roman soldiers. The girl was huddled under a bench, and the shopkeeper was busy pulling the wine jars that had been set into their slots in the counter for the day's trade back out again. He stopped long enough to pick up a knife and slap it down on the counter beside him. Everywhere along the street, people were diving into buildings and pulling shut their doors.

Forst saw that the Romans were fighting with a mounted German war band, caught between the foot soldiers who were pouring out of the fort and the cavalry troop that had chased them into the town. The Germans were armed with oval shields and heavy fighting spears, and they had swords slung from their belts as well. Some of the cavalry troopers were wounded, and a few were riding double behind their mates.

The Germans must have ambushed a patrol, he thought, and caught the worst of it until the fighting had swept into the town itself. Forst flattened himself back in the doorway as a German horseman toppled a cavalryman from his mount. The Roman fell and lay still in the mud, with a red hole in the scales of his cuirass. The troop horse screamed and crashed into the unshuttered front of a food stall, upsetting the iron brazier that was burning on the counter. Another cavalryman plunged toward the German, who pulled his own rearing mount up and looked for a way out as the stall's awning fell and caught fire from the brazier. There were unlit torches in brackets on the wall, and the German pulled one free and stuck it in the flames. He whirled it around his head and into the roof thatch of the next shop as the cavalryman closed in on him and they disappeared again into the melee in the street.

It was then that the odd thing happened, the thing that Forst remembered over all the rest of the skirmish. Someone shouted *"Fire!"* and suddenly there seemed to be two Roman armies in the street. The foot soldiers' commander gave an order, and his troops split like two forks in a stream. One pursued the now retreating Germans, while the other became a line that passed buckets of water from the channel that supplied the fort, to pour them on the flames of the shop. For a while the fighting raged around the bucket line, but they only put their shields over their heads and let it pass by them, never stopping the water.

Their commander stood with his optio beside him, and, watching him, something moved into place inside Forst. It felt like a window being flung open, he thought, grasping for the idea that had come to him so quickly and completely in the chaos. Whatever else might be an ill with Rome, the Romans were builders. They would take the land they had conquered and make something of it. In the Black Forest over the last ten years, they already had. Forst had seen that when he had first come back to the Rhenus. His people, if they took the land back, would burn everything in it that was Roman. And that would be wrong now. Forst watched the flames sink under the steady splash of the water and watched the faces of the German shopkeeper and his girl as they stood to one side, out of the soldiers' way. The towns and the people here were too Roman to go back. That was what it came to in the end. And so was he. There was a dead German warrior in the street, one hand outflung in the mud, his knotted hair pulled from its pins and trampled with it. Forst looked at him sadly, a man he had never seen, a boy come to his sword since Forst had last ridden with a war band.

Wet ashes drifted down around him. *Too much gone*, he thought. Too much water gone by in the river and too many men dead. These were new men, this new chieftain and his warriors. Forst had a new tie, a new child, and a wife for whom he had fought as hard as he had ever fought for Nyall Sigmundson. And no one stepped in the same river twice, not ever.

Most of the fire was out, and the bucket line moved aside as another cavalry troop splattered past them through the mud. Ranvig was going to lose. One more warrior in his war band wasn't going to make the difference or bring Nyall back. Forst knew that, and knew that he had lost his belief in lost causes. He would say a last prayer to the German gods that Nyall had found his peace, then he would go back to Emer. And that was a Roman way to think. Somehow Rome had made a Roman of him.

XXI
Fiorgyn

YGERNA TOOK ONE LOOK AT THE COMMOTION IN THE STREETS, barred the door, and sat down beside it with the silver-handled knife that Julius Frontinus had given her.

"It's mostly our own men," Flavius said, lifting a shutter and looking out at the foot soldiers milling outside. "The Germans will be a mile down the road by now with the cavalry on their tails." He had come in search of Correus, who was wanted to interpret the emperor's midday ultimatum, and found him already gone to the fort.

"It's your men I don't trust," Ygerna said. "Not in this mood. They are jumpy with these raids, and they have left off thinking. This is a German house. They may not care which Germans they chase."

As she spoke there was a flurry of angry Roman voices almost under the window, and someone shouted, "There! There's one of them! Get the heathen devil!" Flavius saw a junior officer of the Claudia lying propped against a hedge with a gash in his leg. Angry voices chorused around him, and he shouted an order that no one listened to. They were nearly out of control, and as he ordered them furiously to hold, the soldiers saw a man from Ranvig's delegation in the distance and began to move that way up the street, picking up their pace.

"Mithras god! Fiorgyn!" Flavius hurled himself at the door and wrenched the bolt back. "Bar it behind me!" he shouted, and ran.

The junior officer of the Claudia was trying to stand up. He saw Flavius and fell back against the hedge, white-faced. "I couldn't hold them," he said. "If you don't stop them, they'll tear that place apart!"

Flavius swore at him and ran on without breaking stride. He turned the corner into a street of thatch-roofed houses and saw them battering at the front of the hall where Ranvig's

people had been lodged. The man they had chased had been
pulled inside by his fellows, but they hadn't been able to get
the door barred in time, and the fighting was halfway into the
house, the German warriors being pressed back by sheer weight
of numbers. The street was full of bales and boxes, broken
open and trampled in the mud, and one of the thralls was lying
among them, dead.

"Burn the bastards out!" A legionary at the rear of the press
looked around him for fire.

Flavius grabbed him by the neck and pulled him backward
into the street. He flung him down in the mud, and the man
began to come up sword in hand. His eyes widened when he
saw Flavius.

"Stop it!" Flavius shouted. "Hold! Fall back!" They didn't
hear him, and a pilum sailed past his ear, aimed by a German
who had caught it and sent it back again. The soft shaft at the
head was bent, and it didn't fly well, but the range was short
and Flavius was wearing only a light parade cuirass. He dived
into the cover of the legionaries jamming the front of the house
and began to fight his way through them. "Hold, damn you!
Back off!" They didn't hear him over the shouting, or they
didn't care. He fought frantically to the doorway and braced
his back against one of the posts. He had his sword out and
blocked part of the doorway with it as they surged around him.
In the hall beyond, he could see the Germans backed into
another doorway behind a bristle of spears, with three or four
dead at their feet and Ranvig in the middle. He had a sword
in one hand and a spear in the other, and his crooked face was
set in a blaze of fury. Ten or twelve more were fighting in the
hall itself. In the room beyond, someone was screaming. Flavius saw with horror that there were women among the fighters
in the hall.

"Hold! *In the emperor's name!*" He threw himself completely across the doorway, and the onslaught slowed as they
began to recognize him. "Hold! *That is an order!*" He turned
quickly to see what was going on behind him. The fighting in
the hall had not stopped. There was a flash of blue cloth, and
he saw Fiorgyn with a knife in her hand, fighting furiously as
two soldiers pulled her away from the rest. Flavius swung his
sword and caught one of the soldiers across the helmet with

the flat of it. The man spun around, hesitating as he saw Flavius. The soldiers at the door had halted, and with a snarl the Germans began to close in on them.

"Friend!" Flavius shouted in German. "Friend! Ranvig, call them off!"

Ranvig's eyes met his over the scuffling men in the hall. "Damn you! What about my dead?"

"There'll be more dead if you don't call them off!" Flavius shouted. "I can't keep them back if you don't!" The men outside the door had begun to press forward again, still angry, still ready to put a pilum in any German they could catch. Flavius pulled the second soldier away from Fiorgyn and flung him against the men in the doorway. His lorica crashed against their raised shields, and they staggered back a step. The other men in the hall had begun to fall back as the Germans came after them. "Get out!" Flavius shouted at them. "Get out while you can. You know the punishment for mutiny." They looked at him warily and backed away. "Ranvig, call your men to heel!"

Ranvig gave an order in German, and his warriors halted, spears leveled, glaring at Flavius and the Romans behind him. Flavius let his breath out.

"Is this the way the emperor of Rome makes a treaty?" Ranvig said sarcastically. There were dead and wounded on the floor. Lady Morgian came out from the back room with the priest and began to look at them. Two Roman bodies were among them, and Flavius called four of the legionnaires back.

"Take them to the surgeon," he said wearily.

"They're dead, sir!" one of the soldiers said. He took a step toward the Germans.

Flavius raised his fist. "Get them out of here! And get yourselves out before something worse happens to you." They knew what he meant, and they picked up their dead and went. The punishment for mutiny was death by stoning.

Flavius turned to Ranvig grimly. "This is your fault, Ranvig. Your raids, your ambushes, your tricks did this. Not the emperor." He turned his back on him and strode across to Fiorgyn. "Are you all right?" he asked softly.

"Yes." She had put her knife away and was rubbing a bruised wrist.

"Come out of here," he said in a low voice.

She nodded and began to follow him to the door. Barden was chanting a low, keening song over one of the men who lay with unseeing eyes on the plank floor, and Morgian was tying a strip torn from her gown around the arm of another. Signy was helping her. She had a cut cheek, and tears and blood were running down her face.

"Fiorgyn!"

Fiorgyn turned back to Ranvig. Her hair was coming out of its braids, and there was someone's blood turning dark on the front of her gown. "I will be back at midday," she said, and went out after Flavius.

"Let her go," Signy said unexpectedly, her voice shaking. She held the bandage while Morgian pinned it. "Let her have this morning. It's the last one, but at least she will have that. I am thinking she is lucky for that."

Ranvig looked at her curiously and dropped down on one knee beside her. "What is it, child?" He turned her head up to him and wiped away the blood with one of Morgian's bandages to look at her cheek. "You've a cut on your face."

"At least she has a man who wants her for her!" Signy flung at him. "Not just because she needs a home and can have babies!" She burst into tears.

Ranvig put his arms around her, and she huddled against his chest, sobbing. He looked helplessly at Morgian.

"These men will live, or they will not," Morgian said. "There is nothing you can do. I will send Barden to put salve on her face when he has finished here."

Ranvig looked at the sobbing child in his arms and picked her up. He went into the back of the house, holding her.

"There will be no peace," Flavius said dully.

"Did you think there would be?" Fiorgyn said.

"No." He sat miserably on the edge of the bed, looking up at her. "But I always told myself there would be a little more time." The time was gone now. He had taken a room at the only good inn in the *vicus* because of it. It didn't matter anymore.

"No," Fiorgyn said. "No more. Only until midday." Because Ranvig was going at midday to tell the emperor one last lie. He would send his people out of the *vicus* before that, in case the emperor should choose not to believe it.

Flavius's face had grown desperate. "Stay with me," he said suddenly now. "Stay with me. Go back to Rome with me."

"No," she whispered. "Don't even try." She backed away from him. "You are the other half of me. I love you. But I can't go with you. Don't make me say it for both of us."

"No. No, I am sorry. I couldn't take you if you could go." He stood up and laid a hand along the side of her face, lovingly. "But go somewhere else, somewhere you'll be safe. Do that for me. If the emperor doesn't like Ranvig's answer, he may decide to hold all of you."

"It wouldn't do him any good," Fiorgyn said. "The tribe has Ranvig's orders not to buy him or any of us back if it comes to that. He made them swear an oath, and he put the chieftain's curse on the man who breaks it."

Flavius had been in Germany long enough to know that that was no laughing matter. The chieftain's curse was reputed to kill—always the man who was cursed and sometimes also the chieftain who had set it. Ranvig's men wouldn't break that oath. "I will tell the emperor that," he said, relieved that he could discourage Domitian from hostage-taking with a clear conscience. After this morning, he didn't care what the emperor did with Ranvig, but Fiorgyn—Fiorgyn was another matter. But there was still going to be a battle, and Ranvig was still going to lose. "Please," he said desperately, "please go away from here, away from Ranvig and his damned war. They will take prisoners afterward. I don't know what might happen."

Fiorgyn put her hand on his. "Flavius, think. If it were the other way—if your soldiers were outnumbered, and the tribes had called up a great war band to fight them, and if I told you not to fight, but to go and sit in a hole somewhere safe—what would you do?"

He looked into her eyes, sky colored, honest, stubborn. "I would like to say that is not the same thing," he said. "But I suppose it is, really, isn't it?"

"I matter too much," she said. "Even if I wanted to go and hide, I cannot. I am Nyall Sigmundson's widow and Ranvig's kinswoman. That counts for too much among the tribes. My place is with my own kind. And I am thinking that maybe I owe Nyall that much, now."

"I know," Flavius said. And the bitter part of it was that he did. Before Fiorgyn, he had never thought that a woman had more to do than to follow the man chosen for her and to let his loyalties be hers. He had never understood Correus's German wife, Freita, and her divided heart. Now, miserably, he did. He would never ask a man for whom he had any respect to desert his own kind with a war coming. Now he couldn't ask Fiorgyn, either. Slowly, trying to make it last, he pulled the silver caps off the ends of her braids and shook the pale hair loose, and she came into his arms for the last time.

It was cold in the room, but they didn't notice. They lay on the bed and traced their hands across each other, memorizing every line and scar and curve. There was an old scar on Flavius's cheek, souvenir of a hunting mishap, and she ran the tip of her finger along it as if she would remember even that. He cupped both her breasts in his hands and put his face against her throat and lay there, letting the misery wash over him until finally it ran away, spent, and there was only the woman in his arms. The cold air stung his back, and he pulled the rough blanket up and wrapped his body around hers under it.

She tilted her head back to look at him and shivered as he entered her, a familiar touch now, welcome, need calling to need. He rocked back and forth gently, and the white legs tangled around his own. Her breath began to come faster, but it was his face that she gave her mind to. A sharp-angled face, dark-eyed and olive-skinned, a Roman face. But no longer alien. A beloved face, sure and familiar, a face she could call up in dreams. *Don't let me forget his face*. She could bear it, she thought, if no one again could ever touch her body as Flavius did. But not if she forgot his face.

It had begun to rain outside, driven on a wind that came through the shutters like a knife, but neither of them felt it. They could have frozen there, still locked together, and they would not have known. Finally, in the still heaviness of spent passion, he rolled a little away from her, but his hands were still tangled in her rippled hair and he couldn't bear to move them.

"There is a last time for all things," he whispered. "I didn't think until today that that was unfair."

"We have been lucky to have had this long. Everything must change." *Let me remember his face.*

He lifted his hand and touched her cheek. "Then maybe it will change again." His natural optimism began to creep into his voice. He had always thought that one did better with some hope to hang onto. "Maybe it won't be forever. Maybe—"

"Maybe," Fiorgyn said, unwillingly. That was more than she wanted to hope for. It was too easy to break your heart on hope. If they did meet again, he would still be married. And so would she. It would have to come to that now, and there were one or two men in the tribe who would be willing to marry a chieftain's widow, even if she was carrying another man's child. For a moment she wanted to tell him, if only to take away the loneliness. But she knew what he would say if he knew, and it would solve nothing and only give them a quarrel to part on.

"We have an hour left," she whispered. There was no more that her love for Flavius could do to her. She would take the hour, she thought, in payment, and put a whole life's love into it.

"The chieftain has stalled long enough," Correus said flatly. The emperor on one side and the chieftain on the other stared across him implacably at each other. The midday sun was dark behind the boiling rain clouds. Water splattered on the roof tiles and fell in a torrent from the eaves.

"The emperor asks too much," Ranvig said. He glanced at Domitian and spoke directly to Correus. "I cannot accede to that. We are the Free People. Even after the last war we managed to hold our land. I cannot give it to Rome now."

"I never thought you could," Correus said. "What do you want me to tell the emperor?"

"That I will talk one more time with my council. But that I am doubtful."

"The chieftain says that he is doubtful, but that he will try to persuade his council," Correus said. "He is lying."

Domitian nodded. "Tell the chieftain that he is out of time.

He has an hour to get out of my fort. And a day to get his people out of the Agri Decumates back where they belong."

Correus translated, but he knew Ranvig had understood well enough. "The emperor thinks you're lying. The emperor would keep you for a hostage, but he knows that if he does, your people will fight. He still hopes that that may be avoided. He hopes that you will go home and stay there."

"Until he has leisure to come and see to us." Ranvig dismissed all that. "*You* told him I was lying."

"I did. What did you expect?"

"No more than that." Ranvig stood. He raised a hand to the emperor, or maybe to Correus; Correus wasn't sure. Then he was gone. The two warriors who had come with him stalked out behind him. Their horses were tethered in the rain outside the Principia, and they kicked them into a gallop as they hit the saddle.

The Romans didn't stop them. Ranvig hadn't thought they would. He had learned what he wanted to about the new Roman emperor in the months he had sat quibbling over a treaty that would never be written.

At the fortress gate, they swung their horses east through the *vicus*, toward where the rest would be waiting for them. Beyond the Roman zone was his war host: Arni with the Semnone warriors who had ceased their raiding in the Roman zone and pulled back to meet them; and Steinvar with his borrowed men, sent from Dacia by Decebalus. The Semnones had been chafing for months for a real fight, a battle with more honor in it than the raiding that Ranvig had kept them to, and Arni had been hard put to hold in line the hotheads among them. Arni hadn't liked it himself. So many factions to quarrel with each other, Ranvig thought. But if he won, the Romans would look no more at Semnone lands. Not for a long while anyway, and that was the most that could ever be said of Romans.

XXII
Autumn Battle

"Oh, Rapax troops are afraid of the dark,
    And Adiutrix's generals are crazy—"

The cheerful voice drifted over the glow of the cookfires,
and an angry shout came back from Velius Rufus's camp.

"The Ninth can't be beat at sounding retreat,
    And all of Augusta is lazy!

So who pulls you out when the heathen box you in?
Who do they send for when the going's getting hot?
Gemina! Fourteenth Gemina!
Gemina, the best of the lot!"

The singer's mates joined in the last chorus and drummed
their mess tins on the ground. Correus grinned. The Fourteenth
Gemina still didn't have a legate, but they had lost their sulks
and malingering and had earned their Eagle back fairly. They
had had enough of building roads, and of sabotage and fouled
water, and of raiding parties that dropped out of trees, while
the Rapax and the British detachments under Velius Rufus were
fighting proper battles with the Chatti. But Marbod's Chatti
warriors had proven to be as dangerous as Ranvig had pro-
phesied, and now the other wing of the army had been called
in too, to smash them and end it. The Fourteenth Gemina was
plainly feeling set up about it, and the singer renewed his insults
happily. Correus considered stopping him before he provoked
Rufus's generals too far. He decided not to. The Gemina needed
to feel proud of itself.

The singer began improvising a new verse, and Correus
went back to his dinner, which Eumenes was serving in his
tent—a legate's tent, red leather and gilded fringe, with rugs

341

on the floor. Correus knew wistfully that he wasn't going to keep it. He didn't have enough service behind him for a legate's posting. Not yet. But for this battle it was his, and the legion was his. Even with his failure to make Ranvig see sense, and now the uncertainty as to just how many men Ranvig was pulling into his war band, Correus couldn't help feeling pleased with himself. It was no easy thing to turn a legion around when it had been spoiled, especially one that had been paid for it. A commander willing to bribe his men could have their total loyalty until the money ran out. It would ruin them in the long run, but Vettius hadn't cared about that, and the common legionary didn't think in those terms. The legionary served for twenty-five years in one legion, and it was his commander who shaped his life. The legionary thought only in the here and now. Correus's first commander, Messala Cominius, who had a legion of his own now somewhere on the Danuvius, had taught him that. It had proved to be the most useful, and dangerous, thing Correus had learned in eleven years in the army.

The tent flap popped open, and Centurion Quintus came through. "All locked up, sir," he said. "Pickets posted, and the watchword is 'laurel.' I'll quiet our nightingale down when I go back through." Quintus's belt buckle proclaimed him as a man of the Gemina now. Centurions promoted from the ranks generally did not reach cohort level and so rarely changed legions, but Correus, serving as both legate and primus pilus of the Gemina, had asked for Quintus as a staff aide. It had seemed better than disturbing the precarious balance of the Gemina by pulling a man from its ranks for the job, and the Gemina First Cohort's second centurion was going to have his hands full with Correus in the legate's post.

Correus pushed away the remains of his dinner, and Eumenes splashed watered wine into the cup. "Have the scouts come in?" The emperor and Velius Rufus had scouts of their own out, of course, but Correus believed in firsthand information when he could get it. Tonight, it seemed, there wasn't any.

"They're in," Quintus said. "But all they had to say was 'Same as before,' so I told 'em to go clean up before they came on to you. They smelled like bog trolls."

Correus dismissed Quintus and sat watching the lamp flame in his wine. If he were Eilenn, maybe he would see something in it. Correus just saw wine, so he drank it and told Eumenes he was going to bed. Outside, the singer ended his song abruptly—that would be Quintus—and the camp began to doze. The scouts could report their lack of success in the morning. They knew that the Semnones were also massing their war band at last and were circling upriver to join the Chatti, but they kept shifting about, and so far no one had been able to tell whether or not Ranvig had all the allies he had claimed. There were other scattered tribes whose land lay between the Agri Decumates and the Semnones. They might ally with Ranvig, or they might lie low and hope the storm would pass them by. None had so far been willing to ally openly with Rome. Maybe Marbod would refuse alliance since Ranvig had left him to fight the Romans alone for so long, Correus thought hopefully. He turned over and went to sleep, counting Germans in his head.

Marbod was willing to ally. He needed the men, and he knew it. But he wasn't willing to listen to Ranvig's strategy. He scowled, his wide, thin salmon's mouth snapping at his red mustache. "That is a cowardly, Roman way to fight that I might have expected of one who has sat in the Romans' holds for a year, drinking wine like a woman."

"Of course," Ranvig said sarcastically. "And Marbod is a great warrior whose strategy has driven the Romans back to Rome. Those are trolls that we saw camped yonder in their tents."

Fiorgyn looked at Ranvig suspiciously. She thought he was deliberately prodding Marbod. Ranvig didn't like Marbod, but it also had something to do with the argument he had had earlier with some of Arni's men over his orders, and with the Dacian men in the peaked caps who had ridden in with Steinvar. She wasn't sure what. Her face grew interested, and she laid a hand on Arni's arm when he started to intervene. Arni might learn to keep his tongue between his teeth by the time his hair had gone gray, but she doubted it. He stood shifting from foot to foot and glaring furiously at Marbod and Ranvig both. Marbod's insults bit too close to the tribe's honor. But when Arni was through fighting Marbod, he wanted to fight the Romans, and he didn't like what Ranvig was saying, either. Beyond Arni, some of the other Semnone warriors were nodding vigorously when Marbod spoke, while Steinvar stood stolidly, arms folded across his wolfskin jacket. The men in the peaked caps had sent none of their own number to the council. They seemed content to let Steinvar or Ranvig speak for them.

"We could have driven the Romans back across the Rhenus by now, back all the way to Gaul!" Marbod shouted. "If the Semnones had sent the men they promised!"

"I promised nothing," Ranvig said. "I gave you a piece of advice that you chose to ignore when you insulted the Romans' emperor to his face."

"And now you bring me foreigners out of Dacia and say they may not fight!"

"Their lord cannot afford their loss just now," Ranvig said. He shrugged and looked amused. "He has other uses for his war host, so that was our bargain. If the chieftain of the Chatti will listen, the Dacians will be useful without fighting. And I have not brought them to you. They are my men, Marbod."

Marbod exploded. "We will not fight in any cowardly Roman fashion, with holding back and running. And if Ranvig of the Semnones does not lead this war band, he may go and sit and spin with his women and his foreigners and let his warriors follow me!"

The lord of one of the Semnones' outlying clans pushed his way forward, with two others trailing him. "The chieftain of the Chatti is right! We did not come here to play children's games with the Romans!"

Ranvig considered him, and his crooked face grew angry. "I had assumed that you came because the Romans are a danger to the Free Lands, and because I am your chieftain." He eyed Marbod and the other man as if they smelled. "We fought in the last war while Marbod sat and got fat in his hold. Are you wishful now to break the oath you swore to me, for *Marbod*? So much for your honor!"

"We will not run!" The clan lord stamped his foot. If he had been a horse he would have laid his ears back. "We will fight like men, in a battle like men!"

It was supposed to be a meeting for the chieftains and their tribal lords, the men who carried a vote in council, but they were making so much noise that others began to crowd around, too—small holders and younger warriors and any man with a mind to make his voice heard. Ranvig, who was normally willing to shout his council to a standstill if they pushed him too far, eyed Marbod consideringly and seemed more pleased than not, Fiorgyn thought. *He is setting them to quarrel with each other*, she realized suddenly. He had thrown his plan into their midst like a bone to a pack of hounds and was sitting back now to watch them fight. There was a thrall's tale that Ranvig had the elves' blood in him, and he looked much like one now, his crooked eyes watching with veiled amusement, his long fingers playing idly with the red-gold band around his wrist, while mortal lords quarreled among themselves for some dim purpose of his own. Fiorgyn looked at him, exasperated. Whatever Ranvig was up to, the elves had nothing to do with it, and now was not the time to be goading Marbod or the discontented among the Semnones.

Gradually the rebellious lord and his two allies had moved so that they stood beside Marbod, four in a row, glaring at Ranvig.

"You are oath-sworn to me," Ranvig said when they had finished shouting, "but if you wish to fight the Romans in one charge like stampeding cattle, I will release you from your oath to me. It will make the ravens happy." He swung around to look at the arguing crowd of men behind him. "Any man of mine," he said deliberately, "who wishes to ride with them is free of his oath."

There was a surprised murmur and then a shout, and a small wave of men spilled forward. Fiorgyn narrowed her eyes as she counted them. Hotheads and quarrelers every one, men who were berserkers in battle and trouble at home. Every man among them had been called before the council over and again for provoking some grievance.

They slammed their spears against their shields and shouted that they would lay the Romans in a red grave. Arni started to move, and Fiorgyn dug her fingers into his arm. "No! Not you!"

* * *

"Where in the name of Pluto and Persephone are they?" Velius Rufus was an unlikely sight sitting on the edge of his camp bed in his undertunic, with his bowed legs wrapped in a blanket. His thick shock of hair was flattened at the back from the pillow, and his expression was pop-eyed and wrathful.

"Out there," the decurion of the frontier scouts said. "And that's about as good as we can get." He was dressed in German breeches and wolfskin jacket, with sheep's-wool leggings for warmth. His hair was long and braided like a German's, and he had a bristly beard going gray around the chin. The cultivated Latin of an educated man was incongruous when he spoke.

Velius Rufus snorted. "And you cross-eyed fools have managed to lose Marbod, too? This isn't a game of hide-and-go-seek with your sister!"

"He isn't lost," the frontier scout said, "but he's moved east, presumably to meet up with the Semnone warriors, and they're none of them sitting still long enough to make a count or pin down their base camp." He wasn't impressed with the general's temper. He'd been out with his men for three days, crawling through bogs and forests so thick a man couldn't see his hand in front of his face, and if no more of the Germans had been found than traces of old campfires, it was because they were taking pains not to be. He leaned one hand on the tent's center pole, waiting for orders. He was cold, wet, and more than annoyed with his own lack of success, and he didn't feel much like standing at attention, but he knew Rufus well enough not to sit down unless the general said to.

"I left orders to be waked up when you came in," Velius Rufus said, "because we are supposed to be fighting the Germans, not bouncing around like hoptoads trying to find them! That was on the assumption that *you* would have found them because that is what the army pays you for, not for looking under a few bushes and coming sniveling back to me that you don't see any Germans! If the rivers freeze again this winter, you'll see Germans coming up through the hypocausts if we don't catch up to them now. And as you may have noticed while you were out picking flowers, there isn't a whole lot of fighting weather left. This army is breaking camp tomorrow and heading for where you *think* the Germans have gone, but I don't want to chase 'em so far that they come circling back on our rear. So get *your* rear onto your horse and hop it out of here, and don't show your face in my camp again until you can point a pilum at the Germans!" Rufus lay back down on his camp bed and pulled the blanket up over his ears. It was as cold as a Vestal Virgin in the German mountains at night.

"I hear and obey, lord." The decurion salaamed, Eastern fashion, and Rufus chuckled under his blanket. The frontier scouts never had had any respect, but if anyone could find the Germans before the Germans found *them*, it was the scouts.

"Go and get something to eat first," Rufus growled. The cold wind whipped in under the tent flap as the decurion lifted it. "Go and wake up a cook. It's a fine night to try to start a fire."

In the morning, the army was on the march. The camp's defenses were destroyed at first light (no Roman army ever made the enemy a present of a fortified camp), and they moved out through the knee-high mist that came from a tributary of the Moenus and still rolled along the high valley. The four British legionary detachments and the auxiliary cavalry, in scale armor over their gold and scarlet, went in the vanguard. The auxiliary infantry fanned out ahead of them to scout the way, and the pioneers marched behind them to clear it, if necessary, to let the bulk of the legions pass in battle order. Behind the pioneers were the emperor Domitian with his staff, his Praetorians, and his generals Velius Rufus and Julius Frontinus, and then the gilded Eagles of five legions, with their troops marching six abreast: the Twenty-first Rapax and the four garrison legions of Upper Germany, the Eighth Augusta, the Eleventh Claudia, the Fourteenth Gemina, and the First Adiutrix.

With them were the legionary cavalry, the artillery mules with disassembled field catapults, the generals' personal baggage, and, at the rear, just ahead of another auxiliary unit of foot troops and cavalry, the legionary baggage carts, the hospital wagons, and any civilians who had the general's permission to be there. Those who didn't, the most determined of the camp followers and entrepreneurs, would be strung out behind, at a safe distance from any official eye but close enough to catch up to the baggage wagons for safety if things got hot.

Correus, riding with the legates of the other German legions,

just ahead of their column, could see the shadow of the Eighth
Augusta's Eagle flung out on the trampled meadow to his left
as the mist burned off, but it was the baggage wagons that he
had his mind on. Against his better judgment, he had sent the
children back to Moguntiacum with Eumenes and their nurse
(Eumenes cursing nonstop under his breath), and let Ygerna
come with the column. It was probably safe enough, but he
had never done it before, and he had argued against it furiously,
while Ygerna just sat there and said, "I am coming, Correus.
If you don't get the general's permission, I will ride behind
with the wine sellers and Rhodope's whores, but I am coming."

"Why, in Typhon's name?"

"Because I have had enough this year of sitting in a house
somewhere and wondering if you have been killed," she said
frankly.

"So you want to come with the column where *you* can get
killed."

"I doubt that. With almost all of five legions and pieces of
four more, and cavalry and auxiliaries, and the Morrigan knows
what else? You said yourself we are going to win."

"We are," Correus said. "But not everyone is going to survive the experience. We don't know how many men Ranvig
has got, and the Chatti fight like wolves. You never know
what's going to happen in a battle. I don't want you there!"

Ygerna's black eyes glowed, and her mouth set in a tight
line. "I am coming! I will *not* sit back and wonder if you are
dead, not this time! I will stay with the baggage and behave,
or I can make myself useful in the hospital, but I am coming!"

He started to say that she didn't know what it would be
like, and stopped. She had gone with Julius Frontinus's army
when she was thirteen. More than the other legates' wives,
more than anyone but the soldiers themselves, Ygerna knew
what a battle and an army on the march were like.

So now she was back with the baggage wagons, riding her
gray mare and putting on the charm for the chief surgeon. And
Correus was going to have to stop thinking about her, or he
would find himself worrying when he was supposed to be
fighting, and that was a good way to end up in the surgeon's
tent himself. Or worse. He had told Ygerna that legates didn't
get killed, but that wasn't quite true. Anything that wasn't

supposed to happen could happen in a battle, and the Fourteenth Gemina still had a few rickety spots. It was unlucky to think that way before a fight. Correus pushed both Ygerna and his own prospects to the back of his mind, and tilted his head to hear what the legate of the First Adiutrix was saying.

"I hope Rufus's scouts know more than mine," Adiutrix's commander said sourly. He was an old soldier, nearly twice Correus's age, his legate's post the cap of an uneventful career, and he was inclined to take a dour view of things. "No good will come of gallivanting over these mountains like a pack of brats after butterflies." The eagle feathers on his helmet nodded in agreement as he bobbed his head gloomily.

Claudia's legate laughed. "I'll send over some liniment for your old bones, Sulpicius, and you'll see the world some better. It's that nag you're riding that sours your viewpoint."

The Adiutrix legate's mount was a hammerheaded hack with a jolting gait. The older man shook his head. "I've had this beast a long time. At my age, a man doesn't like changes. Better to retire, maybe, after this campaign, him and me both. Find a farm somewhere." He lapsed into thought, and the Claudia's legate turned to Correus, kindly including him in their talk.

"What about you, Julianus? This is your first legionary command. What do you think about it?"

"I'm too unnerved to think," Correus said frankly. "I'd assumed we'd have a new legate by now." He wouldn't have traded this chance at command for all the sunken gold in Atlantis, but he was admittedly unsettled by the rush of events and uncomfortably aware of his scarlet cloak and helmet crest among the purple and eagle feathers of the legates.

"The Fourteenth does seem to have gone through commanders lately," the Augusta's legate said.

"Ill luck," said the legate of the Adiutrix.

"I doubt that luck had anything to do with it," Augusta's commander said shortly. "Grattius Benacus was a good man, and Marius Vettius was a danger to the empire, and I'm quite certain I see a connection. The only curse on the Fourteenth was Vettius."

"Thank you, sir," Correus said. "Mithras knows he did it

no good. But I was wondering if I was the only one who'd seen it."

"Oh, no," Augusta's legate said grimly. "It was plain enough." He gave Correus a serious look. "How are they now? Will they hold?"

"Oh, yes, they'll hold," Correus said. He hoped to Hades they would. They were much improved, but it hadn't been very long, and obedience had to be a habit, or it might not last.

"You've done a good job with them, I'll say that," the legate of the Twenty-first Rapax put in. "I haven't seen worse than what you started with, except maybe the men they sent over from the Ninth Hispana. They were a mess, and it took Rufus a month to knock them halfway straight. He bounced two of their commanders, did you know that?"

The legate of the Claudia whistled between his teeth, and Correus thought of the Ninth Hispana, which had nearly mutinied in Britain. There was something wrong with that legion, some rot at the heart of it. Queen Boudicca of the Iceni had cursed it twenty years earlier, and maybe it had stuck. But he kept quiet about it. That was an ill omen for the march.

They were winding into a mountain valley now, away from the little river and toward the high pastureland and the forests of the Taunus. It was cold, and the wind whipped their cloaks around them and ruffled the horses' manes. Correus, looking down the length of the valley, thought that it would be no good place to meet the Germans, but there was winter coming. Velius Rufus had decided to waste no more time and trust to numbers to make up any disadvantage in terrain. It was the largest army the Romans had assembled at any one place in Germany, the equivalent of five full legions, and it would be broken up again when the season was ended, Correus thought. It was too large for safety. Marius Vettius wasn't the only man who would think of making a bid for the purple with the temptation of an army this size to call on. In the meantime, it was a comforting bulk at his back. It would be nice, he thought, if the Germans found it as impressive.

Marbod, sitting on a rock under a pine tree and chewing his mustaches, had found it most impressive. The troops that Velius Rufus had brought against him earlier in the season had been nearly tripled in number by the addition of Julius Frontinus's legions. And for that he had listened to Ranvig at least enough to let the Romans get onto unfavorable ground—but no more than that. A pair of warriors ran through the trees, and one dropped down on the ground and scraped the pine needles away with his hand.

"Here, lord." He drew the little valley into the dirt. "They come this way, as we thought."

Marbod nodded. His war band was gathered behind him, stretching away through the dark forest; the Semnone cowards, who were men with no honor, would be hooted away from Valhalla's gates when they died. Marbod stood up, and his spear-bearer put his heavy war spear and shield into his hands and checked the fine red lacing of his sword scabbard. "Now!" he shouted. "Now is the last battle, and we leave the Romankind for the ravens!" He swung himself up onto his horse and waved his spear. They streamed out of the forest behind him, the lords and warriors of the Chatti and the rebels from Ranvig's camp, a wild, unruly horde that bayed like wolves as they crashed down the mountainside.

From his place on the opposite hillcrest, Ranvig watched them go. He sat on his own horse, with the cold wind ruffling his braids and an odd light of satisfaction in his eyes as the troublemakers of his tribe streamed along the valley floor with their lords before them, neck and neck with Marbod of the Chatti for the honor of first kill, first blood, first place at the victory feast after they had danced on the Romans' graves.

"Now we fight!" Arni shouted. He was practically hopping in the saddle beside Ranvig. "Now we fight before we are too shamed to go home again!"

Behind them the Semnone warriors tensed their hands on their spears, and the Dacians in their peaked caps looked interested. It was not their war, but any war interested them.

Steinvar sidled his horse over to Arni's and put his lean, scarred hand in Arni's face. "Be quiet, or I'll tie you up and leave you with the Dacians. We won't go home at all if we fight like those fools." He nodded at the howling mob that was pouring down from Marbod's hill, screaming taunts and curses at the Romans. The Roman scouts had seen them, and the auxiliary infantry was already forming their lines while the cavalry and the legions came up behind them, a solid wall of scarlet and bronze packed tightly across the valley floor. A Roman trumpet sang out, and the heavy boom of a German war horn answered it.

"Are we going to let them fight while we sit here?" Arni exploded.

"Yes," Ranvig said harshly, still watching the valley floor. "We fought once while the Chatti sat by. I remember."

"We are all that is left of the Semnones," Steinvar said. "We have boys of twelve in this war band. If we go home on our shields, then it will all be gone."

"This is a shame and a dishonor, and the gods will curse us for it!" Arni shouted. His usual flyaway smile was gone, and his face was furious. "These men rode here with *me*! If you won't take them down, I will!" He raised his arm, and Steinvar grabbed it and wrestled it down to his side.

Ranvig wasn't looking at him. Slowly he raised his own arm, spear in hand, and the Semnone warriors shifted a little in their places behind him, every eye on the long white hand with the red-gold bracelet. Below, the leading edge of Marbod's war band crashed with a scream like demons out of Hel into the Roman lines.

Steinvar twisted Arni's arm behind him. "You will wait until he gives the signal, or I will flay you alive and find my daughter another husband."

Ranvig dropped his spear, pointing down to the valley, and another war horn bellowed above him. Steinvar let go of Arni, and the war host of the Semnones poured down the ridge.

Correus heard the shouting and the trumpet calls from the front of the column only an instant before he saw the dark wave that rolled down the hillside toward them. He pulled his horse around and rode at a gallop for his legion, third in line in the column behind them. The other legates were doing the same, the emperor and Velius Rufus had drawn up to the side, and Rufus was shouting orders to three optios at once. Two couriers raced by Correus, heading for the rear, as he swung Antaeus in at the head of the Fourteenth Gemina.

"What in Typhon's name is going on up there, sir?" the Second Cohort commander asked.

"Germans, Centurion," Correus said briskly. "Form them up." He looked around him for Quintus.

The Second Cohort commander slid off his horse, and an optio on another horse took its reins and galloped for the rear. Down the line the other officers were dismounting. The legions were infantry, and an officer stood and fought with his men.

Quintus pushed his way through the crowd. "Looks like we found 'em, sir," he said. "Nasty spot for it."

Correus looked at the valley's width. It narrowed where the head of the column was deployed. The Germans had chosen their timing carefully. "I'm betting we back up," he said to Quintus. "Tell them to get ready." As he spoke, another trumpet sounded the "Fall Back and Regroup" and a courier from Velius Rufus leaned down from his saddle.

"General's compliments, sir, and we're pulling back. Half a mile." He spurred his horse on down the column.

"You'll make general yet, sir," Quintus said cheerfully, and trotted off to pass the order. The narrow valley ahead would have kept two-thirds of their troops jammed up behind the rest. By pulling back, they would both blunt the first fury of the Germans' charge and gain enough ground to put their advantage in numbers to some use.

Ranvig saw the column begin to back up and re-form, like a single living body, and he swung his mountain-bred ponies and their riders in a wider arc along the slope. Below them, Marbod's warriors were screaming challenges as the Romans fell back before them. Marbod would know the Romans weren't running, but his war host, in a battle fury, wouldn't stop to care. Marbod might hold his own men, but never the renegade Semnones. And Marbod's men would never let Semnones take the lead. Ranvig had given the chieftain of the Chatti an ill gift.

The Romans had drawn their lines up across the widest stretch of the valley floor now, the auxiliaries to the fore with the scarlet weight of the legionary troops behind them, studded with the golden standards of cohort and century, and the great Eagles of the legions. The cavalry was forming up on the wings, but the wings ran right up onto the mountains' slope, and the cavalry ponies, not bred to these hills as the Germans' were, were finding it tricky going already.

Marbod's men, blue and red and ocher with war paint, their wild hair streaming out behind them, were tangled now with the auxiliaries of the front lines. They were naked from the waist up, many of them, save for the dark iron collars and the paint, and they fought with a fine red fury. The auxiliaries were beginning to buckle under their onslaught when the Roman trumpets sounded again. The auxiliaries fell back through the opened ranks of the waiting legions, and Marbod's men howled after them.

Ranvig's horses came down the last of the slope on their haunches, the loose pebbles from some long-dead streambed rattling under their hooves and the Semnone foot fighters at their heels. The ridge above them was bare of men. As the legionaries flung their pilums into the mass of Marbod's warriors, Ranvig's war host swept around the Roman cavalry and into the Roman flank.

There was blood in the air already, along with the worse smells of battle, men who had vomited or lost control of their bowels. Ygerna had smelled it before, and she thought sickly of the destruction that that smell meant and went on laying out bandages. Labienus, the chief field surgeon, a lean, plain-faced man in his forties, had set up his hospital tent among the baggage wagons, and already the wounded were being brought to the rear. Auxiliaries, mostly, but Ygerna knew that the Romans always began a battle with their auxiliaries. The men from the legions would come in soon enough.

Cottia and a surgeon's orderly were struggling to unfold the camp beds and laying out canvas on the dirt floor for the men the beds wouldn't hold. Labienus, in a bloody apron, was using a deep, cup-shaped spoon with a hole in the bottom to pull a barbed spearhead out of a man's shoulder while a junior surgeon held him to the table. Cottia had a white line around her mouth, but she worked grimly and cuffed the orderly indignantly when he looked at the writhing auxiliaryman and stopped to retch.

The wounded were coming faster now, faster than Labienus and the legionary surgeons and their juniors could deal with them. The orderlies laid the least desperate of them on the canvas and heaved the worst onto the surgery tables almost before the last man had been moved.

"Go and help Labienus," a junior surgeon panted, taking Ygerna's arm with a bloody hand and pointing her in the right direction. He didn't stop to ask if she could stand it, and with gritted teeth she told herself that she could. The junior surgeon disappeared somewhere into the chaos and the animal moaning that came from the men on the floor.

Labienus was pulling long splinters of what might have been the man's own shield from the red wreckage of an arm, and with a lurch in her stomach Ygerna saw that the man's belt buckle bore the Capricorn badge of the Fourteenth Gemina. She thought at first that he was unconscious, but then the man's eyes opened in narrow slits, frantic with pain. Labienus shoved a clay cup in her hand.

"Lift his head and get as much of this down him as you can." He had a pair of bronze forceps in one hand and a probe in the other, but Ygerna looked at the arm and knew that that wouldn't be the end of it. It was smashed above the elbow, and splinters of bone stuck up whitely among the wooden ones.

She slipped an arm behind the man's head and held the cup to his lips. "Drink this, it will make you better." She didn't know what was in it.

The man choked and gagged, but he got most of it down and his eyes began to dull. "No..." he whispered, and she saw with horror that Labienus had a saw in his hand.

"What is happening?" she asked, partly to distract him from the terror that still came through the cloudy veil of the drug and partly because he came from Correus's legion.

"Spearmen..." he whispered. "Germans..." and she realized that he didn't know. To a legionary in the line, there was no pattern to the battle but his own three feet of space. He gagged again and heaved on the table, and Ygerna heard the sick grinding sound of the bone saw. She put her hands on his shoulders and held him down and put her face close to his so that he would look at her and not at Labienus.

"Hold them!" Correus shouted. "For Rome! For your Eagle! Push!" A legate's place was at the center of his men or with the generals on some vantage point, with a courier to send his orders, not in the front line where death was the likeliest prize. But the Fourteenth Gemina was a legion too newly disciplined for that, so Correus was in the forefront with the Eagle-bearer beside him, cursing them, cajoling them, screaming himself into hoarseness at them, over the screams of the wounded and the wild howling of the Germans. A German spearman staggered toward him, and Correus pulled Antaeus up on his haunches a split second too late. The spear cut a gash along the horse's shoulder, and Antaeus screamed and lashed out with iron-shod hooves. The German fell back with a ruined face, and Correus swore. A Roman short sword was no use on horseback, but if he got down, his men couldn't see him, and that was the point. "Give me that!" Correus dropped his useless sword as a legionary caught the German's spear and tossed it up. It was a war spear, long, heavy, barbed at the end, with a bloody collar of speckled feathers around the shaft. Correus had learned to use one when he was eighteen. From Forst. He swung Antaeus around and drove the blade into a snarling German face. Blood welled up to cover the blue and ocher paint and the dark iron ring around the German's neck.

Marbod's men came on, like hunting wolves over the bodies of their dead. The Romans met them, still wedged solidly across the valley mouth, but the torn bodies of the Roman dead were growing, and the wounded who could not fall back were trampled underfoot. On the left flank, the Roman lines had begun to cave in a little on the center, jamming those behind them more solidly together, and the cavalry, on horses less adaptable to the steep terrain, were pushing gallantly against Ranvig's host, with bad results.

The emperor Domitian and his generals, on a slight rise above the right flank, watched the pattern of the battle while the emperor slammed his fist into the purple silk of his saddlecloth. "That is more men than you thought, Rufus!"

"There is also bad weather coming, and the emperor wishes to conclude the campaign this season," Rufus said. "Another ground would have been more favorable, but time was important. As we discussed."

"Marbod's men aren't rested," Julius Frontinus said. "Ours are. That will tell, sir, in the end."

"And so will bad judgment when the Senate counts our losses!" Domitian snapped. He wanted a triumph, not a Pyrrhic victory and a slaughter.

Rufus and the chief of Engineers glanced at each other and kept their thoughts to themselves. It had been at Domitian's insistence that they had pushed for a conclusion before winter. There were beginning to be loud noises in Rome that this campaign grew too costly, that the emperor was not the warrior his father and his brother had been. Domitian needed a clean, decisive victory—quickly.

Wherever they could stand clear and fight, the Romans cut down the German host, but it was like wading through heavy sand or waist-high water. There wasn't enough room, and the Germans still loped howling into the front ranks. The front ranks began to thin. For each man killed, another moved up from the press at the rear, but the dead were growing. Still, there was a limit to Marbod's men, and the warriors in his host had been lost from his control almost from the start. They threw themselves at the Romans like berserkers, and like berserkers they went to Valhalla by the thousands.

The air had grown thick and oppressive under lowering clouds, and the light was gray with the coming dusk when the last remnants of Marbod's war host wavered. The Roman lines surged forward over them. Those who had been battling the men of Ranvig's host, who had slashed their way through the Roman cavalry to hammer at the infantry's flank all day, braced for one last charge. They were bone weary, spitting blood, their breath coming in gasps, but they would have to do it alone. If they sank under Ranvig's charge, the front lines would never be able to turn in time to stop him. They raised their shields for one last push, one last time, and then halted, puzzled—because the Germans were gone.

Correus, whose Fourteenth Legion had swung around from the front to try to reinforce the faltering flank, halted his men, also. The Semnones had pulled back as suddenly as they had come, their hill-bred ponies scrambling up the slope, with only the ragged remnants of the Roman cavalry stumbling after them. Ranvig must have drawn off his foot-fighters first—it was only horsemen that streamed away up the hillside. Correus's weary, heavily armored legion and the legions of the flank would only waste their time and lives on that hill. Almost as soon as he gave the order, a trumpet sounded the "Hold" to echo it and the scattered cavalry turned back as well. The sky above was dark with boiling rain clouds as well as the growing dusk. It was too late to chase the Germans tonight.

Mithras god. Too late forever, maybe. Strung out along the ridgetop, opening their ranks to let Ranvig's fleeing horsemen through, were spears and men unending, a black line that stretched the length of the valley and back into the dusk.

The general had seen them, too. The trumpets called "Regroup" and the footsore legions stumbled to their places, but the Germans didn't move. Then, while Correus watched from Antaeus's back, his mouth dry and every limb aching, the low sun broke through the cloud just once behind the ridge. A single horseman moved from Ranvig's lines and raised his shield and spear, black against the sun. The men on the ridge turned around, and, while the Romans watched them uncomprehending, they walked away into the dusk, and the horseman turned and followed them.

"They're gone, sir." Quintus saluted and staggered slightly.

"Sit down, man," Correus said. "What do you mean they're gone?" He had counted his dead and seen the wounded sent back to the rear, and now he was sitting on a rock under a tent flap, trying to start a fire in the rain.

"Where's your optio?" Quintus said disapprovingly. He sat down and began to poke twigs in the fire. "They're gone. Gone clean out of the territory by the look of it. Not a smell of them, and the scouts say they're still traveling. I don't get it, but the gods be thanked anyway. We couldn't have fought another like this one today."

"Out of the—?" Suddenly Correus began to laugh. The ground was getting soft in the rain, and one of the tent poles shifted and a corner of the flap came down, but Correus didn't seem to notice it. Quintus watched him nervously as Correus sat there while his fire went out and the rain ran down his collar, and laughed.

The army had buried its dead by lantern light and tipped the Germans, of whom there were many, into a common pit in the rain-soaked ground. The Agri Decumates belonged to Rome. In the morning the weary men of the legions would parade by the graves of their dead in the shadow of their standards, and the commanders would call out the names while the emperor intoned the Prayer for the Slain. The emperor would send his dispatches back to Rome, and the Senate would vote him a triumph.

Ranvig of the Semnones had not wasted the year that he had spent playing at treaties with the emperor of the Romans. He knew Domitian now. Knew what he wanted from this campaign and had given it to him. And if the warning not to take more than had been given had been somewhat pointed, neither the emperor nor his generals would mention that in Rome.

Ranvig had never meant to hold the Agri Decumates. He had thrown Marbod of the Chatti and the troublemakers from his own tribe to the Romans to let the Romans' emperor take the land in the way that would best please him: with a great battle, and a fine victory, and the robes of a triumphant general. And then there had been the warning: *No farther. No farther if the emperor wishes to keep his triumph.* Beyond the Agri Decumates, on the borders of the Suevi lands, they would be waiting, in case the emperor should be so foolish as not to listen.

He would listen, Correus thought. He laughed again, noiselessly now, half bitterly, at himself earnestly counseling Ranvig not to take on Rome. There was still something missing, some last piece of Ranvig's game to be played, but it would come. He was as sure of that as he was that Ranvig had won. As sure as the dead men in their grave in the driving rain.

Quintus brought him his dinner, hard wheat biscuit and bacon, camp rations, with olives and wine from the officers' mess, and he was eating it when Ygerna picked her way through the muddy camp with a lantern in her hand.

"You are alive," she observed. "And you are sitting in a tent and swilling wine, while I have been wondering if you were dead."

Quintus eyed her warily and backed out of the tent. Correus put his wine down and held his arms out to her. "Flavius was here. I asked him to find you. Didn't he?"

"In this?" They had camped where they had fought, in the

churned ground of the valley, and rain was sheeting down outside the tent. She set the lantern down, and he saw that her gown was soaked in blood under the mud and water.

"What have you been doing?"

"Helping Labienus to cut a man's arm off," she said shortly.

"Dear gods." He put his arms around her, and she buried her face in his chest.

Epilogue

SPRING, AND THE TREES ALONG THE RHENUS BUDDED INTO green bloom. It was pretty country in the spring, Correus thought, but he wasn't terribly surprised to find that he would be leaving it. There was trouble on the Danuvius now, and he couldn't sorrow over much, because trouble always meant promotions, and his had taken the form of the command of a Danuvius fort. Not a legionary fort, but a fort all his own, and a good step up. If there was a good war, he might have his legion before a year was out.

He wasn't going to put it that way to Ygerna, he thought, with his orders tucked into the palm of his hand. Ygerna was pregnant again and was going to have to go back to Rome. He would miss her desperately, but he wasn't going to let her have a baby on the frontier, not after the hard time she had had with Eilenn. At that, he was happier than Flavius, who had lost his last babe, and been told by his wife's physician that if he fathered more children on her, he would run the risk of losing her too.

The house in the Moguntiacum civil quarter seemed to be very full of people when he got there. He was not surprised to see Lucius Paulinus, who had kept his promise and stayed in Germany to make his peace with Domitian; but judging by the amount of baggage heaped on a mule cart outside, and in the green-tiled atrium, Julia had arrived, as well.

She threw herself at Correus, and he grinned and kissed

her, and then looked quickly at Ygerna to see how the land lay. Ygerna had a grim look in her eye, and Julia's face was flushed and rebellious. The air between them crackled.

"Mama! I have found three frogs in the garden!" Felix hurtled through the door, and the frogs, which he appeared to have brought with him, bounced wildly across the tiles.

Ygerna caught him by the wrist. "Frogs are not for the house. And the cat will catch them and eat them. Very likely on my bed."

"Yes, Mama."

She looked at him sternly. Then they both giggled.

Julia stiffened. She looked at Felix unhappily. He was bigger. And he loved Ygerna. He hadn't even seen her.

Ygerna took a deep breath. She shoved Felix gently away from her. "Your aunt Julia is here."

He swung around, and his green eyes lit up like the sun on seawater. In a moment Julia was staggering back against the atrium wall with Felix in her arms. Her eyes met Ygerna's over his head.

"He does not forget you," Ygerna said. "Must it be one or the other?"

Correus and Lucius looked jumpily from one wife to the next, but after a long moment, Julia shook her head. "No. It would seem not." A frog hopped onto her big toe, and hopped off again, startled. She began to laugh.

"I can travel with Lucius and Julia," Ygerna said chattily, "so you can take Eumenes with you." She perched on the end of the bed and watched him pack. Correus decided that if he lived to be as old as his father, he would probably never understand women, so he would give up trying now. "But I am coming to the Danuvius when the baby is born," Ygerna said. She looked interested. "Julia says it is wild country, wilder than the Rhenus."

"Getting that way," Correus said.

"Why are they sending you there?"

"The Dacians are looking too busy across the Danuvius." Correus slung a tattered copy of Julius Caesar's memoirs into the trunk, with the head and broken-off shaft of a German spear. A bedraggled collar of feathers hung around its neck. "We are being sent to look back at them."

Ygerna eyed the spear. "What is that?"

"Souvenir," Correus said shortly. "A reminder not to underestimate the enemy. I took it away from one of Marbod's men."

"Did you underestimate Marbod?"

"No, he underestimated Ranvig. And so did we."

Ygerna yawned. "You can explain that to me when I get to the Danuvius." She curled herself up on the end of the bed. She seemed to want to sleep all the time. It must be the child. "If you stay long enough for me to catch up to you."

"Oh, I shouldn't worry about that," Correus said. "This is going to take a while." And it wouldn't be long before half the legions in Germany were following him, he thought. Dacia was just the place Ranvig would pick if he could order up a new war for Rome. Far enough away to take the emperor's mind off Germany and just in the right spot to make the German legions the most likely reinforcements.

"I should like to see Dacia. That will be nice," Ygerna said comfortably.

The chieftain of the Semnones sat by the hearth of the great hall of Ranvigshold and polished a hunting spear. There were children playing outside, shrieking like fiends in the spring sun. A ball bounced past the open door as he watched. His son tumbled after it, head over feet, brushed himself off, and scampered on, with a smaller child behind him. Ranvig found it pleasant to watch the children. These would have time to grow now, and Signy had another babe at the breast, a girl this time, with Signy's rose-gold hair.

The chieftain and his young wife had found matters somewhat easier between them of late, with no older women in the hall to overshadow her. Morgian had gone away home to Steinvarshold, and Fiorgyn was married as well, and with child. Ranvig had his own ideas about that, but he would keep them to himself. She had picked a brown-haired man for her husband.

Arni had done his best to get himself killed in the fighting, but he hadn't, and he had just ridden in to say that the spies in Moguntiacum said that the Romans were posting men to the Dacian frontier. Ranvig grinned silently and held the hunting spear sideways to the light to see if the rust was gone.

Glossary

aedile   Roman political official in charge of games, markets, temples, and public buildings

Aesculapius   god of healing

amphora   large, narrow-necked jar used to store and transport wine and food

Annwn   Celtic land of the dead

Aphrodite   goddess of love

Athena Nike   virgin goddess of wisdom and power, in her aspect of goddess of victory

atrium   the central room of a Roman house, frequently built around a pool

augurs   a priestly college at Rome, the business of which was to take the auspices on all important occasions

auxiliaries   cavalry, light troops, bowmen, etc., recruited from the provinces; term applied to all units other than the legions; the officers were Roman, and the men received Roman citizenship upon their discharge.

Avernus   lake in the crater of an extinct volcano, supposed to lead to the underworld

Bacchus   god of wine

basilica   public building housing law courts and exchange

Cassandra   prophetess daughter of Trojan King Priam; Apollo, whom she had repulsed, caused her true predictions always to be disbelieved

century	a unit of eighty men; six centuries made a cohort
Charon	boatman who ferried the dead across the River Styx
cohort	six centuries; ten cohorts made up a legion
confarreatio	the old religious form of Roman marriage witnessed by senior priests; divorce was nearly impossible
consuls	formerly the two highest Republican magistrates in Rome; under the empire a much less powerful office, but still a great honor; the emperor was generally a consul
corona aurea	Roman army decoration for extraordinary bravery
corona civica	Roman army decoration awarded to a soldier who has saved the life of a fellow citizen, at risk to his own
corvus	"crow's beak," the iron spike at the end of a Roman boarding ramp, used to punch through the deck of an enemy ship and hold it to be boarded
cuirass	close-fitting body armor covering the torso
Diogenes	Greek Cynic philosopher, reputed to have gone about in daylight with a lantern, looking for a man with the proper human virtues
Donar	German god of thunder, protector of men
Eagle	the standard of a Roman legion; it personified the legion's honor, and its loss was a disgrace
the Eagles	the Roman legions
Eir	German goddess of healing
Epona	Celtic goddess of horses
Erebus	the darkness through which the souls of the dead travel to Hades

Europa	Phoenician princess carried off by Zeus in the form of a bull
the Fates	three goddesses who spin, fix the length, and finally cut the thread of life
Flavian Amphitheater	later known as the Colosseum
Furies	avenging goddesses
the Goddess	Earth Mother in her many forms
Gorgons	three frightful sisters whose look turns the beholder to stone
greaves	lower leg armor
Hades	lord of the underworld; also the name of the underworld itself
Hector	chief Trojan hero in the war with the Greeks
Hel	German goddess of the underworld; also the name of her domain
Hercules	hero god famed for great feats of strength
hortator	on a ship, one who sets time for the oar strokes with a mallet
hypocaust	Roman hot-air system
Isis	Earth Mother in her Egyptian form
Janus	two-faced god of beginnings and endings of all undertakings
Juno	wife of Jupiter, goddess of marriage and childbirth
Jupiter	Roman name of Zeus, all-powerful father of the gods, protector of Rome
latrunculi	literally "bandits," Roman board game
legate	commander of a legion
legionary	the enlisted man of the legions; he was a Roman citizen
lilies	small, sharp spikes set in a defensive ditch

lorica	body armor of several types; at this time, scale or segmented plates
Lugh	Celtic sun god
maenads	priestesses of Bacchus who worked themselves into a frenzy at his festivals
Mercury	god of commerce; messenger of Zeus who guides the shades of the dead to the underworld
Minerva	Roman name of Athena
Mithras	Persian god of light and truth, mediator between man and the supreme god; his worship was popular in the Roman army
the Morrigan	Celtic goddess of battle; Earth Mother in her warlike aspect
the Mother	Earth Mother in any of her many forms
naiad	freshwater nymph
Neptune	Roman name of Poseidon
Olympus	mythical home of the Roman gods on the summit of Mount Olympus in Thessaly
optio	aide assigned to an officer
Persephone	maiden abducted by Hades to become his wife; doomed to spend six months of each year in the underworld
phalerae	Roman military decorations in the form of medallions worn on a leather harness across the chest
pilum	Roman military javelin
Pontifex Maximus	the chief priest of Rome
Poseidon	sea god and creator of the horse
Praetorian Guards	the home guard of Rome, the elite of the army, and the personal bodyguard of the emperor

praetorium	the commander's quarters in a Roman fort
primus pilus	commander of the First Cohort; in the field, second-in-command of the legion
principia	headquarters building in a Roman fort
quinquireme	galley with five oarsmen, but probably only three actual banks of oars
Rome Dea	goddess personification of the City of Rome
Romulus	legendary founder of Rome
Saturnalia	Roman winter festival when slaves impersonated their masters and vice versa
sidhe	in Celtic legend, the hollow hills of the faery folk; here used to mean a dwelling of an older race
Sign of Horns	invoking the Horned God (similar to Pan) to ward off evil
spina	central divider of a chariot track
Tartarus	lowest level of the underworld
tribune	officer in a legion, generally a young man serving a short term before beginning a political career
trireme	galley with three banks of oars
triumviri capitales	Roman officials who inquired into all capital crimes, apprehended criminals, had charge of prisons, and carried out sentences
Typhon	fire-breathing monster and creator of hurricanes, said to have a hundred heads and terrible voices
Ulysses	hero of the Trojan War
Valhalla	German paradise for the souls of slain heroes

Valkyrie	maiden messengers of Wuotan sent to choose the slain in battle and serve them mead in Valhalla
Venus	Roman name of Aphrodite
Vestal Virgins	priestesses of Vesta, supposed to be incorruptible
vicus	the civil settlement outside a Roman fort
vine staff	a centurion's staff of office; literally a cane cut from vine wood
Wisdom	a Celtic board game resembling chess
Wuotan	German chief of all the gods; sky god; god of light, war, and knowledge, giver of life and breath to men; he had two ravens, Hugin and Munin, who perched on his shoulders daily to tell him the news
Ziu	ancient German tribal god of war